"*Winging It with You* is everything you'd ever want a rom-com to be—fun, sexy, and overflowing with heart. I'm #Thasher and Chip Pons's biggest fan."

—Hannah Grace, #1 *New York Times* bestselling author of *Icebreaker* and *Daydream*

"I've waited so long for a book just like this! It checks all my reader boxes: sharp prose, dimensional characters, heart-clenching romance, reality TV setting, and dialogue made of dreams! Contemporary romance magic!"

—Christina Lauren, #1 international bestselling author of *Love and Other Words*

"*Winging It with You* is all about taking chances on the heart—and seeing them pay off in glorious Technicolor. Asher and Theo's chemistry is off the charts from their first moment on the page, and watching them trek through their unexpected love story was a pure delight."

—Lana Ferguson, *USA Today* bestselling author of *The Fake Mate*

"Chip Pons writes with such heart and honesty—it's impossible not to fall in love with his characters. His stories pulse with emotion, leaving you thinking about them long after you've turned the last page. Chip Pons is the fresh voice in romance we've needed!"

—Sarah Adams, *New York Times* bestselling author of *Beg, Borrow, or Steal*

"*Winging It with You* is heartfelt and hopeful—a truly dreamy love story! Asher and Theo are electric, and their indomitable joy will have you cheering for them from the very first page and long after you read the last."

—Lyla Sage, *New York Times* bestselling author of
Lost and Lassoed

"Emotional, sexy, and deliciously fun. Chip Pons delivers a heartfelt romance with *Winging It with You*. Asher and Theo have sparkling chemistry that leaps off the page, set against the backdrop of an adventurous bop around the globe. I can't wait for everyone to get their hands and hearts on this book."

—B.K. Borison, *USA Today* bestselling author of
the Lovelight series

"The definition of delightful, *Winging It with You* is soon to be your favorite romance of the year! The high stakes of reality TV meet the sexy situationship of fake dating. Chip Pons gives us characters you can't help rooting for."

—Julie Soto, *USA Today* bestselling author of *Forget Me Not*

"*Winging It with You* is tender, sexy, and brimming with hope. Asher and Theo have my whole heart—their moving growth journey, their genuine joy, their sizzling chemistry. I adored every page!"

—Chloe Liese, *USA Today* bestselling author of
Only and Forever

ALSO BY CHIP PONS

You & I, Rewritten

WINGING IT WITH YOU

A NOVEL

CHIP PONS

G. P. PUTNAM'S SONS

NEW YORK

PUTNAM
— EST. 1838 —

G. P. PUTNAM'S SONS
Publishers Since 1838
1745 Broadway, New York, NY 10019
An imprint of Penguin Random House LLC
penguinrandomhouse.com

Library of Congress Cataloging-in-Publication Data

Names: Pons, Chip, author.
Title: Winging it with you: a novel / Chip Pons.
Description: New York: G. P. Putnam's Sons, 2025.
Identifiers: LCCN 2024041748 (print) | LCCN 2024041749 (ebook) |
ISBN 9780593853504 (trade paperback) | ISBN 9780593853511 (epub)
Subjects: LCGFT: Romance fiction. | Gay fiction. | Novels.
Classification: LCC PS3616.O616 W56 2025 (print) |
LCC PS3616.O616 (ebook) | DDC 813/.6—dc23/eng/20240930
LC record available at https://lccn.loc.gov/2024041748
LC ebook record available at https://lccn.loc.gov/2024041749

Printed in the United States of America
1st Printing

Book design by Daniel Brount

The authorized representative in the EU for product safety and compliance is
Penguin Random House Ireland, Morrison Chambers, 32 Nassau Street,
Dublin D02 YH68, Ireland, https://eu-contact.penguin.ie.

To everyone courageous enough to leap when that long-awaited moment presents itself—you know the one. The one you've been quietly dreaming of. The one that will change everything. Even if it's daunting or scares the hell out of you, I hope whatever it is turns out to be infinitely more beautiful than you could have ever imagined.

"Grab your passport and my hand."

—DR. TAYLOR ALISON SWIFT

1

ASHER

'm sorry, Asher . . . but I can't go on this trip—"

The last words I expected to hear coming out of my long-term boyfriend's mouth at the airline ticket counter. After months of meticulous planning—countless hours of my life I will never get back, painstakingly stressing over cost-analysis documents and packing lists and risk waivers—*this* was the one travel hiccup I could not have thought to plan for.

"Did you forget to pack something?" I ask, lining up my luggage as I try to visualize the now-packed to-do list I've been ticking items off from one by one. "There's definitely still time to head back home . . ." But when I turn back toward him, there's something about the way his overplucked eyebrows are pinched together that tells me a different departure is on the horizon.

That, and he's awkwardly left about two feet of intentional space between us.

My fist clenches around the boarding pass the ticketing agent—Susan, I learn looking down at her name tag, which is bedazzled with glitter hearts—literally *just* handed me after rather rudely being the human version of sunshine this early in the morning, and I instantly start to sweat. Her big, empathetic blue eyes are pooling with pity as she stares back at me, a hand extended out toward me slightly as if somehow she's personally going to be able to fix this humiliating situation.

"I don't think I can do *this* anymore . . ." Clint's voice cuts through my thoughts, more nasally than normal, and I swear the way he just emphasized *this*, like being here with me is the world's biggest inconvenience, makes my skin crawl.

"The competition?" I ask daringly. "Weren't you just telling me in the Uber over here how excited you were?"

He scratches the back of his neck uncomfortably.

I now notice that our awkward confrontation is holding up the growing check-in line. Maybe it's the unflattering fluorescents or my sudden unbridled rage for the man, but Clint Hanson has never appeared more unattractive than he does right now in his too-small sweat suit with his matching fanny pack and hideous shoes that he insisted on numerous occasions all the celebrities and influencers were wearing. Based on the way he's dressed, one might *almost* believe, if they really tried, squinting, that perhaps he's the age he's still pretending to be.

Just so we're clear, he's pushing forty.

"Clint, this entire trip—everything we have planned and saved for these last few months—was *your* idea," I say, trying to use the calmest, most monotonous tone humanly possible to avoid being labeled as dramatic or emotional.

Again.

He hasn't made eye contact with me since his sudden change

in plans—both travel and life, something he's really perfected during all the conflicts we've ever had. Instead, he is annoyingly playing with the buckle of his luggage tag.

"I'm just not sure we want the same things out of this," he says after a painfully slow moment.

"*This*? Clint, what are you even talking about? What is it that you 'wanted,'" I ask, putting aggressive air quotes around the word, "when you signed us up for this competition?" I take a deliberate step forward. "Or better yet, what about these last seven years? What's changed about what you've *wanted* this whole time?"

Clint stands in silence as my questions are left unanswered.

I have spent the better part of the last decade carefully molding myself into the perfect boyfriend for him. We rarely argued about anything serious, and when we bought our house together, I made sure he felt like it was *his* home too despite his horrible taste in decor. I always remembered his family's birthdays and anniversaries and never once brought up the fact that he was losing his hair. When he sent me unsolicited dick pics, I most certainly didn't let him know how little it did for me— both on-screen and in real life—and when given the choice between joining him and his weirdly pretentious friends at their weekly themed charcuterie nights or doing just about anything else, I always chose him. Because that's what you are supposed to do in your late twenties when you are in a relationship. You choose your partner.

Except standing here in the international terminal, sleep- and caffeine-deprived, I realize he isn't choosing me or us, and instead of the usual panic or involuntary mental lists that I'd expect to begin forming about my imminent singleness, I'm overwhelmed with a surprising sense of relief.

"I just know that if I get on that plane, I'll regret it," he admits, a blow to the gut.

He'll *regret* it. I am legitimately at a loss for words right now.

"Let me get this straight—" The edge in my voice makes a timely and most welcome return as my anger rises. I notice a few onlookers are now being far less subtle about their interest in our preflight drama. "Somewhere between me sucking you off last night after making sure all *our* stuff was packed and this morning"—several teens waiting with their families can't choke down their laughter at my lewd bluntness and it only sharpens my resolve—"you had some soul-shaking revelation that you, the one and only Clint Hanson, can't do *this* anymore."

He stumbles toward me, nearly tripping over our luggage. "Keep your voice down," he hisses through thin, dry lips and narrowed eyes. Ah, that's right. He'll do anything to avoid the world's perception of him being tarnished. "Why don't we go outside and talk about this? Somewhere private."

An almost feral laugh escapes my lips.

The life I had been meticulously cultivating was just obliterated in an airport terminal and I'm laughing.

"There's absolutely nothing to talk about. You decided you can't do this anymore," I say, waving my hands between the two of us. "So, we aren't going to do this anymore. End of discussion." I turn to try to divvy up our matching luggage, another unnecessary purchase to appease him, pushing mine toward Susan, who tags each of my overly crammed suitcases one by one.

"What are you doing?" he asks, looking between me and my luggage in confusion.

"I have a plane to catch."

He grabs my arm before I can turn to walk away. "You can't be serious."

"Let go of me, Clint. *Now*."

Sensing the growing number of eyes on us, including those of a very concerned Susan from behind the ticket counter, he thankfully listens.

"Asher, just hold on . . . Give me a moment to explain." His tone and gaze soften as we seem to be entering the eye of the breakup storm that's been violently building around us. For the briefest of moments, I'm tempted to hear him out. Considering all the time we've invested in each other, I should, right?

There's even something behind his tired brown eyes that I can't quite put my finger on. Something I haven't seen in a long time.

Compassion? Remorse? Perhaps even . . . regret?

"You can't do this alone," he says.

Well, that lasted all of two seconds.

"Fucking watch me, Clint," I spit back, and the nosy teenagers, who now feel like my brothers-in-arms, hoot and holler. Turning away from him, I storm off toward the escalator with the cheers of approval solidifying my decision and strengthening my resolve.

"Excuse me, sir . . . um . . . Mr. Bennett!" Susan yells after me, hurrying around the ticket counter. "You're going to need this."

She places my passport in my hand. I stare at the cheesy cover—a recent and thoughtful gift from my mother, one of a matching set whose twin is safely tucked away in Clint's pocket. I run my thumb over the phrase she printed in small, gold script. *Away We Go!*

"Thank you." And away I go.

/////////////////////

After barreling through security, I find solace in the least likely of places.

An airport TGI Fridays.

"I'll take another."

I wave my empty glass in the direction of the bartender—a gentleman in his mid- to late forties, I'd guess. Judging by his glance of indifference, I can only assume he's used to passengers who are eager to drown their sorrows or quell their flying anxiety before their flights.

He places my third (fourth?) mimosa in front of me—it's basically juice, right?—and lingers momentarily. "Can I get you anything else?" he asks again, because it feels like I've been here for a full afternoon already. One of the downsides of traveling with Clint was always his irrational need to be at the airport hours before a flight. I'm not just talking about some wiggle room to make sure you're checked in and have enough time to grab food without having to race through security. No, the man is notorious for wanting to spend a full day at the airport, lounging in uncomfortable chaos with a terminal full of strangers, *just in case*.

I lean forward, peering dramatically over the bar. "You got a man back there who isn't spineless, selfish, and a worthless bag of dicks?"

His expression shifts from suppressed laughter to total annoyance. He might have even scoffed at me, which to this day, I hadn't realized people did in real life, but here I am learning something new. He could just be my new best friend.

I glance down at his name tag. *Mick.*

"Are you married, Mick? Someone special in your life?"

"I, um . . . I'm not," he says quietly, averting his gaze as he haphazardly wipes a pint glass with a rag I'm sure hasn't been washed in *quite* some time.

"Alright, can you just pretend with me for a moment? What kind of man convinces his partner of almost six . . . no, seven years—*seven years*, Mick . . . to uproot his entire life—literally begs him to put a giant pause on any sort of personal and professional plans he may have—"

A pair of handsome pilots pulls up to the other side of the bar, momentarily tearing his attention away from my story.

"Stay with me, Mick . . . we're getting to the good part."

Conflicted, he gives the duo a sympathetic nod. "And what's that?"

"This partner has asked you to do all this for a reality television show."

"Which show?"

Mick isn't a man of many words; I like that about him. "*The Epic Trek*. You know, the show where you trav—"

"I know the show," he says, cutting me off. Mick leans back against the bar, crossing his arms. "But did you have to say yes?"

He's got me there. "I thought that's what a good partner does—agrees to things they don't want to do. Even if that means spending the last four months training for an intense global travel competition that would pull me away from my friends and my career."

"I don't see the problem here. Your man wants you to travel the world together and have a chance to win some money. Could be worse," he says. "Do you need anything else? I have other customers."

Perfect. Another man just itching to get away from me.

"I'm all set," I say, reaching for my glass of water and feeling just how pathetic this all is. "What am I doing here?" I groan, dropping my head into my hands, rubbing the ache growing behind my temples. The airport bar is buzzing with excited travelers. Families and couples and passengers flying solo like me. I thought about calling my parents, but each time my finger hovered over our family's home number, I set my phone down. We don't have *that* type of relationship—the one where some version of a panicked phone call from their oldest son would be met with anything but a laundry list of questions and an *I told you so* tone.

That's not to say we have a bad relationship. I love my family and I know they love me. Unconditionally. But my mother would make that pained *tsk*ing sound when I told her about Clint and me. And my father? Well, he'd go down some rabbit hole about things like *follow-through* and *integrity*—two of Edward Bennett's unwavering measurements of good character—and if he loses faith in your ability to adhere to those ideals, you're screwed. And right now, neither of those things would be entirely helpful.

I've always been the reliable one. The one they didn't have to worry over when it came to life decisions. They'd had their reservations when Clint and I told them about the reality competition, but when I laid out my plan, accounting for every penny of the prize money and how I intended to use it to start a science, technology, engineering, and mathematics program for LGBTQIA+ students, those reservations quickly faded, because in their eyes, the son who never caused them any stress had a plan.

Asher Bennett always has a plan.

Except for today, dumped and teetering toward tipsy in an airport bar with only a few hours to figure out my next move.

What am I going to do?

For the first time in my life, I don't have a solid grasp on which direction to move. Since Clint's confession, I think I've been operating solely on rage and adrenaline—and mimosas—but now? Emotions like humiliation and confusion and a deep sense of regret wash over me. I cycle through the last couple of months, searching for some sort of sign that this was coming, some indication that Clint wanted out, and come up blank. We'd been happy. Happy enough to still plan for a future we'd both wanted. Or so I thought. Which is why I believe his choice to end our relationship wasn't something he'd just decided to do on a whim. Knowing him, it was probably something he'd been silently stewing on for quite some time. Waiting for the perfect opportunity to rip the rug out from under me.

The idea of it being premeditated hurts even more.

Perhaps I was too professionally driven? Maybe I wasn't driven enough? Did I say no to too many threesomes? Or yes too many times?

I really need to know where we stand on threesomes.

Was all *this*—the breakup, the last few years of my life, the fact that I stupidly agreed to go on this show to begin with—payback or some sort of cosmic karma?

And speaking of the show. Could I . . . still go?

The whole not-having-a-partner thing really screws me here. But what if I could find a replacement? The rational part of my brain is holding up a cardboard sign that reads *Dumb* triple underlined as my relationship with Clint rushes through my mind. Years of putting my hopes and dreams on the back burner so he could shine. Years of saying no to myself so I could say yes to him.

Years of allowing someone else to dictate whether it was my turn.

I think about what this money could do. How many students in my own community could benefit from the Own Voices in STEM program I've been silently dreaming about for years if by some miracle I walked away with the prize money. Despite the odds being heavily stacked against me, I know with certainty I have to try.

After all, what kind of Bennett man would I be if I didn't have "follow-through"? I finish my drink, allowing myself just another moment or two of self-pity before I figure out what comes next. I scroll through my phone, looking for someone I could call to be a last-minute partner on the show.

A lifeline in my moment of need.

My brother is the first person to come to mind. But I'd never ask him to miss classes, and anyway, competing together would result in one of us killing the other. Outside our last names, we have literally nothing in common.

There's my colleague, Simon. He's mentioned on more than one occasion that he's completed several marathons over the years, so I suspect the physicality of the challenges wouldn't be an issue for him. As my thumb hovers over his contact, though, dread coursing through my veins, I remember he's just a few weeks, if not days, away from getting married. I doubt his future bride would be okay with loaning me her groom-to-be for a high-stakes international travel competition.

A knot of frustration coils tightly between my shoulder blades as I realize just how unfair of me it is to even think about asking someone to drop their own responsibilities to help me out like this. Another Edward Bennett–ism comes to the center of my mind.

A lack of planning on your part doesn't constitute an emergency on mine, he'd always say, and honestly? Fair.

I set my phone on the counter face down, resisting the urge to chuck it clear across the bar, entirely overwhelmed by just how hard it is to think of someone, anyone, I could ask—even if I were to be that selfish.

Holy shit. Do I not have any friends?

It shouldn't be this hard to think of a single friend who's *mine*. Not Clint's friend. Not a colleague. Not an acquaintance. An honest-to-goodness, call-you-up-way-too-late-to-vent-about-boys-or-work-or-both, always-down-for-margaritas-on-any-day-that-ends-in-*day*, ride-or-die *friend*.

The realization sucker punches me right in the throat, sending a wave of pitiful regret straight to my bones.

I used to have friends. Loads of them, actually. Those first years of undergrad were a hazy blur of nights spent with various smatterings of friends I'd collected. Two a.m. laughing fits shared over double cheeseburgers and cheap vodka or delirious nights cramming in the library fueled by burnt coffee and Tastykakes. But now? Could it be that I'd met Clint and, somewhere along the way, just completely forgone any basic human connection beyond him and us?

The very same anger I felt this morning churns in my stomach as the departure time on my boarding pass stares up at me from the counter. A reminder of the self-imposed ticking clock I've volunteered to race against.

What the hell was I thinking? Slumping in my seat, trying to knead the tension throbbing behind my temples, a thought pops into my head.

"Can I get you anything else?" Mick says; his sudden reappearance startles me. "Some food, perhaps?" His question reminds me I've been drinking on an empty stomach.

"I'll take more water when you have a moment," I say, pushing my empty water glass in his direction. "Oh, and some mozzarella sticks, please."

Mick nods, punching my order into the computer, and makes his way around the bar. I glance at the now-thinning crowd in the restaurant. The handsome pilots are still on the other side of the bar. And suddenly, I see it. A plan—a rather stupid and almost entirely unrealistic one—comes barreling into focus.

2

THEO

Can you believe they're grounding me?"

The flight into Boston deplaned faster than usual. Tagging along behind the last of the passengers and crew making their way up the jet bridge, I was finally able to check my email. Sitting in my inbox was the dreaded answer from my supervisor. I'd maxed out my flying hours for the month, and the bottom line: I was forbidden from piloting any more flights.

Effective immediately.

"You're being dramatic, and you know it," Mark says as we cross the threshold into the busy terminal. "They aren't *grounding* you, Theo. It's protocol."

"Cállate," I say, and he laughs when I give him the finger. But shutting up isn't something Mark is known for. Especially when he's right. "Please don't give me the whole protocol spiel," I groan. If there's anyone who knows the FAA rule book front to back, it's Mark. He can, notoriously, rattle off random regulations in every conversation.

"Theo, listen to me," he says, grabbing my arm, halting us in the middle of Terminal E. "Maybe *this* is your sign to slow down a little bit." He nods to the phone that's still in my hand. "I know it's not what you wanted to hear, but you're the only pilot I've ever met who doesn't travel for themselves. Or even just use the time off you've earned. Whether you like it or not, these rules and limits are in place to prevent burnout. You know . . . safety and all." Mark puts an arm around my shoulder. "You know what Amelia asks me every time you leave?"

"Hmm."

"She asks if I think you're happy. Like *actually* happy."

There's no hiding anything from Mark's wife. "And obviously you tell her that happy is my middle name, right?"

"Something like that." Mark laughs again, dropping his arm and grabbing the handle of his rolling carry-on. "Look, I'm not going to tell you how to live your life. Never have, never will. But we've all watched you charm your way through the last couple of years, cracking jokes, making everyone laugh, so, this?" he says, pointing back at my phone. "This is an opportunity, Theo. An opportunity to seize some semblance of *normalcy*." It's hard not to notice the emphasis he places on that word. "I know we don't really talk about your military service . . ."

I step back, the sharp turn into more delicate territory taking me by surprise. "Yeah, I think it's a little *too* early in the day to be unpacking all our emotional damage, sir," I say, sarcastically glancing at my watch.

"Hear me out," he says in response to my attempt to redirect the conversation. "You're one hell of a pilot, my friend. One of the best I've ever seen. Shoot, I feel like I learn something new from *you* every day."

His compliment means everything. Flying has always been my dream, and honestly, no matter how overworked or tired I am, there isn't a single moment when I'm in the sky that I forget that. It's the one thing in my life that I feel good at, and now? Having that taken away from me? It scares me more than I will ever admit.

"But do me a favor and try to remember there's more to life than work, okay? Take some risks. Stop putting off that trip home. Strike up a conversation with a stranger. I don't care what you do, but be spontaneous and step outside your comfort zone."

"It's like you don't even know me at all." More to life than work, huh? What a foreign concept. On every level, I know he's right. But I can't brush off the fact that I've spent the last couple of years on autopilot—show up to work, sleep when I can, and eat. Rinse and repeat. And while it may be easier to just avoid . . . everything, is that really the life I want to be living?

"I'm serious, Theo." His voice is now filled with concern.

"As am I. I promise to talk to strangers and will do my best to remember there is more to life than work." I place three fingers straight up. "Scout's honor."

"You're so full of shit," he says, rolling his eyes. We both turn and continue making our way through the crowded terminal. "I know you're mentally drafting a rebuttal email."

He's not wrong.

It's useless, though. Decisions like this aren't something that can be reversed, no matter how much I beg, plead, or throw back-to-back fits. And as much as I love a good professional grovel, I have to accept the fact that my flying days are officially on pause.

Once again.

"Speaking of," I say, unlocking my phone to the email and handing it over to him, "have you ever seen something like this?"

Mark adjusts his bag on his shoulder and takes my phone mid-stride, reading aloud the email that's already seared into my brain. "'Mr. Fernandez, it's come to our attention that you've exceeded the maximum flight hours allowed by the Federal Aviation Administration . . . '" He looks up at me before continuing, his lips drawn into a hard line like some disappointed father. "'. . . for the *third* quarter in a row. Upon further review of your flying history and in coordination with the airline's human resources department, we are mandating a three-week administrative leave, effective immediately.'"

I can't tell you the last time I took leave, let alone three weeks' worth.

Come to think of it, as I'm standing here in the middle of the terminal, I can't even remember the last time I had fun. Honestly, after twenty-five, what even is that?

"Go on," I say, tipping my chin in his direction. "Read the last little bit there."

Mark cocks an eyebrow but lowers his gaze back to my phone's screen and continues reading. "'After consulting with our Aviation Medical Examiner, and in alignment with the airline's policy to assess the physical and mental well-being of each of our pilots . . . ' They've involved the Aviation Medical Examiner?" he asks, and I can hear the surprise in his tone.

"Oh, just keep on reading," I say, crossing my arms as I lean against the wall.

He narrows his eyes. "'. . . we are additionally requiring proof that during your administrative leave, you've taken the necessary steps to prioritize a healthier work-life balance and your mental health fitness."

Mark hands me back my phone. "I've never heard of anything like this. Have you?"

"Nope."

His brow furrows as he clearly tries to wrap his brain around this predicament. "How the hell do they expect you to provide *proof* that you're prioritizing work-life balance?"

That's the part of this that's bothering me the most.

I could easily spend the next three weeks locked in my apartment. Well, *easily* is subjective, since all this so-called self-care is a foreign concept to me. But I could at least try. Hell, I could probably use the extra sleep. But this? This *proof* they're asking for? I have no idea how I'm going to pull that off.

"Who knows, maybe I'll take up manifestation or start a YouTube channel and document every second of my day." Is YouTube still a thing? Who knows.

"You could . . . become a plant dad," he offers with an unamused expression.

"I think the phrase you may be looking for is plant *daddy*. But sure, let's go with that. I could do that." I pause momentarily. "Well, my friend . . . since I suddenly have *all* this free time on my hands, wanna grab a bite?" I say, nodding my chin in the direction of our favorite spot just ahead.

"Of course," Mark says, smiling as he dodges a very frazzled-looking family. "But it'll have to be quick. I've got two more flights today and I need to close my eyes before my next weather briefing."

"Rub it in, why don't you!" I shout as a gaggle of kids weaves their way between us.

//////////////

If I were a betting man, I would never put money on an airport-terminal TGI Fridays becoming a time-honored tradition of mine.

But here we are, seated at our usual spot at the bar—yes, we have a usual spot—about to eat our weight in mozzarella sticks, something Mark and I have gone out of our way to do every time we pilot a flight together. The airport seems busier than usual today, which only adds to my frustration about the whole grounding thing. People are flying and those flights need pilots and instead of doing what I'm best at, I'm being forced to hang around.

I watch Mick place down a plate in front of the blond man who's been chatting his ear off across the bar. "Hey, Mick! When you have a moment, can we grab an order of mozzarella sticks?"

Mick looks exhausted, which makes sense because it's pushing closing. "Sorry, boys, the kitchen's closed."

I'm sorry, what?

"Hold up," I say, sitting up straighter on my stool. "I just watched you deliver an order to that guy over there."

Mick looks back at who I'm referring to, eyes rolling and shoulders slumped. "Yeah, well, he actually got the last batch, so take it up with him."

"Oh, come on, Mi—" I start, but he puts his hands up, cutting me off.

"Look. I don't know what to tell you—we're short-staffed, the fryer's been on the fritz all week and no one from corporate seems to want to do anything about it, and I need . . . I need to get out of here."

With that, he turns and heads back through the kitchen doors, seemingly unworried that there are a few remaining customers who I'm sure want to close out their tabs.

"It's fine, Theo," Mark says, pushing back his stool and starting to get up.

"It's tradition," I snap, putting a hand on his shoulder to prevent him from moving any farther. "Stand by, I'm going to get you those sticks."

"I really wish you wouldn't," Mark says, already exasperated by my nonsense, but it's too late, I'm afraid. My plan is already in motion as I round the bar, eyes on the cheesiest prize sitting untouched in a red plastic basket.

The man doesn't move when I pull out the barstool closest to him. Not even a raised eyebrow at the unintentional screech of the stool's leg against the dated linoleum flooring. His attention is focused instead on whatever he's furiously typing away into his phone. He's striking in a subtle way. Dark blond hair falls haphazardly into place. Long legs tucked awkwardly underneath his stool. And while I'm privy only to his sharp profile from this angle, vibrant green eyes peek out from beneath thin tortoiseshell glasses and manicured eyebrows.

I clear my throat. Nothing.

"Excuse me," I say, both unnerved by this man's lack of situational awareness and envious of his ability to tune out the rest of the world. "I noticed you haven't touched your mozzarella sticks."

He puts his phone down, slowly turning to face me. "I'm sorry . . . what?" He's dressed in one of those matching athleisure sets Amelia is always trying to push on me, with white Chucks laced loosely around his ankles.

"Your mozzarella sticks," I repeat, noticing the fullness of his lower lip and the narrowed green eyes I'm now realizing are the color of moss. "You haven't touched them."

He blinks, shifting his eyes from mine to the basket of fried cheese in front of him. "I'm . . . what?" He pinches the bridge of his nose. "Did you need something?" Exhaustion seeps off every syllable.

"Sorry, how rude of me," I say, extending my hand in his direction. "I'm Theo Fernandez."

He straightens on the stool he's sitting on as he sheepishly takes my hand in his. The unexpected warmth of his skin sends the smallest tingle across my palm, but I ignore it.

"Uh . . . I'm Asher?"

"You don't sound too sure about that." He scowls at me, quickly letting go of my hand and allowing his own to fall back clumsily against the bar.

"It's been a . . . day." His voice trails off, and before I can ask why, he turns his gaze away from mine.

Not a fan of small talk, I see. I reach into my back pocket, pulling out my wallet to get straight to the point. "I'll give you twenty dollars for them," I say, sliding the bill across the bar toward him.

"What?"

"Your mozzarella sticks—I'll give you twenty bucks for them."

He opens his mouth to say something but quickly shuts it, the faintest of smiles forming as he fidgets in his seat. "Um. I don't think so," he says, reaching to pull the goods closer to him.

Okay, blondie. We're playing hardball, I see. "Look . . ." I glance down at his airline ticket, hoping to learn his full name. ". . . Asher Bennett heading to Los Angeles by way of Dallas.

You seem like a nice guy," I toss out there, hoping a little flattery will soften whatever standoffishness I'm picking up on. "I don't want to bother you during your little mimosa and mozzarella stick snack—solid combo, by the way. Real nutritious." He fails at stifling a laugh. Now we're onto something. "But do you see that guy over there?" I say, pointing across the bar to where Mark has been watching from his seat, a grimace splashed across his face.

Asher Bennett's gaze lingers on mine, hesitating as if he's trying to decide whether to actually entertain whatever this is, but finally, he looks toward Mark, who waves.

"That handsome devil is my best friend, Mark. He and I have this little tradition where after every flight we fly together, we stop in here for some mozzarella sticks. It's kinda our thing."

Asher looks at me, unamused, resting his elbows on the bar as he leans forward in his seat. "That's nice."

"It is . . . it is. But you see," I say, angling my body more toward his. "You appear to have gotten the last batch."

"How unfortunate."

"Incredibly. Are you a superstitious man, Asher Bennett?"

He shakes his head. "I prefer to spend my time based in reality, actually."

"Ah, I see . . . a man of science. I can respect that. Well, Mark, on the other hand, he's *incredibly* superstitious, and I'd hate to think what would happen if our little cheesy tradition here got ruined."

"It would be *such* a shame." He's leaning closer now. Intrigued? Perhaps.

"Are you really willing to risk the lives of all those innocent passengers when Mark has to get in the cockpit for his next flight? I can only imagine the headlines . . . and who they'd blame."

"Let me guess . . . me?" he asks, pointing a finger at himself, lines dancing around his eyes as his mouth curves into the briefest of smiles.

"I mean, I'm not one to point fingers."

"Yet, here we are," he says, rolling his eyes. "I'll tell you what," he continues, reaching into his bag on the seat next to him and holding up a quarter. "I'll flip you for it. Heads, the sticks are yours." He pushes the basket toward me, a sly grin spreading across his face. "But tails . . ." he says, rolling the coin across his knuckles. "Tails, you're going to have to do something for me. Deal?"

"Anything you want, it's yours."

"Be careful what you offer." There's a forced edge to his voice, one that leads me to believe whatever forwardness he's presenting doesn't quite come naturally to him. I watch as a million little gears turn behind his big green eyes. As they catch the sun coming in from the window, giving me a calculated once-over, I realize I might not be at all ready for what's to come.

3

ASHER

United Flight UA2325—Seats 3A & B
BOS–LAX

So, are you finally going to tell me what's in Los Angeles?"

Shit. I still haven't found the right time to bring up the competition. Not as we waited to board in unbearable silence. Not even as we awkwardly navigated around each other once we made it to our cabin—a surprise upgrade to first class after Theo had a brief, friendly conversation with the gate agent. And not when we settled into our seats and took off.

The poor guy has no idea what he's gotten himself into.

It was almost too easy to get this man with me onto the plane—which is probably why my palms are sweaty and every red flag in my arsenal is flying on high alert. The coin we'd flipped bounced off the bar's counter and skidded across the greasy restaurant linoleum between a few rolling carry-ons before settling near the host's stand.

I thought he'd object when we both walked over and saw

our fate, but instead, Theo put his hands in his pockets, shoulders raised and head cocked as if to say, *Your move.*

Tails.

For sure he'd backpedal on his whole *anything you want, it's yours* line he so carelessly threw out there, right? But when I told him he needed to book a flight to Los Angeles, the man didn't flinch. He just stepped away for a moment, cell phone in hand, as his friend—Mike? Mark?—trailed after him, a growing mixture of concern and confusion plastered across his face.

And here he is, intently staring in my direction, waiting for my answer.

Time to rip off the Band-Aid, Bennett.

"Oh, you know . . ." I say, fidgeting with my seat belt. "Sunshine, million-dollar listings . . ." Deep breaths. "And just a silly little production crew waiting for us."

Theo tilts his head in my direction. "What was that last one?" he asks, now leaning ever so slightly in my direction.

"The million-dollar listings? Yeah, there's a whole reality television series about them, actually, and they're like, super popular with the gays and . . ." My voice trails off as I watch smile lines form around his amber eyes and his full lips curl up at the corners of his mouth. A dimple makes an appearance front and center on his cheek and it transforms his profile into something far more endearing than the initial impression I had of his picture-perfect face.

"What's this about a production crew?"

My heart is racing and I'm not sure if it's because I'm actually an anxious flyer, or the fact that I'm about to reveal a horrifically concocted plan—which, for the record, is not at all a reflection of my normal decision-making skills—or that I keep getting whiffs of whatever spicy cologne is radiating off Theo's larger-than-life body.

Saying that Theo Fernandez is attractive doesn't quite cut it.

The first thing I noticed was how much space he takes up. His features are dramatic and angular. Arms and legs long enough to swallow you whole. I sneak a glance over at how he's sitting in his seat. *Those thighs.* But it was his soft smile and kind eyes that made me question if the dizziness I was feeling back in the restaurant was from the mimosas or him. Neatly cropped dark, thick hair and manicured stubble accentuate his tanned skin, and while I know next to nothing about him, Theo exudes an aura of confidence that makes me shake with both excitement and unease.

"About that," I say, wiping my hands on my pant legs. He's following my movements, back and forth, until he finally raises his eyes to meet mine. "Don't freak out."

"I don't freak out," he says casually.

"Really? Everyone freaks out from time to time, especially under stressful cond . . ." He arches a brow as I begin to ramble. I'm doing it again. "Right. So, the production crew. Well, for starters, the reason I was at the airport today is because I've been selected to compete on the upcoming season of *The Epic Trek.*"

"The travel competition show?" he asks.

I nod.

"The one that's competed in pairs?"

He's onto me.

I nod slower this time, willing myself to look anywhere but his questioning gaze. Theo opens his mouth but then quickly reconsiders, leaning his head back against his seat. He may be bold at first glance, but I'm deducing he's far more measured than he lets on.

"And considering I met you alone at the bar . . ." His voice trails off as he reaches up and runs a hand through his hair, cleverly constructing the puzzle that is my conundrum with little to no help from me. As I sit quietly, debating how to proceed, I see he's looking at me, waiting, eyebrows raised and leaning in even closer than before.

"I don't have a partner," I say. Well, it's more of a whisper.

Theo looks genuinely confused. "How does that wor—"

"He dumped me," I shoot back. "My boyfriend and I showed up today after months of planning, and he dumped me at the check-in counter." It's not lost on me how pathetic this entire ordeal sounds coming out of my mouth.

It's the first time I've allowed myself to *feel* the intensity of my new reality. I'm single for the first time in years, and I'm livid. Clint gave up on us, on me, like it was the easiest thing in the world. Like I meant nothing to him. We weren't perfect, far from it . . . but we had a life together, and now, it's evident to me that none of it mattered or meant anything if it was that easy for him to just end things.

Theo's already kind expression softens even further. "Mierda," he says, his sudden Spanish jogging the list of curse words I'd committed to memory in high school. "I'm sorry." He puts a large hand on my knee, which causes me to shift in my seat as the heat from his touch sears straight through the fabric of my pants.

"Wanna know the kicker?" I ask, doing my best to hold his stare like a functioning adult. "The *whole* thing was his idea."

"No," he says, shaking his head in disbelief. "Seriously?"

"Oh yeah." I lean against our shared armrest, aware that

Theo's hand is still firmly planted on my leg. "It was one of those bucket-list or *someday* type of dreams for him, and he'd been talking about doing it for years. How could I say no to that when he finally decided to go after it?"

That just wasn't something I did, and I think on some level, it's not something that would have gone over well if I wanted to. Clint Hanson was raised to believe that he was in fact God's gift to humanity. His parents instilled such an unshakable sense of self-confidence and worth that he fundamentally believed his approach to life was the only one worth exploring. So, it became easier to go along with the plans he made or what he wanted to do because anything beyond that would upset the world order or throw the earth off its axis or something dramatic like that.

"Why go through with it now, then?" he asks. "If this whole thing was someone else's idea, why are you . . . here?"

I think back to Clint's words at the check-in counter. *You can't do this alone.* And maybe he's right. Maybe this will be the single greatest mistake I've ever made, but I don't have anything to lose, and right now, I want nothing more than to do the exact opposite of what he'd think I'd do.

To be the exact opposite of the person he said I was.

"I just need to prove I can," I say, without offering any further explanation. But Theo just nods, seemingly understanding that some things are better left unsaid. For now.

"So, what was your plan? Sit at that terminal bar all day and just pray you happened to stumble upon a potential partner?"

"Something like that," I say, shrugging my shoulders.

"I just *had* to come along asking for those damn mozzarella sticks," he says, his grin growing wider. "Mark is never going to let me live this one down."

"The first of many regrets you'll have since meeting me, I'm sure." That came out far more self-deprecating than I intended, but this has been the day from hell, so I'll allow it.

"I'm assuming your whole *be careful what you offer* spiel . . ." he begins, the smile lines forming around his eyes. "Bonus points for only being slightly ominous and murdery, by the way. Well done." I roll my eyes at him but struggle to hide my own amusement, which appears to make his toothy grin grow wider. ". . . Sorry, where was I? Ah, right. I take it your ominous warning means that you were planning on withholding the whole needing-a-partner bit until *after* we touched down in LA?"

He's not wrong. "When you put it that way, it sounds far more malicious than I intended," I say, crossing my arms over my chest. I totally *was* planning on telling him . . . eventually. Solidifying the fact that I am a horrible, *horrible* human being. "In my defense, I'm in new territory here. I hadn't thought through all this fully and then . . ." I reach back, massaging my neck in an attempt to root out the tension knot that's doubled in size. "There you were."

"I see," he says, pursing his lips. "Well, if you're done being a tiny little lying liar who lies about your intentions with me, I just have a few questions for you, if that's okay?"

"Of course." I feel every ounce of blood in my body settle behind my cheeks.

Theo sits up a little in his seat, turning his body to face me fully now as he crosses one leg over the other. "How long is the competition?"

"So, I don't have a definitive answer for you, considering it's all elimination based? But I was told during the application process that the entirety of the show shouldn't be more than four-ish weeks." Theo nods slowly, perhaps doing some sort of mental math or planning. "I'm asking a lot, I know . . ."

"Four weeks. That's . . . doable. And the reward?" he interrupts, resting his chin on his hand, before I can get the rest of my thought out. "The prize money. What's our incentive here?"

I could kick myself.

Why didn't I lead with the prize money? "It's quite a lot," I say, remembering how animated Clint was when he relayed the details to me all those months ago. "This is actually the show's twenty-fifth anniversary, so they've doubled the pot."

"To how much?" Theo asks, his eyebrow raising with intrigue.

"*One million dollars*," I whisper, and I'm not entirely sure why. It's not some secret that's going to get me killed if the wrong person is within earshot.

Theo blinks. "And . . . we'd split that?"

"Oh my gosh, of course! If we were to win, I would absolutely split the lump sum with you."

His gears are turning, and I make a mental note to remind myself that if he agrees to this, I want to ask him what he'd use his half of the money for.

"Alright, guapo," he says casually, like I'm someone who's used to being called that by an *actual* handsome stranger on a recurring basis. "Last question."

"And what's that?" I ask, trying, and I'm sure miserably failing, to remain calm at his compliment.

"What are *we*?" he asks, eyeing me with suspicion. Oh, he absolutely knows what *we* would be and he's probably just wanting to hear me say it out loud.

I clear my throat, nervous how he's going to react to this oddly specific detail, because honestly, if it were me? I'd run.

"They're expecting me to compete with my boyfriend."

No reaction.

Nothing.

My palms begin to sweat as I wait for him to say something. Anything.

"Which I know is ridiculously unrealistic considering we just met so I completely understand if you—" I'm pretty sure several people turn their heads in our direction as the near-hysteria rising in my voice echoes through the cabin.

"Boyfriend, huh?" he interrupts, finally speaking. He removes his hand from my knee and I am a little too aware of its absence. "I could be your boyfriend."

I repeat his words over and over again in my mind.

I could be your boyfriend.

Theo says it like he's being asked to shift plans ever so slightly—instead of getting Italian for dinner, he's fine with getting Thai. Or like a longtime friend called asking if they could meet up for coffee on Sunday morning instead of Saturday afternoon.

Like he's the most agreeable human on this planet and being asked to be a stranger's fake boyfriend is a regular occurrence in his life and not some huge, cringe-worthy ordeal, as my rising blood pressure would lead you to believe.

"Why?" I ask, completely suspicious about what kind of person would willingly involve themselves in something like this.

Theo bites his lower lip, a sign that he's thinking or, under different circumstances, perhaps an invitation—either way, he says, "Let's just say you caught me on a good day."

"I'm serious," I press.

"So am I." Theo slides more comfortably into his seat, his legs invading my space. "You want to know what Mark and I were talking about before I came over and—"

"—you tried to steal my snack?" I interject.

He groans. "More like politely offered to *buy* your snack, but if you want to hold that grudge, that's fine, I guess." Theo laughs, a rich, throaty sound, and when he does, his entire face lights up. "Anyway, before the whole mozzarella stick debacle, Mark was telling me how I needed to do something spontaneous. To shake up my life a little bit and step outside my comfort zone." His gaze lowers to his phone resting in his lap. "In fact, work demands it."

Now I'm the one leaning forward. "Meaning?"

He straightens in his seat, perhaps uncomfortable being put on the spot by a stranger, and right then, I see the smallest crack forming in the charming facade I was initially introduced to. "Let's just say I haven't been the best at maintaining a healthy work-life balance and leave it at that for now."

I'm intrigued, but if he is telling the truth, this whole thing would almost be *too* serendipitous.

"This is *very* unlike me, and this whole thing may just be a disaster waiting to happen," he says, which feels like the understatement of the century. "But I've got the time, and unless I missed the long line of volunteers begging to be your partner . . ." he says and places a hand to his forehead as he theatrically scans the nearby passengers.

I slow-blink at his poorly timed sarcasm, but I can't ignore the fact that he's right. This handsome stranger sitting next to me seems to be my only viable option if I'm going to go forward with this whole thing.

"If you're in, I'm in."

I don't know why, but I trust the sudden seriousness in his voice. Every instinct of mine is screaming that this is crazy, but there's something about the way he's looking at me that makes me feel like I can trust him.

Or he's just exceptionally good at pretending.

"What do you say, Asher Bennett? Shall we?" Theo offers his hand and the same smile I was met with at the bar returns to his face.

This is it—the now-or-never moment that just might be a defining one for my sanity. Are we doing this? Pretending to be boyfriends after a fifteen-minute conversation and knowing absolutely nothing about each other?

Fuck it.

Seriously, fuck everything about it. After today, what more do I have to lose?

I take his big and firm and surprisingly soft hand in mine. His smile widens, and I think the sight of it rushes all my blood to my head.

Or maybe this is just the Theo Fernandez Effect.

We shake, and when he returns my hand, the warmth of his touch still crackling over my palm like a flame refusing to be extinguished, he leans back in his seat and we continue our ascent. He's charming. Charming and direct and very obviously gorgeous and seemingly up for anything, at least far more than I am, which feels like a dangerous combination if you ask me.

He seems like a good time.

And I could use a good time after the day I've had.

Like him, this just might be the most spontaneous and out-of-character thing I've ever done. I'm terrified and my insides feel like they are melting from stress or unexpected excitement or maybe even a genuine fear that all this—my life and Theo and the fact that I am so far out of my comfort zone here it's bordering on hysterical—is going to tragically implode around me with all of America watching.

4

THEO

Los Angeles International Airport—Baggage Claim
Los Angeles, California

The jig is up.

Asher and I spent the flight in a comfortably uncomfortable silence, exchanging the exact amount of pleasantries and common courtesies warranted when traveling with someone you've known for all of three hours. He'd been on edge since we took off, head constantly swiveling, quietly excusing himself to go to the bathroom at least half a dozen times, and fidgeting with his seat belt. Based on the way he kept stealing glances at me as we crossed the continental US, I get the feeling he's sizing me up every chance he gets.

It's obvious he's spiraling.

Or at least hurting.

The guy is practically one big tightly wound ball of stress, and it only gets worse as we deplane after touching down at LAX. I watch his slim shoulders rise as we step onto the escalator, descending into the sea of eager passengers clambering to grab their belongings.

That's when I see her.

She's short with dark hair pulled back into a low bun. Dressed in all black with an annoyed expression plastered across her face, she stands holding a simple white sign that reads *Asher Bennett and Clint Hanson*. Even behind her tinted aviators, I can tell she's quietly judging everyone heading in her direction.

Asher nudges me, his sharp elbow landing right in my gut as if I hadn't already been scanning the room for every exit to be prepared when this all blows up in our faces.

Her head tilts in recognition and she lowers her sign. We're still about twenty or so feet away, but I can sense her looking between Asher and me.

We're now ten feet away, and if we make it through this unscathed, I swear I'll never eat another damn mozzarella stick in my life.

"Hi, um . . . that's me. I'm Asher Bennett," he says as we begin to close the space between us. I don't have to know Asher that well to know he's about as nervous as one can get. "And this is my boyfriend . . ."

She ignores him, stepping directly in front of me.

"Bullshit—who the hell are you?"

///////////////////

"No, Dalton . . . *You're* not hearing me. We've got a situation with the ga . . ."

Our firecracker of a production handler has been on back-to-back phone calls from the front passenger seat. After Asher and I wheeled our luggage to the curb, she seemed dead set on preventing us from stepping foot into the navy van, *The Epic Trek* written along the side in large, white block font.

"She was just going to say *We've got a situation with the gays*, wasn't she?" I whisper to Asher from the back seat and his lips twist into the faintest of smiles. We're still parked outside the pick-up zone.

What sort of equal-opportunity disaster did we just walk into?

"Don't mind Jo," our driver finally says, composed. She shoots him a look. I lean in my seat to peek in the rearview mirror and see he's dressed in a black linen bowling shirt that's unbuttoned at the neck, revealing a chest full of graying hair that seems to be stealing the spotlight from the thinning wisps atop his head. With one hand resting on the edge of the open window and the other casually resting on the steering wheel, he's every bit what you'd expect of a television crew member. "This job is her life . . . but she's one of the good ones," he says, staring back at me through the mirror. "Arthur Davis at your service. Cameraman, designated driver, and not one for forced small talk." I instantly love everything about his blunt honesty.

"Nice to meet you, Arthur," I say, wishing I were able to shake his hand. "I'm Theo Fernandez and this is my . . . *boyfriend*." That's going to take some getting used to for both of us. "Asher Bennett." I keep glancing up at Jo, who taps her watch, a nonverbal cue that prompts Arthur to start the van, pulling out of LAX's bustling loading zone and into the afternoon traffic.

"Pleasure," Arthur says politely. I keep glancing up at Jo, who's slowly shaking her head in what I can only imagine is frustration. Arthur nods his head toward Jo, a smile growing across his face. "She'll get you boys squared away. Don't you worry." Arthur's got this whole *I'm not going to worry about things I don't need to worry about* attitude.

Just then, Jo turns in her seat, removing her sunglasses and hooking them on the neckline of her shirt.

"I'm sorry about all that," she says after a painfully awkward silence. "I see y'all are already fast friends with my bestie, Arthur, but I'm Jo Bishop, your production liaison during filming, here to make sure that you"—she turns toward me—"*both of you* are set up for success throughout the competition. Care to explain to me how all *this* came to be?"

I raise an eyebrow in Asher's direction.

He swallows. "Long story short? Clint, who you were expecting, decided he couldn't do *this* anymore, whatever that means when spineless men say such things. Insert Theo."

Jo looks less than amused when I give a friendly salute.

"We met at the airport and after I explained my situation, Theo offered to pretend to be my boyfriend so that I could at least try to make it on the show."

"I'm sure splitting the million-dollar prize had absolutely *nothing* to do with this selfless act, right, Theo?"

I choose to ignore her not-so-subtle character insinuation. "That and I just couldn't resist the opportunity to use this experience to launch myself into being a full-fledged influencer. How does this sound," I say, plastering the biggest smile across my face. "*Swipe up for a ten-percent discount on this organic, all-natural facial cleanser. Use code THEO10 at checkout!*"

Jo and Arthur crack a laugh at my best Insta-famous impression.

"There won't be any issue with the . . . partner switch-up?" Asher asks after a moment.

"Yeah, about that." Jo gives us both yet another once-over.

She reaches beneath her seat and pulls out a thick black binder. "After talking it through with the rest of production, I went over your application paperwork and it appears we were thrown a bone." Jo begins riffling through the laminated pages, her manicured brows pinching together in concentration. "Ah, here we go," she says, pulling out whatever sheet of paper she'd been searching for. "It would seem that as long as *you* are here and competing," she says, nodding in Asher's direction, "we're in the clear."

Asher takes the page she extends to him. "I'm not following," he says, scanning the document.

"Cliff? Colin?" Jo starts.

"Clint," Asher corrects.

"It doesn't matter," Jo says, and I can't help but snicker. I like her too. "He filled out the paperwork with you listed as Contestant One."

"Meaning?" Asher looks as confused as I am.

"Meaning," Jo says, taking the application back from Asher to slide back into its spot in her binder, "that as far as production is concerned, you're the only contestant liable for competing this season. 'Asher Bennett and Partner,'" she reads.

"Liable?" he groans. I watch as Asher physically retreats into himself, putting his head in both hands. "This was a massive mistake," he says quietly. I feel the urge to comfort him, but honestly, I don't want to say or do the wrong thing when he probably just needs a moment to sort out his thoughts. I know I would.

"*Liable* is an aggressive word," Arthur says, weighing in for the first time. "I think what Jo means to say is that as long as you and whoever your partner is"—he raises an eyebrow at me—"show up and fulfill your end of the contract with production, there won't be anything to worry about."

"Exactly," Jo says, nodding in agreement. "*We* deliver a couple for our viewers to root for and *you* don't get sued for breach of contract."

Asher groans again, melting into the seat next to me as Arthur gives Jo a questioning look. He clearly is the more mellow one of the duo.

"And how exactly is *that* aspect of all this supposed to work?" I ask, finally sensing an opening in this conversation to interject. "The couple thing. How are we supposed to address the fact that we aren't actually dating?"

Jo appears to mull over my question, her eyes pinched shut as she taps an index finger to her lips. "Here's what we're gonna do," she says after a moment. "Truthfully, I'd be willing to bet that my boss wasn't listening to a thing I was saying on our call. He just kept shouting at me to fix it."

Arthur shakes his head at the mention of the show's host, and I can't help but wonder what the history is there.

"And that's what I'm going to do," she continues. A small crack appears in Jo's overly competent facade. This is obviously an unexpected wrench in her plans. A hiccup she absolutely didn't anticipate waking up to this morning. "All sorts of couples have been featured on the show, right?" she says, turning toward Arthur, who nods in agreement. The pair couldn't be more different, but watching Jo brainstorm in real time, it's abundantly clear they are entirely in sync.

"Who's to say how long the two of you have been together?" she asks no one but herself, really. "Maybe instead of an established long-term couple, we pitch this as more of a new fling. A couple nauseatingly in their honeymoon phase."

Arthur nods against his headrest. "They'll eat that up."

"Right? Okay, what if we do this," Jo says enthusiastically, twisting over in her seat to address us. "Let's keep it vague—elusive, if you will. The only people who know about the true nature of this relationship are currently sitting in this van." She seems pretty confident that Dalton has already brain-dumped their prior conversation. "So, if someone asks either of you about how long you've been together or starts getting into the nitty-gritty details of your dating timeline, just brush them off with something nondefinitive. Think you can do that?"

Asher remains silent.

"Seems simple enough," I say, feigning confidence in Asher's and my ability to pull off this whole charade. "How long have we been together, you ask?" I act out, turning toward Asher and nudging him with my elbow. "Oh, I don't know, babe . . . it feels like a lifetime!"

Asher's cheeks burn. "Kill me," he groans.

Jo's face drops. "That's . . . a start," she says, returning to facing forward. Asher's got his arms crossed now. He's leaning dramatically away from me and staring out the van's window. My uniform is bunching in all the wrong places cramped in the back seat next to him, California's perfect weather sending streams of sweat down my neck. As we drive in silence, I'm aware that this is the first real moment I can truly process what I've gotten myself into.

What pretending to be someone's boyfriend will *actually* entail.

On national television.

With everyone in my life watching.

And while meeting Asher the way I did is quite literally the answer to all my aviation problems served on one hell of a silver platter, the fact that my parents are going to be witnessing me race around the world with my so-called boyfriend is a can of worms I don't know that I'm ready to open.

Especially considering how well that turned out last time.

The travel will be easy. Between my time in the Navy and the tempo of my profession, I'm used to living entirely out of a suitcase for days on end.

The boyfriend part? That's another thing entirely.

I've missed about a dozen texts from Mark, his concern incrementally growing with each message, so I fire off a *you're the one who wanted me to be spontaneous* text with a promise to check in periodically, hoping that'll pacify his overbearing protectiveness. A twinge of something close to homesickness pulls at my chest when I think of Mark, but out of habit, I shove whatever that feeling is down to focus on the matter at hand.

Asher turns to look at me with wide eyes. "Do you really think we can do this?" he asks, his voice quiet. I'm not sure if it's nerves or if he's trying to exclude Jo and Arthur from this conversation. He's taken off his glasses, hanging them on his shirt collar. "Convince people we're dating?"

"Dating?" Jo says, chiming in before I can respond. The woman clearly has hypersonic hearing.

Even though she's not facing us any longer, I watch as Jo shakes her head. I'm determined to make her like me. "I need the two of you to be more worried about convincing the entire world you're head over heels and disgustingly in love."

Oh, right. *That.*

5

ASHER

The Ambrose Hotel—Room 201
Santa Monica, California

The second we step into the hotel lobby, Jo shoves something rectangular into my chest.

"And what is this for?" I ask, grabbing the phone before it can fall to the floor.

"I could be wrong," Theo says, abruptly getting up from one of the hotel's overstuffed armchairs, "but I think it's one of those new devices all the kids are talking about that lets you send messages to one another?" He walks over, those big arms crossed over an even bigger chest.

He laughs as I roll my eyes. "Wow, thank you, Captain Obvious."

Theo bows theatrically. "It's what I do. It's who I am."

Jo, whose expression gets more and more pained at our back-and-forth, clears her throat. "Are you quite finished?" she snaps, stowing the binder she'd been flipping through back in her canvas tote with a huff. "We need a picture of the two of you."

"What kind of picture?" I ask, turning the phone over in my hand.

But a rather bored-looking hotel concierge finally makes an appearance behind the check-in counter, pulling Jo's attention from us to making sure our rooms are ready.

"Nothing complicated, boys," Arthur says from his seat. He'd pulled out a rather worn-looking sudoku booklet the second we sat down and seemed to find it incredibly easy to tune us all out. "Just a photo Jo can post introducing you to our viewers."

"Will a selfie work?" Theo asks, and Arthur nods in approval. "Alright, how do you want to do this?" he asks, turning to face me.

I slide open the phone's camera, making sure it's on selfie mode. "Here, come stand next to me."

He shuffles over so we're now standing shoulder to shoulder. "Three, two, one . . ." I say, taking a burst of photos.

Before I can even open the camera roll to review them, Jo's attention returns to us. "Oh, look, Arthur—Mr. Grumpy Pants is posing with his brother," she says sarcastically. "Or better yet, his roommate."

Theo chuckles, but scrolling through the string of photos I've just taken, I am horrified to see that she's not wrong.

If someone told me we were supposed to *like*—not to mention *love*—each other based on this photo, I would have laughed in their face. I have a grimace pretending to be a smile plastered across my pained face. A perfect mix of awkward terror and unexpected constipation disguised as some botched attempt at happiness. But by comparison, Theo's smile is wild and genuine. There's a hint of excitement in his eyes, and the dimple I noticed earlier makes a timely appearance. I fight the urge to run my finger over it on the screen.

"Here," Theo says, offering his hand. "Let me try."

I hand him the phone, glad to be free of photographer duty.

"Is it okay if I put my arm around you?" he asks, his voice calm but direct. I nod.

Theo takes a measured step closer, closing the polite distance we naturally placed between us, and lifts one arm around my shoulder, outstretching the other to take a picture. But he doesn't just drape his arm around me—he pulls me flush against the length of him, our bodies all but fused together.

The sudden closeness to Theo sends electricity down my spine. It's the first time we've *really* touched each other. There's a sudden intimacy to how we're now positioned, something typically reserved for just Clint, but based on how Theo's body practically swallows mine—there's no comparison.

"Nothing complicated, remember," he whispers just for me, and I force a swallow. I almost bust out in a fit of nervous laughter, because there's nothing *not* complicated about any of this. He must have taken a photo because from one second to the next, he frees me from his grip, and the warmth of his large body against mine slowly seeps away from me.

Theo shows me the phone's screen, revealing a moment of candid intimacy between the two of us that feels both nothing like me and yet not at all forced.

"Hmm" is all I can say, and Theo takes that as some sort of approval, because he has already passed the phone back to Jo.

A small smile spreads across her face as she reviews it. "That'll work," she says, pocketing the phone and reopening her binder. "Here is your room key."

Room key.

Singular.

"There's only one room?" I ask, hoping the twinge of unease in my voice isn't as obvious to them as it is to me. Sharing a room with Theo is yet another detail to this whole charade that I hadn't quite thought about.

"Obviously there's only one room," she says dismissively, still flipping through her binder. "One room for our happy little *couple*. Do I have to remind you boys about the whole disgustingly in love thing we talked about earlier?" Neither Theo nor I say anything. "Look. I don't care what the two of you do behind closed doors—be friends or don't. Fuck, if it floats your boat. I *truly* could not care less. But here? On my turf and when filming is concerned? I'm going to need you both to hold up your end of the bargain and convince me you have what it takes to pull this off. Got it?" She crosses her arms, waiting for some sort of acknowledgment from us.

I'm pretty sure if I make eye contact with Theo at this very moment, I will melt into the marbled hotel lobby floor.

We both nod, a nonverbal agreement to her frightening terms, and I reach forward to grab the room key from her outstretched hand.

Our room key.

////////////////

Lying next to a complete stranger in bed is just as awkward as I'd feared it would be.

Even more so considering I'm wrapped up in the thick white duvet like a sad little burrito, afraid to move a single inch, while Theo couldn't appear to be less bothered, sprawled out next to me in his briefs.

Only his briefs.

After our lobby lecture from Jo, Theo and I rode the painfully slow elevator in not the most comfortable of silences. I'd used the key card to open our room's door, revealing a space with walls a deep navy that blended seamlessly into the dark velvet blackout curtains on either side of the long window. The sophisticated, monochromatic look is everything you'd expect from a swanky Los Angeles hotel.

But it was the very plush, very *singular* bed centered in the room—the very one we're currently attempting to sleep in—that sent my heart sprinting up my throat.

We'd taken turns freshening up in the cramped bathroom, sidestepping around each other like two stubbornly repelling magnets. I may or may not have snooped through Theo's open toiletry bag he left on the counter, surprised to see both how meticulously organized it was and that he seemingly always traveled with enough lube, condoms, PrEP, and poppers to supply an entire gay kickball team for a long weekend in Puerto Vallarta.

"Are you awake?" Theo asks quietly, his question interrupting a snowballing thought about the apparent abundance in Theo's sex life.

"Mm-hmm." How could I not be? Even though today has felt like the longest day of my life, there's no way in hell my anxiety about this mess is going to let me sleep.

"Jo's a little . . ."

"Intense?" I say, finishing his sentence. That's an understatement.

Theo snorts in the dark. "Very. I thought she was going to rip my head off the second we made eye contact."

That's definitely something I could envision. "I'm sure *this* is not something she is happy about dealing with."

He's quiet again, and for a moment, I think maybe he's fallen asleep. "Do you want to talk about it?" he then asks as he turns on his side to face me.

"Talk about what?" I ask, feigning naivety. I'm grateful for the darkness of our room, because Theo's question almost sends the pent-up emotions I'd been warding off all day teetering over the edge of whatever self-control I've managed to hold on to.

And the last thing I need is another man labeling me as emotional.

"Your ex. The competition. This whole fake-dating thing," he says quietly, every ounce of his words flooded with a sudden sincerity that feels more like a punch straight to the gut. "Any of it."

Today has been a blur. My nerves feel fried, and there's an incessant throb deep behind my eyes that's slowly been driving me mad. But since I put both time and distance between me and that terminal, my body and mind have been on autopilot.

And sadly, I think it took getting dumped this morning to realize that the last couple years of my life have been on autopilot. Some carved-out version of myself just going with whatever flow Clint dictated, because somewhere along the way, I gave him permission to slowly chip away at everything that made me . . . me.

Flashes of my life with Clint snap into focus while I ponder Theo's question.

Clint's comments about my anxiety disguised as some sort of partnerly teasing.

His lack of interest in—and oftentimes belittlement of—my professional accomplishments.

Looking back, the double standard of the life we'd built together seems endless, and while I can't pinpoint when exactly I settled for it all, becoming this shrunken shell of a human being, my biggest takeaway from today is that no matter how I tried—no matter how perfect I was—I was never, *ever* going to be good enough for Clint Hanson.

"It's just . . ." I start. But where do I begin? How can I possibly explain to Theo that right now, I'm more upset with myself than I am at my ex? That my self-worth feels absolutely depleted and if I really allow myself to spiral over the events of today . . . or the last seven years, really . . . I fear I'll slip into some sort of impenetrable self-loathing depression and never leave this bed? "You know what? Forget it. We should get some rest," I say instead, once again grateful for the darkness as tears streak my cheeks. "We have a busy day tomorrow."

He doesn't press the issue when I turn my back on him— away from his warmth, his unnerving kindness. He just lets me be. Gratitude swells inside my chest as I stare at the wall, praying he succumbs to his own exhaustion sooner rather than later. Praying for my silent sobs to end in the pitch blackness of this strange room.

6

THEO

The Ambrose Hotel—Room 201
Santa Monica, California

H ey, boys, mind if we steal you for a sec?" Arthur catches
us just as we step out of the elevator the following morning. "It'll only take a moment," he adds, quickly turning and
weaving through the hotel lobby.

Asher gives me an annoyed side-eye. Judging by his grumpy
demeanor all morning, I gather he didn't sleep well last night.

Once we step out of the brushed-bronze revolving door, Arthur leads us around the expansive building to a blocked-off
section of the grounds where Jo, who's simultaneously on a
phone call and aggressively typing one-handed into her tablet,
is standing waiting for us.

"Gotta run," she says, quickly hanging up. Her hair is pulled
back into a short ponytail under a simple baseball cap and once
again, she's dressed head to toe in black, a Jo Bishop staple, I'm
learning. "There are my favorite faux-bros! Feeling rested?
Ready to get this competition started?"

When I glance at Asher, he's fidgeting with the strap of his backpack.

"That good, huh?" Arthur says, shaking his head when neither Theo nor I say anything.

"Anyway," Jo says, not really caring that it's very clear we'd much rather be anywhere but here, "we need to capture a quick social media stringer—the first of many, actually, before the challenges start."

I immediately don't like the sound of this. Social media and I have a love-hate relationship. I pretend to be above it all and *act* like I'm indifferent to it in general, but I'd be lying if I said I didn't get stuck in a social media wormhole from time to time.

"And what's a stringer?" Asher thankfully asks, because I was wondering the same thing. Arthur busies himself with the sturdy tripod and begins setting up his large camera, adjusting the settings while assessing the current lighting situation.

"Just a series a video clips that we produce to either be split and posted online in shorter segments or, depending on the content, run as a whole video." Jo sets her trusty tablet down and grabs us each by the arm, like a mother leading a pair of oversize toddlers through life, and all but drags us in front of Arthur's lens.

"Okay, if you two can just . . . yup, stand right here, Asher—" she says, physically adjusting his stance to one that feels absolutely the opposite of natural. "And Theo, please scoot in . . . yes, right there. And put your arm here," she says, manipulating my arm around Asher's shoulder after she forced me to stand practically on top of him, clipping on a wireless mic before she turns away.

Asher looks less than amused when I cast my eyes in his direction.

"Eyes forward, please," Jo demands. Amid her puppeteering, Arthur has turned on two small but incredibly powerful lights, instantly bathing us in the heat of mobile stage lighting.

"*Fuck*, that's bright," I grumble under my breath, raising an arm in a measly attempt to shield my eyes. Asher, whose arm is now involuntarily wrapped around my waist, is drumming his fingers against my hip, his agitation building. "Mics are about to be hot," Arthur says, messing with the little box that allegedly turns our neck mics on and off at the touch of a button. "Camera's on, Jo . . . ready whenever you are." The camera's recording button glows to life, and I feel Asher's body become rigid against mine.

Several nosy onlookers have stopped beyond the barricade to watch us awkwardly stand while Arthur and Jo take their places behind the camera.

"Okay, Asher, let's start with you." Jo says, crossing her arms and looking between the real-life two of us and the two of us being captured on the camera's viewfinder. "Why don't you introduce the both of you and tell our audience what you're up to."

"Sure," he says, clearing his throat. "I'm Asher Bennett and this is Theo Fernandez, and we are competing on this season of *The Epic Trek*."

Jo and Arthur look at each other, neither of them saying a word, and I feel a slight tremor radiate through Asher, his entire body tense.

"Was that . . . horrendous?" he asks, the pitch of his voice rising ever so slightly.

"No, no, my boy," Arthur says, adjusting his camera settings. The red light turns off. "We just want to give the lovely people watching at home a little more to work with."

Jo silently nods in agreement. "Yeah, that was pretty bland." Arthur shoots her a look. "What? It was!"

An idea pops into my head.

"You know what the best part of reality television is?" I say, leaning in close enough that Asher's the only one who can hear me. Asher looks up at me, his eyebrow raised in curiosity. "It isn't real," I whisper, my lips just barely brushing his temple. "And you don't have to be either. So, who do you want to be, Asher Bennett?"

He bites his lip, a flush creeping up his neck, and I can practically hear the individual gears churning behind those green eyes. "Okay if I try it again?" he asks Jo and Arthur after a moment.

They both nod, the red light reappearing.

Asher takes a deep breath, his grip on my waist tightening when he does. "Hi everyone," he chirps with a level of cheerfulness so unlike the grump who could barely mutter three words this morning when our alarm went off. "My name is Asher Bennett and this handsome specimen next to me is my boyfriend, Theo Fernandez."

He yanks me even closer to him, turning his head slightly away from the camera. "Can I kiss you?" he whispers, his voice low and just for me.

I smile when our eyes meet, hoping he takes that as some nonverbal cue to proceed.

Asher leans up and places his lips lightly to my cheek, and whatever part of my brain that regulates how I'd normally respond to a cute boy kissing me feels conflicted.

His kiss is brief, casual, and logistically, I know it's strictly for the cameras, but that doesn't stop my body from reacting to this unexpected display of affection from . . . well, my boyfriend. I'm probably supposed to say or do something else, right? But judging by Jo's wide grin from behind Arthur, something tells me that whatever this was is exactly what Jo wanted.

"We're about to set off on our first challenge of this season's *The Epic Trek* and hope you'll be following along with us!" he adds, waving enthusiastically at the camera like a trained spokesperson who knows his audience. With the camera still rolling, Asher keeps smiling but rests his head on my shoulder, and I'm painfully aware of how awkward I must appear, standing there with a shocked smile painted on my face.

The red light finally turns off and Asher snaps out of whatever role he's just been playing, dropping his arm from its spot on my waist and taking a rather intentional step away from me. "Will that work?" he asks, putting his hands in his pockets.

"That was . . . oddly perfect," Jo says, clasping her hands together. "I didn't know you had it in you, Bennett," she teases.

Neither did I.

He adjusts his glasses. "It's all part of the game, right?"

But Asher turns toward me now and silently mouths, *Thank you.*

"You've got some downtime the remainder of the day," Jo says, swiping across the overly populated calendar on her tablet. "And then tonight, we have a quick preproduction all-hands with the crew, where you'll meet Dalton, his team, and the rest of this season's contestants." I'd wondered if there was going to be some sort of formal introduction to the pairs we'd be competing against. "But I'm begging you," Jo says, the familiar all-business tone returning to her voice, "please ensure you get some rest tonight considering we've got an early showtime tomorrow before wheels up for the first challenge." We both nod obediently as she rattles off additional travel details. She then turns on her heel and heads back toward the hotel with Arthur like some hyperpunctual mother hen, Asher and I trailing behind as her ragtag group of little hatchlings.

///////////////////

Stepping into the hotel's event space—which has been entirely taken over by the production team—instantly transports me back to high school.

Everyone's nervously scanning the crowd to see where they fall among the *cool kids*, their chatter an octave higher than normal as they do their best to appear unfazed by it all.

Jo dragged Asher toward the bar after escorting us from the lobby, in some attempt to loosen him up, if I had to guess. He'd shot me a nervous glance, his glasses falling down the bridge of his thin nose slightly as Jo weaved the two of them in and out of the minglers. Arthur ditched all three of us the second we crossed the room's threshold, his entire face erupting in a shit-eating grin when he joined a group of acquaintances, who seemed to have a bottle of beer waiting for him.

Which left me momentarily alone.

I don't mind doing my own thing. Don't get me wrong—I love people. My sister, Elise, would always get so annoyed at me growing up because I'd stop and talk to just about everyone I met out and about, quickly learning the obscure details of their personal lives.

But a few moments of mental quiet here and there are fine by me.

I retreat to the room's back wall and lean against it, closing my eyes in an attempt to tune out the conversations around me until they're nothing more than a soft murmur in the background. Mark always joked about how jealous he was that I could seemingly ignore the world around me as we navigated bustling airport terminals together. I bought him a pair of ear-plugs.

"I'm glad to see we're not the only ones bad at faking it," a distinctive Midwestern voice says from my left. Faking it? How can they tell? I open my eyes to see that I've been joined by a pair of women who look like carbon copies of each other, but separated by a generation.

"I'm not . . . we're not . . ." I begin to stammer defensively.

"Oh, you don't have to pretend with us, dear," the older of the two says. She's middle-aged with kind eyes and a joyful smile. When she places an oddly comforting hand on my fore-arm, an unexpected pang rattles around my chest as I think of my own mother.

"*This* is all so exciting, don't you think?" she says, removing her hand from my arm and waving it around the room. My gaze shifts to her companion, who I'm assuming is her daugh-ter, as she shakes her head, looking entirely inconvenienced by the whole situation. She's inherited her mother's fresh-faced features, but instead of long, chestnut hair to frame her heart-shaped face, hers is box-dyed a black so deep it's almost blue, with blunt bangs she's fiddled with a dozen times already. "I think it's okay to be a little nervous about it all. I know I cer-tainly am."

Relief washes over me when I realize what sort of *faking* she was alluding to. "It's very exciting, ma'am," I say, looking down at her small hand still on my forearm.

"Goodness, look at me, just chitchatting away," she says, shaking her head as if she's just recalled a more urgent thought. "Where are my manners? You're probably wondering who in the heck these charming and attractive strangers are who've invaded your space like a couple of nosy Nellies."

"Really, Mom? Charming and attractive?" her daughter groans, tilting her head back against the wall in annoyance. She can't be older than her late teens. "I apologize for my mother—she doesn't get out much," she says to me, looping her arm through her mother's. Despite her sharp tone, it's clear there's a lot of love between them.

"Shush, sweetie. I'm Jennifer Hale, but please, feel free to call me Jenn." Those drawn-out Midwestern notes cling to her every vowel. "And this snarky young lady right here is my pride and joy—my daughter and competition partner, Ellie."

"Theo Fernandez," I say, shaking their hands one after the other. "Lovely to meet you both."

"Likewise, Theo Fernandez," Jenn says, a soft smile spreading across her kind face. "Now, dear, who are you here with and why do I have to yell at them for leaving you all alone over here?"

Ellie barks out a laugh. "Have you considered the possibility that your new friend Theo *wanted* to be alone? I know it's a difficult concept for you to understand, Mother."

Jenn ignores her daughter's quip. "Nonsense. Theo wouldn't be standing all the way over here if he didn't secretly want someone like us to come and talk to him. Isn't that right, Theo?"

"You caught me," I say, putting my hands up, which only makes Jenn's smile widen.

"I like you," she says, patting my shoulder. "Now seriously, are you a part of the crew or are you competing this season?"

"I'll be competing this season with . . . him, actually." Right on cue, Asher makes his way back to where we're standing, a cocktail glass in each hand. "Jenn, Ellie, this is my boyfriend, Asher," I say, hoping I didn't place too much emphasis on our new romantic label.

"Hello," he says coolly, passing me whatever much-appreciated and expertly timed drink he's brought. As I put the flimsy cardboard straw between my teeth, the smooth bite of gin hits my taste buds. "I wasn't sure what you wanted, so I just got a gin and tonic. Hope that's okay," Asher whispers.

I wouldn't say gin and I are enemies, but after a few questionable nights out with Mark over the years, we certainly aren't friends. Nodding, I take another sip from the straw. "It's perfect. Thank you."

"Well, don't you two make quite the pair," Jenn says, which sends a soft flush of pink behind Asher's cheeks. He seems tired, indifferent even, but he smiles reluctantly at Jenn's compliment.

Her daughter rolls her eyes. "And that'll be enough of *that*," Ellie says, dragging her mother away by the arm. "Later, boys," she calls over her shoulder before the two of them saunter off toward a nearby table.

Asher visibly relaxes the moment we're alone.

"I'm just going to issue a blanket apology for whatever hell I've gotten you into," he says, the small crease just above his glasses smoothing. "Do you think all this is going to be hard?"

I arch an eyebrow. "What's that?"

"The whole *boyfriends* thing. On television." A flush of red creeps up his neck.

"I think it's only going to be hard," I say, softly tapping my index finger against his temple, "if we allow ourselves to get stuck up here."

His eyes bore into mine now, and for the first time, I take

note of the copperish flecks floating in the deep pools of green. Precioso.

"So, your plan is to just wing it?" he asks, and I can tell he hates everything about that.

"Winging it has gotten me to where I am today . . ."

Asher looks at me skeptically. "Traversing the globe with a complete stranger after having agreed to accompany him on a reality TV show? Hmm . . . Your excellent decision-making skills aren't impressing me, mister."

I lift my glass in his direction. "To winging it," I toast.

"Or something like that." Asher smiles gently, tapping his own glass against mine. "So, I've been thinking."

"Is that supposed to surprise me?" I interrupt. "Because if so, you're going to need to try harder than that."

Asher leans against the wall. "Oh, fuck off," he says abruptly. An attempt is made to sound authoritative or serious, but a smile tugging at each corner of his mouth gives him away. *There he is.*

"The sharp tongue on this one," I murmur against the rim of my own glass.

I watch as Asher retrieves a small notebook from his back pocket, setting his drink down on a nearby high-top table. "It's probably best if we get to know each other a bit better," he says, opening the notepad and tapping his finger against the page.

"You have . . . a list? A written list of questions?" Of course he does. "When did you have the time to do this?"

He shrugs his shoulders.

"Lay 'em on me," I say, crossing my arms.

Asher gives his list a once-over. "What is your favorite day of the week?"

"Sunday."

I watch as he scribbles down my answer in the margin of his notepad. *Nerd.*

"Why?" he asks, an eyebrow cocked.

"Because it's the one day I give myself permission to not feel guilty for doing absolutely nothing."

He smiles. "I like that . . . Okay, next question. Chunky or creamy peanut butter?"

My answer is typically divisive. "Chunky," I say quietly.

"Get out."

I *literally* laugh out loud. "What?" He looks at me like I just stole money from the elderly or said I don't believe in climate change. Which, of course, I do.

"I'm serious. That's heinous, Theo." But he's smiling again, and I think I like Asher a whole lot more when he smiles. He takes his time jotting down some remark next to his peanut butter question—something character-damaging, I'm sure—then continues his line of questioning.

"Where are you from?" he asks, angling his body in my direction.

"Just outside Madison, Wisconsin. We grew up on a lake."

He smiles and I'm curious to know why. "Do you have siblings?"

"I have an older sister, Elise. She and her husband, Stefan, have been together for what feels like forever, so I've always considered him to be like a brother too. Elise just opened her own pediatric clinic in our hometown and Stefan is a chef. Their schedules couldn't be more opposite, but they make it work for their kids." I can't help but smile when my niece's and nephew's faces pop up in my mind. "I'm rambling, I'm sorry!"

Asher just smiles, jotting down another note, *Guncle*, and underlining it. "And your parents? What do they do?"

I haven't been this intensely interrogated in a while. "My mom's a schoolteacher and my dad is a carpenter."

The familiar smell of sawdust and pine floats to the surface of my memory, sending a wave of nostalgia straight to my core. Summers and weekends spent side by side with my father in his woodshed as he crafted pieces of furniture from nothing, conveying each step of the process as he went.

My mother would bring us horchata when the weather was nice and then take her usual spot reading or knitting on the dock my father built.

"And how are they going to feel about you gallivanting around the world with some *boyfriend* they've never met? Won't they be confused?"

"Oh, I don't see it being a problem."

Which isn't a lie. It's playing by the unspoken rules my family has seemingly agreed to.

Don't talk about it. Don't shake things up. Be the old Theo they all know and love.

He quietly raises an eyebrow at the ambiguity I know is lingering behind my words.

"Seriously, my parents aren't the ask-about-your-boyfriend type," I say when I can't bear the silence any longer. "They don't ask about my love life and I don't volunteer the information." Not that there's anything to discuss anyway. "It works just fine for everyone."

Asher is a perceptive man, or at least I believe him to be, because he changes the subject without a second thought. "What musician would people be surprised to learn you have downloaded on your phone?"

"Too easy," I say, relieved to be wading back into shallower waters. "Ashley Tisdale."

He cocks his head at the immediacy of my response.

"Okay, wait," he says, leaning forward. "Are we talking *High School Musical* Ashley Tisdale? Or . . ."

"All of it," I say, unlocking my phone and opening my music library before passing it over to Asher. "The Tis must be protected at all costs."

I watch with zero shame as he scrolls through my extensive collection of certified bops. I like what I like.

"Alright then, someone's *clearly* a fan," he teases, handing my phone back to me.

"What can I say, I'm a man of exceptional taste."

"I can see that," he says, chewing on his bottom lip. "Moving on from Disney starlets, if that's okay with you?

"I'll allow it."

Asher shakes his head. "When you were growing up, did you have to have your bedroom door open or closed?"

"I'm sorry," I say, raising an eyebrow. "Was something supposed to have changed between growing up and now? Because every single door must be properly examined before bed and shut completely. Come on, Asher . . . I'm not a psychopath."

Another Asher eye roll. He begins trailing a finger down his never-ending list of questions, but I think it's my turn to pull out a few of his closet's skeletons. "That'll be enough of that," I say, swiping the notebook from his grip and tucking it under my arm. "I have a few questions of my own. Let's start with the basics—when's your birthday?"

"May eighth."

Ah, a Taurus. That tracks.

"Excuse me. What's the face for?" he asks, pushing my arm playfully.

"Just piecing you together, Asher Bennett," I say, and his nose scrunches up. I'm pretty sure he hated that entirely. "Okay, how about what you do for work?"

He folds his arms across his chest. "I'm a biomedical engineer."

"A what now?"

His face reddens.

"No one ever knows what I do when I mention that," he says, reaching for his glass. "We develop the technology and equipment to help diagnose certain medical conditions. Like right now, we're working on this incredibly exciting and even more frustrating artificial liver . . ." He's lit from within and it's the most animated I've seen him. "You know what? That's not important."

"Makes mental note to ask Asher all about artificial livers. Got it," I tease.

His cheeks flush. "What about you?" he asks.

I slow-blink. "Really? Are you forgetting where you met me?"

"Uh . . . right." Asher runs a hand through his blond hair. I bet it's soft. "Do you enjoy it?"

"Flying is flying, I guess."

Asher clearly picks up on my unintentional change in tone. "Is there something else you'd rather be doing?"

That's a loaded question. "You could say that. I was a naval pilot in another life."

"Oh, that's amazing," he says, and I can tell he's being genuine. "Thank you for your service."

I never know how to respond when someone says that, so I just smile and continue with our little game. "Anyway, I'm the one asking questions here, mister. If we win this thing, what would you do with the prize money?"

A faint smile grows across Asher's face. "That's a pretty big *if.*"

"So. Dream with me."

He's quiet for a moment, his gaze suddenly a million miles away. "*If* we were to somehow win," he says earnestly, "I'd use the money to start a program for LGBTQIA+ students in STEM. I've always wanted to work with students who have an interest in what I do, and it just seems like a great way to give back." He stares into my eyes from behind his tortoiseshell frames. "I don't know . . . that probably sounds boring."

I shake my head. "Definitely not boring."

Silent appreciation flashes across his face. "Thank you for saying that. What about you?"

Well, now I just feel like an ass. "My answer isn't as . . . philanthropic as yours."

His grin returns. "So? Tell me." Asher leans in a little closer, seemingly interested in whatever it is I have to say.

"I've been saving up for my own plane for a while."

He nods his head. "Considering your profession, that makes sense."

"Not just any plane," I say after taking a sip from my glass. "I've had my eye on this 1981 Cessna twin-engine for ages. It needs a little love but it's worth it." Asher's looking at me like I'm speaking another language, which is about how I felt when he was going on about robotic organs or something like that. "It's a small four-seater plane. Nothing special but everything I'd need."

"That's incredible," he says, smiling. "If we win, you owe me a flight."

"If we win," I say, handing him back his notebook, which he slips into his bag, "I'll be your personal pilot for life."

He throws his head back and laughs. "Deal," he says as the lights around us dim and dramatic music begins to blare throughout the room.

"Ladies and gentlemen, let's give a warm welcome to the man who makes it all happen—your host, Dalton McKnight!" an unseen voice echoes. There's no mistaking the show's long-time and historic—by reality television standards—host as he flits across the stage.

Like most actors turned reality television hosts, Dalton has had a long career in front of the camera, getting his start on the sets of the soap operas my mom and Elise used to watch. But if I remember correctly, it wasn't until this gig that his career really took off, making him one of America's most beloved household names.

Truthfully, that may be a stretch considering his stints in rehab and his seemingly never-ending list of toxic relationships, which without fail end up spread across the tabloids.

"Alright, trekkers, who's ready to kick off the historic season twenty-five of *The Epic Trek*?" Dalton shouts.

I've never wanted to sprint toward an exit faster in my life.

"They're *still* clapping?" I hiss in Asher's direction as Dalton seems to take his eighth clasped-hand bow following his introduction.

When Jo mentioned tonight's mixer, I hadn't realized it would be this . . . *theatrical*. Dalton is clearly the type to thrive on public validation, his ego visibly expanding to dangerous levels with each clap, threatening to suffocate us all.

"It's so refreshing to be back with you all—my family," he says from behind an alarming megawatt smile, resulting in a drawn-out collective *awww* from everyone around us. "I can already tell that *this* season is going to be incredible. Can you feel it? Because I can!" he asks the crowd. Their applause, now bordering on hysteria, is a resounding yes. He's in his element, the beloved master of ceremonies taking his rightful place in the limelight, and I've got to give it to him—he sure knows how to work a room.

"Before we wrap up for the evening, we've got a few house-keeping items to go over. Jo?" he says, turning toward where she's waiting in the wings before joining him on stage.

Dalton may be Mr. Flashy, but Jo is all business.

And I'm getting the sense she's really the one in charge around here. She takes the microphone from his outstretched hand, ignoring the strained smile he's throwing her way. "Thanks, Dalton. First and foremost, we are on a *tight* schedule that doesn't leave a lot of room for flexibility." A shared groan ripples through the crowd, but Jo doesn't skip a beat. "You all have been given detailed itineraries, so please, do me—and yourself—a favor and follow them. *Meticulously.*"

She flips through the pages of her clipboard, clearly double-checking she isn't forgetting anything. "We've got an early departure tomorrow—our hours are going to be long and tiring, trust me . . . I get it, so please try to get some rest while you can."

People must take that as some unspoken cue to leave, because one by one, the chairs around us start emptying. "Can I have the contestants hang back for a moment?" she asks, sitting on the edge of the stage and setting her clipboard and mic down next to her. She waits for the others to leave.

"I'm going to level with y'all . . ." Jo says, the bite to her all-business tone replaced with something more relatable, friendly even. "You're about to embark on some of the most tiresome and draining weeks of your life. You didn't hear it from me, but production has made a lot of changes recently, especially to the challenges . . ." Her brow furrows in a way that makes me think she isn't at all happy about said changes. "So don't go into this thinking that if you've watched previous seasons of this show, you've got it all figured out."

How reassuring.

"Social media is going to be key to this year's challenge," she says, waving her tablet in the air. "We've set up each team with a joint social media account that will be managed by their producer. Your success in this competition will rely not only on how well you do in each of the challenges but also on audience participation and engagement and by how you connect with people online," she continues. "So make sure you put your best foot forward when the cameras are rolling. We'll be coming around shortly to collect your personal phones, so if there's any last-minute messages you need to send, now's the time to do so."

I already messaged my family earlier, typing up a succinct explanation of the last twenty-four hours, so when the production team member comes around with a container, Asher and I each place our phones inside it without objection.

I can't say the same for the others. Jenn looks like she had to pry Ellie's phone from her hands mid–frantic typing.

"Before we call it a night, I want to run through the list of competitors this season," Jo says, crossing her legs. "Whether you choose to be friend . . . *ly* . . . or not is up to you." I'm pretty sure she's looking directly at Asher and me when she emphasizes this point. "Either way, we get a good show, so it doesn't make a difference to me, I suppose."

Jo flips through a few more pages on her tablet and begins reading.

There's Bianca and Jackson Mitchell—a twin brother and

sister duo with fiery red hair who look more prepared to go into battle than to mingle with the other contestants. Their pinched facial expressions lead me to believe they'll be exceptionally pleasant to be around.

We've already met Jenn and Ellie, who are waving enthusiastically at everyone. I like them. Jenn is clearly filled with a warmth and kindness that is just so stereotypically Midwestern, and Ellie, well . . . I can tell she's quickly going to become a favorite of mine.

Ivan Morales and Eddie Green, a pair of lifelong friends who served in the Army together. Honestly, I could tell they were veterans right away by the way they carried themselves. Despite their age and it no longer being required of them, they still have their hair cut in the classic military high and tight style.

The newlyweds from Florida—Griffin and Alana Peters. They're allegedly on their honeymoon, but no amount of forced PDA could make me believe those two aren't secretly miserable.

Garrick and Ivy Conners, a father-daughter duo from the Pacific Northwest, wave enthusiastically before foot-stomping the fact that Ivy was accepted to each of the eight Ivy league schools. How ironic.

Kiara and Ruby Moore are next—a pair of sisters and small-business partners from Nashville who allegedly have an organic candle business they plan to expand upon.

Dallas and Cameron, a pair of Gen Z influencers hoping to use this platform to raise awareness for . . . I'm not sure what exactly, to be honest.

And then there's us.

Asher Bennett and the schmuck just dumb enough to join him on this crazy adventure. All I want to do is find some food, take a hot shower, crawl into bed, and try not think about cameras and social media and all the ways I'm going to completely fail at being Asher's boyfriend.

I've never had much luck with that title.

Why would now be any different?

7

ASHER

Ben & Jerry's Flavor Graveyard
Waterbury, Vermont

Neither of you are lactose intolerant, right?"

Jo ambushed us the second we stepped out of the production van, her eyes wide with an excitement that I could only assume came from the first day of actual filming. Before Theo and I could even finish shaking our heads no, she'd pushed two shirts—each branded with *The Epic Trek*'s logo—into our direction and rather forcefully led us by the arm toward the tent.

I'm exhausted.

She wasn't kidding when she said we'd have an early morning. After tossing and turning all night—because let's be real, there is no way in hell sharing a bed with Theo will ever feel *normal*—Theo and I were showered, packed, and taking off to our first destination: Waterbury, Vermont.

"How much time do we have, Jo?" I ask, crossing my fingers that I can find some quiet corner for a few extra moments of sleep.

"Less than five minutes," she says, walking ahead without looking up. We cross a small patch of lawn sandwiched between two industrial compounds, and oversize sliding doors open as we arrive, revealing all the trappings of a makeshift set. Taped-down cords rope their way along the floor and massive clusters of lights hover above us, professionally positioned to capture every detail of our first challenge.

"Alright, my boys," Jo says, fastening a wireless mic to each of our collars. She turns to Arthur, who gives her a thumbs-up. "This is where I leave you. Listen to the rules, work as a team, and remember . . . what gets shared on the internet literally lasts forever, so *think* before you open your mouths. Make Mama proud."

Panic floods my veins. I don't think I'm ready for this.

The internet. If I wasn't half-frozen with fear before, I certainly am now as she pushes Theo and me in the direction of the chaos in front of us.

I'm definitely not ready for this.

"And we're rolling in three . . . two . . ." a voice calls out. The familiar tones of the *Epic Trek* theme song blare from speakers in every corner of the room, vibrating every surface, straight into my bones.

"Ladies and gentlemen," a hidden announcer's voice booms through the speakers. "Please give a warm *Epic Trek* welcome to your legendary host, Dalton McKnight!"

A faux round of applause fills the air as Dalton steps onto the platform in front of us. We're basically standing shoulder to shoulder with the other contestants, who I'm struggling to remember by name. Except for the newlywed couple, Alana and Griffin, who, thanks to their more aggressive communication style, have each enunciated every single letter of the other's name at least a hundred and eighty times since we've been around them.

Beyond the platform that Dalton is now standing on—the dramatic lighting magically taking ten, if not more, years off his face—are rows of giant silver vats, wooden pallets stacked high with boxes, and eight tables covered in various unidentifiable tools.

I literally could not even begin to discern what the hell we are walking into.

"Welcome to season twenty-five of *The Epic Trek*! I'm your host, Dalton McKnight." His voice, as animated as it is, is almost robotic. "Today, we're filming inside a Ben & Jerry's factory where thousands of gallons of ice cream are created and packaged each day."

Dalton's monologue catches my attention. Ice cream?

"But here, in Waterbury, Vermont, there's a sweet little one-of-a-kind secret," he says, turning toward the back of the room as another set of doors opens, revealing a sign in the background.

The Flavor Graveyard.

"What makes *this* Ben & Jerry's factory special," Dalton continues, gliding across his platform as several cameras follow his every move, "is that this is where discontinued and limited-edition ice cream flavors . . ." He pauses for dramatic effect. ". . . come to be buried. Figuratively, of course."

I watch the shared confusion ripple across the contestants' faces, and I'm thankful I'm not the only one who's seemingly lost. Dalton is now joined by a young woman who's casually dressed in a pair of slacks and a polo branded with the ice cream empire's recognizable logo.

"Here with me today is Ana Harrison, creative director at

Ben & Jerry's. Ana, care to share today's challenge with our contestants?" Dalton says, making space in front of the camera for his companion.

"Sure thing, Dalton," she says with a subtle twang of an upbringing far from here escaping her red, glossy lips. "Thanks for that introduction. Like Dalton said, what makes *this* specific factory location unique is our famous Flavor Graveyard—where, sadly, some of our more obscure flavors are discontinued and ceremoniously laid to rest."

A graveyard—an actual graveyard, complete with ornate tombstones and benches for grieving sugary-dairy aficionados, lies just beyond the open doors.

"Today, each pair will work together to re-create one of our retired base flavors using all of the ingredients behind these doors," she says, waving a hand at what I'm guessing is a wall-to-wall refrigerator to our left.

"But there's a catch," Dalton says, reclaiming his place in the glaring spotlight. Of course there is. "In order to re-create your assigned flavor, each team must match each ingredient here." Dalton continues his expert glide across the platform to the side that's been slightly hidden from our view by several camera operators. But now that they've shifted, an odd square grid of ice cream containers mounted ahead of each team comes into focus. I quickly count the rows: ten squares by ten squares, a pint of ice cream resting neatly in each one.

"One at a time, each contestant will take a turn at their respective grid with the goal of matching the ingredients needed to make their designated flavor." Dalton goes to the grid, randomly removing two containers from their spots. "Most flavors only have a few ingredients," he says, opening one of the pints to reveal a neatly printed *cream* under the lid. "So, as I'm sure you can guess, most of these pints are *not* a match." He opens the other and holds the lid up so we can all see the large red X beneath it.

It's essentially a life-size game of Memory. I'm sure there's a logical approach, but it really comes down to a combination of subtle strategy and pure chance. I start doing the mental math. There are one hundred containers of ice cream in each of the grids, and if we're meant to match them in pairs, that means there are . . . 4,950 possible opportunities for a match. I'll have to remember to thank my father for this mathematical competence when this is all over—he wouldn't let my brother or me leave the kitchen table each night until we went through some variation of times tables, long division, and quick-on-your-feet numerical scenarios.

"Once you find a match, however," Ana says, joining Dalton at one of the grids, "you will then race to the refrigerator to locate the ingredient. Once you do, it'll be a mad dash to bring it back to your individual mixer to get it added in," she says, waving to the row of tables intended for us beyond them. "The first team to match all their ingredients and get them properly mixed wins."

Seems straight forward enough.

"Our friends at Ben & Jerry's have also come up with something fun to sweeten the deal," Dalton says, once again finding his light directly in front of the panning cameras.

"That's right, Dalton," Ana chimes in. "The winning team will have a chance to resurrect a discontinued flavor of their choice, and, for a limited time, their ice cream—complete with their likeness and branding—will be available to the public!"

Theo nudges me. "I've always dreamed of having my face

plastered all over the desserts in the freezer section," he whispers, a smirk spreading across his far-too-smug face as he crosses his arms.

I can picture it now. Someone in middle America reaching for that pint of their favorite ice cream after a long, draining day of work and being utterly confused when they find Theo and me staring back at them from our spot in the frosty freezer. A laugh escapes me at the thought of us being actual *dairy queens*, and I make a mental note to try to weasel that pun into some conversation today. Theo slowly turns his head in my direction, puzzled by my reaction to the joke he's not in on, but I pretend I don't see it.

"Alright, contestants, are you ready for your very first *Epic Trek* competition?" The faux applause reappears. Were we supposed to clap, hoot, and holler? I almost join in but decide against it when I look around and see my fellow competitors are as still as statues. I don't want to be *that* guy.

"And the *trek* officially begins in three, two, one . . ." Ana and Dalton shout together before a loud buzzer goes off.

All at once, the other competitors take off toward the tables before them. Theo aggressively grabs my hand, his hot touch taking me by surprise, and I have no choice but to follow him at a near sprint. Any and all civility between us competitors quickly flies right out the window as elbows are thrown, and I'm pretty sure I see Bianca attempt to trip someone as we all race around Dalton's platform.

Theo weaves us through the chaos to our assigned table, with Arthur following closely behind. We find an envelope with our names on it and I instinctively rip it open, pulling out a thick piece of cardstock.

RAINFOREST CRUNCH—FIVE INGREDIENTS

"What's it say, babe?" Theo asks, his choice of pet name momentarily catching me off guard until I remember that yes, I am in fact his *babe* for all intents and purposes. I silently pass him the card and take off toward our grid of ice cream containers, randomly selecting two, noting that we need to locate five matches.

Shit. Both red X's.

Theo's turn. He selects one pint that lists an ingredient, *vanilla*, but then another red X and puts them both back.

I quickly step forward, grabbing the *vanilla* pint he just put back and selecting another at random—a new ingredient, *cream*. I roll my eyes but take a mental picture of where both ingredient pints are so I can start making pairs in my mind. I notice that at least two other teams have made their way to the refrigerator.

Theo strolls back over to the grid, selecting another set of pints without any rhyme or reason. He shrugs when he realizes they're both red X's and puts them back, his demeanor completely absent any sort of urgency.

Normally, I couldn't care less about anything competitive. But with the lofty prize money on the line? The dreams I have for my science program—unrealistic or not—flash in my mind.

"Nice try, *babe*," I say when Theo makes it back to our table, hearing the twinge of annoyance that's starting to build. "But it's a race, remember?"

I watch as Theo's brows pinch together before I jog over to our grid, and once there, I grab the pint I know says *vanilla* and reach for another. *Vanilla.* Our first match. I run back to the table, placing the pints down as I pass by and continue to the massive fridge—shaking my head at Theo's unwarranted but kinda cute congratulatory cheers. It takes me no time at all to locate the small container with *vanilla* written on it, and within seconds, I've grabbed it and emptied its contents into our mixer, the sweet aroma of the vanilla extract trailing behind me.

Back and forth Theo and I go to the grid in the hope of finding the rest of our matches. He's picked up the pace, which I'm thankful for, but neither of us has made another match, and I can feel myself getting frustrated.

Just as a not-so-subtle comment disguised as encouragement is on the tip of my tongue, he randomly procures a match from the wall: *condensed milk*. Theo runs toward the fridge, athletically avoiding two of our rivals who turned at the same time to collect their own supplies, and races back to our table to pour the contents into the mixer.

After about a dozen rounds of back-to-back red X's, Theo matches *sea salt* and quickly gets that added to our mixture. I fail to find a match on my next turn, but Theo unexpectedly matches our fourth ingredient, *cream*, and runs off toward the fridge. There's no way of knowing how many matches our competition has found at this time, but it makes me feel a hell of a lot better about our standing knowing we only have one more ingredient remaining.

However, neither Theo or I find a match on our next two turns, and any hope I had quickly evaporates.

Theo finally selects a pint labeled *milk*, but unfortunately, pairs it with yet another red X. I watch as his shoulders slump in frustration.

I go to grab the *milk* pint he just put back and do my best to remember the zones we haven't been routinely pulling from. While it isn't necessarily a strategy, I've been mentally sectioning our grid into smaller ones that I've rotated between with each turn. Right or wrong, it's how my brain makes sense of things like this.

Out of frustration, I snatch for the pint almost dead center of the grid and hope for the best.

Milk.

Finally. I flash the lid to Theo, who throws his fists in the air in exhausted celebration, and I take off toward the fridge in search of our final ingredient.

"Come on, milk . . . where are you?" I mutter to myself as I rummage through the various containers. I'd imagine it would be in some sort of glass. Maybe a pitcher?

I spot it just as I get bumped from behind. *Hard.*

It's Jackson. "Move," he growls, pushing past me to grab whatever ingredient he needs.

Oh, hell no.

Gripping the handle of the thick plastic pitcher, I quickly but carefully make my way back toward our station, where Theo is standing next to the waiting mixer, a wide grin plastered across his face. The pitcher is oddly heavy, and some milk sloshed over its rim on my way back. Even though I'm using both hands, I don't have confidence in my wet grasp.

"Here, let's do it together . . ." he says, reaching for the handle as I'm about to start pouring it in.

"I've got it," I snap despite my tenuous grip, but he ignores me, and something about this makes my blood boil. "Wait, don't . . ." I choke out, trying to maintain a solid grip on the handle—and my patience—but it's too late. His hand collides with my slick one, eliminating what little hold I had on the pitcher, and it slips straight through my fingers onto the ground in painful slow motion, the finale a big *clang*. There's an audible gasp from around the room as Theo and I are left dripping with our fifth and final ingredient.

A random bell goes off, and Dalton's annoying voice returns booming throughout the room. "And we have a winner!" he shouts. I don't even have to turn to face his general direction to know who won.

The twins.

I angrily wipe the milk from my eyes with the back of my hand. I am completely soaked. The chilled liquid is sloshing in my shoes and dripping down my neck and I'm certain I swallowed more than a mouthful in shock amid the sudden dairy downpour. What was Theo trying to do, grabbing the pitcher like that? Especially at the finish line.

We were *this* close to being done.

Movement around us ceases as the remaining pairs realize the challenge is over.

"What the hell was that?" I hiss when I turn to face him.

Theo flinches, his facial expression unrecognizable, shifting quickly from stunned to remorseful to entirely confused.

"I'm sorry, I just thought . . ." His voice trails off, his gaze dropping to the floor. "It was an accident."

"An accident! Theo, that was just plain careless," I bark. I'm more confused than anything. Neither one of us had *helped* the other like that with any of the other ingredients. "I said I had it and you didn't listen to me," I press, realizing this has very little to do with Theo and everything to do with the fact that I've spent the last few years being ignored by Clint.

Disregarded.

Belittled.

Like who I am and what I bring to the table were so insignif-

icant that it was the easiest thing in the world to just wave
me off.

"I said I had it," I repeat, my voice a mere whisper this time.

He opens his mouth to say something but decides against it.

"Uh-oh . . . sounds like there's trouble in paradise." *Shit.*
Dalton's voice reminds me of where I am and the fact that
Arthur has been hovering just out of sight the entire time.

He for sure just got all that on camera.

Great.

Epic Trek? More like Epic Disaster.

///////////////

Theo isn't in our hotel room when I finally make my way back
up there.

Even though I want nothing more than to watch as the
remnants of our failed challenge wash down the tub drain, I
decide against a quick shower because squashing the tension I
created, figuring out a real path forward so that every challenge
doesn't end in one of us scolding the other, is far more important.

It doesn't take long to find him.

He's sitting on the side steps of the quaint hotel, a serene
patio that stretches out into the wildness of the surrounding
Vermont woods. Theo's leaning back on his hands looking up at
the immense northern sky, whose colors are quickly fading
from hues of pinks and burnt oranges to deep and endless blues.

I pray the peace offering I thought to grab on my way down
will be enough to smooth things over. I may not *actually* be
dating Theo . . . but the last thing I'd want to do is make him
feel a sort of way because of my shitty behavior. I'm not myself
right now. There's no sugarcoating that Clint royally fucked

every part of me that cared about anything, and while I can't see that side of me going away anytime soon, I have no business being rude to be people who genuinely don't deserve it.

People like Theo.

Especially because, and I know I have to do a better job of reminding myself of this, he *is* doing me a huge favor.

"Can I join you?" I ask, hoping the nerves in my voice aren't as apparent to him as they are to me.

He looks up, unfazed and seemingly happy about my arrival. A warm and very much undeserved smile spreads across his face. "Of course."

"I brought you something," I say after I've sat down beside him, handing over the pint of ice cream I snagged from the production fridge when no one was looking.

Theo takes it from me, turning the container over in his hands. "They sure do move fast," he says, tapping the label with his thumb. *Bianca and Jackson's Peanut Butter and Jelly* in all caps is written in Sharpie across a piece of painter's tape on the side of the pint. "Think it's any good?" he asks, raising an eyebrow in my direction.

"Let's find out." I pass him one of the spoons I brought with me as he pops open the container and sets the lid down on the cool paver between us. The ice cream has melted slightly from my walk here in the summer heat, making it easier for him to scoop out a heaping spoonful before passing the pint back over to me.

The rich vanilla ice cream is complemented by the sweet and tart flavors of the blackberry jelly and, much like anything in life, the creamy peanut butter just makes it all the better.

"I hate to admit this," he says, reaching for the pint again and taking another big spoonful. "But despite Bianca and Jackson being absolutely bitter human beings, they taste pretty damn good."

He's not wrong.

"Seriously—I could eat this all day," I say, almost forgetting why I brought it in the first place. I sneak a glance at Theo, observing the smile still plastered across his face as he's between bites. It reminds me that he just may be the happiest, most carefree human I've ever encountered.

Which ultimately makes me feel worse.

I exhale, smelling the sweetness of the jelly on my own breath. "I owe you an apology," I say, my voice retreating like the colors of the sun. I can feel the heat radiating off his body the moment his head turns my way, but I don't want to look at him.

Not yet.

"You really don't." There's no emotion, good or bad, to his voice.

"No, but I do—" I catch him eyeing the pint of ice cream still in my hands. I pass it to him, which makes him smile once more. "I do, Theo," I repeat as he sets the container down next to its lid, but not before taking another bite. "Today was—"

"A mess?" he says, finishing my sentence with a slight smile.

"A mess and unnecessary and I can only say how sorry I am for the way that I acted."

He leans back on his hands again. "I don't take that kind of stuff personally," he says after a long moment, releasing the clutch his silence had on my heart.

"Still, I was wrong for how I treated you and I'm very, *very* sorry." My apology lingers between us, leaving me worried both that it's not enough and that my outburst earlier has definitely scared Theo off. I wouldn't blame him—I'm usually much better about keeping everything bottled up.

"Most couples argue during tense moments, right?" he asks, picking up the pint again and taking another bite. He angles it in my direction, and I take it, our fingers grazing this time. "Most couples bicker and say things they don't mean in moments of anger."

He's normalizing my reaction, which saddens me and makes me feel slightly better at the same time. "Of course, but . . ."

"They can move on from weird moments of conflict, especially when one or both parties apologize."

I swallow the ice cream that's now partially lodged in my throat. "Right . . . but we aren't *most couples*."

"Here, we are," he says matter-of-factly. "Here, we are just like everyone else: a couple who has good days and bad days and everything in between."

Theo sets his spoon down on the paver beside him and wipes his hands on his joggers. "But I appreciate the apology . . . and the ice cream," he says, nudging me with his shoulder. "The challenges are only going to get harder from here and I don't know about you, but I don't think I can stomach a Bianca and Jackson victory lap."

Ugh. Just the thought of them winning another challenge makes my stomach knot. "I know."

"But we'll be okay. You and I are just figuring each other out," he says, and I want to believe him. But I'm frozen at the possibility that I'm damaged beyond repair. That it's only a matter of time before Theo realizes the colossal mistake he's made, leaving me here to face this all alone. "As partners . . . and as a couple."

8

THEO

Old Stagecoach Inn—Room 204
Waterbury, Vermont

'm going to hop in the shower, if you don't mind."

I peel off my clothes, which are now awkwardly stiff and emitting a smell resembling a sour bar rag from the dried spilled milk, and turn the water on as hot as it can go, stepping into the shower's spray before the water has a chance to warm up.

I'd be lying if I said I hadn't been looking forward to this very moment all afternoon.

A moment to just shut my brain off.

Away from the cameras and Jo's bossiness.

Even a moment away from Asher.

His apology meant a lot. Not that I needed it, but it was nice to know that deep down, he's not the kind of guy to just unload on someone else—whether they deserve it or not—without feeling some semblance of remorse.

As soon as he pops up in my mind, my head instinctively swivels in the direction of the bathroom's door.

In my haste to get under the water as quickly as possible, I realize I didn't shut the bathroom door. Like at all. Modesty has never been an issue for me. Am I in the best shape of my life? Absolutely not. I'll never be one of those shredded gays deemed most valuable on Grindr or social media. It's taken a while, but I love my body just the way it is. And unless one were sitting at the edge of the bed, staring directly into the oversize mirror hung above the low dresser across from it, which has a perfect view of the all-glass shower I'm currently fully nude in, my error with the door shouldn't be an issue.

The now-scalding water feels incredible, and within seconds, I feel the tension in my body begin to loosen. I massage the sweet-smelling soap across my skin. Tilting my head from side to side, I make small circular motions at the base of my neck, trailing a hand over each tired shoulder. As my hands glide over my stomach, Asher's reflection catches my attention from across the room.

He appears to have plopped down on the floor and is leaning himself against the foot of the bed in some sort of attempt not to get the bed dirty—something I'm deeply appreciative of.

The tall glass shower door is already covered in a layer of thick condensation, so my view is pretty obstructed. Like looking through a camera lens unfocused, the general shape and outline of what I'm looking at is distinguishable. But the details? Not so much.

However, movement catches my eye. Is he . . .

No mames. Is he jerking off?

Steam billows from the heat of the water pouring down on me as I watch a blurred version of him in the mirror. My breath catches in my throat, fearing that if I exhale, somehow he'll know that I'm looking and my own personal show will be over before it really even started. I feel like a voyeur in our hotel room, silently watching from a safe distance as the unsuspecting object of my wildest desires carries on with his business.

I shouldn't be doing this but my cock throbs anyway.

There's no question about it. Asher is definitely jerking off. He's leaned his head back against the bed, his face turned upward as I watch his arm move up and down from behind the steamed glass. Slow and steady at times, more sporadic at others.

I definitely shouldn't be touching myself to this.

But I can't help it.

I quickly lose my battle of self-control and slide my hand down my wet body, grabbing my own cock and timing my movements to his.

My hand feels so damn good, and now that I think of it, I can't recall the last time I got off. But cumming would literally solve all my problems right now, and sneaking a glance at Asher, it would appear he feels the same.

A choked-out moan nearly escapes my lips as I watch Asher bring his hand to his mouth, return it to his cock—an impressive one from my view at this distance—and resume his strokes, his head now slumped forward in pleasure. Emboldened by the entire situation, I reach up, using my forearm to wipe the shower's glass and create a peephole, hoping it doesn't cause him to freeze.

Or stop.

Time feels like it has ceased to exist and if you told me I was somehow still breathing as I waited for some indication from Asher of whether this is okay, I wouldn't believe you. But after a painfully torturous moment, his expression—now in sharp clarity—darkens. From across the room, his green eyes latch onto mine, a not-so-subtle signal for me to continue. He's like a siren calling to me from behind glass, his song begging me to fulfill whatever deliciously devious thoughts my sex-fueled brain can muster.

Talk about a plot twist.

Slowly, we each resume our movements, pleasuring ourselves like we have a million times before behind closed doors. Watching Asher watch me just might be one of the sexiest moments I've ever accidentally stumbled upon. I wipe the glass more than once, removing any and all condensation blocking his view. I even angle my body in his direction so he knows without a shadow of a doubt that this—this moment and the one he's getting me dangerously close to—is just for him.

I can feel myself reaching the point of no return. We're both furiously jerking off our own cocks, and if I were feeling any braver, I would wave him in to join me under the shower's spray. But I decide not to push my luck. Gripping myself tighter and tighter, I watch as Asher's chest heaves, a silent cue he's on the precipice of release. He looks like a goddamn fever dream with his mesh athletic shorts—and, to my surprise, a black jockstrap twisted down around his thighs. What I wouldn't give to be between them.

Or have him between mine.

Higher and higher I climb as my dick begins to throb in my hand. *Fuck.* I want this so bad. No, I fucking need this—the brain-scrambling, body-tingling numbness that only comes from an orgasm. And it's almost here. My breathing spikes as I watch him pump his cock over and over again, a mirror to my own frenzied movements. *Fuck.* I'm about to blow and as my balls tighten and my breath catches in my throat, I have to grab the top of the shower door, bracing myself for what's to come.

Asher's body shudders as mine splinters apart. He lifted the hem of his shirt just in time, taking it between clenched teeth. Rope after rope of his thick load paints his exposed stomach in time with each well-practiced stroke, and my own coats the shower door right behind his in the most euphoric and needed of ways. My mouth waters at the thought of tracing the lines of his mess with my tongue, lapping him up as he lays there panting. Leaning my head against the shower wall, my wild breathing slowly returns to its usual cadence as I watch Asher get up from his spot against the bed, pull up his jock and shorts—expertly adjusting his still-hard cock up into his waistband—and step entirely out of view like I haven't just watched one of those Sean Cody scenes I've had favorited for years come to life. Worry over how this could complicate things starts to creep in, though, replacing the fading tingling sensation in my hands, my face, and every nerve ending in my body.

If some line was crossed, there's no coming back from this.

///////////////////

"Here," I say, shoving Asher the grease-soaked paper bag containing a breakfast sandwich—a bacon, egg, and cheese on an everything bagel—from the only food option open at this hour. "I grabbed you this." Our flight boards in less than an hour, and the only detail I could get out of Arthur on the way to the airport is that we're headed to South America.

Asher looks at me from his spot sprawled out on the terminal floor, exhaustion swirling behind his glasses. "I'm fine," he murmurs.

After our mutual . . . festivities . . . last night, he completely closed himself off. Again. He'd tiptoed around me like some cringe-worthy changing of the guard after I cleaned up the mess I made in the shower, getting ready for bed and crawling in without a word and avoiding all eye contact.

"Come on, you should really eat something," I insist, more forcefully this time. "I overheard Jo telling some of the crew we won't have an opportunity to grab something when we land. Besides, how long has it been since you've had anything in your system?"

"You keeping tabs on me now, Fernandez?" Asher shoots back, a hint of a smile forming from the corner of his mouth.

"I believe that's what boyfriends do, *Bennett*," I say, echoing his nickname of choice, which makes that smile of his fully appear. I slide down the wall, claiming the spot on the floor next to him, our shoulders pressed against each other. Part of me was worried he'd flinch at the sudden physical contact, but he doesn't seem to mind. Instead, he takes the bag from my outstretched hand, his glasses slipping down the bridge of his freckled nose as he opens it. "You've been . . . quiet. Alarmingly so," I add.

Asher picks at the bagel but doesn't say anything.

"If this is about last night . . . If I made you uncomfortable or anything, I'm really sor . . ." But my words trail off when Asher speaks.

"You didn't."

His shortness leads me to believe he's not entirely telling the truth. "Are you sure?" I prod. "You seem to be avoiding me."

"If you haven't noticed," he says, bumping his thigh against mine. "It's kinda hard to avoid you." I hate thinking I'm unavoidable. Some big burden that's just in everyone's way, even unintentionally. I've always been too much. Too loud or too impulsive. I'm pretty sure I used to drive my abuela crazy by bouncing all over the house when I was younger, and once I was old enough to know better, I somehow figured out a way to channel the bubbly energy that came in waves into something a little more grounded.

Something that doesn't make people leave.

"I just think I'd feel more comfortable if we had some rules," he says quietly.

"For . . . ?"

"Rules to make sure *this* . . ." he says, flailing a hand between us. "Rules or guidelines or whatever you want to call them, so it's not immediately apparent that we aren't *actually* dating and rules to make sure we don't get carried away."

"Ah, so this *is* about last night."

"You said it yourself, Theo," he says, and I'm now realizing his thigh is still pressed against mine. "We're partners. And the last time I checked, partners have rules."

"I guess that's fair," I say, but my intrusive thoughts shout something about how rules always end up getting in the way of fun. I would know. "What are you thinking?"

"No sex," he blurts out almost immediately. And loudly too. Loud enough that several passengers waiting at our gate nosily crane their heads at us.

I choke out a laugh. "That's both presumptuous and mildly disappointing."

The flush returns to his cheeks. "I don't mean to be presumptuous," he says earnestly, but if I didn't know any better, I could have sworn his gaze shifted down to my lips and back. "I just feel like it'll only, you know . . . complicate things."

"Well," I say mulling over his proposed "rule." "We wouldn't want this entirely normal and not at all staged situation to be even *more* complicated." A gentle laugh slips through his pursed lips. Reaching into my bag, I grab a pen and whatever loose paper I can find. "I feel like we should be writing this down to, you know, make this whole thing even more official."

Asher groans as I write in all caps *NO SEX*—underlining it twice—and I have to remind myself I'm now allegedly forbidden from liking these little sounds of his.

"Well, if sex is off the table, you aren't allowed to fall in love with me."

"Love?" he hisses, appearing to nearly choke on the bite he'd just taken. "Who's the presumptuous one now?"

"Listen. I'm afraid it's bound to happen," I say, hoping Asher picks up on the humor in my voice as I write *NO FEELINGS* on our scrap of relationship paper. "We're going to be sharing hotel rooms and kissing for the cameras . . ."

"Kissing, huh?" he repeats, and I'm trying hard not to stare directly at his now-parted lips and wonder if they are really as soft as they look.

"Oh, tons of kissing. Loads," I say, intentionally laying it on thick. "You heard Jo. They're expecting romance and fireworks. A couple that both checks the diversity box *and* is actually into each other. And last time *I checked*, couples who are in love definitely kiss. I mean, come on . . . we're literally sharing one bed. Have you seen any rom-com within the last twenty years? It's bound to happen."

"Hm" is all he can manage. I've screwed myself by mentioning kissing and the fact that we are indeed forced into such close proximity, because all I can think about now are things that would *definitely* be violating our very first rule.

"You have to stop looking at me like that," he chokes out after a moment.

"And how might I be looking at you, Ash?" I tease, knowing full well how I'm looking at him. Like I'd watched him come undone right in front of me last night and I'd be lying if I said I didn't want to do it again.

"Like someone who hasn't met a rule he didn't take as a personal challenge," he says, nudging me firmly with his elbow. "It's like there's always something *else* behind those eyes of yours." Which is rich, because he's the one staring at me from behind two deep emerald pools I could easily and willingly drown in. The thought surprises me, but then again, so has Asher.

"Have you considered that this just very well might be my face?"

Despite his need for so-called rules, Asher seems lighter.

Still as tightly wound as ever but, I don't know, more playful?

Slightly less guarded?

He shakes his head. "No, sir."

I swallow hard. Okay, that *has* to be intentional. "Sir, huh? It's like you're trying to tease me now."

"Oh, don't start," he says, shaking his head again at my ridiculousness, but even though Asher needs rules and is fresh off a breakup . . . after last night? I think we're just starting to scratch the surface of his flirtatious charm.

"You know I prefer to be called *sir*," I say, quickly correcting him. "Keep up, Bennett."

He rolls his eyes. "Rules. Let's focus on the rules."

"Ah, yes. *Those.*" I scrunch my face like I've just eaten something sour. "Let's see . . ." I tap my pen to my lips. "We've got no sex—which, let's be honest, is a rather bleak way to kick off this whole rule thing." He ignores my side-eye. "And no feelings—again, good luck with that, babe." Asher looks like he could kill me. "What else?"

He wraps up the second half of his sandwich, quickly tucking it away in the front pocket of his bag. "Let's just make a pact to be honest," he says after a moment. "I know we're lying practically every second Arthur's camera is on us . . . but let's not lie to each other."

His voice is sad, and I could be reading too much into things, but maybe it's possible that all this—the breakup, the competition, even me—is weighing too heavily on him. I don't know what it is about this man that sends my protective instincts into overdrive. From the little I've been able to piece together about Asher, it's not hard to tell he's experiencing one hell of an emotional whiplash. I wish I could peel back his guarded layers and really get a sense of who this man is. People have always been easy for me. To charm. To understand.

To sleep with, if I'm being completely honest.

But there's something I can't quite pinpoint about Asher Bennett. One minute he seems so nervous to be around me he might pass out, cheeks red, all limbs, and the next, he's cold and unreadable without a single warning. Then there are moments in between where he seems less extreme. Soft, content moments where there's a warmth burning just beneath the surface.

That's the man I'm determined to know.

"No sex. No feelings. No lies," I say, recanting our list of rules. "Too easy."

Asher fidgets with his bag strap, something I've noticed he does in the lulls of conversation. "I also think we need a safe word," he whispers.

"A safe word? Explain . . ."

"I know myself, or at least I used to," he says. "I'm going to need a word or a phrase I can say when this whole charade feels too big and too complicated. I don't want to get confused or say or do the wrong thing, so it would help if we had something that would ground us back in reality. Is that dumb?"

"It's definitely not dumb." I hope he believes me. "I think I understand. You need something to hold on to. Something real. That's not dumb at all."

He stares at me with something that looks like relief.

"My friend Mark," I continue. "You know, the guy I was trying to steal your mozzarella sticks for?" He nods. "We joke and troll each other all the time, so he and I have this thing that when we want to talk about something serious, we say a phrase I introduced him to from my time in the Navy—*Whiskey, Tango, Foxtrot.*"

He blinks. "You say what now?"

His momentary confusion is adorable. "*Whiskey, Tango, Foxtrot*—the phonetic alphabet for WTF, or what the fu—"

"Oh," he interjects. "Of course! That's . . . cute. But why?"

"Honestly? I can't remember how it started, but it's become our version of a 'friend check' and we've been using it ever since. The moment either of us says it, the other knows it's about to get real. We could use that if you'd like?"

"We can't use *your* thing with your friend. That's supposed to be special."

I shake my head. "The entire US military uses that expression; I think we're fine."

"Nope, we need something that's ours."

"Ours?" I ask, the word choice making me smile. "I've got it."

Asher signals me to go on with his free hand, clearly eager for whatever it is that I've *got.*

"If either of us says *mozzarella sticks*, it's on," I say, hoping it'll elicit some sort of laugh or smile from him.

He barks out a laugh. "Mozzarella sticks? That's what you're going with?"

"Listen, it's how all this started, so, if you ask me, that's as official as it gets," I say, extending my hand in his direction.

"Attention passengers in the terminal, Flight DL2302 will begin boarding in ten minutes."

"Asher Bennett, do you consent to our newly finalized rules for this season of *The Epic Trek*?" I ask, doing my best Dalton impression.

Placing a warm hand in mine to seal the deal, Asher nods. "I'd be foolish not to."

9

THEO

Three miles off the coast of Buenos Aires
Buenos Aires, Argentina

Can we get an extra life jacket over here?" Jo yells into her headset.

Once Arthur successfully parked and managed to drop us off at the marina, we were quickly ushered across a large dock built into the island's peninsula. We climbed the set of stairs leading up to an expansive boat deck, where several of the other teams had already begun getting into position, and followed Jo to our spot.

"An adult extra-large should be fine," she barks after taking another glance at me. How humbling. Jo shrugs innocently when she realizes I've been hanging on her every word. Ellie catches my eye through all the commotion and gives a small wave, rolling her eyes at everyone running around with filming about to begin. Asher and I are sandwiched between the Army pals and the newlyweds, both of whom appear to be squabbling like old couples.

"Here," Jo says, pushing the life jacket she's been holding into Asher.

He looks at it like it's venomous. "Must I?" But she ignores him and he does as he's told, quickly securing the offensive flotation device around his tall body and fastening the clasps one by one. A PA runs across the deck toward us with another life vest in tow, which Jo quickly rips from his grip and tosses at me.

"Okay, listen up," she says, pulling her tablet out of her bag. "I can guarantee that neither of you is going to be too pleased about today's challenge." Before either Asher or I has a chance to react, she preemptively cuts us off. "I don't want to hear it. After the whole ice cream fiasco, I need you two to give a little bit more than *this*, okay?" she says, gesturing at us.

I glance at Asher, who's now fiddling with the straps of his life preserver while I fasten mine. He's pale. Paler than normal, which is saying something. The boat then lurches forward, and I wonder if he has an issue with motion sickness.

"When you say this . . ." I ask, turning my attention back to Jo.

"Guys, seriously," she says, folding her arms. "I've had dental procedures with more convincing chemistry." A laugh catches in my throat, but when I look at Asher, I see he's shoved his hands deep in his pockets, either uncomfortable or annoyed.

Or both.

"You two assured me that when the cameras were rolling, you'd sell one hell of a love story. It's time to pay up," Jo says. "I'm looking at you, Asher Bennett."

His head snaps up when Jo singles him out.

"If there's any part of you that wants to make it to the finale, you're going to need to try a little harder. Understood?"

Asher nods, his cheeks reddening at the public callout, and I fight the urge to say, *Yes ma'am*. The snap behind Jo's tone makes me stand up a little straighter, and the others have stopped to observe the two grown men who just got scolded by their stage mother.

"Go easy on them, Jo," chimes in Arthur, who, unlike his counterpart, is all smiles this morning. He tinkers some more with his portable sound equipment. "I've got you boys hooked up with a nice little waterproof camera on your boat. I mounted it myself. Hated doing it, though," he says, his lips pulling into a thin line. "It's the first time it's being used so do me a solid and don't break it."

Out of nowhere, Dalton comes careening through the chaos of crew members finalizing whatever shot they'd been setting up. "Alright, people, let's get this over with," he calls out impatiently.

Jo steps between us and places a hand on each of our shoulders. "Do not let me down."

I'm not usually one to feel the pressure of others' expectations, but as Jo backs away, her eyes shoot daggers at Asher and me, and I immediately have the urge to make her proud.

Zoom in on Dalton.

The show's intro music fills the open air from the speakers along the boat's perimeter and Dalton takes his mark in the center of it all.

We're rolling in three . . . two . . .

I watch Dalton's face transform. From one second to the next, he's changed the annoyed grimace for which only Asher could give him a run for his money into the dazzling and charming face of a master of ceremonies.

"Good morning and welcome to yet another exciting episode of *The Epic Trek*," he says. The main camera operator side-steps around him, panning to ensure the expansive ocean paints the perfect backdrop. "I'm your host, Dalton McKnight, and tonight, we are surrounded by hundreds of miles of ocean as our contestants face their next challenge."

Hundreds feels like a stretch considering we were only moving for about fifteen minutes, but okay.

"In just a few moments, each of our teams will be dropped off on their own sailboats that have been anchored off the Puerto de Buenos Aires. Using whatever is available to them, and with the help of some basic instructions, they'll work together to assemble their sails, navigating their way back to our starting point in La Boca."

I sling an arm around Asher's shoulder and lean in close. "We got this in the bag."

Doubt takes center stage on his face as he mouths, *The bag?* at me but remains quiet, allowing Dalton to continue his monologue.

"Remember, while both speed and accuracy are important in all our challenges, no one on *The Epic Trek* is ever fully safe," he says, turning his attention from the camera to us. "Our loyal viewers at home will *help* decide which teams advance to our next challenge"—I keep forgetting that this isn't just a race and that the votes from the viewers are taken into consideration—"*and* who will be sent home."

The camera operator swings wide, panning to us at Dalton's cue as we stand lined up alongside the other contestants. Jo not-so-subtly signals our attention and mouths, *Chemistry*, her facial expressions extra dramatic from beyond the view of the operator. I remember to smile and inch a breath closer to Asher. His hand brushes mine, soft and hesitant, but it's the first time he doesn't jump out of his skin at my touch. In fact, it feels like he's purposely keeping his hand in place as the camera's lens lands directly on us.

His fingers lace through mine for the first time, the slightest tremble behind his touch, and when I look down at the simple gesture and then back up to his waiting gaze, he just shrugs like the act means both nothing and everything. A slow smile tugs at the corner of his mouth, one that spreads as if it's deciding in real time whether it wants to reveal itself. But when it does? I'm thankful the cameras have found a new subject, because no one needs to watch me forget how to breathe in high definition.

All this receives an enthusiastic double thumbs-up from Jo.

Dalton wraps up his spiel, and we continue toward our respective boats. But all I can think about is how it feels to have Asher's hand in mine. The firmness of his grip and the way I can feel the severity of his nerves. I find myself thinking of something reassuring to say, something that will remind him that we're in this together or that he can count on me. But the moment passes as production begins dropping each team one by one onto much smaller boats.

Of course, we're last.

"Remember," Jo calls after us as we climb down the rickety rope ladder to our own boat. "We need chemis . . ."

But the sound of the waves slapping against the boat's hull drown her out. We step down onto the wood of the small sailboat and bob up and down in the chop of the rough water. Jo and the crew get farther and farther away from us, becoming pinpoints where the sky meets the sea. Nostalgia washes over me as my so-called sea legs adjust to the unnatural movement of the boat. I haven't been on a sailboat like this in years—not since my sister and I would spend nearly every waking hour on the lake on the old Sunfish my father surprised us with when I was in middle school. Elise and I would take turns piloting the boat around the lake, jumping off the deck into the water to cool off when the Wisconsin sun became too unbearable. Asher, however, has immediately claimed his post on the built-in bench, his knuckles white as he grips its ledge, a look of abject horror painted across his face.

"You okay . . . babe?" I ask, adding the relationship-appropriate pet name when I notice the camera Arthur mounted.

"I'm fine," he whispers through tight lips. Every muscle of his lanky body is tense and rigid. Judging by the way he's also breathing, slow and intentional, it's clear he's anything *but* fine.

"It helps if you look at the coastline," I say, sitting down next to him.

"Huh?" Asher cocks his head but keeps his eyes glued to the boat's deck.

"For motion sickness," I say softly. "It helps to scan the coastline and keep your eyes moving instead of looking down. Try it."

He doesn't move.

"Come on, Ash," I say, the nickname slipping out accidentally, but I can't guarantee it won't become a thing. "Just try it. I promise it'll help."

Slowly, he lifts his gaze, maintaining his controlled breaths of the salty air in the process. I watch his shoulders relax slightly as he shifts his head from side to side, taking in the distant coastline just like I instructed.

"Better?" I ask, hoping it helped a bit. Do I rub his back? I know I'd like that if the roles were reversed, but since I haven't quite gotten a grasp of what Asher's comfort level with physical touch is, I all but sit on my hands.

"Better," he says between inhales. Relief flashes behind his wide eyes when they meet mine. "Thank you."

"Of course." I linger next to him longer than I probably should considering we are officially mid-challenge at this point, but a large part of me is concerned that he'll get sick.

"So," he says, wiping his palms on his pant leg. "Shall we?"

"Are you feeling up to it?"

"Do I have a choice?" he says, forcing a smile. There he goes, putting on his facade like armor. I want to press the issue, to tell him it's okay if he needs to collect himself for a moment, but he's on his feet in no time, hands on hips and ready for business. The sailboat is midsize, I'd estimate around thirty feet in length, with a thin but completely bare mast. At the far corner of the stern sits a wooden box covered in *Epic Trek* branding, so that seems like a good place to start.

Asher beats me to it.

On unsteady legs, he opens the lid, revealing a folded heap of canvas and a thick loop of white rope. Running the rope through his hands, one over the other, he looks up at the mast behind us, his expression laced with equal parts determination and fear. "Alright, Mr. Midwest, any idea where we begin?"

It's been years since I've been on a sailboat, let alone assembled the sail. That was something my dad always did, but when Asher passes me the rope, a lifetime of memories comes crashing back. "I think the first thing we should do is unfold the sail to make sure we get it laid out in the right direction."

I watch Asher's eyes scan the thin mast, and I begin to lay out the large canvas between us.

"Here," I say, holding the rope out to him. "As I roll it out, follow behind me with the rope and weave it like you would a shoelace through these grommets here," I say, tapping the metal rings along the sail's edge.

He takes the rope from me, inserting it through the first grommet, and then another. "Like this?" Asher asks. We're both kneeling now, practically nose to nose, and I'm not sure if it's the way the light is hitting him or the reflection of the deep hues of the ocean, but his eyes have never appeared this vibrant. Depths of jade stare back at me, and for the briefest of moments, I'm too stunned to talk.

Come on, Fernandez. Focus.

"Is this wrong?" he asks, insecurity lingering in his voice.

"No, that's perfect," I say, shaking my head.

We work in tandem, me pulling and stretching the sail to make room for Asher as he continues weaving the rope in and out. When we're finished, we each stand up, admiring our handiwork before we need to attach the sail to the mast.

"We just need to get this . . ." I stretch up on the tips of my toes, trying to get the end of the rope through the pulley at the top of the mast. ". . . there. Now, we should be able to pull this all the way down . . . Yup, just like that," I say, as we work together to pull the length of the rope up and back through the pulley, effectively securing one portion of the sail to the mast.

Almost done.

"Ash, you see that line right there?" I say, nodding to the other end with my chin. He picks it up, quick to understand where I'm going with this. "Yeah, that one. If you can just run it through the pulley over there on the other end of boom, we should be all set," I say, tapping the long, horizontal pole attached to the mast.

He does what I ask, repeating the hand-over-hand movement we just did together on the mast.

"Alright, the last thing we need to do is attach that rudder to the stern—the back, sorry—of the boat and we're golden."

Asher picks up the removable rudder, inspecting it from behind his glasses before placing it in the groove at the back of the boat. "Here?"

"That should be good?" With the sail and boom in the way, I can't be completely sure, but once we hoist the sail, I'll be able to adjust if necessary. "Can you come and help me with this?"

"Aye aye, Captain," Asher says, giving me a half-assed salute that my former commanding officer would have had a field day with.

"We're going to raise the sail now, and when we do, we just need to remember to watch out for the boom," I say, patting the thicker piece of metal between us. "Ready?"

"Let's do it," Asher says, his demeanor now absent any seasickness he may have been feeling earlier. He almost looks like he's having fun—an important first for us.

He's so close now. Close enough that I can feel the warmth—his warmth—radiating off his sun-kissed skin.

Focus, Theo.

"Pull!" I shout.

We do, with all our might, our hands clumsily trampling over each other as we raise the sail inch by inch until the crisp white fabric reaches the top of the mast, bucking as it finds the wind. We're practically flush against each other now. Two random puzzle pieces at first only pretending to fit together, but somehow, even though they were plucked from two entirely different boxes, starting to realize that perhaps, by some stroke of actual fate, they do.

I'm starting to think I don't care whether it's all for Arthur's perfectly placed camera.

Or if Jo's words are ricocheting around his brain like they are mine.

Chemistry.

All I know is that Asher Bennett is looking at me in such a way that makes me think he's weighing his options. Like he's trying to logically calculate the odds against his next move. And maybe, out here in the middle of the waves and the chop and the warmth of the now-setting sun, he's figuring out if I'm one of them.

"You know what I'm thinking?" I ask, my voice a barely there whisper. I lean into him to ensure my lips are concealed from the camera's lens.

This is it.

The point of no return. The one that could change whatever dynamic has been brewing between the two of us, and if I'm wrong—if I'm wrong and somehow miscalculated whatever signals or insinuations that kissing me is something Asher is even remotely interested in—my humiliating rejection will find its permanent home in some depressing corner of the internet for me to relive at my leisure.

"What's that?" he asks, his chest rising and falling rapidly from the sudden increase in cardio. His hair is wild, and his glasses are tilted ever so slightly on the bridge of his freckled nose. If I didn't want to kiss him before, seeing a genuine smile dance across his face as he stares into my eyes seals the deal.

Something's clicked this afternoon.

Something that has made the thought of kissing Asher Bennett stop feeling like something I'm supposed to do and instead feel like something I want to do.

Like if I don't taste that smile on my own lips, this moment will somehow be forgotten.

An unexpected dip in the waves shifts our bodies suddenly, and with the sail's ropes in one hand, I reach down to place a steadying hand on Asher's waist, doing my best to hold him in place.

"I'm thinking a real couple would probably kiss right now," I whisper through halting breath, intentionally grazing my lip on his temple.

Asher slumps against me, and I'll never know if it was because of the force of the sea or my words but watching his lips part makes my stomach flip.

"You know, for the camera," I add, reminding him of the roles we've agreed to play.

"Right," he says, swallowing hard. "That."

"Can I kiss you, Asher?" I ask after a lingering moment, our cheeks now pressed together, and he doesn't hesitate to nod, slowly nuzzling his way toward my lips. My grip on his waist tightens, and I pull him even closer as he tilts his face to mine, a bracing hand intentionally placed on my chest.

It would be cruel to drag this out any further. To lean back and allow every second—every unexpected detail—of this moment to reveal itself like a candid Polaroid. Sliver by sliver and then beautifully, all at once.

But Asher's pressing the entirety of his body against me now, so whatever patience I've tried to exhibit reaches its limit. With my eyes pinched shut, I search for his mouth, my lips dragging across the expanse of his stubble. His breath hitches, and if the wind hadn't been forcefully funneling into the sails around us, I'd know with certainty if a soft moan just escaped his lips or not.

Desperate to have both hands on him before our lips fully collide, I fumble with the excess rope between us to tie it around the hook of the boat's mast when a massive gust of wind comes barreling toward us from behind.

The boat lurches forward, its fully furled sail stretching against the force of the wind. Asher and I are ripped from each other and thrown backward.

We slam into the back wall of the stern and reach out for the lip of the boat or anything we can get our hands on to avoid toppling overboard.

But the rudder—and Arthur's camera—weren't so lucky.

Between the violent gust and our bodies careening backward, the rudder was knocked off its groove and sent crashing toward the ocean floor.

And Arthur's camera and its entire mount follow right behind it.

"Well, that's inconvenient," I say, peering over the side of the boat. Asher slumps down and rests his back firmly against the boat's wall. "What is it they say about sailing in a rudderless ship?" I can't help but laugh at yet another mishap on the Asher and Theo reality show from hell.

He looks at me, glasses askew on the bridge of his nose and mouth agape in disbelief. "I'd be willing to bet it's nothing good."

"Nope."

//////////////////////

"Well, now what?"

After scanning the boat for something, anything, with which to rig some sort of makeshift rudder—we even tried hanging off the stern of the boat and plunging our arms as deep into the water as we could reach—we gave up.

"Now, we wait," I say, furling the sail and securing it back to the mast. Without a rudder, we'd be sailing around directionless, so there's no point in leaving the sail up. "I'm sure production planned for some sort of mishap like this." I hope.

Asher and I sit side by side in silence on the boat's bench.

The burn of his scruff against my lips is still there. Same goes for the way I felt so pulled to him. And honestly, it would be so easy to straddle him where he sits now, grab his face in both my hands, and pick up right where we left off. But judging by his quiet demeanor and the deep flush climbing its way to his cheeks, I'm fairly positive whatever *almost* moment we had is officially over.

"Arthur's gonna be pretty pissed about that camera," he says after a moment, breaking the silence.

"Yeah, I'm glad it wasn't me who knocked it in," I say, nudging him with my shoulder, in response to which he chokes out a laugh.

"Oh, so you're just going to rat me out like that? I see how it is," he says, poking me back. "Where'd you learn how to do all this? The sailing."

I shrug. "It's something my dad taught me."

"Did you spend a lot of time on the water or something?"

"My family's house is on a lake," I say, and as soon as I do, every detail of the lake house flits through my memory. The faded shingles. The dock I helped my dad build. All of it. "Being on the water kinda comes with the territory."

Asher seems to mull over my response. "That must have been amazing."

"Yeah, my sister, Elise, and I would have to get dragged back home from the lake by our parents. But when I first started sailing, the bobbing motion, even the slightest shift in the water, would make me so sick."

"Can't relate," he says dryly, rolling his eyes. "Thanks for the coastline trick, by the way."

"Of course. What about you? I take it you didn't spend much time on the water?"

He shakes his head. "Absolutely not. I'm sure this won't surprise you, but my family is not the outdoorsy type."

"You don't say?" I mock, feigning surprise.

"Don't be mean," he says, elbowing me in the side, and I don't think there's a reality where I could ever be mean to him. "I *did* go to camp every summer, but again . . . it wasn't outdoorsy by any means."

"Tell me more about this non-outdoorsy summer camp."

"I'll pass," he says, but before he can double down, I interrupt him.

"Mozzarella sticks."

Asher throws back his head, letting out a loud laugh that ricochets all around us. "Seriously?" he snaps, but even he is unable to contain his smile. "This is what you want to use *that* on?"

"Mm-hmm," I say, nodding my head. "If I don't know everything there is to know about a young Asher Bennett attending summer camp, I'll die. Did you all wear uniforms? What about bunkmates or counselors?" Asher rolls his eyes as I sling an arm around his shoulder. "Oh, did you have a camp crush? Tell me everythi—"

"Okay, okay," he says, shoving me off him. "I'll tell you *everything*," he says, drawing out the word. "Although I can assure you you're going to be sadly disappointed by the lack of salacious stories about science camp."

"Science camp, huh?" I repeat, trying not to laugh but failing. "You know what? That makes sense."

Asher smiles wide. "If you think I'm embarrassed about that, you're wrong. In fact, my summers at camp were some of my happiest memories growing up."

"I hope you know I was only teasing," I say, bumping him with my thigh.

"Oh, I know," he says softly, but even in the dimming light, I can see Asher's thin face fall as he looks out across the water. "It was the first, and honestly the only, place I ever felt I belonged. I didn't have to worry about fitting in or being made fun of just for being myself. That does something to a kid. Something others grow out of or can shrug off more easily. But for me, if I wasn't the nerd . . ." He takes a deep breath, turning now to face me. ". . . I was the faggot. It was always one or the other. Without fail. So, showing up to that camp in the middle of the woods each summer meant that I could just be Asher."

He straightens from his spot on the bench. "And that's enough."

The weight of *that word* lingers between us.

One that I can guarantee has been hurled at every gay man our age on more than one occasion out of spite or ignorance or just plain hatred. I remember when it had been directed at me for the first time. It was during an away basketball game in sixth grade, and I'll never forget how Jordan Farrell looked at me when I started changing into my uniform next to him before the game. I wasn't out—hadn't even begun thinking about boys that way or the fact that I might be different. But he grabbed his clothes and labeled me with that word anyway before I truly even understood what it meant. It stuck like all nicknames and labels do.

Especially the hurtful ones.

And when I think about how much of my childhood was wasted trying to be the opposite of what Jordan and everyone else called me, it both breaks my heart and fills me with a rage I can't put into words.

But before I can tell all this to Asher, to stand with him in painful solidarity of this shared life experience during some of our most formative years, we're both blinded by a tidal wave of light.

"*Mantengan tranquilo,*" a robotic voice blares, and a sleek boat comes into view. I'd argue we've done a pretty good job of remaining calm given our current predicament. "*La ayuda va en camino.*"

How mortifying.

Both Asher and I leap to our feet. Gratitude for our lost-at-sea adventure being over has quickly replaced any momentary embarrassment from having to be rescued in such a dramatic manner.

Standing front and center of our mid-ocean extraction is Jo, a worried crease growing between her brows even though she appears to be doing everything in her power to hold back a smile. "Seriously?" she yells, as we are thrown a rope by a rather annoyed-looking guardsman. "The Argentinian coast guard?"

Asher is pulled up over the side of the boat while several other members of our ragtag rescue crew secure our sailboat to the side of theirs. A rough hand then reaches for mine, pulling me up as well and delivering me next to a waiting Jo.

"We were worried about you two idiots," she says, pulling us both in for a hug the moment we are safely standing on the deck. "What the hell happened?"

Asher and I exchange glances.

"Weren't you the one who wanted chemistry?" I say as she grabs both sides of my face, shaking her head. "Well, chemistry happened."

"Mm-hmm," she mutters, a sly little grin returning to her face. She lets go of her mama-bear grip on me and pulls out her tablet. Clearly, she's already begun teasing the whole ordeal online, because when she pulls up our social media feed and points out that #Thasher is trending, clip after clip of Asher and me sitting side by side on the boat appear on the screen. In more than one instance, expertly altered memes of the infamous *Titanic* shot of Rose and Jack floating on the door with our faces Photoshopped onto their chilled bodies fill the frame, leaving me both in awe and utterly terrified of the power of the internet.

"Wait . . . how?" I ask, wondering where this salvaged footage came from.

"The camera set up on your boat was streaming video back to our computer. So, we were able to get a nice little chunk of today's challenge up until you two threw it overboard—Arthur's livid, as I'm sure you expected," she adds, and I can't help but laugh. "Nice work, you two." Jo nudges Asher with her hip, but he doesn't pay her any attention—his eyes haven't left mine, and for the first time, I feel like he's made the intentional decision to be okay with someone else seeing him. Truly seeing the quirks and the scars and whatever it is that goes on behind those questioning eyes of his. In the middle of the ocean, where there was not a soul around but us, walls that had been so firmly rooted by their foundations were lowered, even if momentarily.

Our boat speeds off back toward the shoreline where today's challenge began. Asher's eyes are on a constant scan of the horizon like I'd instructed earlier, and he's bathed in the soft, pale glow of the moon's light, every nook and crevice of this man now illuminated so clearly. The salty air fills our lungs, and for the briefest of moments, there's no more hiding.

I can't pinpoint the *what* or the *why* but whatever curiosity or intrigue or even just baseline attraction I've felt toward the man I'm supposed to be dating is now inching its way toward an unignorable part of my brain.

The part that is starting to blur what is just for the show and what will break all our rules.

10

ASHER

Mio Buenos Aires Hotel—Ballroom C
Buenos Aires, Argentina

When we return, we'll reveal the team America has decided to save."

Camera one on Dalton still . . . and cut.

There were a lot of annoyed glares when Theo and I finally made it back to production's staging area, where the rest of the contestants were waiting in various states of exhaustion under the bright production lights. Even Ellie looked like she was ready to strangle us. In fact, the only person who seemed at all concerned for our well-being was Jenn. She practically threw herself at us, angry-whispering how worried they'd all been.

Judging by the fact that Bianca and Jackson have been staring daggers at Theo and me since we stepped off the dock, I highly doubt that. From the safety of Jenn's embrace, I have the urge to stick out my tongue at them. And when I do, I'm met with an award-winning eye roll from Bianca.

Dalton drones on and on, and I can't help but steal glances

at Theo's profile. He's all smiles, per usual. It's uncanny how the explosion I'd been bracing for after the whole rudder ordeal never came. How he never once allowed whatever frustration he was feeling, if any at all, to surface. He shifts his weight from foot to foot next to me, bored or anxious, or maybe planning his great escape from the personal hell I've inflicted upon him.

My chest tightens because as much as every relationship I've been in has conditioned me otherwise, Theo might just be the exception. Someone capable of not sweating the so-called small stuff. Who never goes to bed angry and would probably always kiss his partner goodnight.

He flexes his hand in mine as if he can read my thoughts, and the more I think about it, the more I believe Theo might have some superhuman ability to know what everyone around him is thinking and adjust his actions accordingly.

And then there is the kiss.

Well, the *almost* kiss.

The kiss I didn't know I wanted but now can't stop thinking about. Theo's big hand on my waist, pulling me tight against him. The way my mouth watered as it lingered in limbo waiting to connect with his. It was unexpected and entirely for the cameras—as he'd pointed out—but dear lord, it was hot as hell. And honestly, *almost* kissing Theo was unlike any other *almost* moment I've ever had. Certainly not like kissing Clint, which surprisingly makes the whole thing even hotter.

Camera two, roaming. Camera one, back on Dalton.

My body is flooded with a new kind of energy—a raw, sensual, and curious buzzing that twists my stomach into knots and makes my brain do all sorts of mental gymnastics over how to get Theo's hands back on my hips and his lips on mine. For real this time. I fail to remember when I've felt this big of a sexual urge for someone else. I sneak another glance at Theo before Dalton's irritating voice floods the space around us.

"Welcome back, trekkers," Dalton says directly into the camera in front of him. "Before the break, we recapped today's challenge, which, unfortunately, wasn't smooth sailing for all our competitors." He looks directly at us as he issues yet another jab at Theo and me from behind a row of luminous veneers. "Let's take a look at the leaderboard."

Dalton turns toward the large screen behind him, his camera following his line of vision as the rows of all our names begin to flash and shuffle. Heat radiates from Theo's hand. Our fate is once again determined by random reality-TV enthusiasts across the country. When I turn to meet his gaze, he gives me a little nudge.

The leaderboard continues to flash, and the sound crew fills the unbearably tense silence between us with upbeat but suspenseful music. It's only a matter of time before someone is informed that their time on the show has come to an end.

The shared elimination limbo is probably the worst thing about all this.

In one moment, your life can be turned upside down and you're left figuring out if the planning and the personal and professional sacrifices were worth it.

If you were even worth it.

And just when you think you've found some solid ground, the rules change. You get dumped at the airport and a row of flashing lights turns on informing you that you've finished dead last.

I don't think I've really given myself a moment to think about what it would mean to be sent home.

To a house that is no longer mine.

To a joint financial situation that I already know is going to be a battle.

And to a reality that feels more like a tragically comical nightmare.

Everything about my future feels uncertain, and damn, if I allow myself to go down that path—the one that is marked by one unfulfilled and delusional chapter after another—I might just fall apart.

Theo slumps against me as the screen before us comes to life, but I think we knew this was coming after two back-to-back disasters. Arthur circles us now, a little too closely, capturing my disappointment that's echoed in Theo's face.

"There you have it, folks." Dalton is gleeful, and on every level, I believe he's getting some sort of twisted enjoyment out of our public failure. "After two challenges, here is the current ranking of this season's contestants on *The Epic Trek*. Coming in first place, we have our early leaders, Bianca and Jackson . . ." The sound crew plays a thunderous round of artificial applause, to which Jackson responds with a stiff wave and Bianca adjusts her long red ponytail, her catlike features gleaming from the praise and attention. "And rounding out the bottom of the leaderboard are our favorite lovers, Theo and Asher." Instead of applause, someone thought it would be better to let the *womp womp womp* of a sad trombone reverberate across the room. Bianca is practically purring from her spot in front of the main camera, and Dalton's toothy grin is toeing the line between charismatic and sinister at this point.

"Now, our leaderboard isn't the be-all, end-all in this competition," Dalton continues, making his way to the massive LED-lit board with all our names. "Some of *The Epic Trek's* most beloved winners from previous seasons were not front-runners throughout the entire competition. In fact, the votes of our viewers at home have saved many contestants from certain eliminations." Bianca folds her arms across her chest, and her features narrow as if to challenge Dalton's statement.

The sound crew now plays a suspenseful tune, one filled with ominous, drawn-out notes that really just do wonders for my growing anxiety. This is it. I don't even have to see the results to know that Theo and I are moments away from being sent home. I can feel it in my bones. Maybe if I'd tried harder or if I'd been a better partner we wouldn't be in this situation.

Maybe if I'd just been better in general.

My stomach instantly knots when I think about *why* I'm doing this in the first place. My plans for the STEM program and the scholarship opportunities I'd hoped to offer. The experiments and the supplies and the hands-on learning. Half a million dollars won't solve all my problems, but it's a starting point and a solid step forward.

And when I look at Theo, my heart constricts at the thought of his literal lifelong dream of owning his own plane slipping away.

Our dreams, his and mine, both swirl down the drain that is my life, because I couldn't get my shit together and give this competition my all.

"After today's challenge, America has voted . . ."

Regret floods my veins. Regret and shame and disappointment that I didn't make the most of this opportunity, and I'm not even ready to talk about the complicated feelings I'm having for Theo. Infatuation? Lust?

". . . and they've decided . . ." For the love of all things holy, put me out of this misery.

Dalton's purposely drawing this moment out in the most painful manner possible, and while I get the higher the stakes, the higher the ratings, anyone who's ever worried about ratings has clearly never been on the receiving end of a reality television show elimination episode.

". . . that *everyone* is safe from elimination this week."

I'm sorry, what? I turn toward Theo, who looks about as stunned and confused as I feel, and he just shrugs. Arthur nearly trips over himself to capture our reactions as quickly as they form across each of our faces.

That's a wrap on S25E2.

It could be the unexpected relief that's overwhelming my nervous system or the fact that I'm *too* aware of how Arthur and his camera are waiting in the wings for a moment like this, but I launch myself at Theo anyway, wrapping my arms around his neck and holding on for dear life, silently thanking whoever's listening for this second chance.

For the competition.

And for pulling this whole thing off.

Together.

11

THEO

Mio Buenos Aires Hotel
Buenos Aires, Argentina

The sliding doors part in front of me as I leave behind the refreshing bite of the lobby's air-conditioning and step out onto the patio.

Everyone—contestants and crew—gathered at our hotel bar for a celebratory drink. I was surprised to see the perpetually displeased Bianca and Jackson joined. They kept to themselves at the far end of the bar, heads together as they sipped their cocktails. But even they couldn't dampen everyone's good mood.

And while the cameras were definitely *not* rolling, Asher kept his hand in mine the entire time. Probably just to keep up the act with the others.

An unexpected but welcome anchor in a sea of chaos.

Which, ironically, is starting to feel less confusing and more comforting. In the midst of the rowdy excitement of it all, I find myself unable—or unwilling—to tear my gaze away from this version of Asher. His eyes gleam with that same lightness

I saw back on the boat. Even when I left him deep in conversation with Jenn and Arthur about some insect native to Argentina to shower off, I don't know—there was something different about him.

Something lighter. Whole and real and brighter than anyone else in the damn hotel.

Maybe it's the threat of elimination or the fact that we almost kissed back on the boat, but I think it may be time to unpack these not-at-all-confusing feelings toward him.

"There you are," I say when I find him again. I'd only been gone for about ten minutes or so, but when I returned to the lobby, he was nowhere in sight. "Everything okay?" I ask, taking a seat next to him.

"It's nothing." Asher's voice is void of any emotion. He slides me a bottle of local beer.

He's lying, because whatever he's thinking about is written in bold type all over his handsome face. Whatever lightness I saw earlier has been replaced with the same tension from our first meeting.

"Hey," I say, nudging him with my shoulder. "What's wrong?"

"Jo forgot to grab this back," he says, turning her phone over in his hand. I take a deep pull from the bottle he just handed me, the crisp ale refreshing in the Argentinian heat. After we learned we'd all be safe from elimination, the first thing Jo did was hand Asher her phone. She's now got us trained to take a selfie, no questions asked. I wrapped my arms around Asher's shoulders, pulling his back flush against my front, and he snapped a photo that was probably more blurry than not.

The only things in crystal clear focus were our wide grins.

But now I can practically hear his gears turning, and any trace of that smile is long gone.

"When I realized I still had it, I couldn't help myself," he admits, finally, tapping the phone against his hand. "I had to see."

"See what?" I ask quietly.

Asher exhales a long breath. "Clint."

Ah. The ex.

"He's just . . ." His voice trails off. "Well, look," he says, unlocking the phone and handing over the illuminated device. It's open to a group photo posted several hours ago.

A handful of stereotypical men in every shade of white is staring back at me. Each with a raised drink in their hand and a smug look across their face. If I had to ballpark, they're all clinging to their thirties and whoever posted the photo went a little heavy on the editing.

The caption simply reads *Cheers to an epic new chapter.*

"I'm assuming one of them is Clint?" I ask, almost afraid to know the answer.

Asher points to the man smack in the center of the photo. He's . . . not horrible. Not my type, that's for sure. But not horrible.

"*Epic* new chapters, huh?" I read. "That's a little on the nose, don't you think?"

More like a calculated and dickish move.

"It's nauseating," he says, taking back the phone, his fingers lingering for a whisper of a moment. "See that guy?" he says, pointing to a cookie-cutter middle-aged man with his arm snaked possessively around Clint. I nod. "That is—well, was, I guess—our couple's counselor."

That's brutal. It's like Asher's ex isn't even trying to hide his indifference or stupidity.

Maybe he's just downright cruel.

"Well, what's our vibe?" I ask, not really knowing what to say. "Are we angry? Out for revenge? Utterly devastated and heartbroken? I need to know how to proceed here, Ash."

He turns toward me, his smile returning. Slightly.

"What, you have different procedures depending on my feelings?"

"Oh, absolutely."

"Alright then," he says, taking a sip from his bottle. "Let's see how you proceed with equal parts humiliated and enraged mixed with a touch of self-loathing." Whatever smile he managed to force across his face disappears as quickly as it formed. There's an undeniable exhaustion behind his eyes, a weight he's been carrying all alone.

"Ah, the mother lode," I tease. "Well, for starters, I'd tell you that everyone has an ex or a romantic situation or two they're embarrassed by, and if they say otherwise, they're for sure lying."

"Is that so?" he asks, his voice quiet and slow, like he's trying to hide the slight crack I can hear.

"Mm-hmm," I say from behind the rim of my bottle as I take another pull.

Asher nods and picks at his bottle's label. "Do you?" he asks after a long moment, and I really should have seen that coming.

I haven't thought about him in ages.

Or more honestly, I hadn't thought about Ethan since Asher came bursting into my life. Thought about how it felt to have someone, and even worse, to have to move on without him.

"Of course," I admit, realizing it would be unfair to let him wallow in relationship self-pity alone. "Falling in love with the wrong person and then getting your heart broken? That's just another part of life, right? One of those things we all gotta deal with at one point or another."

"And have you?" he asks, turning toward me. "Dealt with it?"

More like ignored it at all costs, but he doesn't need to know that.

Not now, at least.

It's easier that way. To pretend the past is truly in the past. That what happened then has no bearing on today—especially when you're still unsure about who you can or should talk to about it.

I clear my throat. "Sure I have," I say, but even I don't buy my lie. "But the more important question here is how do *you* want to deal with it?"

He mulls over my question, opening his mouth several times but then seeming to change his mind. "I don't want to deal with him or any of it," he says after a beat. "I'm just upset about how it all ended and what that means. The only thing I can think about is how angry I am for wasting so many important years of my life trying to make someone like him happy."

Asher's brow furrows, and I realize now that this isn't a conversation he needs me to interject in. Right now, he just needs to vent, and I'm happy to let him.

"I lost myself, Theo," he says, and his voice is filled with a sudden vulnerability. "I don't know when or how exactly, but somewhere along the way, I lost just about everything I happened to like about myself and became . . . this."

Asher fixates on something in the distance.

"And *this* is?" I ask, hoping to gain a better understanding of how he views himself.

He shrugs his shoulders. "I don't know . . . just a version of myself who I barely recognize anymore. Someone who strategically molded themselves into what they thought was the perfect partner. Someone who said and did all the right things to make sure they didn't inadvertently cross some imaginary line. Someone who made sure to let everyone else shine. And yet somehow, all *that* could never be enough. But I see the relationship for what it was. And more important, what it wasn't."

I hate that. God, do I hate that.

He turns back toward me. "Did you know that last year, my team at work won the Walter R. Fitzgerald Award for Healthcare Innovation?" he asks excitedly, but he must see the blank stare on my face. "Of course you wouldn't," he laughs, shaking his head. "I keep forgetting we've known each other for a literal millisecond."

This sends a slight pang of hurt through me.

"Will you tell me about it?" I ask, hoping he'll elaborate.

"It's . . ." he starts, a flush sneaking up his neck. "It just this award they give to a research lab that makes a significant development in the advancement of our career field. Our department won last year for our work on artificial nerve regeneration and it was a really big deal and moment in my career. I mean, Theo—we developed technology that helps damaged spinal cords by directing synthesized signals to the human brain . . ."

Asher comes alive as he rambles on about artificial nerves and something about sensory injuries. The passion he has for what he does is obvious.

Sexy, even.

"I'm sorry," he says, his chest rising and falling excitedly.

But his apology catches me off guard. "What are you apologizing for?"

"I . . . I don't know, actually," he admits, a nervous laugh escaping his mouth. "I have a habit of getting lost in the weeds once I start talking about this stuff."

"It's something you love, right?" I ask, confident I already know the answer.

He nods, biting his lip, and I know he watched as my eyes briefly darted down to it.

"Don't apologize for something you love, Asher," I say, hoping he believes me. "For something that makes you *you*."

He shrugs his shoulders, setting the beer bottle on the table in front of us. "Anyway, he didn't come with me that night for the award," he says, his eyes brimming with the weight of his frustration. "Or any night that was mine, for that matter. There was always something more important going on in Clint's bubble. His job, family, friends—they were higher priorities than me."

That's bullshit. "And what exactly does Mr. Perfect do?"

"He's in corporate finance."

I snort. "All *this* over a finance bro?" I joke, reaching over and grabbing his thigh. "Come on, guapo—we have standards!"

Asher stares at me and then bursts out laughing. "You're so right," he says, half laughing or maybe even crying at this point. "My brother not-so-discreetly called him a discount fuckboy and I always secretly loved that."

"Your brother sounds like my kinda guy."

A soft little smile that I'd like to trace with my fingertips flickers across his face before he leans his head on my shoulder.

"Thanks for listening," he says, his voice practically a whisper. "I haven't gotten to talk about any of this with anyone."

"What about your parents?" I whisper back against the softness of his sweet-smelling hair.

"Especially them. We don't have that kind of relationship,"

he says, leaning back on his hands. "They're good people and mean well. But they've always had this sort of hands-off approach when it comes to the emotional stuff. I think in their minds, they were setting us up for success by learning from life's lessons alone, when in reality, we probably just needed . . . a hug."

"Are you hinting that you want a hug?" I ask after a moment, partially joking.

"Kinda."

Now *this* is something I can help with. I jump to my feet, extending my hand in his direction. "Get over here."

His cheeks redden as he stands, making the freckles on the bridge of his nose more noticeable in the glowing moonlight. "You don't have to . . ."

Putting my hands on my hips, I do my best dad power pose. "I said . . . Get. Over. Here."

I open my arms as widely and dramatically as humanly possible, calling him over with a nod of my head.

He's clearly on the fence, torn between receiving the hug he just flat-out asked for and figuring out if said hug from the man that's pretending to be his boyfriend is weird.

"Asher Bennett, you better not leave me hanging here . . ."

He doesn't much longer.

Slowly, he steps forward, closing the distance between us and wrapping his long but hesitant arms around my waist. He's stiff and rigid as I pull him tight against me, and I can only imagine the confused and irritated expression on that pinched face of his, but eventually, Asher completely and wholeheartedly exhales.

"I think this trip is going to be good for you," I say, my chin now resting against the side of his head. He smells like cinnamon and clove and his hair just might be the softest thing I've ever felt.

"Why's that?"

"Because *you're* the one with the actual new chapter ahead of you," I whisper, recalling when I rehearsed these words to myself, afraid the honesty behind them might be too much for him. "Not the other way around."

He nods in silent agreement or resigned acceptance, and the two of us are left swaying just slightly in the night air with the warmth of Asher's cheek resting on my shoulder and his arms tightening around my waist.

/////////////////

You'd think Jo's early wake-up calls would start to get easier.

You'd be wrong.

Her thunderous pounding on our door shakes me awake. I would have been pissed, but I feel the heat of Asher's leg pressed against mine, so Jo's aggressive knocking is quickly forgiven and forgotten.

"Morning," he says, eyes squinting in the morning light. Asher's bedhead is something to behold, his blond locks sticking out in every direction. It's both hilarious and wildly endearing. "Sorry," he mumbles and slowly scoots away from me.

If there's one thing this trip has shown me it's that I had forgotten just how nice it is to wake up next to someone. Even if they constantly put space between you.

We each shower—separately—and make our way down to the lobby in search of caffeine and carbs before we have to join everyone else to head to the airport. Again.

Ellie practically runs into us the moment we step out of the elevator, worry all over her face.

"You haven't seen a teal backpack around, have you?" she asks, her voice teetering on the edge of panic. "I know I had it when I came down this morning, but I can't find it anywhere."

Asher and I shake our heads. "Sorry, kiddo," I say. "But we just got down here. We can help you look, though."

Jenn joins us from across the lobby. "Alright, sweetie," she says, wrapping an arm around her daughter's shoulder. "I talked to the hotel manager and asked them to keep an eye out for it."

"Our passports are in there," Ellie groans, covering her face with her hands in frustration. "We won't be able to travel if I can't find it. I'm so sorry, Mom."

Jenn tucks Ellie even more tightly under her arm. "Oh, honey, we'll figure it out. Don't you worry."

"Where was the last place you saw it?" Asher asks, his tired eyes filled with concern.

"I had just come down from our room with our luggage cart and was starving so I set my stuff down there." Ellie points to the small seating area just beyond the hotel's coffee bar. "And I went to grab some juice and toast. When I got back, I noticed the backpack was gone."

If her bag was indeed stolen, it's long gone now, but saying that would be the opposite of helpful.

Asher bites the inside of his cheek. "Well, you both stay with the bags," he says, turning toward Jenn and me. "And Ellie and I can take another lap . . . just in case. You said teal, right?" he asks, and Ellie nods. "Cool. Oh, will you grab me a coffee?" he asks me, placing a welcome touch on my arm. "A little cream and . . ."

"Yeah, yeah. Three sugars," I finish. "I've been paying attention, Bennett."

His face splits into a wide grin. "I can see that."

Jenn and I plop down in the armchairs at the far end of the lobby after helping ourselves to some much-needed coffee and pastries. I loaded two pieces of pan con tomate on my plate, one for Asher and one for me, and my mouth practically floods with drool over the toasted bread and the salted tomatoes.

"I don't know about you," Jenn says, peering over our mountain of shared bags, "but I am exhausted."

"Extremely."

She sips her coffee, raising her eyebrows at me. "So, is this what you expected it to be? The competition?"

I could double over in laughter.

Nothing about any aspect of my life right now is what I expected it to be. Not being grounded from work and having all this unplanned free time. Or competing on a hit reality show.

And I certainly was not expecting whatever is going on between Asher and me.

But before I can respond, a commotion across the lobby pulls our attention.

"So let me get this straight." Asher's sudden raised voice echoes around us. "You just *happened* to find her bag on your floor and were bringing it down to the front desk? I don't buy it."

He's facing off against Jackson, whose arms are crossed against his chest. "I don't *need* you to buy it. That's what happened," he scoffs back, a smirk forming at the corner of his thin lips.

I don't know how, but I instantly know he's lying.

"It's fine, Asher. Really. All that matters is . . ." she says, riffling through the bag's pockets and visibly relaxing when she withdraws what she'd been worried about, "these." She holds the two passports up.

Jenn and I take a step closer, hoping to defuse the escalating situation. "She's right, Ash," I say, reaching out to put a supportive hand on his back. "Let's just go meet Arthur at the van."

"No, we all agreed to the same rules on day one," Asher says, shrugging away from me and taking a step closer to Jackson, who's now rolling his eyes and looking entirely bored. "I want him to admit he was trying to mess with her and got caught."

But the elevator doors ping open and Russell, Dalton's executive assistant and right-hand man, comes strolling into the lobby, his eyes both annoyed and entirely bored by the spectacle he's just walked into.

"I'm sorry, is there a problem here?" he asks like he's just been entirely inconvenienced by our presence.

"You're sweet as sugar to ask," Jenn quickly says, laying on what I'm learning is her signature charm. "But we're all good here, aren't we, boys?"

Asher shakes his head, clearly disappointed he didn't get Jackson to admit to any wrongdoing, but turns and leads Ellie away from the redheaded menace. "We're fine," he says through gritted teeth.

"Good," Russell says pointedly, and proceeds to walk directly through us. "Let's remember our surroundings going forward."

My intrusive thoughts really want me to stick out my leg to trip him, but he speed walks straight out the front door before I get the chance, leaving us in his wake. Jackson follows without another word, which is for the best, and Jenn, Ellie, Asher, and I start collecting our bags to begin loading them outside.

"You good?" I ask Asher, placing a hand on his back.

He rakes his fingers through his blond hair, nodding as he does, and the four of us make our way to the parking lot where our various vans wait for us.

"I'm proud of you," I say, and I really mean it. Watching him stand up for Ellie reminded me of times when I wished someone had stood up for me. Someone in your corner like that, regardless of how trivial the situation, changes everything.

"It was nothing," he says, a slight blush spreading beneath his glasses.

But it wasn't nothing. Instead of telling him so or that I hope all this is helping him stand up for himself with the same passion, I just smile and climb into the back of the van with him.

12

ASHER

Ria Formosa Natural Park
Algarve, Portugal

Y ou boys alright back there?" Arthur shouts over the thunderous sound of the wind from a van full of rolled-down windows. Before we can respond—not that it would matter, because based on the massive grin on his face, Arthur is loving this—he takes a sharp right turn and continues speeding down the barely there path, while our bodies play bumper cars in the back seat.

"I think he's trying to kill us," I whisper to Theo.

"That, or we are currently being held captive during his audition for the next movie in the Fast & Furious franchise."

Theo may be sitting upright, but he's got his arm around me and there's no point in lying about how much I like that. When we're not being told to get close like this for the cameras, I'm itching to get close to him like this. The way I'm able to fit neatly into the natural crooks of his body or the way his lips might feel against mine.

Full and sweet and not a trace of weirdness in sight.

It's been ages since I've felt this level of . . . frustration. Or infatuation. Or better yet, confusion, because everything I now do with Theo for the show twists my rational thinking around like a pretzel, and everything we *don't* do behind closed doors is just . . . worse.

It's maddening.

Logically, this *crush*—the word itself makes me cringe—makes sense. Theo's undeniably attractive, and he's got that whole savior complex thing going for him. But I never felt whatever I'm feeling now for Clint. Not once. I fit myself into his world and wanted to build a life with a partner. The difference? I can't recall a single instance where my stomach waited in knots just to hear his voice or catch a glimpse of his smile.

And now that I've somehow found someone who's forced me to think and feel and fucking fantasize about all these infuriating things, I've ripped my own rug out from under myself by stupidly suggesting a set of rules that all but guarantee nothing will ever happen between us.

Arthur takes yet another unannounced sharp turn and the familiar reality-television-show branding comes into view. Jo reaches forward to turn the van camera off before twisting around to speak to us. "For today's challenge, each team has been assigned a task voted on by our audience. Unfortunately, I have no idea what the individual tasks are," she says, craning her neck into the back seat. "Dalton's been keeping that one under wraps. But I *do* know that they are meant to be competed individually, and I hate to say it"—Jo now officially dons her production-handler hat as Arthur parks the van—"but Asher, this challenge is all yours."

"Great." I groan, placing my forehead against the cool window while everyone else starts to exit the van. Jo and Arthur begin setting up their camera equipment, but when I get out I scan the scene searching for any clue as to what we—*I*—could possibly be getting into. Theo comes up behind me, slinging his big arm around my shoulders and pulling me close to him. "You nervous?"

"I mean, *that's* not helping."

The other contestants begin to join us around the second staging area. Besides the usual sound equipment and cables snaking their way through the grass, there appear to be make-shift individual zones created out of dark fabric hung from PVC pipes, one for each team.

"Here," Jo says, handing me a laminated card with a block number three written in bright yellow. "Good luck!"

Arthur resumes filming, and though it's taken a minute, I've almost gotten used to constantly having his camera in my face.

We're rolling.

Theo laces his fingers through mine, the only thing ground-ing me at the moment.

Camera three on Dalton.

"And we're back with our next challenge," Dalton's voice booms as he steps forward. "But there's a twist. Behind me are individual mini challenges for each of our teams," Dalton con-tinues, circling the camera. "We've watched in awe as they've competed as pairs, but today, we polled our viewers and Amer-ica has voted on challenges that will be competed individually."

Pan to the screens.

"Contestants, if you'll please step forward to the number that corresponds with the card you were handed earlier."

Theo bumps me with his shoulder before pulling me to-ward zone three.

Instant dread floods my veins. The best part of all this has been facing the unknown with Theo. But now, whatever lies behind this curtain, I have to face alone.

"On the count of three," Dalton shouts. "We will reveal the challenge that America has chosen for each of you. One . . ."

Please be something with math.

"Two . . ."

I'd happily settle for some sort of puzzle. I look over at Theo, who's all but vibrating with excitement. I would give anything to have a fraction of his . . . *Theo-ness?* All smiles and heaps of unbridled energy.

"Three . . ."

Oh, you've got to be kidding me.

The thick velvet curtains drop to reveal two large glass tanks.

One is empty, from what I can tell, and large enough for a grown man to lie down inside.

The smaller one is filled with something that makes my stomach recoil.

Snakes.

Their scaled bodies press against the glass, twisting around each other and searching for their escape like slippery magicians straight out of every single one of my nightmares.

No, no, no. I cannot do whatever it is that these production pricks have planned. I don't care that America voted for me to do it, which feels like a giant middle finger to me, thank you very much. But no. Snakes are quite literally my worst fear and the one thing on this planet I've actively gone out of my way to never, ever, under any circumstances, be around.

"You don't look so good, kid," Arthur's voice rips me from my inner panic. He's momentarily lowered his camera—a first.

"Arthur, there's no way in *hell* I can do this."

"That's just the fear talking."

"No, you don't understand," I say, my heart rate spiking. "I can't do snakes . . ."

But before he can respond, we are joined by a man dressed head to toe in every shade of khaki and what exposed skin there is has been tanned within an inch of its life. "Asher, right? My name's Wyatt," he says, extending a weathered hand in my direction. I shake it, or at least I think I do. I'm beginning to think I've fully lost my grip on reality, and all I can do is stare at the sea of swirling serpents just feet away. "I'm the animal handler on call today, and I'm here to walk you through the challenge, make sure that none of the animals get hurt."

I snap my head in his direction, and Arthur chooses that very moment to raise his camera back on me. "You're worried about the *snakes* getting hurt? What about me?"

A sarcastic little laugh slips out of his mouth, and I can't help but glare at him. "Most snakes are harmless to humans, like the boas we have here."

I really don't like Wyatt.

"That's easy for someone to say who doesn't have to . . ." My voice trails off when I realize I have no idea what I'm about to do. "Wait, what's the challenge?"

Wyatt lifts the lid of the empty tank and I step closer. There are dozens of keys in various shapes and sizes at the bottom. "The goal here is to locate the key that opens each lock as quickly as you can," he says, tapping a built-in lock I'm just now seeing on the inside of the lid.

A pit grows in my stomach because I have a feeling I know the answer before I even ask.

"And the snakes?"

Wyatt gives me a look—the kind that confirms my suspicions. "So, if you'll just go ahead and get into the tank . . ."

I look around for my own escape, hoping I can somehow slip away unnoticed, but with Arthur zeroed in on my every movement and the fact that I've already come this close to accomplishing my goal, I know I'm just going to have to suck it up and get this over with.

There's also a million dollars on the line, so that helps put things into perspective.

Theo's hand flexes in my mine, a subtle reminder that he's right here with me.

"I . . . I really don't know if I can do this," I whisper, turning to him.

His eyes find mine. "We can walk away right now if you want to, Ash—you don't have to do this."

He's giving me an out.

Permission to do the thing every cell in my body is screaming to do—run away.

Theo doesn't break his stare, his beautiful eyes reassuring me that money or not, the only thing he cares about is my safety.

Around me, the other contestants are in various stages of their own challenges.

I see Ellie struggling with what appears to be a life-size game of Jenga, using all her strength to lift the giant pieces up and down a set of ladders.

Next to me, Jackson is hard at work sifting through mounds of sand looking for who knows what. There's a large scale hanging behind him that gives me no context as to what challenge America chose for him.

Everyone else is already immersed in their own challenges and then there's me, all but frozen in fear and looking like a deer in headlights. Arthur raises his eyebrows from behind his camera lens. I'm sure he's mentally yelling at me to get my ass in the damn tank or to stop being such a baby or something gruff and Arthur-like.

Well, it's now or never, Asher Bennett.

"You're staying here, right?" I ask Theo before stepping into the tank, still clinging onto his hand like a vise.

"I'm not going anywhere, babe," he says, his eyes flooded with concern. That and only that is enough to calm my over-stimulated nerves. Even if his pet name of choice is just for the show, it's like my brain needs to hear it.

The glass is cool against my sweaty skin. I run my hands along the floor of the tank once I lie down, feeling the edges of the different keys with my fingertips.

Wyatt peers in from above. "You ready?"

Fuck. Fuck. *Fuck!*

Every nerve ending and cell in my body is screaming out in fear. "Just get it over with," I say through chattering teeth. My limbs are shaking, and white-hot adrenaline is coursing through my veins as my natural fight-or-flight response kicks in.

Wyatt lifts the smaller tank to the edge of the one I'm in and a curious—or starving—slippery monster sticks its head out, its tongue flicking in my direction. What is it they say about wild animals? That they are more scared of you than you are of them?

I highly doubt that.

My body tenses harder than it ever has before as I brace for Wyatt to drop them in. Time slows as he stands above me, dangling a box of snakes that are probably are chomping at the bit to choke me to death on national television.

Plop.

A thick yellow constrictor lands in between my spread legs, thankfully not making any contact with my skin yet.

Plop. Plop. Plop.

One by one, more snakes are carefully dropped into my tank.

And then all at once, Wyatt tips the contents of the tank in their entirety over me, completely covering a good portion of my body in miles of slithering scales, and I think I've officially stopped living. The full weight of their bodies swirl around me. There's a good possibility I'm now watching this nightmare unfold in real time from the beyond.

"Just don't make too many sudden movements and you'll be golden," Wyatt says before closing the tank's lid and locking me in from the outside. Is this guy for fucking real? How the hell am I supposed to get out of this death trap without sudden movements? I force my eyes shut and have to remind myself to breathe as I feel the thick scaled body of one of my captors start to wrap itself lazily around my leg.

Don't panic.

Breathe. Find the key. And get yourself out of here.

I slowly fan my fingers along the floor of the tank, bumping into the middle section of one snake and what feels like the tail of another. I grab a key and shakily lift it toward the lock, afraid of those sudden movements Wyatt mentioned that would lead me to become a snake's chew toy.

I line the small key up to the lock, and it doesn't fit into the keyhole. Shit. Okay, next one. I set the key flat on my chest, hoping to avoid using the same one repeatedly.

I slide my left hand along the bottom of the tank again but feel the flick of a snake's tongue on my wrist and freeze. This is most definitely a new ring of hell and someone's plan to punish me for every bad thing I've ever done in my entire life. I have to get out of here. Now.

Slowly but intentionally, I grab another key and lift it to the lock once more. It slides in. "Thank God," I mutter through clenched teeth.

But even though the key slides in all the way, it doesn't budge.

And so, the torturous cycle continues.

Locate a key, realize it's wrong, try not to freak out about the snakes, and repeat.

Arthur returns with the lens of his camera pressed flat against the tank's glass. His eyes are wide at my current predicament. I can only imagine the double chin situation I've got going on from this angle. Here's your money shot, Arthur. You're welcome.

At this point, it's hard to discern where the snakes end and where I begin. They're everywhere. Around my legs, their clammy skin wrapped just tight enough to let their presence be known. On my chest, the entirety of their combined weight moving and shifting as they, like me, figure out what in the sweet hell is going on. I'm pretty sure there is more than one slippery little fucker trying to get comfortable inside my shorts. If I weren't legitimately crawling out of my skin, now would be the perfect opportunity for some *trouser snake* humor.

Part of me feels bad for them.

But the other, more prominent part feels like screaming until my body is no longer capable of producing sound.

Please don't bite me, Mr. Snake, I chant internally. I continue trying key after key to no avail, my pile of discarded keys growing on my chest.

My fingers rake against the bottom of the tank as a curious large white snake makes its way from my chest and along my neck to set up shop near the side of my face, its split tongue inspecting my cheek.

And this is the moment when the panic sets in.

My heart tries to claw its way out of the very center of my chest and every inch of my body starts to shake. Every neuron firing in my brain is acutely aware of the situation I'm in.

I need to get out of this fucking tank.

Now.

"I . . . I don't think I can do this," I choke out in a panicked frenzy as I attempt to push myself up off the floor of the tank.

"Get him out of there," Theo's stern voice growls from somewhere above.

Theo.

"And face guaranteed elimination?" a muffled Arthur shoots back.

I . . . I need Theo.

No, I *want* Theo.

When my fingers make contact with another key, I hurriedly lift it to the lock with squinted eyes, mentally pleading for it to be the correct one to end this madness. It slides fully into the keyhole and, to my surprise, turns completely.

Did I just—

The lock clicks open, propping the large box's lid open ever so slightly. The first thing I see is sweet Theo, his poor face filled with more concern than I've ever seen in it before, and Arthur and Wyatt flank him, standing at the ready.

"Please. Get. Them. Off. Of. Me. *Now*." I hiss at Wyatt, echoing my restless tank companions. I lie perfectly still as Wyatt lifts each snake off me one by one, an agonizing new game of patience and control when all I want is to dive into a pool of scalding hot water.

Or bleach.

"You can get up now," Wyatt says, leaning into the tank and offering me a hand. After however long I was locked in there, ten, fifteen, twenty minutes or seven hundred years, my limbs are rigid with stress, so when I clap my hand into his, every muscle screams out in protest.

I can't believe I did it.

Might as well start calling me Asher "Snake Charmer" Bennett from now until eternity, because not only did I just face the biggest fear of my life, I did so with minimal meltdowns. Well, *visible* ones. But before I can truly wrap my head around the feat of it all, Theo pulls me into those massive arms of his, picking me up like it's nothing.

"Are you okay?" he asks, his scruff on my ear.

"I . . . think so," I mumble, my lips unintentionally against his throat. He releases me just enough to give me a once-over as if he doesn't trust my own assessment. I've not seen this side of Theo before, and I have to admit, I like it. "I promise. I'm fine," I add when I see the worry in his eyes. "A little disgusted and very much in need of a shower, but fine."

His eyes are still surveying me, but they dip down to my lips and for a heartbeat of a second, I think he wants to kiss me.

"Congratulations, Asher, you've successfully completed your individual challenge! You and Theo are ea . . ." Dalton's voice fades to the background, because now all I can think about is Theo's lips.

And why they haven't been on mine yet.

Theo lowers me in his arms slightly, shifting my weight. "You did it," he beams through the widest and most beautiful of grins. Despite Arthur, who's now circling us with his rolling camera, capturing every angle of this moment, Theo's smile is genuine. Just for me.

"I didn't think I could," I whisper. Our situation may be convoluted, and the lines of this relationship may be blurred, but there is no denying the authenticity in his reaction. He's celebrating . . . me. Because I faced a genuine fear of mine today, and it's starting to feel like I've made him proud.

At the end of the day, this moment might not mean too much for the overall competition.

But looking down at Theo's smiling face . . . it also means everything.

"Well, you did amazing today," he whispers, his voice thick and low enough that only I can hear him. We're *so* going to have to reevaluate our rules. "I knew you co . . ." he starts, but I interrupt whatever he was about to say by crashing my lips into his—honestly, taking us both off guard, but it's something I've been wanting to do since being stranded on that damn boat.

I can feel Theo's confusion against my lips.

What are the chances he's wondering the same blaring question I've had every single time he's placed his arm around me or called me *babe*?

Is this for the competition or could this be real?

But I feel the moment he decides he doesn't care, and honestly, my body melts in relief.

Theo slowly slides me down the length of his body, and the moment my feet are on the ground again, I fling my arms around his neck, pulling myself tighter against him as he kisses me back with overwhelming force.

It's not lost on me that this is our first kiss, and I'm praying it won't be our last, because kissing Theo Fernandez is like coming up for air while simultaneously being set on fire and screaming *Thank you.*

He's inhaling me with a passion and urgency that some people wait their whole lifetime for and here we are in the middle of nowhere, caked in dirt and sweat and probably snake slime, so when he reaches up, taking my face in his large hands, well . . . I could just about pass out from the tenderness of it all.

"What are you doing?" he asks against my mouth.

He parts my lips with his, gently sliding his tongue against mine as I claw my fingers into his hair—I want to remember this moment for the rest of my life.

Right on cue, the shuffling sounds of Arthur scrambling to get the close-up shot of this celebratory moment fill my ears and a wave of deer-in-headlights embarrassment rushes over me. I *will* remember this for the rest of my life, because Arthur just captured me throwing myself at Theo like some sex-crazed animal, and he'll be spending his evening happily editing it into some compilation of today's events.

"Winging it," I say, panting because Theo has completely obliterated whatever part of my brain triggers the millions of subconscious decisions needed to inhale oxygen and exhale carbon dioxide.

Theo must sense the sudden shift in my mood, because I can feel his wide smile against my lips. Planting a soft but lingering kiss at the corner of my mouth, he slowly drops each hand from my face, one after the other, leaving my skin tingling at the absence of his touch.

Arthur starts breaking down his camera equipment behind us.

"Asher, my boy—I didn't think you had it in you!" he says

enthusiastically, quite the change in tone from his usual indifference. "When that huge snake—"

"You know what? I think I've had enough snake talk for today." My interruption clearly kills Arthur's excitement, so he shrugs his shoulders and turns his attention toward the rest of his gear. Theo and I make our way back to the parked van, our hands never leaving each other's.

"I mean this in the kindest way possible, but the two of you *reek*," Jo says, her face pained as she dramatically cranes her neck away from us where she stands against the van. "Like, I get it. You've been gallivanting around in the wilderness and exerting yourselves physically, but *dear lord* . . . the combination of smells is too much," she says between exaggerated breaths.

"So, what I'm hearing is," I say, stepping forward as Arthur now joins us, "someone wants a hug!"

"Asher, you know I love ya . . . but if you so much as lay a finger on me right now, I will make sure that you get the worst edit in the history of reality television." She's laughing—we all are—harder than we have since this whole thing started, and I must admit, taking my seat in the smelly van with the three of them, as different as they all are—it's kinda nice. Jo, Arthur, and most important, Theo, whether we wanted to or not, we've become a little found family in the most unlikely of circumstances.

As Arthur shoots the van back into drive and we settle into the comfortable silence of four people who have now learned to just *be* with one another, I bring the back of my hand to my lips, still feeling the burn of Theo's that just might be permanently etched upon them.

I am in *so* much trouble.

13

THEO

Ria Park Garden Hotel
Algarve, Portugal

Asher's kiss kept me up all night.

Every time I found myself on the verge of sleep, my mind had other ideas, reminding me what Asher's lips felt like and sending a jolt of electricity straight down my spine. I also kept secretly hoping he'd climb on top of me, taking me in as each torturous hour passed, but that would most definitely violate our silly little rules. Instead I tossed and turned all night, wildly horny. So, after thoroughly giving up on sleep, I snuck out of bed, quietly threw on a pair of running shorts, and tip-toed to the door, shoes in hand.

Asher's back is to me as I close the door, his hair wild and his long leg sticking out from beneath the comforter. As much as I'd love to burrow back into bed with him, I need to clear my head.

And if I'm being honest, to just have a moment away from Asher and Jo and the cameras.

We didn't say too much last night after the kiss.

Arthur had convinced us to join him and some of the other crew members and contestants for dinner. After a few too many beers and cheese arepas (and some horrific-tasting rum concoction), upon returning to the hotel, Asher and I were finally able to break away. We literally passed out from exhaustion.

"Well, look who's up before the sun," Jenn's familiar voice calls the second I step out of the elevator. She's sitting with some sort of notebook in her lap, dressed both stylishly and comfortably in a white tank top and pair of flowy linen drawstring pants.

"Morning," I say after crossing the tiled lobby to join her. "I was just going to get some air before it got too hot out."

"Perfect . . . I'll join you," she says, closing her book and inviting herself. Before I can find some way to politely decline or stress the fact that I was just looking for a little alone time, she's gotten up from her seat, leading the way out the front door and into the cool morning breeze.

I have no choice but to follow her.

Jenn loops her arm through mine when I flank her outside, and the two of us wind our way through the quiet city. She doesn't say anything at first, her head on a constant swivel as she takes in the local scenery. I think I'm starting to understand that she's a genuinely curious person. Someone who looks at the world with wonder. Like she's trying to memorize every detail around her. Every so often, her pace slows, mine along with it, and she unhooks herself from me. Opening the notebook she's had tucked into her side, Jenn scribbles something down before relocking our arms and setting off again.

Curiosity gets the best of me after our fourth stop. "What are you jotting down over there?"

A warm smile spreads across her face. "Oh, I just have my little lists," she says, opening her notebook so I can see inside. The pages are filled with columns of notes. In some instances, there's just a word or two. In others, a full sentence. "Food we've tried. People we've met. Things I need to remember," she says, trailing her finger across the neat script. "All of it. I don't want to forget anything from this trip, so it's all in here."

That's adorable and entirely in line with the image slowly forming of Jenn in my head. In a lot of ways, she reminds me of my own mother, and there's a small part of me that thinks she feels that.

"Are you at all curious to know what I wrote back at the hotel?" she asks, tapping her index finger toward the middle of the left page.

Check on Theo.

My heart constricts at the thought of being checked on, a dull ache laced with a longing I think I tricked myself into believing wasn't there. When we look at each other, I fail to find the right words.

"Why?" I ask, the only word I seem to be able to mutter when we simultaneously slow to a stop.

Jenn tilts her head in the direction of a bench just up ahead, nestled beneath an overgrown flowering tree, its branches swaying. Sitting together, my movements a skeptical mirror of hers, Jenn folds her hands in her lap.

"Do you remember what I said to you when we first met?" she asks. While I can conjure up the memory of meeting Jenn and Ellie at the contestants' welcome reception, for the life of me, I cannot recall what we talked about.

She laughs with a soft little sound that reverberates throughout her entire body. "No, I wouldn't imagine you would with everything else we've had going on," she says, patting me on the arm. "I'll remind you. I said you didn't need to pretend with me and you looked like you were going to choke." Funny enough, I feel like I could at any moment. "Kinda like you do right now, sweetie."

I swallow, mulling over my next words very carefully.

"Jenn, I'm not sure what you mean—" I start but she literally shushes me.

"Oh, darling, why waste your breath?" she asks directly. "I overheard Jo on night one yapping away on that phone of hers about liability waivers and needing to swap out paperwork for, what were her words? Something like *the grumpy one's faux-beau situation* . . ." Yup, that sounds like Jo—especially on that first night. "I don't know," she says, now laughing again. "Maybe I got that wrong."

I choke out a laugh, turning my entire body toward Jenn. "So, let me get this straight. You've known this whole time about *us*," I say, dropping my voice to a whisper, which now feels pointless, "and you didn't say anything?"

"Now, where would be the fun in that?" she says, playfully nudging me. "Besides, who doesn't love to be on the *inside* of a juicy little secret? Even if no one else knows I know . . . you know?" she adds with a wink.

"Then why now?" I ask, genuinely intrigued.

Jenn pats her notebook. "Like I said, just wanted to check on you. Who knows, maybe *not* pretending might be nice. Even for a moment . . ." There's something else entirely lingering behind her words.

Huh. Not pretending. The phrase swishes around my brain, because after all this time with Asher and the show, it's getting harder and harder to separate what I've been pretending about and what I haven't.

"Sweetie, my husband died last year," Jenn says both abruptly and a little too causally for the weight of that statement. She places a warm hand on my arm the moment I open my mouth. "It's fine—well, not fine," she corrects, her warm facade slipping ever so slightly. "But you know what I mean. We're . . . well, we're managing."

"Jenn, I don't even know . . . I . . . I'm so sorry." I stammer out but the words feel meaningless because an *I'm sorry* from a stranger means nothing after such a huge loss.

"I know, I know," she says quietly, shaking her head. "I appreciate you saying that. I really do. I only brought it up because I wanted you to know I relate. This whole thing—competing on this show, Ellie and I being here together, that was something she was supposed to do with her father, and instead, she got me." The grief in her voice is unmistakable, any icy edge to her normal cheerful demeanor. So much so that it makes my own throat tighten with each breath. "So, the whole *pretending everything is normal* thing you've got going on? I get it."

Without any hesitation, I throw my arm around Jenn and pull her tight against me. She rests her head on my shoulder when I do—a simple act that feels entirely familiar.

"So, you and Asher . . ." she inquires after a moment. "What's the real story there?"

There's that word again: *real*.

The city around us has slowly begun showing signs of life. Pedestrians have started milling around and street vendors have been setting up shop. A familiar smell of smoke and fresh bread fills the air, causing my stomach to rumble.

"It started off as something easy . . . arbitrary, I guess."

"And now?" she asks, a hint of smile behind her question.

I'm starting to picture what really being with Asher could be like. The line between what's real and what's not grows thinner and thinner by the moment. "It's . . . complicated."

An older man pushing a fruit cart stops in front of us, and the aroma of the chopped pineapple invades our space. "Ananás?" he asks through a toothy grin, offering us a large container of the bright fruit.

Jenn gets up without a word, pulling out some of the folded euros that production made sure we exchanged at the airport and offering them as payment. Their transaction concludes silently—a nod here, a smile there—while I just watch it all unfold from our bench. When Jenn reclaims her seat next to me, pineapple in lap, the quiet vendor continues down the street.

"You know what I think?" she asks, tapping the lid of her container.

"What's that?"

"Sometimes, *complicated* is the word people use when they don't want to admit something's actually just . . . hard," she says rather bluntly. "And you, Theo Fernandez, don't seem like the kind of man who shies away from hard things."

I fight the urge to insert a perfectly timed *that's what he said* but decide against it because the reality is, that's *all* I feel I've done for the last couple of years.

With my family and the hard conversations I *know* in my heart we should be having.

Don't even get me started on my dating life—or lack thereof. The second something turns from a convenient hookup to, well, more, *I'm out.*

No, Jenn clearly doesn't know the real me. But does anyone?

Do I, even?

"Right now, I'm not so sure about that," I admit, my throat thick and my palms starting to sweat.

"If I've learned anything over the last year," Jenn says, turning so her eyes lock with mine, "it's that when things happen outside our control—the things that change every single aspect of who we are and what we thought our future would be . . ." Her voice hitches and I want to tell her that she doesn't have to talk about any of this anymore. Especially not for me. But she carries on anyway. "When your heart suffers a loss or takes a hit, all you can do is cling to whatever happiness you can find. Because you will be happy one day. I have to keep telling myself that—over and over again so I believe it," she says, nudging my thigh. "You'll feel the sun on your skin and remember the good times, and while that pain never goes away—because let's be honest, honey, it doesn't—it shifts into something else entirely."

I pray she's right.

Of course she is—she's the mother of a teenage daughter, for crying out loud, and a no-nonsense woman who's been there, done that.

She's a widow.

"I'll take your word for it," I say, hoping she doesn't notice me wiping away a stray tear with the back of my hand. "You gonna eat that?" I ask, pointing my chin toward the pineapple she has yet to touch.

"Oh, heavens no," she says, passing the container over to me. "That shit'll kill me. I'm deathly allergic."

My jaw drops. "Wait . . . what?" I ask, laughing so hard my eyes fill with tears again. "Why the hell would you buy it?"

Jenn stands, shoves her hands in the pockets of her linen trousers, and shrugs. "I hate saying no to people, okay? Stop being so nosy." I can't believe this woman but couldn't adore her more. "Come on," she says, "let's go see if those no-good partners of ours are up yet."

And without another word—or waiting to see if I'd followed her again—Jenn takes off back in the direction we came from, leaving me feeling a little lighter than when she'd found me.

14

ASHER

Ria Park Garden Hotel
Algarve, Portugal

Arthur and Jo wait for the most inconvenient moment to demand social content.

Theo was abnormally quiet when he returned to the room this morning. It's weird—we've been sharing a bed for only a short amount of time yet before I'd even opened my eyes, it's like some part of me knew he wasn't there. We took turns getting ready, the quiet between us twisting my stomach into anxious little knots, and when we made our way to down to the lobby together, it was Arthur's face that greeted us the second the elevator doors opened.

"I promise, this'll be quick," he calls over his shoulder and leads us out the hotel door and around the building. Jo and Arthur have a knack for finding partially secluded outdoor spaces to film these things in, which I'm not complaining about considering doing them with an audience is the definition of my personal hell.

Per usual, Jo is waiting for us while stress-scrolling on her tablet. Arthur seems to have ditched his usual camera setup and is going for something more mobile; I see a phone hooked up to some sort of stabilization apparatus between the lights.

"Hopefully you two are rested and settled into your room. Do you need anything?" she asks, not looking up from her screen. Jo is quite literally the employee who's constantly putting out dozens of professional fires. But I'm learning that regardless of how demanding her job is or the fact that she's constantly juggling nine trillion things at once, there isn't anything she wouldn't do for her contestants.

Theo and I shake our heads.

"Excellent—whaddya say we knock out a social video and then all grab a bite after? I'm starving." She slides her tablet into her messenger bag and crosses her arms. At the mention of food, my stomach growls.

"I could eat," Arthur chimes in as he digs through his own bag, retrieving various cords and plugging them into his setup.

"Since Asher did the last one," Jo says, stepping forward to physically manipulate Theo and me, "I think we oughta let Theo have a turn."

"How kind of you," he says, sticking his tongue out at her, but she just flings his big arm around my shoulder. I have to remind myself I'm not supposed to like having Theo all over me this much. That none of this is real and every time he shows the slightest hint of affection toward me, it's because Jo's making him or it's for the cameras.

But still.

He's unfairly attractive, and being pressed against his body the way I am now all but forces my mind to fixate on how sturdy he feels next to me.

Theo shifts his weight from one leg to the other, causing his thick thigh to flex ever so slightly against mine. I grit my teeth and shove my free hand in my pocket so I'm not tempted to brush against said thigh.

"The two of you are getting a lot of love online already" she says, a smile pulling at the corner of her mouth as she fusses with the sleeve of my shirt. "#Thasher has been trending again. It's cute, don't you think? I love it."

She must decide that my appearance is as good as it's going to get, because she gives up trying to get the edge of my sleeve to lay flat and instead grabs her tablet again, swiping to an already open tab. "See?" she says, tilting it so we have a better view. "I think your parents are even joining in on the online fun, Theo."

"My parents?" he asks, a slight hitch in his voice. His arm flexes slightly around my shoulder. "Can I see?"

"Hmm, I know I just saw that," Jo says, scrolling down the feed aggressively with her finger. "Oh, here." She turns the tablet back over to Theo. In all caps is a post from a Carla Fernandez, his mother, I'm gathering.

BUENA SUERTA, MIJO! Everyone wish our son and his boyfriend luck as they compete on this season of THE EPIC TREK! #THASHER. Watch here!

She included a link to the site where the first two episodes are already streaming. It's weird to see a still of Theo and me standing together, arms crossed and looking exceptionally focused just moments before we took off on the whole sailing blunder.

"Your mom seems lovely," I say, giving his arm a reassuring squeeze.

He doesn't have to say anything for me to pick up on the

fact that something about his mother's comment bothers him. Instead, he lifts his gaze toward the tree line.

"How are we doing, Arthur? Camera ready?" Jo chirps, securing her tablet back in her bag and walking over to where Arthur is now bent over, still tinkering with his equipment.

"Ready when you are," calls back Arthur, who's now placed a large pair of headphones over his ears.

"Whenever you're ready, Theo, just give us a quick intro and set the scene," Jo urges as she steps behind the tripod.

Theo swallows. "Um, sure." I glance up at him and his jaw is clenched. He looks nervous, which immediately feels odd considering this man burst into my life with confidence oozing from every pore of his being. "Um. Theo here . . ." he chokes out.

And then nothing.

Absolutely nothing, and as time itself stops in the most painfully awkward standstill, I can feel heat radiating off every inch of Theo's body.

"Hold on . . . Let's try that again, Theo," Arthur says, his voice laced with a calm empathy.

Something's wrong.

"This is just very casual and low-threat," Jo adds rather curtly. The two of them have officially settled into their roles of Good Cop, Bad Cop, I see. "We just need to get an introduction here."

"Casual. Got it," Theo repeats, and he wipes his free hand on his pant leg.

"Whenever you're ready, son," Arthur says. I see him nudge Jo with his arm, a *tone it down* expression written all over his face.

Theo exhales and the drum of his fingertips resumes. "Hi . . . I'm Theo Fernandez and this is Asher Bennett—my boyfriend." Odd that he's introducing himself so formally, but I smile, leaning into him when he says my name. "We just touched down in Portugal to film the next segment of the reality television show *The Epic Trek*. Actually, it's kinda a funny story . . ." he says, laughing rather loudly. "Our flight was delayed and we almost missed our connecting flight in London . . ." He's rambling and his voice eventually trails off before he can get to whatever was funny about that story, because both Jo and Arthur are looking at him, their mouths open in disbelief at the overly detailed explanation he's begun giving.

So, instead of providing our team with another opportunity to continue their torture, I break free from Theo's viselike grip and step toward them.

"Jo, give me your phone," I demand, extending my hand in her direction.

She hands it over with a look of curiosity splashed all over her face, and I march back to Theo, grabbing him by the hand. "Come on."

No one objects.

Not even Theo, who I'm now forcefully dragging as far away from the lights and camera as I can. I lead us to the edge of the manicured property, through the thick tree line until I've effectively put a barrier between Jo and Arthur, and us.

It's peaceful among the trees and the beautiful green tones of the vegetation. Spongy moss and twisted vines surround us and the melodic calls of local birds float in and out of earshot.

"Can I try something?" I ask quietly. He nods. "Pick me up then."

Theo scrunches his eyebrows at my request. "Just trust me," I say, bracing myself on either side of his shoulders, Jo's phone still in hand.

And he does. Theo lifts me off the ground—with one arm, mind you—and I wrap my legs around his waist, securing myself to him. Whiffs of citrus and spice radiate off his body, and it's not lost on me that our sudden closeness is awfully intimate, even for pretend boyfriends.

I slide Jo's phone up to camera mode and press record, holding my arm out selfie style.

"Hi trekkers . . . Asher and Theo here," I say, doing my best to sound personable and inviting, like the videos that fill my feed daily. "We're just getting settled in Portugal and *this one* over here"—I nod my head in Theo's direction—"complained the whole way about how little leg room he had on the plane." I tighten my grip around Theo's neck.

"Did not," he chimes in, nuzzling against me, but I watch as he flashes a grin for the camera.

"Mm-hmm, sure," I say, rolling my eyes. "Anyway, we are both exhausted and starving so we are going to go find some amazing local cuisine before we succumb to jet lag. Hope you tune in!"

Short, sweet, and zero need for anyone to feel uncomfortable.

I stop recording, and the last thing the camera captures is Theo's smiling face looking up at me. He's still got his head buried in the crook of my neck, and neither of us moves for what feels like an eternity. Theo's holding me like it's nothing, and I can feel the strength of his upper body beneath my arms.

"You can put me down now," I say, my voice just a whisper.

I feel him nod his head in agreement, but he doesn't move an inch.

He's lingering.

I'm acutely aware of his firm grip around my waist, and if I didn't know any better, I'd say his hand most definitely flexed on my ass. I feel my skin flush.

Slowly, he lowers my body down his, and while I know I probably shouldn't have, I'm not going to pretend I didn't just allow my hands to trail themselves over his chest and stomach.

"Thanks," I manage as my feet hit the leaf-covered ground, and I fear my throat may begin constricting. Theo nods in acknowledgment, shoving his hands in his pockets. A slight flash of red makes an appearance across his cheeks. For someone who has literally jabber-jawed my ear off since the moment we met, he's sure settled into the role of man of few words today. "Are you . . ." I start, reaching out for him but suddenly unsure if I should or if saying anything is a bad idea. "Is everything okay?"

But Theo leans into my touch and every uncertain thought melts away in an instant. "I'm alright," he says quietly, a slight rasp to his voice. I search his eyes for anything that indicates the contrary, and I think he must see the concern I'm feeling. "I promise, Ash," he says, adding a slow-spreading smile to really seal the deal.

We walk in silence back to our original spot where Jo and Arthur are waiting, curiosity painted on each of their faces.

"Here," I say, handing Jo's phone back to her. "Will this work?" They replay the video.

"Oh, yeah," she says, a smug smile spreading across her face. "That'll work, alright."

"Good. Anything else?" I want to wrap this up so we can get some food and escape into our room. They shake their heads simultaneously.

"Can we help with any of this?" Theo asks, a hint of frustrated embarrassment woven in his words.

"No, you boys go on and get some rest," Arthur says, already folding down the tripod and placing it in its carrier. There's something fatherly in the way he addresses us, and under normal circumstances, from anyone else, that would rub me entirely the wrong way. But I suspect that's just who Arthur is. A stoic and kind man who shows he cares by handling the little things.

I turn to head back to the hotel, room key in hand, and Theo falls in step next to me. Taking in his sharp profile, I would never assume he'd be someone who needs protecting in any capacity, but perhaps there's far more to the boisterous and overzealous man I've tricked into being my boyfriend than meets the eye.

The elevator seems to be stuck when we cross the lobby, so we silently agree to take the stairs. We're only on the fourth floor, anyway. Theo pauses once we are alone in the stairwell and quietly takes my hand to prevent me from climbing any farther.

"She's never used the word *boyfriend* before," he says out of nowhere. "Neither of us have. So, seeing it written like that, online of all places, just . . . threw me off for a moment." His mother's post seemed supportive enough, though.

Happy and excited, even.

I turn to face him, fully ready to dive headfirst into family trauma and questions about his coming-out experience and a poorly timed jab about his mommy issues, but something in

Theo's expression stops me. His brow is furrowed, like he's weighing his next move, and it hits me all at once that he may not know he can talk to me.

If that's even something he wants.

"You know I'm here, right?" I say nervously, deciding now is as good a time as any to let the man I'm supposed to be dating know I'm someone he can count on. He's been *that* person for me far too many times to count already, and the last thing I'd want is for him to feel like he is alone in whatever it is he's so clearly thinking. "For you."

"I know," he says, but the expression on his face says otherwise.

"Seriously, Theo," I say, taking an intentional step forward, realizing now that it matters whether he trusts me. "Whatever it is . . . you can talk to me." I place what I hope is a reassuring hand on his forearm, and when I do, Theo's expression softens.

"I appreciate it," he says quietly, putting a hand on top of mine. The warmth from his touch makes it difficult to swallow. "It's just . . . This whole thing with my family feels like it should be incredibly black-and-white, you know? And instead, it just feels . . ."

"Complicated?" I offer, and my interruption elicits a welcome smile from this serious version of Theo.

"Yes, guapo, *complicated*," he repeats, but I'm too fixated on how his lips move when he calls me handsome to pay attention. "I guess I just don't know how we got here."

He runs his thumb in circles over the back of my hand—intentionally or absentmindedly, I'm not sure. Either way, it's a welcome distraction. "And by *here* you mean . . ." I prod, hoping to get on the same page as him.

"I don't know," he says, that furrowed brow returning.

"Distant? Just not as close as we used to be. It's like from one second to the next, we all started walking on eggshells around one another."

There's genuine longing in his voice, and while a huge part of me wants to pull him into a tight hug or even change the subject to something lighter, the other part knows Theo probably has needed to talk about this for quite some time.

"So, this has something to do with your sexuality?" I ask, noting that this all seems to have stemmed from his mother's use of the word *boyfriend* online. I really hope that's not the case.

"Yes and no. We never talked about it. Growing up where I did, there wasn't anyone my age who was *out* or for me to date, so, I don't know . . . it never once occurred to me I needed to change anything."

"But then there was?" I ask, sensing a shift in this story's direction.

He looks up, his eyes finding mine. "I guess you could say I met someone who put a lot of things in my life into perspective." Theo leans his big shoulder against the wall and I instinctively follow suit. "And then it ended." There doesn't seem to be any harbored hostility lingering in his tone. Just a mature and neutral *it was what it was* mentality.

"And your family?" I ask, now curious how they fit into all this. "How were they involved?"

Theo laughs to himself, some personal memory probably replaying behind those golden eyes of his. "Oh, they were plenty involved. At the end of the day, I think the whole thing just became something none of us wanted to bring up. So we didn't, and I think we all got pretty good at pretending . . ." he says, his voice trailing off quietly as he drops his gaze to our hands. "I guess you could say we found some uncomfortably comfortable middle ground."

My heart lodges forcefully in my throat as I take in what might just be the real Theo for the first time. Someone who's been pretending for his family. Someone who might be tired of it.

And here I am asking him to carry out yet another charade by being my pretend boyfriend.

"Is this . . . is being here making it worse?" I ask, nervous I might already know the answer.

Theo shifts his weight to his back leg. "I wouldn't say it's making it worse," he says quickly, though the tone in his voice is unreadable. "But I'm not going to lie, it's a little disorienting trying to keep up with what's real and what's . . . for the show, you know?"

Oh, do I ever.

"Is there anything I can do to help?" I ask. I've been so concerned with pulling off the whole *fake boyfriends* bit and how Theo's presence might help me that I haven't really stopped to consider what he needs out of this.

"You're doing it."

"That seems"—I start, but then we lock eyes and for a fraction of a breath, I think he might kiss me—"unlikely." My voice gets trapped in my throat as I watch his eyes drop to my lips, and I could swear he inched forward ever so slightly. But he doesn't move in for the kiss I'm practically begging for, and the hint of disappointment pooling in my stomach surprises me. Instead he just smiles, and it does something funny to my insides.

There's no denying my attraction to Theo. From the second I laid eyes on him, I knew that, conventionally, he was gorgeous. But on days like today, when he's peeling back those layers and showing me who he *really* is, I'm left considering how to make a voluntary amendment to our *no sex* rule I'm now kicking myself for instituting.

"I'm serious. You've gotten quite good at this whole boy-friend thing," he says, winking at me as he pivots our conversation entirely and slings an unexpected arm over my shoulder. His voice is noticeably lighter.

Boyfriend.

That word rolling off his tongue sounds different. Fuller and more . . . complicated. Now more than ever, I'm understanding the razor-thin line between real and reality television Theo was just talking about.

"You're hilarious," I say, trying to ignore the fact that Theo's now pulled me in flush against his body and is leading us up the stairs.

I prod him with my elbow so he doesn't start thinking I like it *too* much.

Because I *am* starting to like it too much.

15

THEO

Ituango Dam
Cauca River, Colombia

'd reconsider eating that if I were you," Ellie says, popping out of nowhere.

Asher and I both freeze mid-bite of the burritos we grabbed from the makeshift production tent and set up shop to eat at an open picnic table. I think I can speak for both of us when I say we're both next-level starving and in desperate need of some actual sleep after Jo's continued assault on our individual REM cycles. And don't even get me started on the way we've been zigzagging all over creation—each flight path and production destination more inefficient than the last.

"Why?" Asher asks with his mouth full, a big ol' glob of sour cream on the corner of his mouth. His cheeks redden slightly when I hand over a napkin, miming where he should wipe.

I'm grateful for the interruption.

Lately, my thoughts have been a confusing swirl of our kisses, now plural.

It's technically only been one.

One on camera and then an almost-one free from prying eyes.

I look over at Asher, who's now wiping his face clean, and wish I knew what he was thinking. He's given me no indication what's going on behind those eyes of his. How much of this is just the game for him? I could have kissed him in the stairwell last night. For a moment, he looked like he even wanted me to. But I promised we'd play by his rules. As much as I'm starting to hate it.

"Hey, I'm just the messenger," Ellie says, putting her hands up defensively and pulling me out of my funk. "All I heard is that whatever they have planned for us today would probably be easier on an empty stomach."

Ugh. Please don't be an eating challenge.

"I'm not eating bull's balls," I groan, and both Ellie and Asher slowly turn their heads in my direction, a confused *the fuck did he just say* expression plastered across each of their faces. "What? Don't tell me you haven't seen that one episode a few seasons back where they made all the contestants eat all that inedible shit?" I ask, in full defense mode.

"I . . ." Asher starts, mouth wide open. "I literally don't even know what to say after that."

I shrug off his comment. "A first."

Ellie laughs. "I'm curious, though—is it just bull's balls you have an aversion to? Balls in general?"

Asher leans forward on his elbows, placing his chin on his fists. "Yes, Theo—do tell the class where you stand on *balls*."

I narrow my eyes at him.

"Oh, *honey*," I say, mirroring his body language. "Only you know the answer to that."

Well, hopefully he's going to.

The flush that's become my newfound Asher obsession returns to his cheeks and he leans back in his seat, quietly retreating from whatever game of chicken we'd started. A subtle smirk makes a timely appearance at the corner of his mouth.

"Um . . . ew," Ellie says through a pretend and overly dramatic gag. "I'm literally *right* here." She shakes her head, quickly turning on her heel before heading back in the direction she came from.

Jo, with a very grumpy-looking Arthur trailing behind her, makes her way over to us before either of us can carry this ballsy conversation any further. She's on a phone call and spewing out one-word responses left and right, but that doesn't prevent her from eyeing our burritos. She purses her lips in such a way that it makes me set down my greasy goodness immediately.

"Can you get them set up?" she asks Arthur, covering her phone with her hand.

"Here you go, guys." Arthur holds out a pair of bright-yellow helmets, each with a small camera mounted on the front. "You'll want to make sure that's on good and tight."

Asher takes one of the helmets and eyes me.

"Let me guess, you aren't going to tell us what we need this for, are you?" he asks dryly.

Arthur makes a show of zipping his lips and throwing the invisible key over his shoulder. "You know I can't do that," he says, prepping the removable mics.

"You're so elusive, Arthur," I tease, and Asher and I pin the small devices to our shirts. "So mysterious and full of secrets."

He responds with a scowl.

"All good?" Jo asks, pocketing her phone. Arthur nods.

"Perfect—we've got to head over to the staging area," she says, turning and leading us toward where the rest of the crew is milling around. Each time we step foot on one of the locations they've set up for a challenge, it's like finding ourselves in some sort of temporary city. Cords and tents and random Pelican boxes piled high. They do a good job of keeping the actual challenge element a "secret," but when we round another row of tent-covered folding tables, there's no way for them to hide *that*.

"What is it?" Asher asks beside me. "A dam?"

But before we get a clear answer, Jo is pulling us each by an arm. "Alright, here's your mark. Please be safe and try to remember to smile!" she chirps, and I'm pretty sure neither of us change our tired expressions. But when I reach for Asher's hand, intertwining his fingers with mine, his own smile makes an appearance.

Jenn and Ellie are only a few yards to our left. We seem to be the last pair in a long row of contestants at the base of what appears to be a massive concrete wall.

"Stand by," a random PA calls out from behind us, and the hum of chitchat dies down as Dalton emerges from somewhere out of view. It's like they intentionally keep him away from everyone to ensure he's happy and unbothered. Like some moody show pony that can only come out when the attention is all on him.

Camera one on Dalton.

He takes his place in the center of the stage with a grimace and an impatient eye roll, rudely swatting away the hand of someone who tries to blot his overly tanned forehead.

We're rolling in three . . . two . . .

And as always, the second the camera's red light turns on, he transforms.

"Welcome to yet another exciting episode of *The Epic Trek*," he beams, and his smile looks more and more like a snarl in disguise. "Today, we're taking our show to new heights . . . *literally.*"

Ugh, cha-ching . . .

Dalton looks up and both the camera operator and I follow his gaze. On some unseen and unheard command, sets of rope ladders are launched from their waiting places at the top of the wall, unrolling messily until they reach the bottom where we're waiting.

Dalton resumes, turning his gaze back to the camera. "Each team will race up the side of the hydroplant behind us here. But as we all know, what goes up . . ."

Here we go.

". . . must come down."

Great.

As Dalton's opening narration continues, several members of production step forward, handing Asher and me each a complicated-looking harness and motioning for us to put it on. Through confused glances, fumbling hands, and multiple failed attempts to get strapped in, we're escorted toward the base of the wall where our respective ladders wait, swaying side by side.

If I wasn't fighting heartburn over the challenge waiting for us, my eyes would definitely be zeroing in on Asher's very visible bulge thanks to how . . . formfitting . . . his harness is.

Arthur has stayed in our peripherals; his camera zeroes in on us as we both keep glancing up the wall. My stomach is in knots and I try to guesstimate the height we'll have to scale—a couple hundred feet, if I had to put a number on it. Heights and me? Yeah, we don't get along.

Never have. Not since my sister left me stranded in that old oak tree when we were kids. We'd made a zip line deep in the woods behind the outhouse, and as soon as we made it to the top, she turned her ass right back around, leaving me frozen, clinging to the trunk of the tree until my dad had to climb up himself to get me down.

"And for our trekkers at home who have been chiming in online," Dalton says, "we heard you loud and clear—which is why for this challenge, each contestant will be tethered to their partner so they're forced to complete the climb as a team."

An overcaffeinated PA steps forward and secures a thick, tightly woven cord with metal clips on Asher and me and then attaches us to our respective ladders.

"Contestants, at the sound of the buzzer," Dalton instructs us, "you'll begin your ascent to the top. The first team to successfully make it up . . . and down . . . will be safe from elimination this week."

His comment is followed by a lingering and unnerving silence.

And then the signaling shriek of the buzzer.

Asher shoots unexpectedly fast up his ladder, and thanks to the tether between us, pulls me right along with him. I match his pace to avoid any unnecessary tension growing between our harnesses—which, considering all the pretending . . . or not . . . we've been doing, seems incredibly fitting. Yet here we are, scaling some ridiculous wall like a pair of spider monkeys.

The rough rope of the ladder burns against my increasingly sweaty palms, and after what feels like a decade of climbing, I make the foolish mistake of looking down, officially and completely halting any progress we've made.

Asher looks back at me when he feels the rope pull against my deadweight. "Everything okay?" he asks, an eyebrow raised.

"Funny thing . . ." I say, through clamped-shut eyes. "We might just have a tiny problem here."

"Huh?"

"A problem," I repeat, clinging to the rope now. "I have a problem with heights."

Asher climbs down a few rungs of his ladder so he's now parallel to where I'm rooted in place. "I don't get it, you're a pilot. How is that possible?"

"Um, that's flying."

He nods in agreement. "Right . . . in the sky. Certainly higher than—"

"Hey Ash?" I cut him off, my eyes now snapping open and finding his. "You may or may not realize this, but *that's* not exactly helping."

"Sorry, sorry," he says urgently, putting a warm hand on my back. "What can I . . . ? Do you want to turn around?"

No, I'm not going to let this irrational fear of mine be the reason we miss out on the prize money. "I . . . I just need a minute."

"Of course." Asher keeps his hand on me, and it's unnerving how much I like it.

"How much farther ahead is everyone else?"

"Don't worry about them," he says, craning his head up the wall to where our competition is. "We're fine. But while we wait, why don't you tell me about your mom?"

His question catches me entirely off guard. "What . . . why?"

"Come on," he pries. "What's the first thing that comes to mind when you think of your mom?"

Flower pins.

"I guess she would always wear these pins on her jackets. Flowers," I share, easily picturing the different fabric florals she'd adorn her outerwear with.

Asher smiles. "What else?"

It dawns on me that my mother will eventually be seeing this play out when I stare directly at the camera mounted on Asher's helmet. The last thing I want to do is make it appear like I don't want to talk about her. I try to hide the twinge of annoyance I feel toward Asher and the fact that he's decided *now* is the time to bring this up. On television. "She's a simple woman," I say, adjusting my grip on the rope. "Simple but time-less and one of a kind."

"Take a step with me," Asher says. "Take a step and tell me what makes her one of kind."

Oh. He's distracting me.

And weirdly, talking to him—about this, of all things—is working.

I take a step and so does he. "I guess it was her quiet stabil-ity. Her guiding hand that led me to grow up in a home with someone I could count on," I add, taking another step. He mir-rors me.

"That's really special," he says, not breaking eye contact.

It really was. As I've gotten older, I've realized that like most parents, her everyday sacrifices went mostly unnoticed by all of us. Her vintage and well-worn style wasn't because she genu-inely enjoyed sifting through the piles at our local consignment shop like she'd said. She'd done that so my sister and I could start each school year with the new clothes we thought would help us fit in.

"Come on, take another step with me."

Or how on every first morning in January, she'd declare that this was finally the year she and my dad would take that belated honeymoon to Europe they'd been talking about since 1987. But each year like clockwork, Elise would discover a new, and expensive, hobby, or I would outgrow my basketball shoes. One of us needed braces or wanted to vacation with a friend.

"It was special. She used to say she was happy to live a small life so that we could live a big one," I say, a small lump growing in my throat. "And it took me a really long time to understand what she meant by that."

We're moving in sync now—hand over hand, rung after rung—in an attempt to make up for the time I'd wasted.

"You're doing so good, babe," Asher says across the space between us, the pet name rolling off his tongue quite naturally as he continues his encouragement every step of the way. "We're almost there."

For the longest time, I haven't felt like someone who needed encouragement. Hell, I haven't let someone get close enough for them to even have a desire to encourage me. But coming from someone like Asher—smart and successful and a little all over the place in the best ways—I'm beginning to think it could mean something different.

Something more.

Like allowing yourself to need someone doesn't automatically equate to weakness.

I glance up after a moment, my arms and legs feeling the strain of our climb, and see that he's right, we're nearing the top. And as much as I'd love to continue a conversation of this magnitude while strapped to the side of an oversize slab of concrete, I pick up the pace, closing the distance between us and the top of the ladder with Asher following suit.

When we reach the top—our hands finally gripping the edge—and we're able to pull ourselves up and over, a pair of production techs comes and begins removing the tether between us. But a more permanent one just might have formed on that climb.

Some link or invisible string tying our lives together.

Me to Asher.

And I like the promise of an us. Or at least I think I could. The weight behind that word and what it would mean nearly knocks me on my ass because wanting it—wanting it so badly with *him*—is really the only thing that matters right now.

Asher launches himself at me when he's finally free, fitting himself perfectly in my arms, and I can feel his smile against my neck.

"Hi," he says, leaning back to look up at me, but I tighten my arms around him so he can't go too far.

"Hi."

His eyes find mine and really hold them. "You did it."

"I have you to thank for that," I say, pulling him closer. "You've been saving me a lot lately, Bennett."

Asher's smile widens. "Some would argue you saved me first."

But I'm interrupted before I can tell him I'd do it over and over again as long as it gets us to where we are now.

"If you two will step over here . . ." a voice calls from behind us. "And we'll get you down."

Down.

After the climb up, and now having Asher in my arms, I'd completely forgotten that we still need to get down somehow. I should have been paying more attention during Dalton's not-so-vague opening monologue.

Hands locked, Asher and I walk over to the other side of the landing, where we're met with another set of harnesses.

"Think they get some sort of sick enjoyment out of tying us up?" Asher asks, leaning in.

"I would," I say with a wink, which makes him laugh. Maybe we should take some of these ropes back to the hotel room.

Asher and I are marionetted by the crew. Moved and adjusted and strapped in tighter and tighter. We stand face-to-face as we're fastened to each other.

"We're about to jump, aren't we," I ask, trying to mask my growing nerves with a smile.

"Looks like it," Asher says, searching my eyes. "You okay?"

I nod—unconvincingly, I'm sure. "Mm-hmm."

We're escorted to the daunting ledge, shuffling awkwardly, and when we reach whatever spot has been determined we'll leap from, thick red cords are attached to our harnesses. Our pending descent becomes more and more real in my mind, and all I can think about is my mom.

Either because of Asher's questioning or, more honestly, I just miss her. And though she's never done anything like this before, I just know she'd be fearless in a moment like this.

"Ready?" we're asked, and I for one am certainly not.

Reaching up to place a hand on either side of Asher's helmet, I adjust his head slightly so the lens of his camera is right on me and just hope that Arthur uses this clip when he's editing it all together.

"Hola, mamá," I say, speaking directly to her because I now know she's watching. "Te extraño y te amo. This one's for you!"

Asher looks back up at me when I've finished, a tenderness behind his expression. "You're kind of amazing, you know that?"

"Oh, I don't know about that," I say, looking down and away from his compliment.

He reaches up and places a hand on my face, forcing my gaze back to his. "I do."

His sudden honesty makes me swallow hard. "You realize you're going to be the one to get us over the edge, right?"

He smiles. "I've got you," he says and wraps his arms tightly around me. We're practically fused together now, standing on the edge of this free fall. Which isn't something I've ever wanted to do or would even remotely consider doing.

But here I am, doing it for Asher.

There's the prize money, sure. But being strapped together on the edge with Asher Bennett is an added bonus.

Something changed on this climb.

Something I'd been hiding from for far too long. And it took Asher's prying nature to open my eyes to just how much I'd been holding on to that lingering familial baggage. I look back in the direction we just climbed from and it's as if this climb was some cosmic nudge for me to leave everything I'd been grappling with on the ground behind me.

"Whenever you're ready," one of the crew members shouts over the wind, and it almost makes me laugh, because it feels like I've been waiting a really, really long time to be *ready* for a moment like this.

This moment with him.

Asher finally places his lips to mine, a soft reassurance that we're in this together, and before I can think about it for another second, we're falling.

Oh, shit, am I *falling*.

16

ASHER

United Flight UA803—Seats 21E & F
Somewhere over the Atlantic Ocean

Oh, I'm sorry, dear," the sweeter-than-sugar flight attendant says when she realizes I'm struggling to recline my seat. "That one's broken."

Of course it is.

Theo offers to switch, but I shrug him off, an exhaustion that's been building over the last few weeks finally setting in.

This is our life now. Time marked by takeoffs and landings with Theo and I sluggishly moving along until we hope to find an hour or two of sleep in the comfort of an airline seat.

A broken one.

He puts his hand on my thigh at the same time that I rest my head against his shoulder. I have to admit that it feels nice not to question it anymore. We've settled into some nonverbal agreement that we're just doing what feels comfortable at this point.

I've also stopped asking where we're going. Not that Jo or Arthur seem inclined to tell us anyway, given that they seem to find immense enjoyment in seeing the shock, confusion, or whatever other emotion must ripple across my face when we reach our destination.

Over the last few weeks, Theo and I have logged an ungodly number of hours cramped together on every mode of transportation known to man. Every once in a while, Arthur will swing by with a camera practically in our faces, capturing a few moments of our travels, but for the most part, this time sitting side by side is just for us. It's one of the rare occasions where we can just exhale and find solace in the downtime.

And in each other.

Theo, without even trying, has become my safest of spaces. A much-needed breath of fresh air amid all the chaos—the hand I instinctively reach for now. He's the person I've placed every ounce of my trust in.

Which feels incredibly odd and unnatural considering how recently we met. We've gone from skeptical strangers to inseparable lunatics in a matter of weeks, and the breakneck speed of it all is enough to give anyone whiplash. I've never allowed myself to get swept up this quickly with anyone before. But it's different with Theo.

The thought causes me to sneak a glance at him.

His face is relaxed as he leans against the airplane's wall. I've never met anyone who can succumb to sleep as quickly and deeply as Theo can. I'm both envious and in awe. His skin is sun-kissed and he's probably a week or so overdue for a haircut. We both are. His dark stubble is almost a beard at this point, not that you'll hear me complain about it. The burn against my skin literally makes my mouth water.

He's quite lovely, in every sense of the word. There's a softness to his current expression that reminds me of early Sunday mornings. He smiled when I told him that after a night of drinking with Jo, Arthur, and some of the other crew. A soft smile at first that spread little by little across his whole face.

But what I've come to admire most about Theo Fernandez is his overall sense of goodness. This man has a heart of actual gold. Not in the way people casually throw around when describing someone who is generally kind or giving. No. I'm convinced that beneath that impressive chest of his lies an eighth wonder of the world—a heart so pure and genuine and *good*. One that gives so much and expects very little, if anything, in return.

If I'm being honest, it's a little overwhelming to think about, since I'm the one constantly on the receiving end of his sunny disposition. That I'm somehow and suddenly worthy of a heart like that.

He squeezes my thigh gently, as if in his sleep he's noticed my absence from his side. Reclaiming my spot on Theo's strong shoulder, my tired eyes beg for rest. The memories of the last few weeks flutter through every corner of my subconscious.

We were dropped at different entrances to the world's largest maze in Denmark with nothing more than a flashlight and a pair of binoculars. For being fairly competent adults, Theo and I were quickly lost in the labyrinth of trees and shrubs that went on for miles and miles. I don't know how we finally managed to find our way out, but I'm fairly confident that neither of us want to ever experience something like that again.

Or talk about it.

No one was eliminated after that challenge, shocking everyone again.

We herded llamas in Peru, working in tandem to successfully get all the incredibly cute but exceptionally stubborn mammals from one corral to another. I'm pretty sure Theo whispered to at least nine of the llamas that he'd adopt them—a promise I have a feeling he'd make good on in a second if he were allowed to. Jenn and Ellie faced elimination after they struggled to get their own llamas to cooperate. Luckily, they were saved and Dallas and Cameron were sent home instead.

From there, we traveled to Toronto, stopping by one of the most breathtaking libraries I've ever seen, where we worked to reshelve dozens of books. The catch? We had to use a very old, very complicated wooden decoding device to decipher the library's organizational system. Everyone but Jenn and Ellie, who miraculously cracked the code within moments, struggled with this challenge, and I'm pretty sure Theo had to stop me from throwing our decoding device across the room on more than one occasion. Thankfully, our viewers decided that #Thasher would live on for another challenge, resulting in the father-daughter pair from Washington to be sent packing.

And somehow, amid the televised conundrums, Theo and I appeared to reach some semblance of an understanding.

Of the competition and each other.

Each stop along the way brings us closer. In the darkness of yet another hotel room or cramped against each other on another endless flight, I feel we've both quietly envisioned just what this could be.

///////////////////////

"Wake up." Theo's voice is but a whisper in my ear.

I don't remember when I finally fell asleep, but I needed every second of it. My body is stiff and I'm fairly positive I'm going to have permanent fabric lines from Theo's pullover etched into my face.

"Ash, come on. You have to see this," he says, nudging me with his thigh.

I nuzzle into his neck in silent protest.

"Please," he breathes, his lips lingering on my skin. Okay, now I'm awake.

"I'm up, I'm up," I groan, pretending that seeing his signature grin when I finally force my eyes open didn't just completely punch me straight in the gut.

He shakes his head at my theatrics but turns toward our window and slides its shade up, leaning back so I have an unobstructed view.

"Theo, it's . . ." My voice trails off because I quickly realize I don't have the words to describe the picturesque beauty before me.

We are weaving in and out of a sea of endless clouds. Miles and miles of velvet softness painted in the amber morning light surround us. Their subtle shifts in the wind allow sun streams to make a divine but fleeting appearance.

It's like we've woken up within a painting. Our very own billowing fresco stretching from every corner of the horizon.

"Every time I step into a cockpit, *this* is the moment I look for," he says, and my heart melts at the fact that he wanted to share it with me. "My mom shared a quote from Leonardo da Vinci, or one of those interchangeable old guys everyone is always quoting, with me when I was younger. Back when I wouldn't stop talking about being a pilot and always had my head in the clouds . . . *Once you have tasted flight, you will forever walk the earth with your eyes turned skyward, for there you have been, and there you will always long to return.*" He reaches over and takes my hand in his. "Or something like that."

I'm speechless. At the beauty we've found ourselves amid. At the borrowed words that clearly mean something to him.

At this man who feels more and more like the rays of sunshine peering through the clouds surrounding us every time he opens his mouth.

"So, you always wanted to be a pilot, then?" I ask when I finally find my voice again. I trail my fingertips over his knuckles as Theo leans in to me, his head now resting on mine.

"I did. My family used to go to the air show that would come to town every summer. They are some of my earliest memories," he says, his voice growing quieter. Most of our conversations have been centered around the competition or one of us complaining how tired we are, so it feels like a treat getting little glimpses into Theo's real life.

"I loved everything about it. The thunderous noise the jets made as they flew overhead, their impossible maneuvers, the way everyone would sprint to meet the pilots as soon as they landed—I was hooked."

Picturing a young and enamored Theo causes my heart to constrict. "And the Navy? Was that always part of the pilot plan too?"

"Not at all. That chapter of my life was definitely unexpected." I feel him shake his head against mine. "No, when I was younger and pictured my future life as a pilot, I was convinced I'd be flying NASA shuttles into space by the time I was sixteen."

"I see you've always been realistic."

"Obviously," he murmurs, struggling to choke back his laugh.

Somewhere in the golden mesh of clouds, it's the last sound I hear before drifting back to sleep.

17

ASHER

Hotel Piazza di Spagna—Room 308
Rome, Italy

D o you want to get out of here?"

Theo's been pacing our hotel room for the last fifteen or so minutes. I lost track after he crossed my claimed spot in our room's armchair for the ninety-second—no, wait . . . ninety-third time.

"Out of here?" I ask. "Where to?" We touched down in Italy in a sleep-deprived haze but were elated when Jo told us we had the rest of the afternoon to ourselves before filming resumed tomorrow. I heard Ellie and Jenn excitedly talking about all the gelato they were going to try and how throwing a euro into the Trevi Fountain for luck is an absolute must as the cast and crew excitedly dispersed in the hotel lobby.

Not me.

Nope, I plan to sit my happy ass in the comfort of this hotel room, take a long shower where I don't care about using all the hot water, and not move an inch. I am exhausted. Scratch that.

I'm whatever word is the word beyond exhausted. Something that would describe how every muscle in my body is feeling. Theo and I have been running on fumes. Literally dragging our feet from one airport to another, agonizingly loading the bags into the van with Arthur and having to deal with the migraine that is Bianca and Jackson's incessant snark every time the cameras start rolling.

No, thank you. I'm perfectly fine staying right here.

"Anywhere. I think I'll lose it if I have to spend another minute in a hotel, Ash." I fight a hoard of demonic butterflies every time he calls me that, but something is clearly off with him. Theo leans against the dresser, his brow furrowed. He's been noticeably quiet most of the afternoon, but I chalked it up to him being as drained as I am.

I close my book, setting it down on the small side table. "Lead the way," I say, knowing I'd do just about anything for this man.

His brow is cocked, and the smirk I've come to both roll my eyes at and live to see spreads from the corner of his mouth. "I thought you'd put up more of a fight."

"First of all," I say, "get to know me. I'm full of surprises. And second of all, what kind of maniac would I be if I said no after all your pouting?"

Theo snorts. "My pouting?"

"Your pouting." I get up from the comfort of my chair and cross the room toward him. "Ever since we touched down today, your shoulders have been slumped, your usual golden retrieverness is all but depleted. I *cannot* be counted on to be the sunshiny one in this pairing, Theo Fernandez, so either snap out of it or tell me what's going on up there." I give the side of his head a playful tap with my fingers, his smirk spreading even wider across his face.

He opens his mouth but decides against whatever it was he was going to say. "I . . . I'm probably just tired." His lie isn't as convincing as I'm sure he believes it is, but Theo just leans forward, closing what little distance remains between us, and I momentarily forget how to breathe. "Has anyone ever told you your eyes have flecks of amber in them?" he asks, his warm breath washing over me, threatening to swallow me whole.

"Uh, what?" I stammer out, disarmed by our sudden closeness.

"Right here." Theo places a soft hand on the side of my face, and the heat from his touch seeps straight into my veins. His thumb brushes gently under my eye and if he's pointing at something, I'm unable to focus on anything other than his now-parted lips, which are only a whisper away from mine. I could just lean in—

"Shall we?" he asks, his hand dropping to his side. My skin instantly longs for his touch again. I don't know whether it's disappointment or desperation or some horny combination of the two, but whatever it is, I'm definitely the one pouting now.

I do my best to plaster on a smile, the one reserved for moments of forced fun and things well outside my comfort zone. "Sure, let's do it."

Theo turns to head for the door but reaches for my hand before he gets too far. I don't know exactly when this whole hand-holding business started when the cameras weren't rolling, but I've stopped questioning it. For once, I'm doing my best not to spiral in a fit of mental gymnastics and just do what feels natural, because this? I look down at his hand, our fingers now intertwined. This feels right.

If I can't lose myself in his kiss, the deliberate back and forth of his thumb over my knuckles as we head down toward the lobby in the cramped elevator is a consolation prize to smile about.

The lobby feels alive when we make our way out of the ancient elevator.

I've been to Italy once before. My grandparents took me on a surprise tour across the country when I became obsessed with Pompeii in school. We went from city to city, learning about the rich history and beautiful culture. At every stop, I remember thinking how everything felt like it was buzzing. Even at my young age, I could tell that the Italians lived differently, throwing their whole hearts into every day, every meal, and every conversation they had. I was in awe.

It's no different today—people are shuffling in and out of the grand hotel door, their bags packed and their eyes wide with excitement.

Some familiar faces come into view as the crowd parts. Jo and Arthur are sitting across from Ellie and Jenn at the cramped hotel bar, a round of half-enjoyed cocktails between them.

"And where are you two off to?" Arthur asks, his gruff voice reaching us over the hum of the crowd as we approach.

Jo looks down at our hands, which are still intertwined. She takes a small sip from her crystal tumbler and struggles to stifle a grin.

"Just need to get out. Maybe someplace the locals would go to?" Theo says, jamming his free hand in his pants pocket.

Arthur downs the rest of his drink, nodding as he gets up from his seat. "Come on, I know a place."

////////////////

There's nothing like a group of tightly wound, sleep-deprived American tourists trying to blend in with Italian regulars.

We follow Arthur down the winding cobblestone streets, each of us with our phone, which production so kindly passed back out, practically glued to our face, snapping away at the gorgeous architecture and local scenery. Our collective *oohs* and *ahs* as we loudly point things out to one another raise more than one eyebrow, but what's the saying? When in Rome?

Arthur leads us directly to the bar when we enter the small stucco building and points at a nearby vacant booth before he disappears from view. I find myself sandwiched between Jenn and Ellie as Jo and Theo slide in across from us, immediately jumping into animated conversation.

He seems more himself. As soon as we left the hotel, his entire demeanor shifted. More relaxed and less antsy?

I missed whatever Jo said that made Theo throw his head back in a fit of laughter, but I'm endlessly thankful for it.

There he is.

"This place is neat, huh?" Jenn says, panning the room with her phone. Ellie rolls her eyes.

"Did you get that incredible church as we walked here? It was stunning," Theo says, which causes Jenn to light up. His kindness is something I've deduced is one hundred percent genuine. He mouths, *Be nice*, to Ellie.

"I sure did," she says. "Here, look." Jenn scrolls back through her camera roll, handing her phone over to Theo, who smiles as he watches the video on the screen.

"Oh my God, Mother. No one wants to see that," Ellie groans under her breath.

I nudge her with my shoulder and give her *the look*. Jenn has quickly become everyone's favorite and has happily assumed the role of stand-in mother for just about all of us. Despite being as exhausted as we all are, her positive disposition has not once waned.

Arthur returns with a tray. A couple of mystery bottles and six glasses clink against one another as he sets them down in front of us. "This place has some of the best limoncello I've ever had," he says, uncorking the tall bottle. He pours a little of the bright-yellow liquor in each glass and Jo passes them around.

"Cin cin," he says, holding his glass up for a toast. He's a simple man, filled with fortitude and grit, and most days, he seems perfectly fine off by himself with a book and his cigarettes. But tonight, his eyes are brimming with a quiet contentment.

"To health and happiness," Jo says as we all raise our own glasses.

The lemon liqueur is fresh and fragrant. Strong enough for celebratory sipping, but definitely too sugary for me to have more than one. It's delicious and refreshing though, like breezy summer nights and tart sorbet.

Theo's stare never leaves mine as he takes his sip. There's something exhilarating behind his eyes. Something building beneath the amber light of the lounge—something raw and magnetic and full of life, and the all-too-familiar push and pull of Theo Fernandez leaves me only wanting more.

Drinks magically appear with each wave of straggling crew members. There's an eclectic mix of nineties pop playing on a vintage jukebox across the way that accompanies the infectious sounds of boisterous laughter and conversation around us. Jenn, who's finally put her phone away, is deep in conversation with Jo about a table of rather handsome Italian men kitty-corner to our booth. Ellie appears to be haggling with Arthur about getting snacks for the table.

And Theo is all smiles taking it all in.

Kiara and Ruby saunter over. "Anyone want to play some bocce ball? There's a little courtyard out back." Kiara's holding what appears to be a dust-covered ball a little larger than a baseball in her hand.

"A game of what?" I ask, blissfully unaware of what she could possibly be referring to.

"Bocce, you dork." Jo elbows me as she maneuvers around me. "I'm in." She leans down and picks up her own ball as our group gathers around them. Bistro lights hang above us and the music from inside trails through the open windows. Though we've all been traveling the globe together, tonight feels like the first time we're all just hanging out. It's nice.

"Why am I not surprised you're not a lawn-sport enthusiast?" Theo's raspy voice says from behind me once we all navigate out into the courtyard, the warmth of his breath on my neck.

"I'm glad my indoor-cat reputation precedes me. I take it you've played?" I ask, wrapping my arms around myself. The combination of the summer breeze and Theo's sudden closeness sends chills down my spine.

To my surprise, he pulls me flat against his chest like it's something we've done a million times. My breath catches in my throat, especially when I recall just how perfectly my body aligns with his. "My dad loves outdoor games like this. We would always play horseshoes or lawn darts or even croquet when the family got together and the weather was nice like tonight."

"That's sweet." I'm only half listening, unfortunately. His

walk down childhood memory lane truly deserves my full attention, but I'm sorry, with his big arms wrapped around me and his lips practically on my ear, I'm distracted.

Everyone rotates in, repeatedly tossing wooden balls across the manicured lawn, trying to have theirs be the winning shot. Ellie and Jo, who seem more interested in flirting with the gaggle of men who've now joined from the outskirts of our group, are quickly defeated by Ruby and Kiara.

Griffin and Alana are up next. I hadn't noticed them join us, but they are defeated rather quickly against the dynamic duo of Arthur and Jenn. Alana shoots Griffin an annoyed look that he simply returns with a half-hearted shrug before sauntering off back toward the bar. They make marriage look so fun.

Arthur and Jenn do their best against the sisters and actually hold their own. Until Kiara surprises everyone with a Hail Mary toss that causes us all to jump up and down in exuberant celebration.

Except for me, of course.

Because I'm quite comfortable playing my own game of control as I lean firmly against Theo. He's resting his chin on my shoulder, the roughness of his scruff an ever-present burn against my own skin. The warmth from his body radiates to my very core.

I could get used to this.

"Asher, Theo . . . get your cute little butts over here. You two are up," Jenn shouts with an extra cheerfulness that can only be credited to the limoncello.

The thought of playing sports *publicly* causes me to physically recoil, but Theo shakes my shoulders from behind. "What do you say, Ash? Should we teach all these ladies"—Arthur clears his throat—"and gentlemen a thing or two about playing with balls?"

Deceased.

"Mm-hmm." Theo talking about balls does something to me. Something bad.

He takes my hand and leads us the short distance to where the rest of the group is gathered, and I instantly miss our spot secluded at the edge of the crowd. Where we could watch from afar. Where I had him all to myself.

Theo proceeds to bend down and pick up a set of wooden balls that have been painted a deep navy. He places one in my free hand. "Ready, partner?"

"Okay, hold on, hold on." I put my hands up. "How do you play this again?" I ask, flicking a clump of dirt off my wooden ball.

"You see this here?" Arthur says. "This is the jack." He holds up a much smaller white ball. "Or the *boccino*, as the Italians call it. We're going to give this a little toss . . ." he says, gently launching the jack in front of us. It lands about twenty feet or so from where we're standing. "And each team takes turns trying to get their ball closest to it."

Theo slings an arm around my shoulders. "Simple enough, huh?"

"If you say so."

We are going head-to-head with Jenn and Ellie now and I'm hoping enough limoncello has been passed around that come tomorrow, no one from our group will remember what I can only assume will be a lackluster athletic performance by yours truly.

"Should we make this more interesting?" Theo whispers so

only I can hear. Chills run down my spine as he lets his lips gently brush against my ear.

"Go on."

"Each turn we take," he says, and I can hear a slow grin forming on his handsome face, "we have to tell each other a secret."

The thought of sharing secrets with Theo makes me giddy, but considering that I am quite literally the most boring human being on this entire planet, his flirty little game is just enticing enough for me to want to go along with it. "You're on, Fernandez."

He laughs, an electric sound that I can't help but smile at. "After you, then," he says, dropping his arm from my new favorite spot around my shoulders, indicating that I should proceed.

I roll the wooden ball between my hands and hate that I can feel every pair of eyes on me. The ball is heavier than I expected, and I have to squint slightly in the dimness to make out the white target I'm supposed to be aiming for.

Am I supposed to roll it like I would if I were bowling? Or throw it like a baseball? Why wasn't I paying more attention to everyone else?

Fuck it. I swing my arm backward before bringing it forward with some attempt at precision and release the ball when my arm reaches its apex. It soars momentarily through the air before landing with an unimpressive *thud* a good ten, eleven feet short of the jack.

There's a slow round of pity applause. Well, that was . . . embarrassing.

"Nice one," Theo says from beside me as Jenn steps up for her turn. He's lying through his teeth, obviously. "But time to pay up." He crosses his arms as he waits for my secret.

"I'm thinking, I'm thinking," I say slowly, hoping to buy myself an extra two seconds. "Uh, I'm double-jointed in my thumbs. Or, I can bend them backwards. Does that count?"

He smirks, feigning interest. "Let's see."

I stick my hands out in front of him and pop my thumbs out with ease, the way I've done for years since I learned I could, the closest thing to a party trick I have.

He smiles and nods in some weird sort of dude approval. "Gross. I love it."

If his smile wasn't the most dazzling thing I'd ever seen, hearing him call my appendage anomaly gross would make me feel a type of way.

Neither of us is paying any attention to Jenn, but the resounding *thud* from behind us indicates it's Theo's turn. He steps up to the invisible line we've all determined is where we're throwing from and expertly launches his own ball toward the jack. It lands about half a foot away from where he intended, resulting in a more genuine round of applause from our audience than I received. I hold back from rolling my eyes.

He turns back toward me, his smile wider than before—if that's even possible—and comes back to reclaim his spot by my side.

"And?" I say, wiggling my eyebrows at him as he gets closer.

But he doesn't stop where I assumed he would. Theo walks so he's directly in front of me and puts a tentative hand on my waist. He leans forward so our cheeks are practically pressed against each other.

"My secret is," he says, his voice a husky whisper against my ear. I shiver when his lips graze my sensitive skin again, each syllable purposely drawn out to maximize contact. "I *cannot stand* mayonnaise."

"Mayonnaise? Really?" I struggle to stammer out. His confession against my ear has practically left me panting. Only Theo could make condiments sound sexy.

"It's vile," he breathes. "The stuff of nightmares."

I laugh, leaning my head against his shoulder. And so begins this new, flirty element to our secrets game. Sure, we throw our little balls and do our best to put up a competitive fight against Jenn, Ellie, and the others. But it makes my heart soar to see how we've both thrown ourselves into this exchange of secrets.

After my next turn, which is far better than my first, I share that I used to tell people I was allergic to peanuts when I was younger instead of just admitting I didn't like the taste. He shakes his head at my ridiculousness. Rightfully so.

I learn that he didn't have his first kiss until he was eighteen. A fact I genuinely have a hard time believing considering just how charming he is.

Back and forth we go, haphazardly tossing balls and leaving our lips to linger longer and longer while we whisper stories to each other. I lose track of how long this tantalizing game has gone on or who wins at bocce ball, and soon, it becomes clear that everyone's energy is dwindling for the evening.

At this point, Theo and I are practically fused together. His arm draped over my shoulder. Mine snaked around his waist. It's the most naturally physical we've been with each other without a camera in sight. And as we walk side by side, back through the lounge and out into the quietness of a town half asleep, Theo and I trail behind the rest of our group.

I don't know if it's exhaustion or lust, but my eyes are heavy, so I lean in to Theo and inhale the sweetness of the summer night off his skin.

"You up for one more adventure?" he asks, his lips now at my temple.

I'm pretty sure I'd be up for anything with him.

But instead of telling him that, I just nod, and the two of us quietly veer away from our group without a single soul noticing.

/////////////

We wind our way through the city's maze and stumble upon a gelateria moments from closing for the night. Eyeing each other with a shrug, we race through the old door and show some restraint in trying every delicious flavor.

Late-night treats in hand, classic chocolate for him and a creamy hazelnut for me, Theo and I walk in a comfortable silence, admiring the grand architecture and charm of the Italian city. I've never really had the chance to travel like this as an adult before these last few weeks—but as we turn down another bistro-lit and cobblestone road, I know this is a place I'll spend the rest of my life longing to return to. Between the passion for food and wine and the fact that there's literally history around each and every corner, what more could one want?

"What are you thinking?" Theo asks, bumping me with his shoulder as he takes a bite of his gelato.

"That I like it here," I say after a beat.

"I do too," he says quietly, expertly tossing his empty gelato cup into a nearby trash bin. "We should come back. Just the two of us."

"Just the two of us, huh?" I repeat, my mouth going dry at the mere thought of truly having him all to myself. It's both hard and incredibly easy to imagine. Theo is so effortless to be around. But that would mean whatever *this* is has turned into something more, and I'm not sure either of us are ready to be there.

Or if he even wants that.

Still, the thought is intoxicating. "We should."

"Mm-hmm," he says, watching me intently as I take another small bite of my own gelato, trying to redirect my attention to something other than him. But I don't think it's doing anything to hide the grin that's quickly growing. My lack of a poker face is less than helpful in times like this.

"Oh. Here," he says, gently grabbing my arm and pulling me to a stop. "You've got a little . . ." He turns to face me head-on, taking a step forward to close the space between us. Theo reaches up, the pad of his thumb hovering ever so gently above my upper lip, and I'm pretty sure my limbs go completely numb.

With his hand soft against the side of my face, Theo slides his thumb across my lip, letting it linger slightly as our eyes meet. There's a hunger behind his gaze, one that's filled with questions and growing impatient. One that just might be tired of biding its time in the shadows.

"There," he says, his voice a husky whisper. Theo removes his thumb from my lip and slowly slides it into his mouth.

For the briefest of moments, we're both still. Nothing happens. Perhaps we're each trying to figure out the other's next move. In the middle of another foreign city, sleep-deprived, jet-lagged, and hornier than I think I've ever been in my life, I feel the battle between common sense and overwhelming lust coming to a head. His eyes find mine—his eyes that have made me feel more seen over the last couple days than any ever have, and I no longer care if this complicates our silly pact.

My mind is filled with one all-encompassing desire: Theo.

I reach for him before I talk myself out of it. There's still ample opportunity for either of us to walk away like nothing ever happened. To go back to the way things were and turn whatever chemistry is bubbling between us on only for the camera.

But we don't.

His hands find my face again and cradle me as the final moments of hesitancy slip between us. I grip his waist with tense fingertips and it's suddenly a race to see who can pull the other closer. The second we're pressed against each other, the most delicious hum radiates in his chest.

Even if this is real—or as real as two horny pretend boyfriends can get—I remind myself it's temporary. But there's something exhilarating about living in the moment. Physically giving in to what I think my body's wanted since Theo sauntered over to steal my mozzarella sticks.

The air around us has reached a breaking point, laced with electricity and longing and whispered *finally*s. And though neither one of us has said a word, our bodies have settled into a conversation all on their own.

Our lips brush, briefly at first, savoring each other's sweetness. But the newness of kissing like *this* when it's just for us draws us in deeper, and we quickly lose ourselves in a dance of frenzied hands, rolled hips, and muffled *oh my god*s.

"Our rules . . ." Theo breathes against my lips. I hadn't realized we'd slowly been moving backward until my back firmly presses against a brick wall. My skin feels like it's been set ablaze under his touch. The warmth of his grip around my wrist, his other hand clawing tightly at my waist. The burn from his scruff as his lips learn the shape of mine, taking his time to memorize every line and dip. I gasp against his kiss when he shifts his erection against mine, rocking me deeper into a blissful oblivion I'd have no problem never leaving.

"Forget them," I think I hear myself say, which feels both nothing like me and also the most honest thing I've said aloud in a really long time.

"Mmm, good," he says, his mouth trailing along my neck and back again until his lips are at my ear. "I need to get you home." My stomach does a backflip hearing him call our hotel room that.

"Here's fine," I breathe, locking my fingers in the thick hair at the base of his neck, arching into him and bringing his lips to mine once more.

He slides his hand from my waist down the front of my jeans, and grabs my straining cock with a squeeze. "What I want to do to you requires a *little* more privacy." Theo laughs against my mouth, a deep, throaty sound that I don't think I'll ever grow tired of hearing.

Especially like this.

Fuck.

He breaks away, and every nerve ending screams in protest. "Come on," he says, pulling my hand after him. We zigzag through the streets, backtracking to the hotel as quickly as two nonlocals can, stopping every so often to press against whatever surface is available, our lips claiming each other in the briefest, most desperate of ways.

What a sight we must be—a pair of American fools, all clumsy hands and hurried tongues, so obviously drunk in lust and lost in the magic of the city. The hotel comes into view as we round a final corner, and we cross the marbled lobby, stepping into the elevator bank. Both of Theo's hands grip my wrist, an inescapable vise as he presses his cock against my ass, and my lips are back on his the second we're behind elevator doors.

When the door to our hotel room is firmly shut behind us, Theo wastes no time pushing me against it, his hands and mouth and hips now moving in sync. One second, he's drawn me back to his mouth, our tongues dancing between ragged breaths, and the next, he's dragging his fingertips down my chest, lowering to his knees as he unfastens my jeans.

"Can I?" he asks, looking up at me with fire behind hooded eyes as one hand massages my bulge over my jeans, the other trailing slowly just beneath the band of my briefs. My brain wrestles to form a coherent thought, but the sight of him on his knees before me, his full lips parted and chest rising, is too much. I nod.

He slides the hem of my shirt up, exposing a whole new area of skin he has yet to touch. He trails his fingertips, then his lips, across my hip bone, slowly and with intention, like he's committing every inch of me to memory. My hands instinctively wind themselves into his hair, begging to have him closer. Theo's teasing me now as his mouth drags lower and lower. His hot breath following every swath of skin his tongue has just skimmed over sends waves of goose bumps under his touch.

Having been at odds this entire time, my mind and body seem to finally come to some kind of mutual agreement. "Please," I pant, arching into the doorway, and Theo's fingers dip behind my briefs. "Please, Theo."

He grips my hips, squeezing so tightly I hope I'll be marked by his touch forever as he traces the lines of my body with his tongue. He slides my jeans and trunks down, freeing my cock and finally ending his relentless torture. Theo looks up at me, his eyes dark and hungrier than before. Without breaking eye contact, he places soft kisses, one after the other, on my tip. But when they start to linger, his wet lips sliding open and his tongue tracing the shape of me, a groan of desire escaping from his chest, I nearly black out.

"You're perfect," he breathes, his breath dancing on my skin.

Theo takes me fully in his mouth, slowly at first, but then like a man driven by an innate need to please. His hands squeeze my ass, pulling me deeper down his throat with seemingly little to no effort, and I know that after what has felt like an eternity of teasing, his expert mouth won't allow me to last long.

"Oh, fuck," I hiss, or at least I think I do, because the way he's slurping down my dick has officially scrambled any hold I had on reality. Each glide of his tongue brings me one second closer to the edge.

My breathing is erratic, and my vision is starting to blur as the primal urge to finish builds around me. "That mouth . . ." I pant, thrusting my hips forward to meet him.

Theo must sense I'm getting close, his movements laced with a selfless enthusiasm, and just before each and every strand that's keeping me firmly planted in this moment is snipped, he slides a finger, slick from his spit, against my ass, a torturous addition to the most delicious and unforeseen crescendo.

"I'm not finished with you just yet, Ash," Theo says slowly, his voice just a whisper, after trailing the length of my shaft with his warm tongue. I want to scream, ask him how he has the audacity to drag me to the brink of ecstasy like this only to inform me I'm not allowed to go barreling over that cliff.

My hands claw at his hair, gently pulling him upward in my

direction. Driven by lust or impatience or some other unseemly need, all I know is that if Theo Fernandez keeps teasing my cock with those perfect lips of his, I won't last another second. "Come here," I choke out between breaths. I hear the hollowed sharpness of my voice, a sound so desperate that under any other circumstances I just might be embarrassed.

But when I peer down to look at Theo, the only thought I'm physically able to concoct is getting him on his feet, free of the clothes separating me from his naked body.

"If you say so," he says, slowly standing up, then immediately pressing me back against the door. I feel the strain in his pants and instinctually reach for it, marveling at the firmness beneath the fabric.

Theo trails his lips along my neck, sending chills down my spine, and when his mouth reaches the corner of my jaw, he traps my earlobe between his teeth, leaving me frozen on the spot. "Asher, I need you. All of you."

His words are my undoing. I push him off me, forcing him back toward our bed, and kick off my shoes and my pants as we go.

I clumsily reach for his shirt, aggressively pulling it up from the hem over his head, and revel at the smoothness of his skin as the backs of his knees collide with the footboard of the bed frame.

A throaty laugh escapes Theo's lips when I impatiently push him down onto the bed and one by one pull off his shoes, not caring where they land. His pants are next, the only barrier to what I need. Theo lifts his hips when I fumble with the button before I peel the dark denim over his thick, muscular thighs and down the length of his long legs, his grey briefs with it.

And there he is.

Naked, on display, and throbbing just for me.

It's better than I could have imagined. *He's* better than I ever could have imagined, and I have to stop myself from diving headfirst on top of him.

"I need that pretty mouth of yours on me, love," he rasps just when I didn't think this moment could get any hotter. "*Now.*"

I've come to know thoughtful Theo. Kind and warm Theo.

But this is something new entirely. Direct, domineering, and *Jesus Christ* so fucking delicious I can't think straight. I crawl up the length of the bed, slowing my movements intentionally to really savor the sight before me. Theo on his back with his muscular arms folded behind his head. His long legs parted wide. His thick cock pointed upward, begging for my immediate attention.

I lower my lips to his right thigh, then his left, before resting my hands on either side of his trembling hips. His back arches when I flick my tongue against his skin and place kiss after kiss up his leg and along his hip bone, mirroring the torturous path he executed on me just moments before.

A low hiss escapes his parted lips.

Theo tenses when I grip his dripping cock in my hand, his fingers digging into the comforter when I trace his tip with my lips.

I wrap my mouth fully around him now, salty precum coating my tongue, and take him in deeper. "*Fuck,*" he moans. "Your mouth feels so fucking good, baby."

Baby. Love. These new terms of endearment don't catch me off guard like they normally would. They instead only make me want to hear them more. And the way he's starting to move his hips right now, he can call me whatever he'd like and I'd say thank you.

I let my hand glide up his length, alternating the tightness of my grip as I bob eagerly up and down on his cock with ease, hungry to take all of him. He feels so damn good in my mouth. So full and thick. His eyes slam shut when I give all my attention to his tip, and when I cup his balls in my free hand, pulling them tight, his hands find my shoulders to hold me in place.

Reaching between us now, he grips the base of his cock with one hand, sliding the other into my hair and grabbing a fistful, slowly guiding me at the cadence of his choosing.

"Look at me when you suck my cock," he whispers, and I find his gaze as I swirl the tip of his dick with my tongue. Right now, I'm his to use, and I've never been happier. There's a tight smirk forming across his face when I look up at him. One that makes my heart race and my own cock pulse in my hand as I time my strokes with his. "I want to watch you take me."

He slowly removes his cock from my mouth but lets his tip linger against my lips as he looks me right in the eye. "Do you like this?" he asks, tracing the lines of my lips with his slick cock.

I can only nod my head.

"Good boy," he says, grinning, parting my lips and sliding his dick back into my wanting mouth. "Now take it all for me." His voice is ragged, laced with need and want, and I've never felt more alive than I do right now with him.

So, I do.

I grip both of his hips, relishing the fact that he's now bucking up against me. I normally don't enjoy sucking dick this much, but there's something about knowing I'm pleasing Theo that has turned the simple act of oral sex into one of the most erotically gratifying experiences of my life.

For the first time in my sexual life, I feel powerful, and

instead of overthinking it or second-guessing it, I'm leaning in to it with everything I have.

Theo deserves that.

I fucking deserve that, damn it.

"Baby, I'm so close . . ." Theo pants, and suddenly, I'm desperate for him to finish. My need to please him takes over and I grip his pulsing cock tighter, swirling my tongue over his thick head as he repeatedly enters and exits my mouth. I'm moving faster now, guided by the not-so-subtle cues his body is giving me, and when Theo grabs my face with shaking hands, I know his release is coming.

"Holy fuck, Ash," he shouts. His back arches off the bed and he slides in and out of my mouth for the final time. My name is the last thing on his lips before he erupts. Rope after rope of his climax floods my mouth, and I'm pretty sure my eyes roll back into my skull as I swallow every drop of Theo's sweet cum.

I don't release him. Not yet. Because I want to make sure that not a single drop of his orgasm is wasted. Theo's breathing slows, his wide chest returning to its natural rise and fall. When his limbs stop trembling, he reaches down with hurried hands to pull me up for our lips to find each other again.

He kisses me like a man possessed. Like he's been ravenous for days on end and my mouth is the only relief he'll know. Parting my lips with his tongue, Theo cradles my face. His thumb glides along my cheek while he deepens our kiss.

"That was . . ." he says, his voice but a breath against my lips, "everything."

Theo sucks on my lower lip and pushes upward with his hips. I'm now seated on top of him, his still-hard cock positioned conveniently against my ass. When I push back against it, he grips my hips hard and holds me right where he wants me.

"Let's take care of this," he murmurs, circling my cock with his hand.

Mmm. The moan escapes my lips involuntarily. Between the burn of his lips on mine, the increased tempo of his glide on my dick, and the way I'm grinding against his length, I am ready to combust.

Theo breaks our kiss, and before I can protest, he spits into his palm and quickly returns his grip to my throbbing dick.

The new sensation is too much.

If I was close to the edge earlier, I'm ready to explode now. Theo quickens his strokes, and I want nothing more than to succumb to his touch.

His dedicated attention to my cock has me clawing at his shoulders, grabbing on for dear life as the inevitable orgasm builds. Each caress brings me closer to something new, threatening to rip me apart brick by brick, and only Theo is the architect who can put me together again.

"Theo," I hear myself whimper, pulling him flush against me now. "Fuck, baby. Oh, God . . . I'm going to cum," I shout against his hungry mouth as the waves of pleasure finally reach their breaking point. But he knows and he's ready. He grips my cock tight, slowing his strokes ever so slightly to time them with each pulse of my dick, bracing me when I erupt. I paint his chest with my orgasm, my legs shaking, and when I feel empty and completely turned inside out, he maneuvers me down onto the bed next to him, my trembling body tucked against his.

"You made quite the mess," he hums, his lips pressed against my temple. My face is numb and my hands are tingling, but I'm just coherent enough to watch him swipe a finger through said mess and bring it to his lips. "Sweet."

Unreal.

Theo Fernandez is unreal. That's the only explanation for the explosive and otherworldly pleasure he was just able to pull from my body.

He kisses one corner of my mouth, then the other, with a tenderness to his touch that's somehow more arousing than before. Everything blurs together in the hazy afterglow, and with his lips still possessively pressed to mine, my eyelids struggle to stay open.

I blink and he's gone, his naked body on display as he heads into the bathroom. When I open my eyes again, he's back, a warm washcloth in hand, gently wiping my body and his.

"Get some rest, sweet boy," he whispers against my temple. He pulls me back into his arms and kisses the top of my head when I nuzzle up against him.

It's clear to both of us I can't fight my exhaustion any longer.

Just like it's starting to become clear I can no longer fight what I'm feeling for Theo.

18

THEO

**Leonardo da Vinci–Fiumicino Airport—Terminal 3, Gate E23
Rome, Italy**

Our flight to London has been delayed for another two hours.

Another two hours stuck at yet another airport. Jo and Arthur are passed out a few rows ahead at our gate. They've clearly become quite accomplished at finding sleep whenever and wherever. Asher's to my right, nose deep in a book. Some medical jargon–laced nonfiction about the quest for the perfect prescription.

Or something like that.

His brow is furrowed. But there is a softness to his expression. As if somehow, despite the heavy subject matter, he's maybe found a moment of relaxation just for him.

Guys with personalities like Asher's have historically never liked me.

The ones who can talk about climate change or politics or

the current state of their investment portfolios for hours on end. The ones who read memoirs. For fun.

I get it. I'm the one who doesn't take life too seriously. The person you can always count on to tell the well-timed joke or laugh off any potential awkwardness. Some might even say I have golden retriever energy. I'm trying to figure out if that *really* is a compliment.

But maybe—

Maybe it doesn't have to be that way.

Maybe with Asher, even though our situation is not completely *real*, I could at least be. I'm starting to think Jenn was onto something when she called me out about pretending. It's exhausting.

He fidgets in his seat, stretching out his long legs in some small attempt to get comfortable, though I know from personal experience it's impossible in these airport chairs.

"Theo?" an unfamiliar voice suddenly calls out from behind me. There could be a dozen Theos in this airport, so I ignore it, considering everyone I know is right here and frankly, I don't have the energy to care.

"Theo Fernandez?" Asher nudges me, a not-so-subtle request to address whoever it is who's now very clearly trying to get my attention.

I rotate in my seat until I see him.

Dressed in his fitted pilot's uniform stands an airline blast from the past. He's definitely familiar with his dark features and styled hair. But I am completely blanking on his name. Micah? Matt?

"Marcus?" I ask, narrowing my eyes and crossing my fingers that's correct.

He wheels his carry-on effortlessly toward us, his eyes locked on me and me alone.

"How've you been, stranger?" he asks, now directly in front of me. "You haven't made a stop in Denver in ages."

Asher looks up from his book, curiosity written all over his face, and he doesn't have to say anything for me to know *exactly* what he's thinking.

"Yeah, I've been mainly on East Coast and international flights these days."

Marcus looks me up and down, and I can see that same *down for anything* energy simmering beneath the surface from when we first met. It's what first drew me to him.

He was, and clearly still is, always down for no strings attached.

"That's a shame," he says, and his gaze shifts to Asher and then back to me. "Hit me up next time you're in town, handsome."

Before I can respond, he's gone, sauntering off in his too-tight pants and overflowing confidence.

I sneak a glance at Asher.

Marking the spot in his book with his airline ticket, he sets his book down and turns slightly in my direction.

"Are you hungry?" I ask, digging out the bag of trail mix I bought earlier from my backpack. I extend it in his direction. He eyes it skeptically but accepts my offer anyway, pouring out a handful of the sweet-and-salty snack into his open palm.

"Thanks," he murmurs, plopping a few cashews into his mouth after handing the bag back to me.

"That was nothing, by the way," I say, out of obligation or maybe a hint of insecurity. I don't want him to think differently of me.

He smirks. "*He* definitely wanted it to be something."

"Fair enough," I say, not being able to deny Marcus's obvious intentions. "But please know that for me, it was nothing."

Asher turns to face me head-on now. "This is all kinda your thing, huh?"

"My thing?"

"I mean, Theo . . . look how *we* met. You wasted no time swooping in like some well-practiced knight in shining armor at the airport."

"Hold on just a minute, sir." I'm not going to let him get away with skewing reality *that* much. "If I recall, you were the one who was in desperate need of a partner and was practically begging me to go along on this adventure with you. What was I supposed to do? Completely blow you off?"

"The begging doesn't sound familiar . . ." he says, an eyebrow cocked, but he smiles anyway, leaning back in his seat. "I'm forever grateful that you didn't. Truly. But then everything that followed—the flirty banter, the nonstop charm, that grin . . ."

I lean forward in my own seat. "What grin?" I ask, hoping whatever smile I'm doing my best to plaster across my face is the one he's referring to.

"That," Asher says, shaking his head and pointing at me. "That right there is what I'm talking about. Normal people can't just turn it on and off like you can."

There's something about his word choice that irks me more than it probably should.

"Hmm" is all I say, trying to tell myself he probably meant nothing by it.

"What?" he asks, a sudden uncertainty now swirling behind his eyes.

Normal. I can feel the blood thump its way to my ears as that word ricochets around and around my skull. "It just sounds like," I say, turning my head in his direction, intentionally locking eyes with him, "you're implying I'm *not* normal."

I'm doing a piss-poor job at pretending I'm fine.

Concern floods his face as he attempts to backpedal. "No . . . I didn't . . ."

I'm suddenly on my feet. "It's fine, Asher. I get it . . ." But I really don't. "You've got me all figured out."

Asher opens his mouth to say something else but quickly decides against it, his cheeks burning red behind his glasses. I'm glad he swallowed whatever sentence was going to come out of his mouth next, because I don't know if I can temper my frustration that much more.

"Do me a favor and watch my bag," I try to ask evenly, shoving my hands in my pockets. "You know," I add, the second the thought pops in my brain, "with everything you've been through, you're the *last* person I thought would put people in boxes."

"Theo, hold on," he says quickly, an urgency—and a hint of frustration—behind his words. But I don't want to fight or even argue with Asher right now. I just need to clear my head.

"And keep them there," I add, feeling the weight of my own words.

His face falls as I leave him and turn toward the quiet terminal.

///////////////////

When I get back, Asher and our bags are nowhere to be seen.

Neither are Jo or Arthur, actually.

I was only gone for maybe ten minutes. Fifteen tops. I'm not usually some heated Neanderthal that needs space or to cool down mid-argument, but there was something about the word *normal* that struck a nerve, and the last thing I'd want to do is say something I couldn't take back.

But obviously I owe Asher an explanation.

Checking the electronic monitor at my gate to make sure I didn't accidentally miss our boarding announcement—I didn't—I plop down in a nearly empty row of seats facing the window to wait for him and our bags.

"Hey, you," his voice says from behind me a few moments later. Asher takes the empty seat next to me, tucking his long legs underneath himself. "Here," he says, passing me a bottle of water. "I got you this." He also lobs something cold in my direction and I catch it against my chest. "This too."

I look down at the rectangular white stick covered in plastic. "A cheese stick?"

A small smile makes its way from the corner of Asher's mouth. "It's the closest thing I could find to a mozzarella stick," he says, his voice just louder than a whisper.

"Is this your subtle way of letting me know you're instituting Rule Number Four?" I ask, peeling back the cheese stick's wrapper. Picking at the top corner of the snack, I pull a cheesy strand and offer it to Asher. He shakes his head, so I plop it in my mouth. "Thank you for this."

He nods, seemingly unsure of what to say or how to proceed.

"I'm sorry," he says at the same time I do, which causes us both to laugh. Laughing with Asher feels so much better than anything else.

He puts a warm hand on my thigh, and suddenly, I'm hit

with the realization of just how much his touch has become a source of comfort for me.

All of him, really.

Which leads me to the next realization, that it's probably time for a little honesty.

He deserves that, after all.

"What you said earlier . . ." I start, but like a jet shooting off an aircraft carrier, Asher all but leaps forward.

"I'm *so* sorry," he says, genuinely apologetic. "I shouldn't have said or implied . . . I'm just really sorry."

"It's fine." I put my hand on his. "Truly, Ash. I'm fine. We're good. For some reason, the whole thing really reminded me of Ethan."

"Your ex?" he asks. Now that I think of it, I don't know that I've mentioned him by name.

I nod.

Asher's eyes gleam at my sudden vulnerability. "Theo, we don't have to talk about this."

"No, it's okay," I say, and I think I actually mean it. He *has* become a safe space for me, so now feels like as good a time as any to open up. For real. "I don't really talk about my time in the Navy. Or why I left," I add, feeling the need to choose my words carefully. This stuff isn't something I enjoy rehashing. "Well, it wasn't by choice. Ethan was one of those people you couldn't help but be drawn to. He was daring and bold and treated everyone around him with an unnerving warmth and kindness that you wouldn't expect to find from someone in the military. He was instantly my best friend and from our very first day of flight training, we were . . . inseparable."

I can't remember the last time I publicly, and voluntarily,

talked about Ethan, but now that the can of worms has been opened, it seems I can't stop myself. There's also something about Asher and the way he's giving me the space to share that makes me want to confide in him. The trauma train has left the station and whether Asher wants it or not, he's getting a front-row seat to the mess that is my life. But as far as I can tell, he's engaged. Nodding his head here and there, positioning himself more comfortably in his seat so his entire body is facing me attentively.

"He was my first *real* ally in the military. Someone I knew was in my corner, regardless of what else was going on. We'd work out, grab a few beers at the on-base bowling alley after work, and spend every free moment together."

I think back to those first few months after graduating pilot training. The anxiety and stress of active duty. The newness of living away from home in an environment that couldn't be more foreign to me.

The undeniable attraction that grew toward Ethan.

The more time I spent with him, the more it became clear that what I was feeling when I was with him was more than just friendship. He would listen to me ramble on about my day—like truly and genuinely listen, in a way that no one had before. He'd buckle over from laughter at all my jokes and light up whenever I walked into the room.

He made me feel special. Seen.

And eventually, he made me feel what I thought then was love.

When we sat side by side that October night on the old couch he helped me load into the back of my truck, everything changed. A random movie played in the background and the buzz of a few homemade margaritas made everything swirl around us. When his thigh slowly grazed mine, I knew it was now or never.

Relief washed over me when he didn't recoil from me leaning over to kiss him.

In fact, it was the most natural thing in the world. Almost as if the entire time he had been patiently waiting for me to come to my senses.

Kissing Ethan was everything I'd hoped it would be.

Slow and tender, like our hearts were choosing to take their time. His warmth was all-consuming and the more time my lips pressed against his, the more it became clear that Ethan and I could never go back to being just friends. His kiss awakened something in me. Something permanent and life-affirming, and when he pulled back slightly, mouthing, *Finally*, against my lips, I knew I was a goner.

After that first kiss, we dated in secret for just over a year.

It's not that we were breaking any rules or afraid of what our teammates would think. We just desperately wanted to keep what we had only for us as long as we possibly could. And I was more than fine with that, because I'd never known happiness like being Ethan Carmichael's boyfriend.

Until the rules changed, and he was promoted.

Because once he was promoted, he officially outranked me. And because he outranked me, us being together became a problem.

"How did you navigate all that?" Asher asks gently, leaning forward in his seat, eyes wide with curiosity.

"We had it all worked out. As soon as Ethan officially pinned on his new rank, we planned to speak to our fleet commander to inform her of our preexisting relationship."

I can remember every detail of what happened next.

Asher, who is probably one of the most astute and observant individuals I've ever met, must sense the toll recounting this story is taking on me.

He squeezes my hand, a small but appreciated sign that he's here.

"To make an incredibly long and heart-crushingly painful story short, a coworker, who had somehow learned of our relationship, had already beat us to the punch. By the time we were able to meet with our commander, we were already in violation for having an unprofessional relationship."

"Stop." Asher covers his mouth with his hands, his confusion mirroring how I'd felt at the time.

"Ethan and I were immediately put on no-contact orders—"

"Wait, what does that mean?" he interrupts, his eyebrows raised with concern.

"It means from one second to the next, I was legally forbidden to speak to, interact with, or be in the same room with Ethan. We were essentially ripped apart and barred from seeing each other during the one moment we needed the other most."

Asher is quiet for a moment. A first. But then he places a hesitant hand on my forearm. "Theo . . . I don't even know what to say."

"Hold on, there's more."

But I have spent the better part of the last three years doing everything in my power not to think about what comes next.

It's too painful.

"They conducted a full-blown investigation into the nature of our relationship." I drop my gaze, picking at a stray thread on my backpack strap. "They started with an in-depth review of our entire military careers, all the way back to our individual officer-training days in college. Then, they followed it up with invasive interviews with our mutual friends and colleagues. And when the time finally came, they sat me down."

I can feel the all-too-familiar lump wedging itself deep in my throat as I prepare to talk about the worst day of my life.

"Moments after I had poured my heart out to my commander about soulmates and finding love in the most unexpected places, I was informed that Ethan had denied the whole thing."

Asher's jaw literally drops. "He didn't."

"He did." I swallow hard, trying to hide the wave of grief that's resurfacing. "He chose his career over us . . . and on some level, I can kind of understand how, or at least why, he made that decision."

"But what about *your* career?"

"As the lower-ranking member, it became clear to me that I was now disposable in this situation. The investigating officers, as well as my own coworkers and leaders, rallied behind Ethan. He was an up-and-coming officer with all the potential. The sure thing."

I turn my head toward Asher to meet his confused expression. "I, on the other hand, was quickly labeled as the officer who didn't follow the rules. The one who disobeyed orders. Someone who selfishly and knowingly went after a superior."

"But that's obviously not what happened," he presses. "What did Ethan end up having to say about all this?"

I sigh. "I wish I knew. We couldn't talk during the investigation, no matter how badly I wanted to, and by the time it was over, what was the point? He'd chosen to trade in what we had for a ticket into the good graces of our commander, while I was eventually discharged for it."

That's the part that hurts the most—even after all this time—seeing how easy it was for him to *not* choose me.

Seeing just how disposable I was.

"I'm confused, though," Asher says, rubbing his temples. "Don't people meet and fall in love in the military all the time? I can literally think of like ten movies and books off the top of my head with that meet-cute being the romantic focal point."

"They do." He's not wrong. I have several military romances loaded up on my Kindle as we speak.

"Then what was the problem with you and Ethan? I know you mentioned that it only became a problem once he got promoted, but was the fact that you're gay . . ."

I don't think I'll ever know what made our situation unprofessional while the countless others I'd seen throughout my career had been accepted, no questions asked.

Do I think it was because we were two men? Absolutely.

But can I prove it? Unfortunately, no.

"All I know is that the military loves to tout the progress and great strides they're making toward inclusion and equity. They pat themselves on the back for hosting lunches and diversity panels and slapping together a few brightly colored social media posts for each observance. But when it's over? Everything goes back to the status quo and the scales get tipped back in favor of the straight, white, cis men who wear the uniform."

"Don't you think that's fucked up?"

"Of course I do, Asher. It's all I've thought about for the last couple of years. I can't help but think how differently the situation would have been handled if Ethan and I were a straight couple. Still, being in the Navy was the best thing that's happened to me. I genuinely don't think I'd have the career and drive I do today if I hadn't."

I mean that.

Even with everything that went down, I don't regret my time in uniform for a second. "But I'm also not going to pretend that the only people who have the unwavering support of the American military aren't those who are firmly in the good ol' boys club."

Asher's quiet again, the reality of my statement left to linger between us. The silence makes me feel like I might have shared too much. Like this information would have been better kept locked away.

"What did your family say about all this?" he asks quietly, like he knows he's tiptoeing around a difficult topic.

I swallow, shifting in my seat again. "They were shocked, I'm sure. But honestly, we only really talked about the career aspect and what I was going to do next. I don't know, maybe they already knew about me or they didn't want to talk about it or they just didn't care, but the whole sexuality conversation never came up, so I just followed their lead."

Part of me wishes I pushed harder back then.

Clawed the Band-Aid off and said out loud what I knew we were *all* thinking.

That I was gay and that I was still figuring it all out.

That my heart was unbearably broken.

That my worst fear just became my reality.

But I said none of those things and they didn't either and somehow, the world didn't fall off its axis. And now, too much time has passed that it hasn't seemed worth it to bring the whole thing up again.

"And honestly," I add, my throat tight, "it was easier to just . . . run from it all."

"I'm really sorry you experienced that. I can't even imagine . . ." His voice trails off, but before it does, a trace of sadness is unmistakable.

"It is what it is." I sigh.

I realize Asher's hand is still on my forearm. When I move my attention to his grip, however, he slowly returns it to his own lap. "Is that how you really feel?"

Is it? I can't be sure. But know I'm exhausted from being angry about it. From letting my anger at Ethan and my resentment of the leaders who failed me weigh on my heart.

"It's how I'm trying to feel about it. I need to believe the things we go through in life—the good, the bad, and everything in between—they are all somehow not-so-subtly nudging us toward what's meant to be."

He smiles, seemingly in agreement with my cheesy way of consoling myself, which makes me feel a little lighter. Like maybe all this—meeting Asher in the airport and competing together—is perhaps where life was meant to take me.

Both of us.

19

ASHER

The Bailey's Hotel London—Bailey's Bar
London, UK

A s we sit side by side with contestants and crew, everyone's collective disappointment after tonight's elimination lingers throughout the swanky hotel bar.

Ivan and Eddie were sent home, a blow to all of us, as they'd inadvertently become the resident *"Have I ever told you about the time . . ."* grandparents we all came to love.

Well, tolerate.

The vibe is mostly somber—apart from a few PAs who have made it a tradition to end each elimination ceremony with a boisterous round of shots. Jägermeister, of all things. What is this, college circa 2008?

The lounge is playing an iconic mix of American divas. Ashanti followed by Shania Twain and then back-to-back singles from Britney Spears. The upbeat tunes and rhythmic bass are incongruous with the overall mood, but even though I was

bummed to see Eddie and Ivan head home, I find myself shim-
mying in my stool. Just a bit.

"I'm going to run up to the room really quick," Theo says,
squeezing my thigh gently. "Don't move." He gets up from his
barstool, smiling with signature Theo Fernandez dimples.
Nodding, I sip on the drink he'd just handed me.

And as Ms. Spears warns the lounge of a certain poison paradise, Theo's former stool is quickly occupied by the master of
ceremonies himself.

Dalton.

We haven't had too much time one-on-one, a fact that I'm
eternally grateful for. But as he makes himself more comfortable next to me, clearly disinterested in the fact that my body
instinctively leaned away from him, I silently pray for Theo's
quick return.

"It's a shame about Eddie and Ivan, huh?" he says, still looking at his phone. When he's not in front of the camera, he's
glued to some other device. On more than one occasion, I've
gotten the tiniest glimpse at his screen to see that he obses-
sively checks his mentions on the app formerly known as Twit-
ter. Out of curiosity, I looked up his account when I had a
moment, and let me just say, the internet has not been too kind
to ol' Dalton McKnight as of late.

Especially the gays.

"But I guess it was only a matter of time," he adds before I
have the chance to respond, swiveling his stool toward me. He
places his phone face down on the bar. The intention behind
the act is alarming. Oh boy. There's no denying that Dalton's
conventionally handsome—or he was in his prime, in a forced
kind of way. He's tall and tan and has an impossibly white smile
that looks more sinister than it does dazzling. But everything

about him, from his clothes and fading blond hair to his lingering expressions and dramatic pauses, is calculated. A strategic maneuver in whatever real-life game of chess he seems to be playing.

He reminds me of Clint in that way.

"Mm-hmm." I say, as an acknowledgment of his presence rather than an invitation to carry on with the conversation.

"Between you and me," he says, leaning in to me—I feel a groan building in my throat, but I force it down—"and don't quote me on this. But I'm honestly quite shocked two *boomers* like them made it this far." The disdain with which he says the generational term is oddly hypocritical considering he's the closest to their age of all of us.

"Really? Boomers?" I ask mockingly, but he ignores me.

"So, I see #Thasher is trending again," he says, reaching for his phone to reopen the social media platform. "Did you see that? The internet just loves you two." He tilts his phone in my direction, scrolling through the hashtag as pictures of Theo and me fill his screen. If his tone was sharp when talking about Eddie and Ivan, his words now could slice through just about anything.

"I hadn't. I don't really pay attention to social media unless Jo needs me to do something." I stab at my drink's remaining ice cubes with my straw, wishing there was more of whatever drink Theo had ordered.

"That's a mistake."

"Is that so?"

"You and your *boyfriend* really need to seize the opportunities in front of you." There's that tone again. Dalton is well aware that Theo and I aren't actually dating—Jo informed him of that fact on day one. And even though she assured both of us it was a nonissue, sitting here at the bar with Dalton and his conniving eyes, it now feels like a problem.

Dangerous, even.

"And what opportunities might you be referring to?" I shoot back, turning to really face him. His thin, dry lips curl into a smirk, and I'm beginning to regret pressing him for more. Even though it feels obvious he's goading me into potentially uncharted territory—one where I knowingly allow him to have the upper hand—there's a small part of me, minuscule even, that's intrigued to hear this so-called industry legend's perspective on Theo's and my newfound online fame.

"Well, for starters," he says, putting his phone back down. "There's money to be made on social media, and anyone who tells you otherwise is lying to you. When you're on a show on a network like ours, it's easy to think that your time in the spotlight will fade when the finale airs. But if the two of you play your cards right, you could position yourself for so much more."

Beyond the prize money, which still feels so far out of reach considering Bianca and Jackson are clearly the front-runners this season, I hadn't really thought about the *after*, when the cameras stop rolling and Theo and I go our separate ways. I'd been so focused on making sure that Theo and I pulled off the whole *hopelessly in love* act to appease Jo and the rest of America that now thinking about what comes next makes my palms sweat.

"And by more, you mean . . ." I ask, almost afraid to know the answer.

"Come on, Asher," he says, crossing his arms in his stool, "you're telling me someone as educated as you can't see what a massive platform this offers? Brand partnerships, public speaking engagements, all-expenses-paid travel, you name it. I'm sure you can use that brain of yours to come up with something creative."

Though every part of me hates to admit it, he has a point. When I originally agreed to go on the show with Clint, the prize money was a huge selling point. And he knew it. There's a fourteen-tab Excel sheet on my laptop allocating where every penny of my share of the winnings would go to set up my scholarship program. But I'd never thought about how being on this show could get my name out there in a different way, regardless of whether I won.

Could it be possible that I just received some valuable life advice from Dalton McKnight?

"And there are . . . *other* opportunities in front of you," he says, his voice dripping with not-so-subtle insinuations as he leans even closer. He reaches forward and places a bold hand on my thigh, the very spot where Theo's had been what feels like just moments ago. The difference in their touch, however, could not be more apparent. Where Theo's had felt warm, familiar, and most important, wanted, Dalton's feels predatory, arrogant, and far too presumptuous for my liking.

I look up and am met by a face oozing with misplaced confidence. He flexes his leathered hand and slowly slides his fingers back and forth across my thigh.

"You know what, Dalton?" I say, pulling my leg away from him with purpose. "I was *this* close to thinking I might have been wrong about you."

His grin widens; he's clearly enjoying whatever one-sided game of cat and mouse he's playing. "Be careful, Asher Bennett," he says, his hand still lingering purposefully between us as if he's betting on me changing my mind. "Or my feelings are going to get hurt."

"I find that highly unlikely."

His eyes narrow at my flippant dismissal. "When you're ready to get serious about what comes next, my offer still stands." If I didn't know any better, I'd say there's a hint of desperation to his manufactured facade. Like the usual confidence that brews behind those narrowed eyes of his has dimmed ever so slightly, so now he's forced to use the power he does have—promises of success, connections, general know-how—to sweeten whatever deal he's negotiating.

Right on cue, Theo's handsome face comes into focus beyond Dalton as he rounds the corner of the hotel lobby and steps back into the lounge. Concern flashes across his face when he sees my bar companion. *Thank God.* His timing couldn't be more perfect, and it gives me all the confidence I need to end this back-and-forth I've found myself in.

"How generous," I say, rising from my stool. Disbelief, or disdain, washes over Dalton's face, at both my exit and my rejection. "But now that I think of it, I've already lain with snakes once in this competition, and I told Jo I won't be making that mistake again."

For once, Dalton McKnight doesn't have a quippy remark or sassy one-liner. Instead, he simply glares after me as I leave him seated at the bar. Will I regret insinuating the host of our show is a snake? Probably.

Was it worth it? Hell yes.

My eyes lock with Theo and he smiles, slowly at first and then all at once, like he cannot contain whatever happy thought just passed through his mind. I immediately find myself itching to know what it was.

"Everything okay?" he asks when we meet in the middle of

the lounge. Part of me can still feel Dalton's displeasure staring daggers at me, but I couldn't care less.

"Oh, everything's just perfect," I say, reaching for his hand and immediately finding comfort in the familiarity of his touch. "But why don't we get out of here. The bar's a little too crowded, don't you think?"

"Whatever you say," he murmurs, nudging me with his shoulder and walking us out of the lounge and into the bustling lobby. I wonder how we look to those around us. Hand in hand and all smiles. Because this whole thing with Theo feels a lot more real than I ever envisioned it could be. Which terrifies me because now, after having him like this, sunshiny smiles and all, the thought of losing him and what we're slowly building makes my heart ache. But right now, all I know is I've never been more at ease with someone else. I may still be figuring out who Theo Fernandez is to me, but it's abundantly clear he's become something more.

A quiet exhale and the safest of spaces.

A shimmering light I hadn't realized was so obviously missing from my life until he came along and lit up every corner of darkness like the goddamn sun.

20

ASHER

Hotel Condes de Buñol—Room 4A
Buñol, Spain

T*hump, thump, thump.*

Our door is literally being *thump*ed right off its vintage
hinges.

"For the love of God, please go away," I groan. Truthfully,
I'm not sure I'm even coherent at the moment, so there is a very
real possibility that I'm making this all up inside my overly
sleep-deprived mind.

Thump, thump, thump. But louder and with more urgency
this time.

"If it's the woman from the check-in desk," Theo mumbles,
rolling over toward the wall, a very clear sign that he most definitely isn't getting up anytime soon, "can you get some more
towels?"

He hasn't even stepped foot in our bathroom to see just
how many towels we already have. A lovable quirk of Theo's—

he needs roughly thirty-seven bath towels at any given time to have a comfortable hotel stay, regardless of the duration.

I swing my legs over the side of the bed, feeling my exhaustion in every joint, and walk over to the door in a daze. I can't tell if it's been five minutes or five hours since we both passed out on that bed, but all I know is that it certainly wasn't enough time.

"What," I say after unlocking the dead bolt and swinging the heavy wooden door open rather rudely considering I have no idea who is on the other side.

But instead of being met by the hotel concierge offering dozens of additional towels for Theo, it's just Ellie. "Come on, we're going out."

"Pass." The only going out I want to do is going out of consciousness. *I made it work.*

"Seriously, guys . . . you aren't going to want to miss this."

Her vagueness must catch Theo's interest. "What is it?" he says, propping himself up on his elbow.

"La Tomatina."

I haven't a clue what the hell she just said, but Theo rather clumsily sits upright. "Stop. *La Tomatina* is today?"

"Mm-hmm," Ellie murmurs, crossing her arms and leaning against the door frame. Theo immediately hops up from the bed, clearly no longer drowsy and instead vibrating with child-like excitement.

"Um, hi . . . hello?" I say, feeling a little left out of the loop. "What are you two babbling on about?"

Ellie and Theo look at each other, their smiles growing more and more mischievous by the second.

"*La Tomatina,*" they say in unison, and practically drag me out the door.

"Mm-hmm . . . you've said that." *Helpful.*

///////////////////////

"Oh, right . . . *this* is what you meant by *La Tomatina*," I say like it's the most obvious thing in the world. "I thought you said *La Tomatino* . . . but of course!" We've found ourselves in the center of a bustling town square a few blocks from the hotel. Theo playfully nudges me in the ribs, knowing full well I had absolutely no clue what I was walking into.

Ellie grabs my hand, strategically leading us through a sea of strangers. The narrow streets of Buñol are bursting at the seams as more and more people pile in from every direction. Theo, Ellie, and I squeeze our way through the excited tourists, and I see that huge sheets of thick plastic have been hung on the storefronts that line the center of town, Plaza del Pueblo. Bucket after bucket of ripe tomatoes in the most brilliant shades of red imaginable are scattered in every direction as far as the eye can see.

"Welcome to La Tomatina . . . the world's largest food fight!" Ellie says, plucking a juicy-looking tomato from the nearest bucket once we manage to find a gap in the crowd large enough for the three of us to huddle comfortably. "Every year, thousands upon thousands of people from all corners of the world make their way to this small city to participate in this historic event."

I review our position in the crowd and feel the part of me that intentionally goes out of his way to avoid *messes* silently scream in protest.

Theo must sense my panic, because he puts a hand on my back, a small gesture but one that immediately lessens my growing anxiety. *Slightly.*

But Ellie could not care less. She just blissfully carries on with her weird history lesson.

"People aren't exactly sure how or why it started, but it dates back to 1944 or 1945," she shouts over the restless crowd, her eyes full of excitement. "Some people think it began as a food fight among friends or as a practical joke—but most people believe that irritated townspeople attacked local officials with tomatoes during a town celebration. Whatever the reason was," Ellie says, laughing as we are bumped by a rather boisterous group of Englishmen who already have several tomatoes in each hand, "it was loved *so* much it has been repeated year after year, growing in size and popularity each time!"

"I'm sorry," I say, crossing my arms, and I can only imagine the disinterested expression plastered across my face. "But it sounds like you ran out of reading materials on last night's train and were forced to read random tourism pamphlets."

Theo snorts and I adore that he thinks I'm funny.

"Oh, my sweet, simple Asher," Ellie mocks in her less-than-sweet tone. "If you hadn't been passed out and excessively drooling on the train, you'd know that production handed out mandatory fact sheets to help us in this week's challenge."

Shit. Whipping my head toward Theo, he discreetly shakes his head. *Ugh.* As painfully annoying as Ellie is sometimes, I have to give it to her—that girl is razor-sharp and incredibly quick on her feet. I'm not usually in the company of someone who comes close to my signature level of snark, so I guess game recognizes game . . . or *something* incredibly cliché like that.

"You little shit—"

"Ah, ah, ah," she says, waving an outstretched finger in my direction. "If you're going to get all snippy and difficult about something I've always wanted to do, you leave me no choice but to officially pull out the birthday card." She sticks her hand in her pocket, retrieving an imaginary card and dramatically flailing it in front of my face.

"Uh, hold on, little one. Didn't your mom say *just* last night at dinner that your birthday isn't until next week?"

"Irrelevant," she says, pinning said invisible card to my chest. "Besides, if I have to spend my eighteenth birthday traversing the globe with a bunch of ancient strangers . . ."

Ouch.

". . . the least you can do is slap on a happy face and give a young girl the only thing in the whole wide world that'll make her happy. Pretty please?"

"Yeah, Ash," Theo chimes in. "Pretty please with me on top?"

Well, that's a fun visual. *Yeesh*, she's really laying it on thick, but on some level, I think she's being serious about wanting to do this.

"I mean, she played *the* birthday card, Asher," Theo says, shrugging his shoulders. "We are contractually obligated as the . . . wait, what did she call us?"

"Hmm, that would be 'ancient strangers,' if I remember correctly."

"Ah, yes, that's right . . . Well, by the rules of all pulled birthday cards, we are officially bound to carry out whatever the card puller wishes. And in this case . . ."

"La Tomatina," we all say in forced agreement. I, however, do it with a groan.

I hate that my natural inclination for adventures that other people—especially Theo—are excited about is total avoidance.

I know I'm capable of having fun—I've been told on numerous occasions how much others have enjoyed the brunches

Clint and I held. That was all me! Always ensuring everyone was happy and fed and never had an empty glass in their hand, that events were paired with the perfect complementary soundtrack, and no matter how last-minute the notice was, I never turned once down the opportunity to host one of my infamous pool parties.

Oh God . . . I'm boring myself.

But deciding to go on this show and randomly choosing someone like Theo to be my partner, someone who is like fifty-two steps above "go with the flow," I've been thinking about how many chances to step outside my comfort zone I've said no to . . . how much of my life I *haven't* been living. *That changes now.*

Several things happen very quickly.

Water cannons erupt from their hidden locations, spewing gallon after gallon of water over the enthusiastic crowd.

Ellie shoves pairs of goggles in Theo's and my direction, which we instinctively put on.

Quickly I grab a tomato, smash it in my hands, and throw it right at Theo's chest.

La Tomatina has officially begun.

Theo appears stunned by my tomatoey sneak attack. "Oh, you're *dead*, Bennett," he shouts over the chaos unfolding around us and lunges toward the nearest bucket of tomatoes, grabbing a fistful of fruity ammunition.

I dart between the swells of bodies, trying to see where Ellie took off to, in my attempt to avoid Theo's impending retaliation.

Smack.

A large and disgustingly mushy tomato collides with the side of my face, exploding tomato bits in every direction, and I whisper a silent prayer of appreciation for Ellie, wherever she is, for having the foresight to bring goggles to this epic disaster.

Smack. Smack. Smack.

One after another after another, tomatoes fly through the air, exploding on impact with whichever target has had the misfortune of stepping into their path. Thankfully, people seem to be squishing them before they wildly aim. *Smack.*

Stopping only once, I stumble upon the smallest gap in the group and turn around. I half expect to see Theo right behind me, ready to deliver his payback. But he's disappeared in the sea of extreme tomato lovers, nowhere to be found, which only adds to the terror of his future attack. *Smack. Smack.* The onslaught of tomato explosions seems never-ending, and I slip with each step.

I should note that beyond the one I threw at Theo, I haven't participated any further. Looking around at the squishy pandemonium around me, the genuine joy is overwhelming. I can't identify any rhyme or reason to who showed up today to take part in this time-honored tradition, but people of all ages and from every walk of life are laughing hysterically as they do their best to combat being hit by an air strike of tomatoes. *Smack.* And as hard as I'm trying to *not* look at my ruined clothing and shoes, seeing the collective happiness around me is delightful. *Smack. Smack, smack, smack.*

I want that.

To be happy simply because I believe I'm allowed to be.

To be . . . free.

Jogging to the nearest cluster of bins, I scoop up a handful of literal bottom-of-the-barrel tomatoes, *really* squishing them to ensure no one will get hurt by my fleeting desire to participate, and scan the crowd for the poor soul who will end up being on the receiving end of my so-called *fury*.

The chaos makes narrowing in on a single individual hard to do thanks to the constant barrage of bodies and relentless smattering of exploding fruit, but when I turn back toward the center of the town square, I lock eyes with a young girl. She can't be more than ten, eleven years old, with her long dark hair in a set of high pigtails. Her determined face tells me she's ready to bring the hellfire.

Absolutely not.

I may not like kids, but there is no way in hell that I'm going to playfully attack a tiny one with an armful of tomatoes.

She raises her hand, palm facing upward . . . and gives me the universal signal to *bring it*. And somehow, it seems oddly fitting, or soul-crushingly humiliating depending on how you look at it, that she is my one and only challenger.

Do I really want to do this? I'd like the record to note that I was born and raised a feminist and firmly believe that all women are the strongest, most brilliant inhabitants of this earth, so my reluctance only comes from the fact that the tenacious warrior before me quite literally comes up to my kneecap.

She must sense my hesitation, because one second, she's standing there looking menacing in an *aw, how adorable* kind of way, and the next, she's charging at me at full force, fearlessly unleashing tomato strike after tomato strike. *Smack . . . Smack. Smack. Smack.*

"Ugghhh!" I yell, dropping my own acidic ammunition so I can properly shield my face. I turn my back to her in an attempt to protect my most, um, sensitive areas, because that just so happens to be where all her throws are repeatedly landing.

"I surrender!" I yell. *Smack. Smack . . . Smack. Smack.* I have no idea how such an incredibly tiny human is capable of throwing objects as fast as she is, but I'm praying that someone is getting this on film so that every pitcher in the history of both baseball and softball can take some notes.

"I said I surren—" I start to shout over my shoulder, but then I slip on the slick pavers while turning around to take a step toward her and go theatrically crashing to the ground. *Oh, fuck me.*

Here lies Asher Bennett.

Physically overpowered by a pint-size fruit assassin, covered head to toe in chunks of tomato, and resisting every urge to curl into the fetal position.

Thriving, am I right?

And just when I thought I couldn't feel any smaller, my petite southpaw bends over my laid-out body and extends the tiniest of hands in my direction, a temporary white flag in the name of good sportsmanship. She struggles to pull me to my feet, but once I am right side up again, she grins and skips off in the opposite direction, clearly pleased with herself for taking down a grown-ass man.

It's useless to attempt to brush myself off considering the sky is literally raining tomatoes. *Smack.* It's in my hair, in my shoes, and I can't be sure how, but I'm positive I just felt a piece of tomato skin slide down into my briefs. I use the hem of my stained shirt to wipe my goggles, hoping I'll have an easier time seeing where Ellie and Theo have been hiding this whole time. I step up on a nearby bench—*smack . . . smack . . . smack*—to get a better vantage point as the crowd swells.

That's when I see them.

Like me, they are each dripping in remnants of this morning's festivities, but instead of being grumpy about it, they're the physical embodiments of pure joy. Ellie and Theo are standing back-to-back, working in tandem as they shower the crowd with the tomatoes they've seemingly been hoarding, their heads thrown back in uncontrollable laughter.

Watching Theo is mesmerizing.

He's erupted with more unbridled happiness than I ever thought one human was meant to. My lips part at the way his soaked white shirt clings to his powerful build, and though I can't quite hear it, I've been around him long enough for me to imagine the infectious laughter barreling through his whole body between throws.

Right now, I'm no longer in control of my body. Every molecule in me is gravitating toward Theo. Without even meaning to, I realize I've stepped down from my spot on the bench and, as if in slow motion, am closing the gap between us.

I know we're approaching a turning point in what's been slowly building between Theo and me.

And the truth is, I've never felt more confident about what I'm feeling.

I've never felt more confident about *him*.

As I weave my way through the hordes of people, all I can think about is intertwining my fingers in that thick hair and crashing my lips into his.

My pace—which is honestly more of a run at this point— picks up with each focused step. I can't get to him fast enough.

Ellie sees me first. She must have some inkling of what's about to happen, because she immediately lowers both hands and drops the tomatoes she was holding. Theo, curious about her sudden ceasefire, turns quickly, the beginnings of a mega- watt smile etched upon his face.

"There you are," he says, running a hand through his hair, now clumped together with bits of tomato. Every other sound around us quietly fades away, allowing the sweetness of his voice to wash over me.

Here you are.

This feels like one of those made-for-television moments, which . . . is ironic because, well, you know. Like the state championship basketball game when Lucas Scott tells Peyton Sawyer *It's you*, except instead of confetti floating gracefully around us, Theo and I are surrounded by, covered in, and choking on tomato guts.

I throw myself at him, which I know takes him by surprise because he staggers backward ever so slightly. But he quickly recovers, wraps an arm around my waist, and pulls me close to him.

And before either of us can say anything that might somehow rip us from the magic of this moment, I crash my lips to his.

Without a single camera in sight and because it's entirely what I want.

What I need.

And whatever has been holding me—both of us—back from breaking that last remaining rule is snipped away with each brush of our lips.

Finally.

21

THEO

Nusa Lembongan Seaweed Farm
Bali, Indonesia

Here, throw these on," Jo says, pushing a rubber-coated bundle into my arms. I untangle the wad of fabric, revealing two bright-blue wet suits, which I hold up for Asher to see. We caught an overnight flight to Bali and I'm fairly certain we're all going on a collective four hours of sleep at this point.

"Great," he says, melting in his chair. "More water." I toss one of the suits at him.

"Fingers crossed this time won't end in us being lost at sea." I rather forcefully pull the tight spandex up my legs and over my shorts.

He scowls at me and does the same. "You're still bringing that up? We got rescued by the coast guard *one* time." But even he can't hide his toothy grin.

"Oh, I'll be bringing up nearly being lost at sea with you for the rest of my life."

These little back-and-forth moments between us are the only things keeping me going the last few weeks. I know I can count on Asher to have some snarky remark ready to go—and to have the last word, always.

"Let's go, people," Russell shouts, emerging through the flaps of the tent, the expected stressed expression painted across his face.

"A little help here?" I ask, struggling with my wet suit's zipper.

Asher comes over and, using one hand as leverage on my shoulder, yanks up my difficult zipper with the other. Before he leaves, he plants a lingering kiss on the back of my neck.

"What was that for?" I ask softly, leaning back into him.

"Oh, you know . . . just in case we die." His chin is now rested on my shoulder, and I can feel him smile.

"Ha ha."

"Now do me," he says. When I turn around, I notice an instant flush of red flooding his cheeks. "I mean . . . don't do me. Oh, God." He closes his eyes and takes a deep breath. "Can *you* please zip *my* zipper?"

"Well, go ahead and turn around so I can do you," I tease. He groans but does as he's told. I slide his finicky zipper closed and let my hands rest on his shoulders. I find myself feeling more emboldened to do what's natural with Asher—to say what's on my mind or follow my body in each moment.

But on some level, I think I'm still holding back.

All this—everything we've been through together—is starting to feel real. And as easy as it is to get swept up in the moment, I haven't allowed myself to get this close to *real* with anyone since Ethan. The thought alone is enough to make me take a metaphorical and physical step back.

He must sense a shift in my energy, because he turns to look up at me with his inquisitive eyes. "All good?" he asks.

"All good," I offer with a smile, and Jo starts to lead us down toward the beach with Arthur circling around us, his camera stabilized firmly against his chest. "Did you think we'd get here?"

The shoreline in front of us reveals some of the bluest water I've ever seen. Miles and miles of beautiful Indian Ocean stretch before us, blending in with a nearly cloudless sky. A lovely contrast to the lush greenery lining the water's edge. Since setting up shop in Bali, everyone has groaned about the heat and humidity, but I don't mind it. Especially since the coastal breeze seems to stir up a sweetness in the air wherever we go.

"To the semifinals?" he asks, pulling at his wet suit collar.

I nod. Dalton is already on his mark, not so subtly hiding his irritation while we all make our way down toward our designated spots. I'm sure if he had it his way, the cameras would always be on him. I swear I've seen him roll his eyes more than once as contestants, myself included, were the subject of a crew member's focus.

"'Shocked' would be an understatement," he says, and then quickly leans up to plant an unprompted kiss on my cheek.

But even that can't calm the wave of uneasiness as we head into whatever challenge production has planned next. It seems that each one proves to be more and more harrowing. I get the whole shock value of it all—fear and drama—and everything that comes with pushing someone outside their comfort zone sells, but it doesn't make it any less grueling.

A man I don't recognize stands next to Dalton, and judging by his half smile—and the fact that he seems incredibly antsy with all the commotion—I take it he's ready for this to be over.

Asher and I, sandwiched between Jenn and Ellie and Bianca and Jackson, halt and stand in a half circle around the semi-raised platform Dalton and his companion are on.

"And we're rolling in three, two . . ."

"Welcome back, trekkers. We're here for this season's semifinal challenge episode of *The Epic Trek*. As always, I'm your host, Dalton McKnight . . ."

I roll my eyes, not even caring anymore if Arthur captures it on film. Dalton's announcer voice is like nails on a chalkboard, and while I know I could never do his job, every time I see him, I wonder how the hell he's still in this industry considering how he behaves when the cameras *aren't* rolling.

"Our contestants have been traveling the world for the last three weeks, and today," he continues, ensuring every syllable is as enunciated as possible, "we're standing on the shores of southern Bali, where the calm waters between the islands of Nusa Lembongan and Ceningan have created ideal conditions for generations of local seaweed farmers."

Seaweed?

I glance past Dalton. Just beyond the contestant staging area are three rows of what look like floating flower boxes in the shallows of the clear water. Each row consists of four of these boxes and they appear to be anchored in place, bobbing up and down in the subtle sloshing of the water.

"As the world's largest seaweed producer, over one million coastal farmers in Indonesia, like Bima and his family here," he continues, patting his companion on the back, "rely on the growing industry to make ends meet during fluctuations in tourism."

Bima steps forward now. "For years, my family and I have cared for and harvested these waters. The seaweed before you," he says, briefly turning toward it, "has been growing for just over a month and has reached its ideal weight for harvesting. Today, each team will collect the seaweed from their floating seabed and hang it by hand so it can be dried and eventually sold."

Both Dalton and Bima step down from their platform and walk toward the water's edge, causing the camera crews to reposition themselves.

"Contestants will alternate using a paddleboard to harvest each seabed. Once you've removed all the seaweed from the bed, you will paddle back to shore to your waiting partner and work together to hang the seaweed out to dry."

There are rows of triangle-shaped drying racks in the distance where I'm assuming we'll hang it all.

"*All* the seaweed from each bed must be hung before the waiting partner can move on to the next," Dalton adds.

I bump Asher with my shoulder. "Seems simple enough, right?" I whisper.

"Famous last words," he hisses back.

He's right. Nothing about anything we've done together has been simple, but I've done my best to remain optimistic.

"Here, take these," I say, handing Ash a pair of rubber gloves and shears. "Why don't you go first?"

"And why is that?" he inquires suspiciously, holding the gloves like he's ready for them to bite.

"Because there are four seabeds and if we're alternating, the farthest one out will be mine." I know he's not the strongest swimmer, and while I don't know how deep the water is, it's not worth risking it. Plus, I hate watching him struggle.

"Good point," he says, failing at hiding the smile now forming.

I place both hands on his shoulders and lock my eyes with his, doing my best to block out Arthur's quick spin around to ensure he captures my precompetition pep talk.

"You've got this. Just try to gather the seaweed and paddle back to shore as quickly as you can, and I'll be waiting right here ready to help you get it all hung up."

"Sir, yes sir." He's mocking me, and he even adds a half-assed salute in the process.

"Let's just take this one seabed at a time," I add, ignoring him.

He pats me on the cheek with his now-gloved hand. "Aka follow the rules directly from Mr. Dalton McKnight himself. Got it."

I want to tell him to be careful. That these challenges have been making me more and more nervous recently because there is so much that could go wrong.

That I worry about him relentlessly.

But Jo comes around to usher Asher toward the water's edge before I have the chance. "Come on, Scuba Steve. Let's get you lined up."

The rows of seabeds bob up and down with the waves ahead of us.

"Contestants, get ready," Dalton shouts. His voice is annoying under most circumstances, but having it ricochet off the water grates on my nerves.

Asher looks back momentarily and gives me a small, resigned shrug. I've learned that, much like the movement of the shallow water before us, his competitive spirit comes at random—both a blessing and a curse considering our current circumstances. On one hand, seeing a fiery rage behind his green eyes is a total turn-on. I've watched as he's thrown himself headfirst into the unknown and surprised just about all of us with his grit and determination and, oddly, his strength.

But on the other hand, I've learned to admire his growing ability to let go of the things that aren't in his control.

"On your marks . . ." Dalton's voice rings through the air. I watch Asher straighten his spine and take a deep breath, turning over the pair of shears he's holding.

"Get set . . ." Adrenaline rushes through my veins, and I'm not even the one about to do anything.

Bianca, who like me, is standing by as her brother is about to kick off the challenge, leans in, expertly knowing when she's in view of multiple cameras. "Don't worry, Theo," she calls over her shoulder. "Production preemptively called search and rescue for the two of you."

I ignore her.

"Go!"

Water sloshes everywhere as the first wave of contestants rushes into the shallow water, trailing their paddleboards behind them. The first seabed is probably only fifteen feet offshore, so Asher gets to it in no time. I watch him loop the rope attached to his paddleboard around one side of the seabed now in front of him, something I hadn't even thought to do.

Arthur and the other camera operators, dressed in matching black waders, follow at a safe distance as they each begin to cut the seaweed. I had originally assumed the actual harvesting would be a simple task, considering the thin texture of the seaweed. But Ellie, for example, keeps glancing over her shoulder at Jenn, who's fidgeting on the beach, clearly aware that her daughter is struggling with her shears. Jackson, on the other hand, appears to have given up on his shears altogether and has resorted to removing the seaweed by the handful.

But Asher—to my, well . . . not to my surprise, because that makes me sound like I've underestimated him, and Asher Bennett is not someone I would dare to underestimate—appears to be more than halfway done with the task at hand.

Jackson finishes first, followed by Asher, who quickly pulls his loaded paddleboard behind him. They reach the shore around the same time, ready to get this seaweed hung so that we can advance to seabed two.

"Nice job, Ash. You really *are* Scuba Steve," I tease when our eyes meet. Arthur cracks a smile behind his camera in my peripheral vision.

"Help me pick this up," he says, practically ignoring me as he bends down to grab one end of the paddleboard. Seems like the fire's back. "One, two, three . . ."

We lift the paddleboard together, ensuring none of the slimy seaweed tips off as we carry it over to the drying rack.

"Okay, hear me out," he says, kneeling down after we've set the paddleboard at the base of the rack. "I cut all this intentionally, hoping it would make the hanging process easier." He picks up a clump of seaweed from the pile. "See how this stem is here?" he asks, pointing to the wishbone shape of the seaweed he's holding. "I cut farther down so we can use this almost as a hook." Asher hangs the seaweed with ease.

"You're a genius," I say, grabbing his face to kiss his salty lips, completely taking him—and myself—by surprise. I'm genuinely in awe of the man before me—the way his mind works and how he thought ahead like this.

"Quit stalling and get to work, Fernandez," he says. A wave of red pools behind his cheeks as he grabs a handful of seaweed to start hanging it. "But I'm glad you're finally noticing."

The two of us work quickly side by side. Asher was right.

The way each chunk has been cut definitely makes the hanging easier. I'm trying to *not* let my eyes wander to how our competition is doing, but I can see them struggling to get the seaweed to stay in place out of the corner of my eye.

Our pile rapidly dwindles, and it seems it's now Asher's turn to give the pep talk. "When you get to the seabed, I'd recommend opening the shears all the way like this," he says, spreading the shears as wide as they can open. "And instead of *cutting* the seaweed, I found it was much easier to *slice* it like you would a ribbon or a banana."

"Whatever you say, boss," I say, hanging the final piece of seaweed on the rack. Bianca is already heading out and it looks like Jenn might be ready to take off on her heels. "Ready?"

"Let's do it."

We hurriedly shuffle through the hot sand, carrying the empty paddleboard to our starting point. Asher hands over the shears as soon as we set the board down in the water.

"Hey, don't forget," he whispers, stopping me with his hand on my arm. "Go deep and slice," he says, and repeats the movement with the shears. As I head out into the cool water, a smile forms on Asher's face—one that a small part of me would like to outline with the tip of my tongue.

Rather than trailing the paddleboard behind me, like I watched Jenn struggle to do once she reached the slightly deeper water, I hop on top of it, placing the shears directly under my chest, and paddle out like one would on a surfboard.

I quickly close the distance between me and Bianca, who is about to reach her second seabed. The water is just above my waist once I reach mine, and I remind myself to tie my paddleboard to the side of the bed as Asher had done.

There are four rows of seaweed growing within the bed, so

it makes sense to work one row at a time to make sure I don't leave any harvestable seaweed behind. Reaching down, I find the hooklike spot as Ash indicated, make my first slice, and place the first bunch of seaweed on my paddleboard.

It's repetitive work: slice, place on the paddleboard, repeat. But a sense of calm washes over me with each ebb of the ocean—a first for any challenge I've been a part of. Being directly immersed in an activity like this, one that is tied so closely to the livelihood of countless individuals and their families, I can't help but feel deeply appreciative to play a small part in it. This whole experience, seeing so many corners of the world from such a different lens, has fulfilled me in a way I wasn't quite expecting.

Traveling has always been some form of work for me, whether in my active duty or civilian life. But until now I've never felt like I've connected with the world around me in such a meaningful way.

Before I know it, I'm almost done with my seabed, and seemingly ahead of everyone else, even Bianca. I scan the rows to ensure I've harvested each piece before turning my paddleboard back toward the shore, half walking, half running with the waves at my back.

Asher greets me with another smile, which sends the butterflies I've been failing to ignore for weeks into overdrive. "My little trick worked, huh?"

"Like a charm," I say, making him beam, so I'm forced to dig my feet into the sand to prevent myself from launching at him. We haul the board back over to the drying rack, invigorated by the small lead we seem to have over the rest of the competition, and work in silent tandem, quickly hanging this next batch and shuffling back toward the water for Asher's second turn.

Arthur hangs back this time. I can only imagine how repetitive this all must come across on camera, so instead, he appears to be capturing some close-ups of the neat rows of drying seaweed along the beach.

"You boys seem to be getting on better these days," he murmurs from behind the lens. "More in sync."

I smile, remembering the epic chaos of the first challenge when Ash and I thought we'd been *communicating*.

"We're trying," I say, though Arthur's attention seems to be on a small crab that's made an appearance amid all the commotion.

How foolish we'd been, thinking two literal strangers could just dive headfirst into being lovestruck boyfriends without there being any hiccups.

At least I don't have to pretend the lovestruck part anymore.

I ignore the way that thought twists my stomach into knots.

Looking to Asher in the ocean, he is, and I think will always be, the first in a crowd to catch my eye. He's kind of a mess with his moppy hair slicked in every which way as he collects the last of his seaweed, and his poor glasses are covered in water droplets.

But damn it, he's *my* mess. The thought of Asher being mine cracks my chest wide open. This could be *it*. The moment everyone always talks about. It scares the hell out of me, but he's mine for however long he wants to be.

With anyone else, self-preservation might kick in.

But Asher? He just might be worth the risk.

"Hurry, hurry, hurry," he pants, dragging the paddleboard onto the sand.

"There's a very real possibility you were a seaweed farmer in another life," I tease, bending over to help him once again as we make our way back to the racks.

"You know what? I wouldn't hate that," he says, fighting a smirk but losing.

Back and forth we go, quickly hanging row after row of seaweed for the third time and hoping that if we move fast enough, we'll be able to widen the small lead we seem to have.

"I know it's probably bad karma to say something like this," Asher says, both hands full. "But we might actually finish first for once!" Excitement fills his voice and flashes behind his eyes.

Well, shit. Now we *have* to win.

Asher hangs the last of his haul up, and I grab the paddleboard, hoisting it over my head with both hands, and do my best to sprint across the beach.

"Theo, wait, don't you need . . ." Asher shouts after me but his voice gets lost in the waves the second I reach the shore.

I launch back into the cool water with the shears secured under my chest one last time and, knowing this lead won't last forever, swim as fast as I can to the farthest remaining seabed. The water is definitely over my head when I reach it, meaning I'll have to completely tread water to finish this challenge.

Bianca gets to her seabed moments after I get to mine. As I start making my first round of cuts, I notice just how rough the waves are this far out. I've swallowed more salt water this round than I'd care to in a lifetime, but I keep at it, alternating between slicing the stems of the seaweed and plopping the clumps onto the paddleboard.

My lungs are screaming in protest and my legs are one tread away from cramping. I need a break, even just a tiny one. I glance over at Bianca and see that she still has a significant amount of seaweed to cut, so I let myself hold on to the side of the seabed, allowing my legs to dangle for a moment.

I take a much-needed deep breath. And then a few more.

And when I feel like I can finish this damn thing, I make another round of cuts. But as I go to place the clump I'm holding on my paddleboard, my hand smacks down on the water.

"What the hell?" I turn and realize my board has somehow come loose from where I tied it and is now floating farther and farther away from me out into open water. "Shit!" I yell.

Placing the shears safely in the floating seabed, I dive off after our paddleboard, swimming against the force of the waves with whatever strength I have left. It seems that the harder I swim, the more distance is put between me and our seaweed-loaded paddleboard, but finally, after what feels like an exhausting eternity, my fingertips make contact with its edge, and I'm able to awkwardly turn it back to our nearly finished seabed.

But when I get there, panting and exhausted and vowing never to go near an ocean for the rest of my life, I see that Bianca isn't at hers anymore. Instead, she's already back on the shore hanging her final batch of seaweed with Jackson.

It's over.

I slap my hands hard against the water, ignoring the spray of the salt water in my eyes. There's no point in rushing now. The competition was intended to be the first to finish, and since Jackson and Bianca secured that title, I give myself permission to catch my breath paddling back to shore.

Asher and Jo meet me at the water's edge with sympathetic smiles.

"Why didn't you tie the paddleboard to the edge like before?" Arthur asks when he joins us, his camera still raised to his face.

"I definitely did."

Asher hands me a bottle of cold water to help rid my mouth of the salty taste. He bends down and looks at our paddleboard's tie. "It's been cut," he says, holding up the rope, which indeed has been severed.

We all look at Bianca, who's now sandwiched between Dalton and Jackson as they capture whatever victory footage is needed for the day's challenge. She makes sure to turn in our direction with a shrug, her infamous oh-so-pleased-with-herself smirk growing wider by the second.

22

ASHER

Mahagiri Resort Nusa Lembongan—Room 416
Bali, Indonesia

Par for the course, Theo and I barely survived today's challenge. On our way back to Arthur's van, Jo lets us know the next elimination isn't for two days, which means Theo and I have an extra forty-eight hours to agonize over the fact that we just might be going home instead of heading into the finals. I'm pretty sure our only saving grace so far has been that viewers keep voting us forward online. Jo doesn't seem to mind, though. She reminds us it's about the "whole package" and, according to her, our standing as the clumsy and borderline-chaotic "couple that could" is as good as reality-television gold.

I'll take her word for it, because judging by the way Theo seems to be in his own head since we left the beach, you could have fooled me.

He doesn't say much on the ride back to the hotel, but I chalk it up to pure exhaustion. But after we take turns showering, doing our best to get rid of the sand lodged in every nook and cranny, it almost feels like our first night sharing a room, tiptoeing around each other. As much as I hate to admit it, there's a growing whisper of fear he's pulling away now that our feelings are getting harder and harder to ignore.

Initially, what drove me to go through with the competition was the promise of what it could mean for my career. But now, though one half of me is still pushing toward the finish line for the prize money, the other half is focused on the fact that Theo and I will probably go our separate ways if we lose.

He's sitting in the armchair in the corner of our room and it dawns on me now that the thought of losing him twists my stomach in knots far more than losing the prize money does.

I'm not entirely sure how to process this information, but what's growing clear is that if I don't fully lean in to my feelings for Theo—or find the courage to talk to him about them—the only thing left to process will be regret.

"What are you thinking over there?" I ask, sitting on the end of our bed, wishing he was right next to me like he normally is.

Theo offers only a small smile. "Not a thing, guapo."

I'd like to think that after spending nearly every waking second with the man, I've come to know Theo pretty well. For the most part, his facial expressions are easy to read, and historically, his default setting seems to be sunshine and rainbows. So this noticeable moody and broody act isn't fooling anyone.

"Interesting," I say, leaning back on my elbows. "Hey, you know what sounds good right about now?"

Theo raises an eyebrow.

"Some mozzarella sticks," I say dryly.

He barks out a laugh, rolling his eyes. "Seriously?"

"Mm-hmm," I say, nodding, extra pleased with myself.

"They sound *seriously* delicious. Spill it . . . or, I mean, hand them over."

He uncrosses his legs and shifts his whole body to face me as a far more serious expression darkens his face. "Asher, I just . . ." he starts, rubbing his hands together. Theo's shoulders are stiff, riddled with a tension I haven't seen until now. I have no idea what I was expecting, but this sudden change in tone is making my palms sweat. "I just don't know if I can do this anymore."

His admission takes the air out of my lungs.

"Oh" is all I can manage, because my brain begins swirling around and around about how all of this is starting to sound just like Clint and his airport terminal confessional.

And then the beginnings of panicked thoughts come rushing in. About the remaining leg of the competition and how we've come too far to stop now.

But the thought of him leaving—of sitting in this stupid hotel room or getting on another flight without him—is a punch to my heart so strong it nearly brings me to tears.

"If I've done something that's made you change your mind about all this," I stammer out, my pulse racing far too fast. "About me. Theo, I . . ." But because I can't untangle my thoughts or get my mouth to formulate what I think I need to say, I just stare at him awkwardly.

"No, that's not it," he says quickly, and for a fraction of a second, I can breathe again. "I don't want to pretend anymore . . ." he whispers, looking down, his voice barely audible.

He doesn't want to pretend? I'm sure under different circumstances, I'd be able to figure out what Theo is telling me, but right now, the only thing I seem to be able to center in my mind is that I'm losing him.

"I can't pretend anymore because it's too . . . real."

That word rolling off the tip of Theo's tongue makes my insides do somersaults.

Real.

He can't pretend anymore because what he's pretending is feeling too real. And like I've been piecing together from what he's told me, when things get too real, he runs.

And then it hits me with the full force of a ton of bricks.

Theo wants to run.

The thought of him leaving is all-consuming and the only thing I care about—the only thing I need in this moment—is to convince him to stay.

Driven by some fundamental need to keep him with me, or because I've finally given myself the space and permission to admit that I want him, I get up from off the bed and cross the room toward Theo. His eyes are wide and filled with something close to concern.

I've never been someone who is good at this.

At using whatever sex appeal I may, or more likely, may not have at my disposal. But something about it being Theo makes me feel more confident in my own skin. Like I'm someone capable of inciting desire or want in someone else, so now, more than ever, I lean in to whatever it is I'm feeling and straddle him in the chair.

Theo raises a questioning brow but stays silent. His hands instinctively reach for my hips at the same time mine snake around his neck. He melts into my touch, which encourages what little confidence I have to do something like this. I've always noted just how seamlessly our bodies fit together when we've been puppeteered by Jo for the cameras, but there's something different when it's just us.

Something that makes me believe in the right person at the right time.

Theo's looking up at me, and it's as if there's a battle brewing behind those gorgeous eyes of his. Desperate to know which opposing team is winning, I place a hand on either side of his face and lean in close, close enough to inhale the sweet spice radiating from his skin. The need to kiss him is stronger than ever, but beyond that lies something more important—the desire to settle whatever doubts he may be feeling about us. Hell, it may be more for me at this point, but that's irrelevant because if I don't have Theo's firm lips on mine right this instant, I might just self-implode.

We're just a few torturous inches apart, and Theo closes his eyes, his breathing wild. "Ash, I can't keep doing this in front of the cameras and then coming back here and . . ." His voice trails off, and when he opens his eyes, they are filled with the weight of all the words he cannot say.

"Tell me," I say, placing my forehead to his, and when I do, a small hum emanates from Theo's chest.

He exhales, his breath hot against my skin. "Acting like this," he says, touching my chest, letting his hand linger along my sternum, "and pretending how I'm feeling isn't real. That this isn't something that scares the hell out of me."

"I feel like you're getting ready to tell me you're leaving," I whisper against the side of his face.

His hand flexes on my hip. "Ash, it's not that sim—" he starts, but I place my finger on his lips, because I need him to know how I'm feeling.

"But please just stay, because I can't do this without you." I hear my own voice crack as my admission slips through my lips. And it's the truth; I couldn't have done any of this without Theo.

Something seems to have unlocked within Theo, because his expression changes. Whatever he'd been thinking seems to melt away. Slowly, as if still a little unsure if this is right or wrong or another way to mess everything up, Theo lifts his hands to my face, and I happily lean into the warmth of his touch. His thumb slides softly against my cheek as his other hand gingerly cradles the back of my head. I can feel him pulling me toward him at the same time I realize he's leaning in to close the short distance between us.

He's going to kiss me.

He's going to kiss me, and I can't think of a time when I wanted anything more.

I can't think at all, actually.

All I know is that Theo Fernandez smells like warmth and new beginnings and he wants this kiss as badly as I do.

"Baby . . ." he whispers, his lips a heartbeat away from mine. I have to close my eyes because I can hardly see straight; the desperate anticipation of having Theo like this is dizzying. There's something different about the way he's touching me. Something inviting about his stare and deliciously unpredictable about his movements. "I don't want to pretend with you."

"Then don't," I whisper, my demand hot and desperate against his lips. "Please don't pretend, because I don't want to either."

That does it.

He crashes his mouth to mine, and I pull him against me with every ounce of strength I have. I snake my fingers in the thick hair at the back of his neck, securing my hold on this beautiful man before me.

He parts my lips with ease, not that I would dare put up a fight, because all that my lips and body and mind want is *more*.

Theo's tongue traces the lines of my bottom lip before intertwining with mine, our mouths hot and full of a matched urgency that causes a groan to build deep in my chest. My want for him was never in question—he's stunning and captivating and everything you'd expect from a man who takes your breath away simply by smiling.

But his heart, his softness and overall goodness, the things that he's allowed me to see, make me want him so badly I could combust right here on top of him.

"I need . . . you on . . . the bed," he says between kisses, and the thought of Theo pushing me onto the bed makes me pant. From one second to the next, Theo is standing with me in his arms like it's nothing. He carries me over to the bed, his lips never leaving mine, and lays us down on the plush white comforter. The second Theo's strong body settles between my legs, every nerve ending burns with an unmanageable need.

I need him.

Our movements are desperate, but that doesn't stop me from committing every second of this moment to memory. The way Theo's lips are parted. The sound of our heavy breathing mixed together. The way I can feel his cock straining against me. Theo slides his hands from my face, resting one around the bottom slope of my neck, the other traveling a little farther, gripping my hip.

But he never stops kissing me. His lips slow and tender against mine, filled with both electrifying newness and comforting familiarity. Until they are thunderous again, leaving us gasping for air as we inhale each other.

More.

I crave his tanned skin, to taste all the flavors I now associate with only him. With frantic hands, I reach down between us to find the hem of his thin shirt and pull, eager to remove all barriers between us. He doesn't object, lifting and angling himself just enough so I can remove it and reveal the broad body I've been mentally running my hands over since the moment I met him.

Thank fucking God my imagination is no longer necessary.

Theo hovers over me and I take in every plane and curve of him. As I trail my hands over his bare chest and down his stomach, he shudders at my touch, and when my hands reach the waistband of his shorts, he collapses back onto me, his mouth claiming mine with a deafening hunger once more.

He invades my mouth with his tongue, gently pulling on my lower lip with his teeth. He trails kisses along my jaw, turning my head with one hand and using the other to slide beneath my shirt, sending shivers dancing across my core. His scruff tickles the most sensitive parts of my neck, and when his teeth graze my earlobe, a growl in my chest bubbles to the surface. But when he grinds his weight into me, the throb of his dick against my own causes me to full-out moan into his mouth.

Fuck.

"Please, Theo . . ." I pant, not caring at all how desperate for him I sound. He doesn't need me to say anything else—not that I could at this point with his sweet lips back on mine. Instead, he rolls us so I'm suddenly half seated, half lying on top of him.

He wraps his arms around me, pulling me tightly so I'm flat against his chest. "Is this what you want?" he asks, pressing his hips upward. The bulge in his shorts teases my ass and I place my hands on either side of his chest so I can really push back against him. All of him. *Fuck.*

"Mm-hmm," I murmur against his lips. I really do. I need to

feel him free of all barriers. I need to watch his face as we finally discover each other, skin to skin.

Theo pushes me back so that I am sitting upright.

With skilled hands, he slowly lifts my shirt over my head, trailing lingering kisses along my stomach and up my chest.

Every new inch of skin his to savor.

He reaches up to lock his hands behind my neck and pulls my face back to his. "Let's get you out of these . . ." he breathes, tugging at the waistband of my sweats. We roll again, Theo's body burying me in the bed, and I raise my hips at the same time he pulls at my pants, his breath dragging across my skin lower and lower, and when he's finally freed me from my clothing, his eyes burn dark with a hunger that makes my mouth water.

"You are," he whispers, his fingertips covering my body, "the most gorgeous man I've ever seen."

His words make me forget how to breathe.

I'm throbbing, my cock begging for his touch, his sweet mouth—something—and as if he can hear the desperation of my thoughts, Theo lowers his lips to my cock, kissing my shaft again and again, flicking my aching head with his wet tongue.

"Theo, please . . ." I pant, and his delicious torture causes my back to arch, my hands to claw at the bedding beneath us.

"You're dripping for me . . ." he says, his lips still against my cock, but now his tongue slides directly over the tip, tasting me. "Mmm. That's my boy." He takes both my hands in his, his grip tight, and pins them on either side of my restless body. The sweet and saltiness of my precum lingers on his lips and when he dips his tongue back into my mouth, his hold on me loosens, so I use the opportunity to slide my hands down his wide back and tug at the waistline of his shorts while I press my body up against his.

"Take these off. *Now*," I pant, his smirk dancing against my lips.

"Yes, sir," he says playfully, and I love it. Theo expertly slides out of his shorts and briefs, and it's my turn to explore his body with wandering hands. I love the feel of his soft hair as I trace the lines where his glorious ass meets his legs, and when I roam around his hips, finally taking his cock, its heaviness makes my eyes roll back into my skull.

Pulling him toward me, I wrap my legs around his waist, positioning his dick exactly where I need it. Theo rolls his hips, sliding himself repeatedly against my hole. His lips are urgent against mine, the desire, need, and impatience he's so clearly feeling matching my own.

He's pressing against me now. Hard and firm, his intent so deliriously direct. I can feel myself open for him. Just slightly at first, but the more he slides and presses against me, the more I feel the arousal taking over, my body demanding what it wants.

Breaking our kiss for the first time in what feels like an eternity, Theo's face hovers just a breath above mine. His breathing is ragged, his eyes brimming with heat, and he's so damn stunning in this moment I pray that time itself stops just so I can savor this moment forever. Ever so slowly, he brings a tender hand to my face, a question lingering behind his stare, one that every gay man knows so well.

Are we doing this? Or . . .

I nod my head, knowing words aren't necessary for either of us right now. Theo's a smart man—there's nothing subtle about what I, or my body, so clearly wants as I'm grinding into him.

"Stay here," he whispers, practically leaping off the bed. I instantly crave his warmth again, the eagerness behind his every touch, the sweetness of his kiss.

But he doesn't leave me wanting for too long.

Theo comes jogging back from our hotel bathroom, naked, hard and on full display just for me, every bit more delicious than I could have ever imagined. I sit up on my elbows, fully appreciating every detail of his body. His strong, powerful thighs. His tapered waist and broad, freckled shoulders. His long arms that I'd give just about anything to have around me like a vise. And that cock . . .

He nearly dives back onto the bed, claiming his place on top of me, and places a bottle of lube and a condom in my hand—an invitation and a choice, one I already know the answer to.

"I'm on PrEP . . . and get tested regularly," he whispers, his breath hot against my ear between searing kisses.

"Uh, I know."

He lifts himself onto his elbows, hair wild and an eyebrow raised as he peers over me. "You do?"

"Yeah, um, I may or may not have . . ." I say, tugging his neck toward me, bringing his lips back to mine, hoping my needy kisses will soften the blow of my nosiness, "snooped through your toiletry bag that first night in the hotel." Thinking back to Theo's PrEP prescription bottle in his open toiletry bag—and the matching one in mine—the choice is clear. I need to feel *him*. All of him.

"Is that so?" he asks, his smile evident against my parted lips.

"Oops," I murmur, letting the slick liquid glide over my fingertips. Theo's watching with patient eyes and when I reach down, coating every inch of him with smooth lube, his eyes burn even brighter.

He presses his forehead to mine when I secure my legs around his waist.

"You sure?" he whispers, his lips parted, the rise and fall of our chests increasing with each passing second.

Ignoring him, I reach around, grabbing a handful of his muscular ass—which will get its moment of appreciation at another time—and pull him toward me.

Pull him into me.

I wince at the sudden fullness and the way he stretches me as I get used to him.

"Right there," I pant, holding him in place. "Just stay right there for a second."

He stills, giving me every ounce of control. I need to take him slowly, something Theo clearly understands as he watches with cautious eyes.

"Kiss me," I plead, wrapping one arm around his back and the other around his neck, pulling myself closer to him.

And he does.

Each brush of his lips eases the momentary tension created from finally having him inside me. It's too much and somehow, despite the burn and ache, not nearly enough. His cock is just the right length and thickness—not too big that it's painfully overwhelming, and with a slight upward curve that I know is going to hit me in all the right places.

"You okay?" he asks quietly against my ear. I nod, and when Theo starts to really move, each thrust unhurried and deliberate, filled with a considerate gentleness that's more of a rarity these days, I begin to unravel around him.

"You feel so damn incredible," he says, his breathing ragged as he starts to glide deeper into me.

I can feel Theo's hungry eyes taking in every second of this moment. Every move my body makes, every sound that escapes my lips. It's as if he's trying to discover what makes me come undone.

He'll always be the same charming Theo I met in the airport bar.

But here? Here, he's a man in control.

He's a man that's taking what he wants and giving it back twofold. A man hell-bent on making every inch of my body sing with pleasure, his touch growing increasingly intuitive as he pumps deeper into me. He's got one hand locked behind my knee and the other slowly stroking my dick. An agonizing sensation that if he doesn't stop soon, I'll explode all over us.

"Unless you want me to cum right now, I'm going to need you to knock that off," I say, tapping his hand on my cock.

"Sorry, sorry," he says, a delicious little smirk growing from the corner of his mouth, and he moves his hand to grip my hip. Theo's kept up a pretty consistent cadence of long, deep strokes into me, but he switches to a few shallow ones, really teasing my hole with the swollen tip of his cock before pulling out completely.

"Oh, fuck," I groan against his lips. "Yes. Oh my God, please keep doing that." Each new thrust elicits a completely new sensation throughout my entire body.

"Yeah?" he asks, delivering another delicious pump. "You like when I tease your hole like that?"

"Hell yes," I say, melting against him, gripping his arms as he continues to slowly enter me ever so slightly before pulling out again. He reaches down to tap the head of his dick against my wanting hole before slowly driving back into me. *Holy shit.* "Please don't stop."

"*Fuck*, Ash," he growls. "I love watching my dick slide in

and out of you like this. You feel so fucking good. So fucking tight."

"I want you on your back," I say, pushing up against his chest. "I need to ride you." He smiles, following my lead, and expertly rolls our bodies without ever pulling out of me so that he's now on his back.

Oh! This new position lets me feel every inch of him as I grind down on his gorgeous dick.

"That's right. Use my cock to make yourself feel good," he says, gripping my hips hard while I roll them against his. The angle of his dick's curve is hitting my prostate with screaming bells and whistles and in such a way that is so powerfully overwhelming it's starting to make my eyes water. I place my hands firmly on his wide chest, using it as leverage to really start to pick up speed, and I push myself deeper onto him. "Yeah, take it just like that. You're riding my dick so fucking good, Ash. *Fuck.*"

I love knowing that I'm making him feel good.

That he's enjoying this as much as I am, because dear lord, I don't think I've ever felt pleasure quite like this.

"Baby, look at *you*," he beams, his eyes roaming over every inch of my body as I rotate my hips up and down on his thick cock. I revel in Theo's praise, fueled by his words of encouragement as I take every inch of him. His strong hands grip my hips for dear life, perfectly meeting each of my thrusts with one of his own, and I marvel at just how perfectly our bodies fit together, like his dick was tailor-made just for me. The timing and intensity of his thrusts quicken as he uses the leverage he has on my waist to really push himself further into me each time.

"I'm fucking loving this," I moan when he continues to hit *that* spot over and over again.

Theo returns his hand to my cock, giving it a squeeze. His eyes are dark. "That's my good boy," he says, a wicked grin plastered on his face. The new sensation of him drilling my ass with his cock and stroking mine in time with his thrusts is too much, and whatever control I've had over my imminent orgasm is fading fast. I lean down and forward, finding his lips again as he continues to bring me to the edge.

"I'm so close, baby," I pant against his lips. "If you keep doing that, I'm going to cum."

"Lose yourself, Asher," he whispers. "Let go and lose yourself. Please, baby. For me." His hand glides over me, mirroring the rhythm of his strong hips, and I can feel my orgasm building. Slowly at first, but soon, my muscles begin to tighten, and I cling to Theo's shoulders, preparing to be thrown over the most satisfying edge. We're both slick with sweat as we breathe into each other's mouths, inhaling each other with every gulp of air.

"Fuck, Ash . . . I'm getting close too . . ." he hisses behind a clenched jaw, his lips still ravenous against mine. He tightens his grip around my cock, the perfect combination of mouth-watering and frustrating stimulation. I can feel him swell inside me with each movement of his hips, and the greedy anticipation of forcing every drop from him sends me flying over the edge.

"Oh, shit . . . you're going to make me cum," I pant like an animal in heat.

Theo's brows scrunch together in determined concentration as thrusts in and out of me so deeply. "Cum for me, baby. I need to watch you come undone."

Knowing that he needs me to finish is what sends me over. "I'm cumming," I shout, not caring if the entire hotel hears me. "Oh, God . . . I'm fucking cumming . . ." The words barely escape my lips when the most earth-shattering and life-affirming orgasm erupts from my core, my release coating what little space remains between us.

"Oh, fuck yes," he growls, quickly freeing one of his hands to scoop up some of my cum with his fingers to taste. "That was so fucking hot."

I feel delirious and spent, and the only thing keeping my eyes open at this point is the desire to make sure he finishes.

Finding his mouth again, I take his lip between my teeth. "I need you to breed me."

Theo's eyes roll back into his skull, a hiss escaping his lips. "Yeah, baby? You want my load?"

"Give it to me," I demand, arching my back so he can really thrust up into me. "I need it." Theo's pace quickens, and he wraps his arms like a vise around me as he fucks me hard and deep.

"Fuck, Asher . . ." My name is the last thing on his lips when he shudders beneath me. "Oh, fuck, I'm going to . . . Fuck, baby, you're making me cum," he shouts, and then stills inside me. His cock pulses repeatedly. He pulls me down deeper onto him, and when he does, I can feel each burst of his orgasm filling me up.

"That felt so . . . Baby, I don't have words for how good that felt," he says between a slew of drunken kisses. Contentment floods my veins, and I relish the fact that I just made him feel that way. That I could elicit this level of pleasure from him. "Just stay here for a second," he says, tightening his grip around me, so I let my entire body rest on his, the exhilarated rise and fall of our chests matching as we come down from the highest of highs.

This is a moment I'll never forget.

Because here, in another random hotel room in yet another country, Theo Fernandez obliterated anything I thought I knew about pleasure and showed me everything I've been missing out on all these years.

And now, after experiencing *that*, I know with certainty I will never want it to stop.

//////////////////////

A surprise for Theo unfolds in my mind the moment I open my eyes the following morning.

We spent the entirety of last night exploring each other's bodies and doing all the things we both so clearly have been holding back. After coming down from the most earth-shattering highs, he'd led me to the shower, where we washed every inch of each other's still-flushed-from-sex skin, idiotic smiles plastered on our faces. Our infinite kisses were only interrupted when I felt the need to drop to my knees under the cascading water. The look on his face when he finished in my mouth will forever be ingrained in my mind. And when we made our way back to the bed, naked and blissed out, Theo held me tight against his chest, repeatedly kissing the top of my head as we both drifted off to sleep.

Sneaking out of bed, away from Theo's gorgeously naked body, physically pains me, but I want to make sure we can at least have some coffee before I spring this last-minute surprise on him.

I throw on a pair of shorts, a T-shirt, and a baseball cap and make my way down to the lobby.

"Well, well, well." Jo's familiar snarky voice greets me as I pour myself a healthy mug of coffee. "I would have thought you two would be locked away for days."

Her comment almost makes me spill the creamer. "Shh, let me at least have my morning coffee before you start speaking in riddles." I take a sip of the hot liquid, willing its magical powers to course through my veins as quickly as possible.

"No riddles needed, my friend." She pats me on the back while I pour another mug for Theo. "I'm just so glad to see you *finally* had a good night's rest."

Between her word choice and the emphasis she placed on them, she's being anything but subtle.

"Mm-hmm" is all I can articulate. "Actually, I need a favor . . ." And I proceed to bombard Jo with my spontaneous plan, which causes her to smile.

"Who are you and what have you done with the prickly Asher Bennett I met a few weeks ago?"

I ignore her jab. "Can I please just borrow it?"

She hands me the van's keys. "I will personally ruin your life if anything happens to it."

"I have no doubt you will." Without waiting to see if she has any additional snarky remarks, I hurry back to our room, coffees and keys in hand, excited to get back to Theo.

He's still sound asleep on his stomach when I open the door, so I tiptoe across the room, set the pair of mugs on his bedside table, and sit on his side of the bed. His hair is a mess, and I could easily spend hours tracing the constellations in the beautiful freckles across his shoulders. He stirs slightly at my touch, so I lean down to plant a soft kiss on his forehead. "Good morning, handsome," I whisper, my lips at his ear.

Theo's eyes are still closed, but I watch a smile form at his lips that melts my heart. I kiss his forehead again. And again. And once more for good measure. "I brought you coffee."

"Have I told you recently how amazing you are?" he says, sitting up and taking a sip from the mug I've just passed him.

Handing his mug back to me, he lets his fingers linger on mine, guiding me in for a sweet kiss.

"Asher. Bennett. You. Are. So. Amazing. And. I. Will. Never. Stop. Telling. You. That," he says, between soft, lingering kisses.

He's quite literally taking my breath away. Again. Something I'm learning he has a general knack for. Before he's able to distract me any further, I kick off my shoes to join him in bed for a few more cuddles. "Only if you're up for it, I have a little surprise for you," I whisper as Theo pulls me tight against his chest.

He kisses the back of my head. "A surprise?"

I nod my head.

"Look at you being all intriguing and elusive. Do we have time for a few more moments here like this?" he asks.

I nod again and pull his arm tighter around me.

"Can all my mornings please start like this?" he asks after a moment of stillness.

"Think of how many we wasted . . ." I say, trailing my fingertips over his forearm.

"Yeah, let's not do that anymore," he whispers, kissing my neck, my cheek, and every inch of exposed skin.

I don't want to.

Ever.

23

THEO

Bali Elephant Sanctuary
Bali, Indonesia

I don't know what's more terrifying: driving through the chaotic, narrow streets of Bali or the fact that Jo thought it was smart to lend Asher the van.

He's sporadically weaving in and out of morning traffic, and on more than one occasion, I've braced for impact in fear of colliding with another speeding vehicle.

Or worse, a slew of unsuspecting locals.

Thankfully, we arrive at whatever secret location Asher was navigating us to unscathed. I'm not going to officially label him as a bad driver, considering we're in a different country. And even though I'm a big fan of the old ten-and-two driving technique, he gets bonus points for holding my hand the entire time.

But I'm also not going to pretend like I wasn't eternally grateful when the car was safely put in park.

Looking over at Asher, I see genuine excitement written all over his gorgeous face. I've seen him snarky and bothered. Unamused, annoyed, and vulnerable, even. But excited? This feels like a first.

We both exit the car only to reach for each other's hands again and walk in lockstep toward the thick greenery before us.

I hear them before I see them.

"Shut. Up," I say, stopping in my tracks. "Elephants? Are you kidding me?"

Asher's face erupts into the most infectious grin.

"Elephants," he says, yanking my arm and taking off in a run through the rows of palm trees and native plants.

////////////////////////

"Hey, um . . . Theo? A little help here." Asher laughs even though there's a slight panic filling his voice.

We are both sitting in a shallow, tiled kiddie pool with a pair of rambunctious baby elephants who are unintentionally smothering us with excited affection. Their skin is thick and rough but somehow still soft to the touch. Their not-so-little trunks effectively challenge us to back-to-back arm-wrestling contests in search of the pieces of bamboo we were provided by the sanctuary staff, which we quickly ran out of.

My jaw has been on the floor since the very moment we stepped foot in the sprawling elephant sanctuary; never in a million years did I think this was something I'd get to experience in my lifetime.

Let alone with him.

"If the two of you have had enough fun with Alba and Aster over here, we're all set for you at the bathing lake," says

Yanie, our smiling guide. She kneels at the edge of the pool, fresh bamboo in hand. Alba and Aster quickly forget that we exist and clumsily charge toward the snack Yanie offers.

Yanie leads the way through the winding paths of the sanctuary as people hurry through the expansive reserve.

"The grounds are larger than I was expecting," I say to Yanie, venturing alongside her through the thick vegetation.

"Our park is set on almost ten acres of land that's been intentionally landscaped to mimic the native home, Sumatra, of our elephants." She points to the greenery all around us. "As Bali's only dedicated rescue facility, everything we do is to ensure comfort and care for these critically endangered animals."

"Critically endangered?" Asher asks, his face full of concern.

"Unfortunately, in 2012, these elephants' status changed from endangered to critically endangered because in a single generation, half their population was lost due to rapid habitat loss and human conflict."

It's heartbreaking. These gentle giants hold such innocence behind their big eyes, and during our introductory tour earlier, we learned just how intelligent they are.

"But as you can see," Yanie says, leading us through a break in the greenery to reveal the most picturesque man-made lake, "we've done everything we can to create a loving and healthy environment for them where they can live out their days free of harm."

At least a dozen elephants of various sizes are escaping the heat, enjoying their time in the water. The playful trumpeting of their trunks fills the air as they splash around like happy children. It's awe-inspiring and a privilege to witness.

"Theo? Asher? Are you ready to meet your new best pals?"

Yanie steps aside and one of her coworkers leads two larger-than-life elephants through the shallows of the water. We step toward the lake's edge and Asher squeezes my hand.

"Asher, I'd like to introduce you to Bernie," Yanie says, patting the elephant to her right. Asher drops my hand to reach out and greet his new companion. He cranes his neck while petting the side of Bernie's big head, the most radiant smile on his face. My heart swells.

"And Theo, this big guy right here is Juno."

I step forward and give Juno a courteous bow, which causes everyone to laugh. "It's a pleasure to meet you, kind sir!" Juno appears to appreciate the formality of my greeting and wraps his heavy trunk around my torso, which I'm choosing to believe is his version of a hug.

"Feel free to give them a scrub with those," Yanie says, pointing to the oversize brushes on our right. "We'll let you all get acquainted."

Juno and Bernie stand side by side while Asher and I grab a brush and uncoil the hose to get to work. I'm honestly shocked he hasn't muttered a single word about the heat or the mud or even the flies I'm just now noticing, but I take that as a sign he might *actually* be enjoying himself. We work in tandem, Asher spraying the elephants' rough and muddy skin and me following behind with a brush, scrubbing them down.

"Isn't this incredible?" Asher shouts over his shoulder, excitedly pointing out the elephants lounging in the water to our left, showering one another with their long trunks.

"It's . . . surreal." It's like a scene from a movie or straight out of a nature documentary.

I watch as both Bernie and Juno dip their impressive trunks into the water pooling at their feet and point them in our direction, showering Asher and me with a watery sneak attack.

"Go ahead and take a dip!" Yanie shouts from where she sits farther down the shoreline.

"What do you say, Ash? Down for a swi . . ." But before I can even finish my sentence, Asher drops the hose and takes off toward the water. I don't know who this adventurous person is that's seemingly body-swapped with my little indoor cat, but I love it.

Reaching forward, I give Juno an ear scratch of appreciation before running off to join Asher. But Bernie and Juno appear to lose interest in us and mosey on their way to join their real friends, leaving Asher and me alone to bob up and down in the lake.

"Can you even beli—" he starts when I meet him where he's treading water.

Now's not the time to talk. I crush my lips to his, cutting him off, and wrap my arms around him as we both struggle to tread water. I pour every ounce of appreciation and feeling I have into him. His lips turn upward into an uncontrollable smile against mine as he weaves his fingers through my wet hair.

"Thank you for this," I say, loosening my grip on him slightly so we don't accidentally drown and cause a scene. I know in my heart that a simple thank-you doesn't even begin to cut it, but it's all I've got right now. "This just might be the best day of my life."

"Honestly? Mine too." Asher kisses me on the cheek, his smirk widening as he starts swimming after Bernie and Juno. "Come on!"

I laugh and follow him, still taken off guard by his spontaneity. If there's one thing I've learned after getting to know Asher, it's not to underestimate him.

We lounge in the shallow waters, feeding the elephants

bamboo and random chunks of fruit and vegetables to their hearts' content and laughing when they spray us from their trunks. We kiss behind a small waterfall and hold hands like real boyfriends do, and not once do I question whether any of this is real.

"So, you and me," I finally ask, my arms tight around Asher. His hair is wild and he's got flecks of mud on both cheeks, but he's never looked more stunning. "We're really doing this, huh?"

"Only if you promise to bring me some mozzarella sticks," he teases, but then gently cups my cheeks and claims my lips.

This day came completely out of left field. But it was everything I didn't know I wanted. And after today and last night, it's getting harder to imagine a future where I don't find comfort when his hand is in mine.

Where his smile isn't the first and last thing I hope to see each day.

A future where Asher Bennett isn't my person.

24

ASHER

Mahagiri Resort Nusa Lembongan—Room 416
Bali, Indonesia

don't want to get up.

Because that means I have to untangle myself from Theo's warm arms and face another elimination. Only Bianca and Jackson, Jenn and Ellie, and Theo and I are left at this point. We've been on the chopping block a few times before, but now, this close to the finals, I can't shake the feeling we might not get so lucky to be saved again.

So I decide against it and nuzzle up closer to him.

Theo stirs behind me, his strong arms still wrapped tightly around me. "We need to get up, mister," I say, turning my head so that I can plant several kisses along his jawline. He hasn't shaved in a few days—neither of us have—but I love the burn his scruff leaves along my skin.

"Mmm, don't make me," he groans.

He pushes his hips toward me—oh, *something* is up—and instantly, my mind starts wandering to the ways he made my eyes clamp shut in ecstasy last night. "No, no, no . . . if you start that, we'll *never* leave this bed."

Theo kisses my neck at the same time his big hand grips my hip, gently positioning his dick against my ass. "Would that . . . be such a . . . bad thing?" he asks between lingering kisses, and each one makes me more and more inclined to say fuck the competition and let Theo fuck *me* instead.

I turn toward him, pushing him onto his back and straddling his body. Theo instinctively places both hands on my waist, holding me firmly in place on top of him—something I will *never* complain about—but I grab them, bringing them up above his head, and pin them there.

Leaning down, I trail my tongue along the edge of his lips before kissing him deeply. "Of course that wouldn't be a bad thing," I say against his mouth, my voice barely a whisper. "But today is the *one* day we have to be on time. Jo will kill us if we aren't."

He's looking up at me with the most dangerous grin on his face. "I hope you know how fucking sexy you are." He gently thrusts upward, pushing his throbbing cock forward. Theo's fighting against me, so I tighten my grip on his hands. "I think I can confidently say that last night"—he leans up, straining to kiss me—"was the best sex I've ever had."

I laugh, and in my momentary distraction, he breaks free from my grip and he pulls me into to him so that our chests are pressed together.

"Oh, please . . ."

"I'm serious, Asher . . . It was . . ." He reaches up as he lets his words trail off, grabbing a fistful of hair at the base of my neck and crashing his lips to mine. Nothing about his touch is strained right now, and when he deepens our kiss, sliding his tongue against mine and sucking on my lower lip, I know that he's not wrong.

Last night *was* in fact the best sex I've ever had, and if he keeps kissing me like this, we're about to have a repeat performance—something I want more than anything but know we don't have time for.

"Theo . . ." I moan against his lips, feeling my body naturally grind against his.

"I know, I know . . ." He kisses me softly and while we both *clearly* want this, there isn't a hint of disappointment on his lips. "I don't think I've told you this before . . ." he says, now cradling my face in his hands. "But I hope you know you always look so beautiful in the morning." He runs his hand through my hair, which I'm sure is standing up in a million different directions. "You look wild and rested and . . ."

"And what?"

"Espléndido."

I don't know what to say to his sweet compliment without ruining the moment with my inadequate words. Instead, I kiss him once more—a slow and lasting kiss that I hope conveys a fraction of what he means to me—before ripping the covers off us and pulling him toward the shower.

//////////////////////

Theo and I could probably break a record for how fast we got ready.

I was incredibly proud of how we were both able to shower, shave—a small part of me already misses Theo's scruff—and inhale a quick continental breakfast, blueberry oatmeal for him, toast with peanut butter for me, before meeting Jo and Arthur at the hotel entrance.

"Morning, Arthur," I say when I see them. Much like Theo, Arthur isn't a morning person, and it usually takes several cups of coffee for his cheerful demeanor to make an appearance.

Jo, on the other hand, is all smiles, leaning against the van. As Theo and Arthur begin loading our bags, she keeps looking at me. *She knows.*

"Well, hello, Asher. Someone looks well . . . rested," she says, adding a wink to really solidify the fact that she knows I know *she* knows.

I stick my tongue out at her. "Mm-hmm. The most rested."

"I'm sure." She loops her arm in mine, forcing me to lean against the van with her. "So?"

"Can we *not* do this?"

"Oh, come on . . . they can't hear us," she whispers. We both look back at Theo and Arthur, who are still loading the bags in a comfortable silence. "How was it?"

"I haven't the faintest idea what you could be referring to."

Jo nudges me with her shoulder. "It's gonna be like that, huh? After everything I've done for you both. After all the strings I had to pu—"

"Okay, okay," I say, quickly interrupting her before her voice gets any louder.

"It was everything you'd expect from Theo," I whisper, even though I know there's no way the others can hear me. "All-consuming, over the top, and just . . . incredible." I can feel myself blushing—*gross*—but I'm tired of trying to hide the smile that he brings out of me.

"You know . . ." she says, leaning her head on my shoulder as Arthur loads the last bag into the back of the van. "If I didn't know any better, I'd say that you somehow stumbled upon something real here, Asher."

That word continues to haunt me.

Real.

"You really think life works that way, huh?" I ask.

"Of course I do."

She lets go of my arm as Arthur and Theo round the back of the van. Theo gives me a soft smile before opening the door and climbing in.

But what if it does?

I climb in after Theo, claiming my seat next to him, and he naturally puts his hand on my leg. It's comforting and foreign and exhilarating all at the same time, an act so small that I doubt he even meant for it hold any significance. But sitting here, on yet another van ride to who knows where, this simple gesture is the only thing calming my nerves.

Since this is the elimination that determines which teams will be advancing to the finals, production has pulled out all the stops, ensuring the wow factor is amped to an all-time high. Jo informed us that previously eliminated contestants would be involved in today's elimination ceremony, but she wasn't at liberty to share how.

"Alright, I'm going to need the two of you to wait here," Jo says after leading us to a makeshift greenroom, her invisible producer hat now very firmly in place. "I know there's a lot going on, but just stay together and I will come grab you when it's time to head out. Cool?"

We both nod.

I'm not used to feeling this much gratitude and appreciation. I've lived most of my life deeply rooted in logic, knowing without a shadow of a doubt that each action of my life will result in a very real equal and opposite reaction. But I don't think Sir Isaac Newton was factoring in matters of the heart when he was hypothesizing his third law. He most certainly never knew a Theo Fernandez because if he did, he'd know that every action could result in a multitude of equally conflicting and enticing reactions that only confuse you further.

I look over at Theo, who's now sitting in a plastic folding chair and fiddling with the strap of his backpack, meticulously rolling it between his strong fingers. I've known from the second I met him that there was something special about him, from the way he sees the world to the way he acts before he thinks. But most important, I've learned to *never* doubt his gut.

I see Theo Fernandez—all of him. Flawed and brave and insecure and perfect and someone I don't know how I'm going to part with.

I take the seat next to him but quickly position it to face him. I take his hands in mine. There's no surprise in Theo's expression, and on some level, I think he's been over here thinking the same thoughts I have, which makes my chest ache.

"Theo, I hope you know . . ."

"Don't," he says, squeezing my hands. "Seriously, you don't have to say anything."

There's a vulnerability in the softness of his voice that makes me want to hug him.

"But I want to." I reach up and place a hand on his cheek. He leans in to my touch, closing his eyes. "Theo, I can't thank you enough for agreeing to do this with me. For dropping quite literally everything for some random stranger you met at the airport—I could have been a serial killer!"

"The jury's still out on that one."

"I'm serious . . . No matter what happens today, I just want you to know that I couldn't have done any of this without *you*. All this has been worth it only because of you, so even if we're not here, I still want . . . this," I say, placing a hand on his chest.

He opens those big, beautiful eyes and stares so intently back into mine that all I can think is . . .

Real.

Theo opens his mouth to speak, but Jo's voice is the only one either of us hear.

"Look alive, boys . . . It's go time!" she says, barreling into the room, mouthing *Sorry* in my direction after sensing her arrival interrupted a moment between us. But I can't hold it against her. This is her job, after all, one she does exceedingly well, even if her down-to-the-second punctuality constantly keeps me on my toes.

He shrugs, slowly standing but keeping my hand in his, which feels appropriate for both this moment and the cameras. We walk side by side behind Jo, ready to face whatever fate this elimination will bring. I focus on the feeling of him slowly sliding his thumb over my knuckles.

While the show isn't filmed with an actual audience present, there's an electrifying buzz in the air tonight.

And now, only three pairs remain.

Bianca and Jackson, who are obnoxiously waving to the cameras like a matching set of pageant queens from hell, have been just one step ahead of us this entire time.

Jenn and Ellie, to everyone's surprise, have miraculously climbed the leaderboard. Everyone loves an underdog, and if we must lose this competition to anyone, I pray it's them, because they are more than deserving. And have souls . . . unlike Bianca and Jackson.

And then there's Theo and me—the fake boyfriends who against all odds managed to land ourselves in the final three.

We join the other two pairs on stage, and looking around, I truly feel like we're part of a television production. There are large screens above us and more lights and cameras than I've ever seen. It's . . . intense.

Dalton McKnight, who I could have sworn just took a long swig from a flask before jamming it back in his pocket, appears before us in tailored athleisure.

"Quiet on the set," someone yells from beyond my vantage point.

I hate that I'm nervous, but selfishly, I really want this. I haven't allowed myself to think about the possibility of winning this damn thing, but being this close to the finish line? Yeah, I want it.

"We're streaming in three . . . two . . . one . . ." The phantom voice trails off, Dalton's cue to step into the spotlight. Like he's ever left.

"Welcome back to another exciting episode of *The Epic Trek*. Together, we've watched as these three teams have battled against the elements, worked together to complete every challenge thrown their way, and even surprised us all with an epic love story." His eyes shift in our direction and his magnetic front-man facade melts away for a fraction of a second, replaced by something that resembles a sneer. *What the hell?*

"And on tonight's special livestreamed episode, we will unfortunately be saying goodbye to one of our beloved duos," he continues without skipping a beat. "But before we get to the official portion of this evening, let's take a look back at some of this season's most memorable highlights."

Camera one on contestants.

The screens surrounding us spring to life, and both Jenn and Ellie jump at the sudden thunder of background music.

Okay, so did I. As the season montage begins, I watch Dalton slip off the stage and disappear into the group of crew members. I try not to give him *any* thought, but he's acting cagier than normal, which makes my already heightened stress spike.

Theo squeezes my hand, gently bringing my attention back to the screen in front of us. It's weird watching it all play back—seeing us struggle and flounder and argue as we make our way through the various challenges.

I cringe when the clip of my snake-challenge debacle fills the frame. Everyone laughs at my very visible discomfort—*great*—but then the camera shifts to Theo.

I can't take my eyes off him.

He has the most genuine concern plastered all over his face . . . I fight the urge to lunge at on-screen Theo and wrap my arms around him. To tell him no one has ever looked at me the way he does.

Camera two on Dalton.

"This has been one of the most intense seasons in *The Epic Trek* history," Dalton says, stepping back into the spotlight, a phrase I'm certain I've heard him say on each and every season. "Bianca, Jackson, Ellie, Jenn, Theo, and Asher . . . it has been a privilege to watch you all push yourselves to the limit and come this far in the competition."

He pauses dramatically, letting the cameras pan over each pairing. I do my best not to look annoyed when it's our turn, and Theo, who is normally indifferent about the whole thing, gives a little wave.

"The first pair who is safe from elimination and will be advancing to the final leg of the competition is . . ."

Suspenseful music plays from a speaker somewhere in the

distance. The whole production crew is *really* trying to mess with my anxiety today, huh?

"Our front-runners . . . Bianca and Jackson!"

Based on the bravado of Dalton's enthusiasm, you'd think there would be a massive round of applause, but instead, his announcement is met with crickets from the production crew. But per usual, the evil siblings from hell are making a scene and jumping up and down; their celebratory squeals make me gag, literally.

"Which means that Asher and Theo, Ellie and Jenn, one of your journeys will sadly come to an end tonight. Can the four of you please step forward and join me?" he says, opening his arms. We all take our places on either side of him, and the intense heat from his spotlight causes several beads of sweat to roll down my back. No wonder he always looks . . . *moist.*

"Jenn, Ellie . . . our favorite mother-daughter duo from the Midwest. Team Jellie to your fans online," he says, squeezing Ellie's shoulders, and I watch with secondhand nausea as she grimaces at their now even closer proximity. "Some might call you two underdogs—not me, of course," he says with a fakeness that no one is buying. "No, I've always known you two were tough . . . Midwest tough, right?"

I lean in to Theo. "Is that a thing?" I feel him tense while trying to hold back his laugh.

Dalton must have sensed the moment a pair of eyes wasn't on him, because he turns in our direction. "And then there's the stoic Theo and deer-in-headlights Asher, the *lovers* who fans have dubbed *Thasher.*"

Ouch—I mean, he's not wrong, but I don't like hearing that coming from him.

"You two have inspired the world with your love story, and it's just so nice to see two people who are so deeply connec—"

But he's suddenly cut off by someone yelling.

Someone whose voice I'd recognize anywhere.

Someone who was supposed to be standing on this stage next to me.

"Wait! I need to talk to Asher Bennett . . . I have something to say." Clint's overly enunciated voice booms from somewhere behind the production team.

The silence after Clint's interruption is deafening.

No one says anything, but I can see the confusion rippling around those closest to me. Jo, who disappeared after leading us to the stage, steps into my line of sight, a worried expression painted across her face.

Straining to see anything beyond our spotlight, I hear someone whisper, "Quiet on the set."

I hear people struggling, the scuff of their shoes on the wood of the platform below.

And when he finally steps into my view, I see the man who left me at the airport.

The man who, just weeks prior, obliterated my entire world and turned his back on me.

"Asher, I made the biggest mistake," Clint says, straightening his bunched-up shirt, a small sign that someone at least tried to stop him. Truthfully, I can't tell you the last time I thought about Clint, but as he steps in front of me, close enough that I can smell the cologne I bought him for our last anniversary, every emotion—sadness, bitterness, resentment, abandonment, rage, relief—comes flooding back, sending my nervous system into a state of shock. I instantly freeze.

"What? Clint, I don't know what you're doing here or how

you even knew we'd be here . . ." I look back at Dalton, at the smile spreading wickedly across his face. "But this is not the time—" I can barely get my sentence out before he interrupts me.

"Just give me five minutes, Asher . . . *five minutes,*" he pleads. There's a desperation to his voice—one I don't think I've ever heard before. He takes my silence as his cue to continue.

Why is he here and why isn't anyone stopping this? Shouldn't a swarm of production members or security be descending on him by now? But taking one look at Dalton's smug face— standing there with his arms crossed as Jo and several others appear to be urging him to do something—tells me that no one is going to stop this, because *this* is gold for them.

Dalton wants this.

A spectacle.

"Asher, letting you walk away was the dumbest thing I've ever done and there's absolutely no excuse for it," he says, clasping his hands together aggressively. He's aged—or maybe he's always looked this . . . exhausted and miserable? Seeing him now reminds me just how blind to my own unhappiness I was for all these years, and a wave of regret washes over me again for wasting so much of my life on a man who didn't value me. Especially after spending this time with Theo.

Theo!

He's still got his hand in mine, but he's looking down, and I don't have to be a mind reader to know that he's crawling out of his skin right now. This is the most embarrassing and cringeworthy moment of my entire existence, and I think everyone in this room can feel that. Glancing around at the faces surrounding us, I see a mixed bag of emotions—confusion, shock, concern.

"What we have—what we had . . ." he says, correcting himself. "It's something that is deserving of a second chance. It's worth fighting for. *You* are worth fighting for. I want our old life back. I want to go back to the way things were before that stupid moment at the airport when everything changed for us. Can we please go back to that? *Please?*"

Never in a million years did I think I'd see the day when Clint would resort to begging—especially for a man . . . he's always had this confusing air of superiority to him. His eyes gleam with sincerity, and if I didn't know any better, I'd think he genuinely believed the words coming out of his mouth, which under previous circumstances would have moved me to tears.

But now?

I feel nothing. A deep and permanent numbness now lives where anything remotely resembling love for Clint used to be rooted. I feel . . . indifferent.

I *know* in my heart that what I had with Clint is something that I would never return to. It was monotonous and surface-level and truly only benefited him.

If I'm being honest, it was painfully boring.

"Clint, please . . . let's just . . ."

But per usual, he ignores me and turns to Dalton instead. "Now," he says, which prompts Dalton to whisper something to a nearby PA. Stepping forward once more, Dalton seems to be resuming his hosting responsibilities despite the chaos Clint's arrival has caused.

"We've got quite the surprise planned for you, Asher." Dalton's announcer voice returns. I watch in horror as the oversize television screens spring back to life one by one, revealing the last faces on earth I would want subjected to this shit storm. "We couldn't let your family miss out on this beautiful reunion!" I don't think I've ever seen Dalton this happy—he's beaming and practically floating on a very visible cloud nine.

This *cannot* be happening.

My father has a pained expression on his face and his arms crossed, either confused or annoyed.

My younger brother looks bored, like he'd much rather be watching college basketball than whatever his dweeb of a brother has gotten himself into.

And my poor mother, with her hands clasped over her mouth, does her best but fails miserably at not letting every emotion have its turn on her face. She quickly waves when we make eye contact, but I know *she knows* this is the worst thing that could be happening to me.

There's no way they would knowingly agree to something like this, and as I try to figure out what lie Clint or Dalton even told them, my legs get dangerously close to giving out.

"Asher, you and I are perfect for each other . . ." Clint resumes from his spot in front of Theo and me.

We most *certainly* are not. I think I hear my dad huff on camera.

"We make each other better."

More like I made you a fraction less insufferable.

"And if you'll have me . . ." Clint drops to his knee at the same time I drop Theo's hand.

Fuck fuck fuck . . . no! What the fuck are you doing? I scream, except not a single sound escapes my lips. I am *literally* frozen in place, and as many times as I might have envisioned this moment with Clint in the past, seeing him here, a breath away from asking me a question there is no coming back from, makes me more anxious and uncomfortable than I've ever been before. I don't know what I hear first—the audience gasping or Clint stupidly asking me to marry him.

My blood feels like it's boiling, and it's entirely possible I might vomit out of sheer embarrassment. A marriage proposal on live television? Just when I thought it couldn't get worse, Clint finds a way to reach a whole new level of cringe. Theo hasn't uttered a single word, but I can feel his eyes watching me with laser-like focus.

I open my mouth to speak, but of course, nothing comes out. Part of me feels that a bout of hysterical laughter and/or tears is coming.

That, or a long-overdue cussing out.

But instead, I stand tomato red and in painfully awkward silence as America, the audience and crew, my annoyed parents, and poor Theo watch me leer at a still-kneeling Clint. I finally regain control of my body and glance over at Theo, who has hurt and confusion etched all over his handsome face, but still, I say nothing.

He shakes his head. "Fuck this," he hisses and storms off.

The room starts to spin when Theo disappears from my view.

Every fiber of my being is screaming for me to chase after him, but my muscles lock and my jaw clenches instead. I realize what I'm experiencing is the start of a panic attack.

"I . . . I need to . . ." My words fail me as I crane my neck to see if I can somehow make out Theo in the distance. After everything we've been through, every terrifying challenge and endless travel day and countless sleepless nights, he's become my comfort and my home and the only person whose hand I want to be holding when life gets too hard. *I need Theo.*

"So . . . is that a yes?" Clint is still on his knee, and the callousness behind his question brings every drop of my blood to a raging boil.

"Let me get this straight," I finally snap, the use of each limb slowly starting to return. I take a step forward, towering over him for the first time in our relationship. "You thought that you'd show up here unannounced, mutter some half-assed words about second chances that I can guarantee you don't actually believe or want, and what . . . I'd just come diving back into your open arms because . . . that would be easier for you?"

"Well, I . . ."

"Because, sure, Clint . . . I genuinely believe in second chances. I think that people and relationships are deserving of them when mistakes are made and a do-over can make all the difference."

He smiles, and I hate how ignorant he is of this entire situation.

"But you? Us? There is nothing to do over, Clint. I threw everything I had into our relationship. I whittled away the best parts of myself so that you could shine, and even then, you . . . our entire relationship . . . was lackluster at best." I watch his face redden in embarrassment. I'm truly not trying to be mean, because what's the point in that? But he needs to hear this, because on some level, he believes with his entire heart that he is entitled to me. "So, to answer the question you so humiliatingly asked me at some weird event you somehow orchestrated—that you shamefully included my family in . . . No, Clint, I will not and have no desire to marry you. Because marriage is a partnership, and you are incapable of loving anyone as much as you love yourself. Now please move so that I can go find my boyfriend . . ."

Boyfriend. Now seems like the worst time to get hung up on the fact that I've never called Theo that . . . and meant it. With the conflicting emotions and the out-of-nowhere drama, even for reality television, I definitely shouldn't be feeling butterflies the size of fighter jets in my stomach right now. *Right?*

Dalton takes a calculated step toward us, ensuring he's now directly in the frame of the camera that has been rolling this entire time. "But he isn't your boyfriend, is he, Asher?"

I have always been a firm believer that violence, especially unprovoked, is never the right answer, but I find myself praying for a little cosmic karma to help me out and wipe the smug look off Dalton's face.

Before I can walk around Clint, he stands to block my exit. "You are unbelievable. While you've been traversing the globe pretending to be this happy couple . . ." He takes another step closer to me. "Did you think about how *I* would feel about that? Do you have any idea how humiliating this has been for me? How many people *I've* had to answer to while you've been off whoring yourself out to some second-rate, corn-fed . . ." He grabs my arm like he did in the airport, pulling me toward him *hard*.

His grip on my arm sets several things in motion.

Jenn and Ellie, who have awkwardly been standing in the wake of all this, are immediately at my side staring daggers at him.

Jo, who's looked unsure whether she should intervene, comes barreling onto the stage, followed closely by two production security officers.

I can hear my father aiming a string of obscenities in Clint's direction through the screen.

He quickly removes his hand from my arm, putting both of them up as the security guards grab him.

"Go home, Clint," I say quietly. I'm emotionally drained and embarrassed and need to find Theo. "There's nothing for you here."

As he's escorted off the stage, I walk in the opposite direction after Theo. I have no idea where he's run off to but I have to find him.

"Asher, wait . . . I don't even know what to say," Jo whispers as she quickly catches up to me. "I am so sor—"

"I really don't want to hear it, Jo," I mutter without stopping or looking at her. I can guarantee that Jo had absolutely no knowledge of what just took place, but I am so exhausted and all I want to do is put as much distance between me and this stupid show as humanly possible. "If you care about me at all, just let me go."

She puts our friendship, if you can even call it that, before the show and lets me walk alone through the complicit crew members.

Where are you, Theo?

25

THEO

Mahagiri Resort Nusa Lembongan
Bali, Indonesia

I feel like I'm going to be sick.

One, for being subjected to that disgusting, demeaning public reunion.

And two, for allowing myself to actually believe there was a chance Asher had feelings for me. Real, genuine feelings.

But seeing Clint show up like that and get down on one knee, and watching Asher contemplate his proposal, was all too much. The lack of an immediate and hard no from Asher very abruptly reminded me that Asher probably hadn't fully moved on. And now that Clint wanted him back, whatever we had been building toward didn't mean much in comparison.

No one tried to stop me when I ran offstage. They all just let me go, either in solidarity or secondhand embarrassment. Now I'm running as fast as I can, faster than I've run in my entire life, to put as much distance between myself and *them* as possible—past all the excess camera equipment and lighting boxes.

When I finally make it to the row of parked vehicles, Arthur, who's leaning against our van, making no effort to hide the lit cigarette between his lips like he normally does, says nothing when I rip open the passenger-side door.

He rounds the van and silently gets in the driver's seat. "Where to?"

"The airport."

"You sure about that, son?"

Arthur isn't a man of many words—it's something I've come to appreciate about him, because far too often, people feel the need to fill every single second with the sound of their own voice. Not Arthur. He speaks when he has something important to say . . . no more, no less.

"Please just drive."

And he does. We sit in silence as he pulls away from the set. Away from Asher and everything we have worked toward the last several weeks. Away from the prize money and the interviews and everything that comes with being on a reality competition show.

Away from the heartbreak.

Because that's what this ache in my chest is, right? Total and utter heartbreak? Not to be confused with the debilitating humiliation I feel or the embarrassment washing over me when I think about Asher with Clint.

No, this is most certainly heartbreak—something I've strived to avoid feeling for a long time, and despite every intention of *not* falling for Asher, I did, and I'll never forgive myself.

It frightens me to think about how quickly I allowed myself

to get wrapped up in Asher. This competition, despite the thrills and the grueling obstacles, showed me that I could open up to someone. That I was capable of letting them in and sharing parts of me that I'd convinced myself were better off hidden away.

I allowed myself to believe I was worthy of love.

But none of that matters now because I'm sure Asher and Clint have already rekindled whatever was left of their toxic relationship, and everyone is swooning over this made-for-TV fairy-tale moment. *Dalton must be loving this.*

Arthur glances away from the road in my direction.

I hold his gaze a beat longer than usual before looking away, turning to the window and the city passing by. I hear a light sigh escape him before he clears his throat.

"I know I don't say much or give my two cents to you boys too often," he says, his voice steady. "But listen to me for a moment, Theo. No rash decisions made in the heat of moment, out of anger or fear or whatever it is you're feeling right now, ever tend to be the right ones."

"I can't . . ." I start, but he removes a hand from the wheel, and interrupts me.

"Take it from someone who's on the move more often than not, son," he says, a sad honesty in his tone. "If you're going to run, make sure you know what you're actually running from."

He doesn't say another word.

We continue driving, and the lights of the airport in the distance eventually make their appearance, a beacon of impending freedom from what's now turned into an instant nightmare. Arthur pulls off the highway, following the *Departure* signs, which loop us toward yet another terminal.

We've spent the better part of the last three weeks in airports, but this time, I don't have to worry about Asher getting lost or complaining that he doesn't have enough snacks.

This time, I'm alone.

//////////////////////

After sixteen hours of intercontinental travel, middle seats, and back-to-back delayed flights, I take an Uber from the small regional airport down familiar tree-lined roads before being dropped off at my childhood home. Grabbing my duffel from the trunk—which was thankfully prepacked ahead of elimination—I take in the lake house before me. The rustic shingles are exactly how I remember them, and the natural stone gleams in the last remnants of moonlight. The ivy on the side of our two-story home is overgrown in some areas, and I can see the subtle glimpses of fireflies dancing down by the dock. As much as I hate to admit it, there's something special about Madison in the summertime. There's a sweetness in the air, one you don't get anywhere else. I walk up the moss-covered pavers toward the soft-yellow front door of the home that raised me. I can see a warm light coming from the kitchen.

Someone's awake.

Someone who I haven't seen in person for many years.

Someone I pray is happy for this unannounced early-morning visit.

I can't tell you the last time I stood outside this door, the one that was always decorated with a larger-than-life wreath for each and every season. I look to the far end of the long porch and see that the American flag is still hung in the same spot between the two white rocking chairs. I smile at the memory of my father raising it when I went off to boot camp all those years ago. Honestly, I don't think I'd ever seen him that proud—when I decided to serve the country his family came to in search of a better life.

But that was before everything changed.

When I was discharged from the Navy, being loved by them suddenly felt like walking on eggshells. It killed me to be away from them when I needed them the most. But at the time, it felt like the best thing to do for everyone. It felt easier.

But being back here again, surrounded by the stillness of what once was, I'm not so sure that was the right decision.

"*Theo?*" My mamá's voice breaks behind me, a sound that ricochets in my chest with an immediate sadness and overwhelming love. I hadn't heard the door open, but the second I turn to face her, she runs across the porch toward me, her soft flannel robe trailing behind, and wraps me in the tightest mom hug. She smells like coffee and floral perfume, and I can tell that even though it's summer, she's been sitting by the lit stovetop fireplace on our back patio.

She smells like home.

"Hi, Mamá," I say, resting my cheek on the top of her head. She squeezes me tightly and sobs against my chest. I know my mother—I'm sure she's convincing herself that if she just holds on to me tight enough, I won't leave again. The thought makes my eyes water. "Oh, Mamá . . . don't cry."

We stand holding each other in the quiet morning light as the sun starts to peek over Lake Mendota. Just as quickly as summers spent on the water with family come crashing to the forefront of my mind, guilt comes rushing after it—at all this time spent apart.

"What . . . what are you doing here, Theo?" my mother asks after a moment, her eyes bright despite the redness. She wipes them with the sleeve of her robe while still holding on to me. Looking at her round face, I can see she's aged gracefully. I've spent my entire life being asked if I was Carla Fernandez's younger brother, a comment that she sure reminded my sister and I of whenever it came up. *Which was often.*

"Can't a guy come home to surprise his mother?"

But really, there's no point in even trying. She's looking at me with the same knowing eyes she's had my entire life. The ones that have always been able to sift through whatever nonsense her children, or anyone for that matter, were trying to convince her of. Like the time in my freshman year of high school when she knew with a single look that Bobby Hale and I weren't *really* going with his family on an overnight camping trip but instead trying to sneak into a senior party to drink for the first time.

"Come on, mijo," she says, patting me on the side of the face before taking my hand and leading me through the front door. "Let's go inside. I'll put on some more coffee, and you can tell me all about it."

My mother busies herself with the coffeepot, the same one my family has had for years, as I take a seat at the wooden kitchen island. I run my index finger beneath the counter, looking for the initials my sister, Elise, and I carved into it with the small pocketknife my abuelo gave me before he passed away. *TF & EF.* If our parents knew about it, they never said anything. It was our little secret. Elise has been, and always will be, my secret keeper—just like I was hers.

"Are you in trouble again?" My mother's back is still turned to me, but I can tell she's nervous to ask.

"No, Mamá . . . It's nothing like that."

"Then what is it, son?" she asks, turning around to face me. Her brown eyes are filled with tears again, and I can see the confusion and hurt in them.

So I tell her everything.

Mostly about Asher. How we met in the airport for the first time, how he looked like he needed someone to be in his corner, and how for reasons I still cannot explain, I couldn't imagine *not* being that person.

I tell her about pretending to be his boyfriend and the hoops we had to jump through to get Jo on our side and all the initial drama the change-up caused.

I tell her about how Asher made me feel—like really *feel*—and it's not lost on me that until now, I've never really talked to my mom about a boy. You'd think that I would be terrified, but the more I talk about Asher, the more at peace I feel.

Sitting in the kitchen, talking to my mom about a boy I'm clearly crazy about over coffee? It feels right. It feels like growth and acceptance and a version of self-love I never thought I would be capable of experiencing.

"You seem happy, mi amor," my mother says, reaching across the kitchen island and taking my hand in hers. "And that makes *me* happy. But Theo . . . you still didn't really answer my question. If everything with this Asher boy is going so well, then what are *you* doing *here*?"

That does appear to be the million-dollar question, huh?

"It's . . . *complicated*" is all I can muster, which isn't a lie. Because, well . . . it is complicated, and before she can twist my arm into getting more details, our private morning is interrupted by my father, who saunters into the kitchen, blissfully unaware of the fact that his black sheep of a son has returned.

"Good morning, querido," he says, coming up behind my mother and wrapping his arms around her, dramatically kissing her on her neck and cheeks like I've seen him do countless times before.

"Alejandro, *quit it!*" My mother's playful objection to his affection makes me laugh, because I know she thrives on the attention. After more than thirty years together, society would have us believe they should be light-years away from the honeymoon phase, but not my parents. They are just as obsessed with each other as they were the day they met.

I clear my throat, hoping to stop my father's very clear morning intentions from becoming a public reality.

When he finally notices me, it's like he's seen a ghost.

"Mijo!" The shock nearly swallows every decibel of his voice. Rushing around the kitchen island to close the distance between us, he nearly knocks my mother's coffee right out of her hands. "*Mijo,*" he sobs, swallowing me in his big arms.

"I've . . . missed you . . . so much, my boy," he says, squeezing me tighter between each choked word. He smells like Cuban cigars and fresh sawdust, just like he always has. No matter how many showers the man has, the distinct aroma of his woodworking shed has permanently fused to his skin.

"I've missed you too, Papá." Every ounce of pain and loss and longing and anger that I've felt over the last couple of years comes rather unexpectedly to the surface. Without permission or any advance warning, my sobs now echo his and I cling to him like I used to as a child.

/////////////////

"Is he dead?"

Frankie's failed attempt at a whisper pulls me toward consciousness. There's an edge of concern to my nephew's voice.

"Didn't you hear him snoring all night? He's definitely not dead," his sister hisses back. Lola is every bit Elise's daughter with her well-intentioned directness.

"*Pssst*, Tío Dos," Frankie whispers, closer this time. They've called me that their entire lives. It began when Lola first started talking. She struggled with the *th* sound in *Tío Theo*, so she'd run around saying *Tío Tío*. Once they both got a little older, though, the family just swapped the second *tío* for *dos*, essentially earning me the nickname of Uncle Two.

He pokes the side of my face. "Mmm," I groan, which makes them giggle. As much as I would kill for another hour or ten of sleep, I love that they want to spend time with me.

"Move. I know what will wake him," I hear Lola say. "Wakey wakey, Tío Dos . . . Daddy made cinnamon rolls." Damn. She knows me too well. My mouth starts to water. *Touché, Lola.*

Everyone in the family fell in love with Stefan's charm and good looks when Elise brought him around all those years ago. Not me. I was skeptical at first, as any brother should be, right?

Until I ate his cooking.

The man is a god in the kitchen.

Which makes sense, considering he's a chef, but his baked goods literally changed my life. At first bite, I was practically planning their wedding for them.

"Morning, munchkins," I say, rubbing the sleep out of my eyes. Frankie hops up on the bed, a wide grin exploding across his face, and launches into my arms. I need to soak up every moment of the guncle love, because I know it won't always be like this. "What do you remember about your dreams?"

Frankie cuddles up and spends the next ten minutes telling me about his battle against dragon aliens and a talking spaceship. Lola sits on the edge of the bed, listening. Even though she rolls her eyes several times at her brother's excited chatter, even she can't hide her growing smile.

I've missed this.

Home.

The warmth of family and being in their lives like this. Being present as Frankie and Lola grow up. As Elise and Stefan continue to be the picture-perfect couple they've always been. As Mom and Dad get older.

I feel guilty. I've wasted so much time holding on to the past in fear of what that meant for my future. And for what?

To make *my* life easier? To avoid confronting my own fear?

"Come on," I say when Frankie wraps up what seems to be part two of his out-of-this world adventure. I rip the blankets off the bed dramatically and scoop them both into my arms, which sends their adorable giggles ricocheting off every surface. "Let's go get some of those delicious cinnamon rolls."

We slowly make our way downstairs, passing wall after wall of treasured family photos. Looking at our family at various milestones is like peering into a time capsule of a life.

Stefan is bent over the kitchen island when we reach the bottom of the stairs. He's carefully layering thick icing on an oversize tray of cinnamon rolls. They smell fresh out of the oven and there's something comforting about the sweet aroma filling the room, so familiar to family and cozy weekend mornings.

As soon as Frankie eyes the cinnamon rolls, he becomes restless. "Daddy, are they ready?"

"Just about, mijo," Stefan says without looking up from the tray before him. I set Frankie on one of the five barstools at the long kitchen island and lower Lola to the ground, their eyes glued to the rich bowl of icing.

Lola quickly swipes a finger into the bowl and plops it into her mouth before Stefan can object.

"Cariña, be patient," he says, shaking his head with a grin.

Lola hugs him around the waist and Stefan sets down the spoon he was using. "Nice bedhead," Stefan says, padding over in my direction and greeting me with a big hug.

He's never shied away from affection, which is a major green flag in my eyes. There have been plenty of Elise's exes who always seemed uncomfortable around her gay little brother. Some would make it a point to offer an extra-firm handshake or give incredibly cold one-armed bro hugs the second I came around. Not Stefan.

From day one, he couldn't help but showcase his natural warmth with every single one of our family members, and it's something I'll always be appreciative of. More male-on-male affection normalcy, please. "Where's everyone else?" I ask when he finally lets me go.

"Your parents went to pick up some carne asada for later," he says, heading back to the kitchen island, "and Elise is at your spot."

I turn my head toward the lake. Stefan grabs a few plates from the cabinet and uses a spatula to serve Lola and Frankie. The cinnamon rolls are as large as their heads, and I don't think I've ever seen them this excited.

"I just put on some coffee, hermano," Stefan says, nodding at the coffeepot. "It should be ready." Bless this man.

I pour us each a mug, handing one to a very appreciative Stefan, and slide two cinnamon rolls onto a plate. Then I sneak out the back door and make my way to the dock while Lola and Frankie are momentarily distracted by their sweets.

I find Elise sitting in one of the two worn Adirondack chairs dad and I built the summer before I went into middle school. Or high school? Beyond being slightly weathered from constant exposure to the elements, they've held up nicely.

She gives me a soft smile when I join her, like she's been waiting for me. I shove nearly half a cinnamon roll in my mouth and pass the plate to Elise.

"If I haven't told you lately that you're my favorite, you most certainly are." She rolls her eyes after taking her own massive bite. "How'd you sleep?" she asks, her mouth full.

"Like the dead."

But truthfully, it felt odd sleeping anywhere without Asher. Hearing his breathing. Feeling the warmth of his arm draped over me. The burn of every sneak-attack kiss he'd place on my neck.

Thinking of him makes it hard to swallow.

". . . until Frankie and Lola decided it was time to get up," I say, a smile spreading across my lips.

"They are the official deciders when it comes to day-starting." Elise reaches over and takes my coffee mug.

"What?" she asks when she sees my mouth agape.

"Nothing's changed with you. Is that . . . my sweatshirt?"

She looks down at the worn Madison West High School crewneck she's wearing. "Seriously? You've not been home in ten thousand years and have lost your claim to anything in your room. Sorry, but whatever you've left behind is fair game."

Can't argue with that.

"Speaking of," she says, tucking a leg underneath her. "How does it feel to be back?"

It's far too early to have this conversation with her. Elise is one of the only people in my life I don't have to worry about being judgmental. But she's also the only person on this planet I can't bullshit. "It's bittersweet. I've missed so much . . ."

"And whose fault is that?"

"You don't need to remind me." I stare off into the lake. The soft morning light dances across the shallow water. "Remember when we decided it would be a good idea to camp out in the canoe?"

A faint smile forms on Elise's face. "I remember *you* deciding to camp in the canoe and me being forced to join against my will. Mom and Dad wouldn't let you do it unless I tagged along."

Even if it was forced at times, she was always looking out for me. When we were kids, it was Elise and me against the world. Two stubborn little messes. She was always guiding me through life, ready to steer me away from harm.

"We were frozen within the first hour," I say, laughing at the memory of the two of us fighting over the single blanket we thought would be enough to keep us warm. "I can still see Dad shaking his head on the dock while we struggled to paddle back in."

I run my hand over the arm of the chair I'm sitting in. I didn't know it at first, but my father had planned to sleep in this very spot. Far away enough to give us the illusion of adventure but close enough to keep an eye on us. Our parents were strict and there were a lot of rules growing up, but somehow, they still managed to let us make our own mistakes and learn from them.

And while neither of them would vocalize it, I'm of the belief they secretly enjoyed having their internal *I told you so* moments whenever either of their children had to learn a lesson the hard way.

"Lola and Frankie are going to be my karma, aren't they?" she says, handing me back my coffee mug.

"Oh, mm-hmm. Most definitely."

Elise's laughter echoes off the lake in loud, thunderous bursts.

"They've really missed their uncle," she says, leaning further into the back of her chair. "We all have."

"I know. I've missed you all so much."

"Are we ever going to talk about it?" she asks after a moment, emotion now filling her voice.

"Why start now, right?" I ask, taking another sip of my coffee.

Her eyes narrow and she tilts her head in my direction. "What's that supposed to mean?"

"It's early," I say, quickly backpedaling and rubbing the back of my neck. "Truly, I didn't mean anything by it."

"No, I think you did," she says, each word more enunciated than the last. "Ay tonto, I swear, hermano." Shit, she's mad.

Or worse, disappointed.

Elise has always felt more like a third parent to me. A bonus guardian who may or may not have had a more direct approach than my actual parents did. And right now, she's sitting straight up in her chair with that third-parent disappointment written all over her face.

She exhales, turning to face me. "Theo, what happened to you was awful. Being outed and exposed the way that you were broke my heart. Lord knows Stefan had to physically put himself between me and our car on more than one occasion as some sort of last-ditch effort to talk me out of driving off, tracking down that clown, and giving him a piece of my mind."

"Seriously?" I say, but it's not at all hard to imagine. Elise is fiercely protective of her family. She always has been.

"That's not the point, dumbass," she snaps. She's also

incredibly sharp-tongued. "If you think for a *second* that we've all just been sitting here turning a blind eye to one of the worst things that's ever happened to you, you're sadly mistaken."

Her big brown eyes stare directly into mine, and I see the hurt and frustration behind them, because on some level, I know it mirrors my own.

"Elise, I . . ." I say, but she cuts me off, holding a hand to my face, and instantly, I'm transported back to the fights we had as teenagers. Drawn-out arguments over who got to use the car on the weekend or whose turn it was to go with Mom to the flea market for the hundredth time.

"Just listen, please," she says. "I love you, little brother, but sometimes, your myopic view of the world and how your family fits into it really clouds your judgment." Ouch.

"I don't think . . ." I start, but she interrupts me.

"Because Theo, I can recall almost every single conversation you and I have had over the last two years, and without fail, you either one," she says, jabbing a finger in my chest to emphasize her point, "tell me about your job or ask me about mine. Or two, give me a full synopsis of the show you're watching."

"In my defense, you *are* a doctor, so I'd consider *that* pretty important."

She scowls at me, expertly moving beyond my attempt at defusing the situation. "Answer this for me. Did you ever go to that therapist I referred you to?"

A scoff escapes me at her intensified line of questioning. "What does that have to do with anything?"

"I'm trying to prove a point. What about that veteran support group I found? The one that specializes in LGBTQIA+ service members," she asks. "Did you ever go and check that out?"

I hadn't thought about either in ages but can recall both

instances clearly. She passed along the information during my depressive fog after separating from active duty, and truthfully, I hadn't given it much thought at the time.

All I can do is shake my head.

"Exactly," she says, the softness in her voice returning. "I sent you those things as an attempt to open the door. To let you know that I was there for you. That after all you'd been through, I was, and always would be, in your corner. Coming out was supposed to be on your terms. It was supposed to be this personal journey that *you* led with the people in *your* life at *your* own pace, and that didn't happen. And it sucks, Theo. It fucking sucks so much, I cannot even imagine how angry you must have felt. Still feel," she adds, correcting herself. "But all of us—Mom, Dad, Stefan—we couldn't force you to talk about a subject we knew was not only deeply personal but exceptionally painful for you when it was clear you had no interest in talking about it. So, we waited. Hoping that eventually, you'd feel safe enough to share when *you* were ready."

"I didn't think you all wanted me to," I blurt out. "I didn't think I could because I . . . I . . ." My voice trails off, because now, I'm recalling every interaction between my family and me.

While I've been sitting here waiting for my parents to acknowledge my identity, they've been waiting for me to acknowledge myself first. Have I really missed out on the last two years because of a . . . *miscommunication?* If I wasn't so confused and throttled by this revelation, I'd laugh at the irony of our situation.

"What are you thinking?" Elise asks after a moment.

"I think I'm more embarrassed than anything." She gives my shoulder a squeeze.

"I'm just going to say this, and then I promise you, we never have to talk about it again." She reaches over and grabs my hand in hers, her grip as cold as it was the night of our canoe-camping fiasco. "Just promise me you won't disappear again . . ." I open my mouth to contest her word choice, but she cuts me off. "Sporadic phone calls and FaceTimes here and there don't count, Theo."

I nod my head. She's right. She always is, and I'm quickly running out of excuses to justify my absence.

"If not for me, then for Mom and Dad. For the kids . . ." Her voice breaks, and the thought of my sweet niece and nephew sends my heart barreling toward my throat.

"I promise," I say, turning my head away from Elise, the tears stinging my tired eyes.

Elise doesn't say anything else but just leans forward in her chair and wraps her arms around my shoulders, letting me turn in to her like I used to when we were kids—awkwardly, given our seating arrangement. "You going to be alright?"

"It's a lot harder being here than I thought it would be," I choke out, my tears now pouring onto Elise's—well, my—sweatshirt. "The guilt from not being here feels like I've gotten the wind knocked out of me and I can't breathe."

She rubs my back like one would to soothe a child. "I don't know if this will make it better or worse for you, baby brother," she says, the calming maternal tone to her voice all too familiar. "But that guilt that you're feeling? You're going to have to learn some way to let that go. It's keeping you rooted in the past. I promise you, Theo—no one is holding a grudge. Not Mom and Dad, certainly not me . . ."

I wipe my eyes on the back of my hands and Elise kisses on the top of my head. "A little home and a little bit of our family chaos will be good for your heart, Theo. You'll see."

Being here with her, in our place, I know she's right.

"Now that we've got *that* out of the way, can you talk to me about what's finally made you come home?"

Here we go. "Seriously, hermana? You couldn't let this very rare, very overdue brother-sister moment last longer than, oh, I don't know, three seconds?"

"Look, you don't want to unpack familial trauma? Fine by me," she says, crossing her arms. "But I would be failing you as a sister if I didn't smack you upside the head right now on behalf of the entire internet and ask: What the hell you were thinking leaving Asher like that?"

"*Me?* Leave Asher?" I shout, pushing up from my chair. "I . . ." I begin, then swallow hard, not really sure where to even start. "It's a little more complicated than that."

"Is it?" she asks. "I need you to explain it to me then, because Theo, I've had my eyes glued to you your entire life and not once have I ever seen you smile the way you did with him."

"You have no idea what you're talking about." I stand up and turn away from her at the edge of the dock.

But, she kinda does. Which irritates me even more.

"Theo, be honest with me," she says, joining me where I stand and putting her arm through mine. "Or at least be honest with yourself, because that's all that matters. You fell for him, didn't you?"

Does it matter? Like, genuinely, looking at this situation as logically as I can, does it matter if I fell for Asher? Even if it was real for me, it wasn't real *enough* for him, and the sooner I accept that, the sooner I can put this whole mess behind me.

"Even if I did, it doesn't change the fact that I was never his. Not really, anyway."

"You don't actually believe that, do you?" Elise says after a moment, leaning her head on my shoulder. "Because I don't. Not after everything we *all* watched you two go through. Not after the . . ."

I reach over and squeeze her hand, silently begging her to stop because my heart can't take talking about Asher anymore. "Elise, please. I can't." My voice is hoarse, and judging by the tears pooling in my sister's eyes, she got the answer she was looking for.

The slam of our parents' back door puts a pin in our conversation.

"Mommy, can I have another cinnaroll?" Frankie shouts, much more loudly than he needs to. His mouth appears to be glazed with the remains of his first one.

Elise groans against me. "Honey? Did you ask your father?" she yells back.

"He said yeah but only if *you* split it with me."

"Oh, he did, huh?" Elise gives me a squeeze before turning to head back to the house. "How will I ever be able to say no to *that* face?"

"Thoughts and prayers, sis."

She makes her way up the wooden steps, pausing before she gets to the top. "I love you, Theo. And I'm so happy you're here."

I smile because I'm happy too.

Happy to be around Elise and her beautiful family. Happy to be with my parents, in a place that is filled with memories around every corner.

Happy I've come home.

26

ASHER

Mahagiri Resort Nusa Lembongan—still in Room 416
Bali, Indonesia

I couldn't tell you if it's been a few hours or a full week since Theo left.

I lie on the pull-out sofa, turning so that my only view is the dark wall. Our king-size bed remains empty. The thought of wrapping myself in the sheets, our sheets, makes me nauseous.

I crush his pillow harder to my chest and inhale the sweet smell of him still lingering on the soft linen. I grabbed it the moment I got back to our room and have held on to it ever since.

Theo.

His expression when Clint dropped to his knee haunts me. It's ingrained in my brain—I've been mentally replaying the pain ripple across his gorgeous face. Cold and alone, I'm desperate to hear him humming in the shower or to feel his hand in mine again.

But he's gone.

He's probably put a couple thousand miles between the two of us now. I would have. His phone is definitely off. Or he's blocked me. Either way, I think I surpassed the record for outgoing calls that went straight to voicemail in an hour window.

I waited for him to come racing back through our hotel room's door. I even called the front desk to make sure an extra key was left in his name just in case he misplaced his. Every sound I heard coming from the hallway made my heart stop, the anticipation of seeing his face sending spikes of adrenaline through my veins. But the moment never came, and it was easier to just succumb to the painful silence of my remorse.

I should have begged. Gotten down on my knees and groveled. Done something, anything, other than just letting him leave. When I should have been screaming that Clint means nothing to me and it's Theo I want to be with, I stood still as a statue, frozen in place and completely debilitated by the humiliation of it all.

Theo, the only man who made me feel something other than doubt and insecurity in who knows how long, left thinking that I'd chosen my past—the one he helped me heal from— over him.

I've spent the better part of my twenties fine-tuning my response to men. Knowing which battles to fight and when to shrug off one-sided tensions was key to every prior relationship. I focused on my professional growth, had as much sex as I thought a good significant other needed, and enthusiastically threw compliments around like confetti. It took years to perfect and was easier than ever to finesse when Clint came into the picture all those years ago.

But all that went out the window when I met Theo, who offered me a mirror. Someone who raised an eyebrow at my bullshit and reflected back every falsehood I tried to wear as a facade.

He called my bluff on that very first day in the airport and has held all the cards since.

I groan. What have I done?

There's a knock on the door. Three solid thumps against the barrier between me and the outside world. I ignore it.

Again, harder this time.

"Please, just go away," I mutter into the pillow.

The peep of the key fob snaps my eyes open. Someone used a key to open the door.

I sit up on the makeshift bed, my heart now firmly lodged in my throat. All the blood rushes to my head, causing my vision to blur. Have I eaten anything? I can't remember.

"Oh hell, you look like shit."

Ellie.

I lay back down, turning away from my unannounced visitor, and wrap myself back around Theo's pillow. "I'm not in the mood, Ellie."

"Are you in the mood to shower, at least? It smells like . . . I don't even know what in here." I don't need to be looking at her to imagine her pinched expression.

I ignore her question. Under normal circumstances, I'd be mortified at someone's insinuation of my bad smell. Right now? I couldn't care less. I'm pretty content continuing my shame spiral, thank you very much.

"Asher, what can I do?" she asks without a trace of her signature sarcasm. She sounds genuinely concerned.

But sadly, there's nothing she could say or do to make the ache in my heart disappear.

I roll over toward her. She's sitting on the edge of the bed, nudging an open pizza box I have no recollection of ordering with her foot. I see her grimace of silent judgment.

"I just want to sleep," I say, covering my eyes with my arm. "Don't you and your mom have to get going anyway?"

"Production has completely halted since . . ." Her voice trails off.

"Since I was humiliated on live television by my asshole of an ex?"

"Well, yeah. *That.* Have you talked to Jo?" I haven't—and frankly, I don't intend to. Ellie gives me a look when I shake my head. "You really should, Asher. She feels awful."

For someone who's prided himself on being a logical and rational thinker, I really am proving quite the opposite now. "There's just . . . *a lot* to unpack here."

Ellie nods, and on some level, she must understand it's not as simple as just talking it out among friends, if we're even considered that, and after everything that went down, I don't know that I want to be. Jo's always been dialed in to *everything* that goes on with this show. Do I believe that she had a hand in orchestrating Clint's sudden appearance and shocking proposal? No. But is there a small part of me that thinks she may have known about it and didn't say anything?

I can't be sure, and that's what's killing me. Jo has talked about ratings and social media engagement and giving the viewers what they want nonstop since the moment I met her. She's literally pushed me and Theo to show more affection and be more playful with each other in the name of good television. Is it really that far-fetched to think her eyes wouldn't light up at the thought of a surprise proposal from a former lover?

"Look, all I know is that since Theo left, Jo has been pacing the lobby, a phone in each hand, trying to make this right." It's easy to picture. As annoyed with her as I am, I'd bet money that Jo Bishop is incredible in a crisis.

"Okay, but . . ." I start, but she interrupts me.

"If Theo means what I think he does to you, and I know you have weeks' worth of photos on your phone that lead me to believe he does, I promise you Jo is the one person who can help you get him back. So do me a favor and just talk to her." Ellie pats my leg, both patronizingly and affectionately.

"No promises," I say, falling back into the bed, but I know she's right.

Ellie gets up to leave, offering one last encouraging smile on her way out. "Oh, and take a shower. Immediately."

"Run along, Ellie. You've been a pleasure, as always," I say, the sound of her laughter lingering before the door shuts between us.

Hauling myself into the bathroom, I crank the shower as hot as it'll go and climb in. The last time I was in here, Theo's arms were around my waist and his lips were trailing over every inch of my body. I miss him so much it physically pains me. Ellie's right, he means more to me than I think anyone in my entire life has.

I go through the motions under the hot water, washing the self-pity and indecisiveness away as I concoct my plan to get Theo back. Ellie was right about one more thing—Jo is my best bet at figuring out where Theo is. Stepping out of the shower, I towel dry my hair and pad back over to my suitcase to grab some much-needed clean clothes.

Ping.

Jo's phone, the one we'd been using sporadically this whole time, lies face up on the plush bedding, its screen illuminated from whatever notification just came through.

Ellie.

I reach for it, reminding myself to profusely thank that girl for swiping it on my behalf, and open up the camera roll. Photo after photo of Theo and me fill the screen as I scroll. Silly selfies in the back of the van as Arthur chaotically drove through yet another city. Candid photos of Theo in various stages of undress, his strong body and handsome face permanently frozen in time for me to ogle whenever I want.

A photo of us kissing, which he insisted on taking with the elephants in the background, makes my chest tighten.

I miss him.

Just as I feel tears of longing pool in my eyes, the phone pings again—a social media notification. And another. And then another. And suddenly, the phone will not stop vibrating. I open Instagram to dozens, if not hundreds, of unread messages. "What the hell?"

I randomly select a message from an unknown user named @phil_d23 that reads *Did you see this????*

Phil has shared a post from another unknown account. I click on the photo and nearly drop my phone.

Theo's handsome face stares up at me from the screen. He's sandwiched between two adorable children, his niece and nephew, I'm assuming, and they're all caught mid-laugh. Frozen forever in time in what looks to be a happy family moment.

The user's name is @efernandez and she's captioned the photo *I love when my brother is in town!* with a healthy amount of red heart emojis.

But then, I notice she's tagged *Eastside Farmers Market*, which pulls up an exact location. Suddenly, I can breathe. Theo. Would it be the worst idea in the history of ideas to just . . . .show up?

I race through my room, stuffing my few belongings into my bag before I talk myself out of it. I don't care what it costs or how I'll get there, but knowing exactly—well, kind of—where Theo is has ignited something within me. I've wasted too much time as it is.

I *have* to see him.

Throwing on my shoes while still shoving clothing into my bag with my passport between my teeth, I'm about to rip open the hotel room door to figure out my way to the airport.

But when the door opens, my escape route is blocked. Jo's standing there, a phone squished between her ear and shoulder and her trusty tablet in hand. The same photo I was just looking at is enlarged on its screen.

"I found him," she says. Her eyes show signs of immense exhaustion. And though she's clearly in business mode, there's a softness there that tells me everything I need to know about her. "I'm on hold with the airline now, but if we hurry, I think I can get you on the next flight out."

She doesn't wait for me to respond but just charges down the hall. I follow her lead like I have this entire time, ready for her to make the impossible happen.

27

THEO

The Fernandez Residence
1201 Stone Hill Lane
Monona, Wisconsin

'm having a staring contest with Lola and losing.

"You're not very good at this," she says, crossing her arms in victory with a smug smile.

"Shush, you." I blink rapidly, forcing moisture back into my old, dry eyes. "Let's go again."

Lola laughs, taking a sip of the double-chocolate malt we each got while Mom, Elise, and Frankie still wander the farmers' market. "Tío Dos, let's not." There's pity in her voice.

Great. My life has been reduced to being pitied by a ten-year-old.

Even though it has only been a few days, we've all quickly fallen into both old and new habits since my return home. Stefan and my mom can always be found in the kitchen, whipping up everything from chilaquiles with homemade salsa verde to a never-ending supply of my mom's famous tacos al pastor.

Elise works more often than not, but when she does not, the two of us take the kids on long bike rides along the lake, stopping to pick the wildflowers that grow by the water's edge. Frankie and Lola run and proudly present them to their abuelita every time we come back, who claps and returns their generosity with besitos on each cheek.

My father and I spend our mornings side by side in his woodshed like we used to. I watch in awe as he uses his nimble hands to create delicate pieces. Fine lines unfurl from the corners of his eyes while he runs a fresh piece of pine through the sander. He's aged, sure, and it may take him a little bit longer to complete orders these days, but everyone on this side of Lake Michigan knows that if they want perfection, they order from Alejandro Fernandez.

We have dinner under the bistro lights and play cards as a family. I'm thankful we don't play for money, because Elise would bankrupt us all in a single round. We lounge on the dock well into the evening, sipping on sweet summer wine and watching with tired eyes as lightning bugs dip in between the reeds. Lola and Frankie end up falling asleep in someone's arms almost every night, until it's time for one of us to carry them off to bed.

Life is sweeter on the lake. Slower and more meaningful. I hadn't realized how badly I'd missed being here until I was right in the thick of it all again. Surrounded by the stillness of everyday life with the ones you love.

Frankie leads my mom by the hand, tugging her along with his usual partially toothless smile that's brighter than the sun. "Look what we got, Tío Dos," he shouts when he's a little closer. I've been told I'm not allowed to say anything about his volume control, or lack thereof, as he's allegedly me reincarnated at his age.

He jumps into my lap, nearly spilling my malt in the process, and shoves a basket of bright-red cherries into my face. "We got your favorite, the sweethearts." My mom sits next to me on the bench, pulling Lola onto her lap and hugging her tight.

"You did?" I ask, tickling him as he squirms in my lap. He reaches into the basket and grabs a cherry and rather forcefully shoves it in my mouth, stem and all. "Mmm, thank you, little one."

We all take turns trying to catch cherries in our mouths, laughing when they bounce off our teeth and noses, and then laughing even harder as we struggle to spit out the pits. Out of the corner of my eye, I see Elise take a few photos of the four of us squished together on the wooden bench and then smile when she looks down at the memory she's just captured. I remind myself to ask her to send it to me.

"Mija, put that thing away," my mother scolds like, her mouth full of cherries thanks to an overzealous Frankie. She sounds just like she did when we were teenagers.

"I'm coming, I'm coming," she says, typing a few more words on the screen before shoving her phone back into her purse. "Um, excuse me, my favorite son in the whole world. Do you have a cherry for your mama?" Elise crouches in front of Frankie, pinching his cheeks as he looks for the perfect one to gift his mother.

"Here you go, Mommy," he says, giving the cherry he's selected a little kiss before offering it to her.

She smiles, her eyes sparkling like only a mom's eyes do, and takes the fruit from his little hands. "Thank you, mi amor," my sister says, plopping it into her mouth.

//////////////

"Is that your boy, Carla?" A man who I'd always thought could pass as Father Time's older brother greets us at the old diner's door. My mom bribed me out of bed the following morning with a trip to Hank's and the promise of my favorite pancakes. "I thought we'd seen the last of you when you took off for basic training."

He extends a frail hand forward, which I take with a firm shake. "It's good to see you, Mr. Greer."

"You too. We were all sorry to hear about your discharge," he says. His voice is somber, but his tired eyes are laced with sincerity.

"Thank you." I don't really know what else to say. I never have.

"It's good to see you, Hank," my mom says as the two share a warm hug.

"You tell Elise she better bring those kids of hers in to see me soon. It's been too long," he says, patting my mom affectionately on the face. "Go on, sit in your usual booth if you'd like. Penny will be right over."

I follow my mom through the near-empty diner to a small booth in the corner. The vinyl cushions are still a deep maroon, and they crack and crinkle when we sit. She passes me a menu that's seen better days, which I nudge in front of me with my knuckle, trying to avoid whatever sticky residue lingers on its edges. It's a formality, really. Our entire family has ordered the same meal for years.

"I've spent so many hours in this booth with Elise," I say, sliding the menu to the edge of the table. "We'd leave school early and eat our weight in short stacks. This place hasn't changed one bit."

There's soft music playing in the background. The lighting is dark but comfortable, casting an amber glow across every surface from the vintage globe fixtures above each booth.

"This place is all Hank Greer has left," my mother says. "His wife passed two . . . maybe three years ago now," she adds.

"I didn't know." Hank and Alice Greer were a staple in our small town. They were front and center at every high school sporting event, decked out in our school's colors. They always made sure everyone felt cheered for. When we would come into the diner, Alice would sneak my favorite snickerdoodle cookie into my pocket, and it was just our little secret.

Without fail.

"A lot has changed since you left," she says, a painful nostalgia filling her voice.

She reaches across the booth, taking each of my hands in hers.

"What happened, mi vida?" my mother asks, her eyes brimming with tears. I don't know how to answer her plea. It took me all of five minutes alone with my mother to remember why I've been avoiding this conversation all this time.

How do I articulate the forever pain of being outed like that? How it felt to have every neatly woven thread of my life so easily undone against my will. Every insecurity and moment of self-loathing laid bare for the world to see as I scrambled to pick up the pieces of the truth bomb that had been detonated on me.

"I don't know, Mamá," I say. A cop-out, I know.

"Can you try? Where did I go wrong?"

"Don't say that, Mamá. You didn't do anything wrong . . . It's not about that," I say, clasping her hands in mine.

"Why? It's the truth. It kills me to say this, but on some level, I led you to believe I wouldn't be there for you when you needed me most." She takes a deep breath, straightening in her seat. "Right or wrong, that's the reality of *your* truth and something we've had to live with all these years. But when you put up that wall . . . I think a part of me has not recovered from that."

I know I was doing what was best for me at the time, but I didn't realize just how deeply my actions impacted those around me. These are the feelings I've been trying to avoid. The insurmountable feelings of loss and shame and knowing now there was so much I could have done differently. So much I wish I had done differently. So much that was outside my control.

All this time, I kept my family at arm's length because it was easier than having to face the judgment I thought would go hand in hand with being an out gay man. The unease and the growing pains of figuring out myself. And when I was outed, the opportunity to sit with that unease on my own terms was taken from me. The words I'd been saving for my loved ones had been spoken on my behalf but were twisted and misconstrued, and instead of correcting the record, it felt easier to run.

"When everything happened," I start. "When everything happened with Ethan," I clarify. "There was a period when I didn't know if life was worth living anymore.

"Ay, dios mío, mi amor," she says, tears spilling over now. "You could have talked to me," she whispers. "You could have

given me all your pain and confusion and I would have helped
you make sense of it. Or at least tried."

"I didn't know where to start, Mamá." And that's the truth.
I didn't even know there was anything to be confused about
until I met Ethan. "It's not like I was living this lie my entire
life. Sure, I may have had moments here and there that gave me
pause. Or made me wonder if perhaps I was different from the
other boys. But growing up, it wasn't some painful existential
crisis.

"Until it was—" my voice catches. "Everything changed for
me. In a single instant, everything about my life—about me and
who I am and who I thought the world would see me as—it all
changed. And I didn't want that. I didn't want to be your gay
son. *Just* your gay son."

"But you've never been just one thing."

"I know that. Now," I say, squeezing her hands in mine. "But
at the time, I couldn't see beyond anything other than the person I loved. The person who claimed to love me for who I am,
taking that choice away from me. They robbed me of coming
out, Mom. They took something so personal and so monumen-
tal to who I am and who I wanted to be and politicized it. They
made an example out of me and guaranteed that I withdrew so
deeply within myself that I couldn't get hurt like that again."

She's quiet, but the tears still stream down her face.

"But if we're being truthful with each other, son," she says,
her hands still warm in mine with the familiar comfort that
only a mother's hands can make you feel. "I know you, Theo.
I've known *you* since your very first breath. So, when I say this,
I say it with all the love and adoration in the world." She looks
at me with knowing eyes. "I think this was more about you not
loving yourself. Or not believing that you were worthy of love

or even that you were scared to live a life that was authentic to you," she says, leaning forward. "And the fact that you're back here, after all this time, I'm afraid that you're still being driven by that fear."

"What do you mean?" I ask, my words barely escaping the lump in my throat.

She offers a small smile. "Te amo, mi tesoro. I've always loved you and always will. You're one of the greatest men I know, and your father and I are so proud of you. I've watched you be there for those around you. For me," she says, touching her chest. "For Elise and for your friends. Without fail, you've dropped whatever you're doing and shown up for them with your loving heart and bravery. But mijo, you don't do the same for yourself. For some reason, you've decided that the best course of action when *your* life gets hard is to run. It's why you dove headfirst into work after leaving the Navy, and if I had to guess, it's why you didn't stay to figure everything out with Asher."

I feel my shoulders slump against the weight of her observation. Every part of me knows she's right; of course she is. I've gotten used to a habit, and as we sit in a familiar booth at Hank's place, I'm not entirely sure how to break it.

But I want to try.

"It's different with him, isn't it?" she says after a moment, rubbing my hands. "With Asher?"

"It *feels* different," I admit. "But I'm scared, Mamá. I'm scared I've opened myself up to someone again and allowed all those feelings to come rushing in . . ." My voice trails off, and I can't fight the lump in my throat anymore. "And I'm scared it was all for nothing." My mother has more strength and honesty than anyone I've ever known. I've watched her hold it together for everyone in my life. And when she gets up from her spot in the booth and sits next to me, taking me in her arms, whispering over and over again how much she adores me, I pray for a fraction of her strength as we all begin to mend what has been disjointed for so long.

We spend the rest of the day as a family.

Running through the tall grass around the lake, the kids giggling and trailing behind me. Looking through old photos with Mom and Elise, each of them dabbing their eyes here and there at how much has changed over the years. Watching my parents curl up together on that old armchair like they have my entire life, still so in love.

"Who is that, mijo?" my father asks, looking out toward the driveway after returning from the kitchen, a blackberry cobbler still warm in one hand and a can of whipped topping in the other. Like old times, we've shared every meal on the patio, the stars above us and the breeze coming off the lake to keep us cool.

I squint my eyes, struggling to see through the summer haze. "I'm not sure . . ." I say, but when I hear the uneven sounds of a rolling duffel against the rough pavement, I know.

Asher.

28

ASHER

Denpasar International Airport
Bali, Indonesia

Jo and I barely spoke as we sped off in the van toward the airport. She'd thrown her phone on the dash as she haggled with the airline representative, playing every card and pulling every string she had in her arsenal to get me where I needed to go. When we got to the international terminal, we shot out like two human cannonballs at the circus. Ripping my bag from the back seat, I turned to Jo, searching for the right words—sincere words for the kindness she'd shown me. But despite the variations of *thank you* I'd strung together in my head, I said nothing. Instead, Jo, sensing my mental fumble, silently pulled me in for a forced but welcome hug.

"Go get him," she said, kissing me on the cheek before practically shoving me toward the ticket counter.

I sprinted through the automatic doors, breathless and running on fumes, making a note of all the things I still needed to say to her. How this competition changed my life, how she'd always been in my corner.

How thankful I am for her friendship.

Racing through multiple airports and across multiple time zones, only one thought kept me going—

Theo.

But after hours and hours of travel, when I see him standing there at the end of the driveway, I suddenly have no idea what to say.

"Hi."

He puts his hands in his pockets. The evening light makes it difficult to read his expression, but he seems neither ecstatic nor enraged to see me, so I guess that's a win.

Before Theo can say anything and the two of us are swept up in the breathtaking reunion I'd been fantasizing about since the moment he left, a tiny human comes running up behind him, screaming from the shadows.

"Stranger danger! Stranger danger! Stranger danger!" His stature is small, but his warning isn't anything to scoff at, because one second, I'm standing in front of the man I'm dying to kiss, and the next, I'm shot.

"What the *fu* . . . *dge*," I yell, clutching my forehead. Somehow, I manage to choke back a string of obscenities I'd love nothing more than to lob at my assailant, but given the fact that he's, what, three—four?—I keep my words G-rated. The little sharpshooter standing before me could quite literally be Theo's mini-me with his thick, wavy dark hair and devilish grin. He stands there locked and loaded, ready to protect his family against intruders.

Theo nearly doubles over in laughter as I peel off the suction-cup dart that basically got me right between the eyes and throw it to the ground. Nice shot, kid.

"This is my nephew, Frankie . . ." he says, his voice trailing off when he realizes Frankie didn't stick around long enough for an introduction. He's instead gone running back up the driveway. "Sorry about that. Did it hurt?"

Truthfully, it didn't feel great, but if anything, I think it just surprised me. "I'm fine," I say, rubbing my forehead and reminding myself not to let Frankie out of my sight.

"Good . . . good." Theo crosses his arms and all I want to do is wrap myself in him. "So, what are you doing here, Asher?" he asks quietly, like he's afraid to know the answer.

"Theo, I—I had no idea . . . I need you to know . . ." But before I can tell him how my heart ached for him as soon as he'd left me or how on the plane ride here I'd replayed each and every moment we'd shared—a continuous loop of some of the happiest moments of my life—I realize we are once again very much not alone.

"Mijo, don't be rude . . . I didn't raise you to allow our guests to just awkwardly stand outside," says a woman who I can only assume is Theo's mother. "Especially when they've clearly been traveling." She loops her arm through Theo's and rests her head against his shoulder.

"Mom, this is Asher," Theo says, his gaze still anywhere but on mine, the hurt in his voice more prevalent than it was just moments ago.

"It's . . . um, lovely to meet you, Mrs. Fernandez," I say, extending my hand in her direction.

"Please," she says, taking my hand in hers, "call me Carla. You must be starving, Asher. Come on, I'll make you a plate," she says, leading me toward the house.

"One sec . . . I need to grab my bags."

"Nonsense," she says. "Theo can do that, right, sweetie?" He doesn't respond, but I can hear him trailing behind us, the wheels of my beat-up roller bag—which is officially on its last leg—screeching against the asphalt with every step.

Carla guides me up the long, curved driveway. I knew little of Theo's family home, but somehow, this is exactly how I pictured it—wildflowers and larger-than-life trees framing the understated but beautiful two-story lake house, and fireflies dancing in the distance, softly illuminating the night in the most fleeting of moments.

Would it be incredibly silly of me to say there's *magic* in the air? Because that's how being here makes me feel. Like at any given moment, something beautiful and entirely out of the ordinary could happen.

I look back at Theo, silently praying it's not too late for *our* magic.

"Alright, mis amores . . . We have a visitor!" Carla says when I step onto a massive brick patio where I've clearly interrupted what appears to be a very lovely family dinner. "Please make Asher feel welcome while I heat him up a plate," Carla says before turning toward the glow of the house.

"Oh . . . you don't have to do th—"

"It's nothing. Please, sit and get comfortable, cariño," Theo's father says, waving to an empty chair.

"Um, hi," I say, giving a rigid wave as I take a seat in between Theo and his father.

"It's nice to meet you, Asher," he says warmly, offering a hand to me, which I shake. "I'm Alejandro. And this is my daughter, Dr. Elise Mariana Fernandez-Perez, pediatric medicine," he says like any proud father would, "and her husband, Stefan."

"Jeez, dad," Elise scolds her father. "Shall I hand him over my résumé and socials as well?"

"What!" Alejandro retorts, laughing loudly with his full body. "Can you blame a father for being proud of his daughter, a doctor?"

She ignores him. "Glad you could make it, Asher," she says, winking at me. I have to find a way to thank her for tagging Theo in that photo and responding to my last-ditch message.

Because without her, I wouldn't be here.

Amid the friendly introductions, Theo abruptly gets up from the table and walks off, hands back in his pockets, shoulders raised. Alejandro watches his son disappear from view, and Elise shoots me a sympathetic look.

"Excuse me," I say, rising from my own chair. I sense each pair of eyes follow me as I briskly attempt to catch up to him.

Theo unknowingly leads me down toward the lake, past a worn pair of Adirondack chairs, until he reaches the far end of the wooden dock. The night sky is void of any stars. A slight breeze sends goose bumps rippling across my exposed skin.

"I wasn't sure I'd see you again." Theo's back is to me now, but his tone has a little more bite to it than when we met in the driveway. "And now you're here, of all places."

"Did you really think I was just going to disappear from your life forever? After everything we've been through?" I take a hesitant step forward, desperately wanting to close the icy distance between us. We've spent too much time apart as it is, but I also know Theo's hurt. I knew coming here was a risk. But judging by Theo's rigidity, I'm beginning to fear I miscalculated exactly how this reunion would go down. It's not like I was expecting to be met with fireworks and an *All is forgiven, Asher* banner, but this? I've never seen Theo like this.

Hurt. Sullen, even.

Broken.

"I don't know, Asher. Maybe I don't think anything any-more." There's an indifference in his tone that stills the blood coursing through my veins. He hasn't moved, but I can see the tension building in his shoulders, like a teakettle just moments away from piercing the silence with its whistle.

"Please, Theo. Look at me—"

He turns, shaking his head, and when our eyes finally meet, my heart shatters into a million pieces. He's blinking back tears. "What are you doing here, Ash? Truly. What do you want?" He's staring at me so intensely, the hurt and confusion behind his eyes is impossible to ignore.

I want you.

It sounds too simple of a statement, but it's the truth. I want him and us and everything that comes with that.

"You have to understand—" I say, my voice breaking, my own tears now streaming down my face.

"But that's the problem," he says, cutting me off. "I *don't* understand. I don't know that I ever will. You said it yourself . . . *after everything we've been through.* La Tomatina. The ice cream, the stupid seaweed, and the elephants. Fuck, Asher. *The ele-phants.*" His voice cracks. "Even after all that, you just stood there."

"What was I supposed to do, Theo?" I feel my own bubble of frustration rising from my throat. "I didn't know all *that* was going to happen. There was no way in hell I could have pre-dicted anything like that ever happening to me. And my fam-ily?" The fury I felt when Dalton and Clint videoconferenced them comes raging to the surface.

"You told me this was real for you," he says after a moment. "You made me *feel* like this was real and not just some detour in your life. I'm a human being, Asher. Fuck, I'm not just some layover you get to take when you're figuring everything in your life out."

"Theo, of course I know—" I start, but he cuts me off.

"And when you just stood there, it was clear as day that *this*," he says, waving his arms between us, "isn't real for you like it is for me." His shoulders slump, and his eyes are pooling with tears. "And maybe that's okay. Maybe months down the line, I'll be able to see all this—you, me, the show—for what it was. A nice little chapter in our lives. You and I don't get the happy ending, and I'll just forever be remembered as that stranger you met in the airport bar."

Panic floods my system. "I hope that's not how you really feel."

"That's the thing, Ash," he says, his voice flatlining. "I don't know how to feel. Not anymore. For as long as I can remember, I've tried to not feel. To not get too close, so I don't get hurt again. But somewhere between mozzarella sticks and here, something changed. *You* made me feel. You reminded me how beautiful it is to be seen by someone and to see them for who they really are. You reached for my hand each night and pulled me close and made me feel safe and whole again. Like I was depended on and needed."

"You are all of those things," I yell, praying he believes me.

"You did all that and it is really unfair and shitty if you didn't mean it." The tears are really falling now. "What about what I want? Because I played the role and did everything you asked and despite you reminding me this wasn't real, I still fell in lo—" He stops himself, choking back the words I've been waiting all this time to hear him say. But not like this.

Don't say those three life-changing words.

Not filled with this much frustration.

"I'm *here*. I'm here and of course I meant all those things," I say, taking a small step toward him. My voice cracks just like my heart has. I take in Theo, standing at the edge of the dock, his arms crossed and eyes wide and red. I need him to realize there was never a choice to make. I had already decided what I didn't want for my life the moment I left Clint standing alone at the airport.

And I decided what I *did* want while sitting with him somewhere over the Atlantic.

And the journey to that decision—everything with him and us and how he's made me feel—was worth it.

He was more than worth it.

"Being here with you," I say, taking another step into the warmth I'd missed so much. "Theo . . . there's nowhere else in this whole world I'd rather be. When Clint showed up, I think I hesitated because from one moment to the next, I was suffocated by years' worth of anger that all came rushing to the surface. Years' worth of biting my tongue and always trying to say and do the right thing. I think my brain and my body just shut down because of all the things I wanted to say to him . . . all the horrible ways he's made me feel these past years . . . and that all I could think about was you."

He lifts his gaze to mine.

"You are the exact opposite of him, Theo. And what we have is so special and so uniquely ours and from the bottom of my heart, baby—I am so sorry that my hesitation or my moment of internal panic led you to believe otherwise."

Theo drops his arms, either in exhausted surrender or wary acceptance. Or maybe on some small level, he acknowledges the sincerity that I've been praying is coming across.

"Because when push comes to shove," I say, taking another

calculated step forward, "the person I want in my life is the person who makes me feel most like myself. The real and flawed and anxious version of me that probably comes with a lot of baggage and whole lot of questions. That's you, Theo. I've spent every single second since you came into my life over-analyzing every moment of every interaction, trying to understand what it is about you that makes me feel the way that I do." Another step forward. "It's the kindness in your heart. The genuine warmth of your beautiful smile. The way you treat everyone around you like they're the most special person in the damn room."

Another step. "So yes, I hesitated, but in that moment, I think there was a part of me that was scared of just how immensely you've changed my life. Of how much I need you."

"Asher, I meant it when I told you I don't want to pretend anymore. I can't," he says, taking his own step toward me, a small one, but a step in the right direction nonetheless. All I want to do is launch myself at him.

"And I meant it when I said let's not," I say, matching his movement, which causes the wooden dock to creak beneath my foot.

"Asher, I can't," he whispers. My fingers flex at my sides, itching to touch him. He's close enough now that I could just reach out if I thought he wanted me to.

"You never have to again." His amber eyes pour into mine—eyes I know in my soul I could get lost in for the rest of my life—and every nerve ending screams for him to hold me in his arms.

And he does.

Theo reaches forward, slowly at first and then like his life depends on it. He pulls me flat against his chest. I wrap my arms around his waist, finally inhaling the most comforting scent of *him* after all this unnecessary time apart.

Neither of us has to say anything else.

If traveling the world together has taught me anything, it's that the feeling of *home* doesn't always have to be a place.

Melting into Theo, I know without any reservation or nagging uncertainty that if you're lucky, home can be a person.

//////////////

After what felt like the deepest sleep of my life, I sneak out of Theo's childhood bedroom, careful not to wake him, to brush my teeth and smooth out my bedhead. A futile attempt, considering the faux-hawk that seems permanently affixed to my head at this point when I glance in the small bathroom mirror before tiptoeing back to the bedroom.

Our reunion last night went differently than I expected. A little cooler than I had hoped, but we got there eventually. We then quietly got ready for the night, sleeping in his full-size bed, and even though we slept strictly side by side, just being in the same space as Theo felt like a dream.

I finally felt hopeful again.

Theo stirs, his eyes slowly opening as he turns in my direction. I want to kiss every inch of his handsome face. But instead, I roll on my side to face him.

I use the silence between us to memorize the freckles that have grown more prominent on the bridge of his nose and along his cheeks. There's so much I want to make sure he knows. And so many things I promised myself I'd tell him if given the opportunity.

"Hi" is all I can muster.

He blinks a few times, his eyelids heavy and reluctant, and he nuzzles deeper into his pillow. "Hi back."

"I've missed you," I blurt out at the same time he asks, "How'd you sleep?"

We both laugh, now cocooned together in the cozy bedding, the glow of the early-morning light coming in through the small window above us. Theo reaches over to pull me closer to him.

"I bet I missed you more," he says, placing a gentle kiss square on my forehead. "Don't move," he mumbles against my skin. I wouldn't dream of it. He quickly hops out of bed, so I crane my neck before he gets too far down the hall to the bathroom for a nice view of Theo in nothing but a pair of black trunks. His wide, muscular back is on full display.

The house is quiet, peaceful. Theo's family was incredibly welcoming last night, calming every nerve I had about barreling my way into town and forcing myself on them.

His room is somehow exactly as I pictured it. Neat and orderly yet still filled with moments of another life lived. There's a row of Hardy Boys books centered on a wooden bookshelf, a small corkboard across the room that holds a string of Polaroid pictures, and a simple metallic desk lamp on the nightstand. I pick up the framed photo next to it, revealing a much younger Theo and a group of people who I'm assuming are his high school friends. I see he's had that same signature grin in every phase of his life.

"I'm surprised you're not rummaging through my drawers, Bennett," Theo teases from the doorway, looking even more delicious than when he left. His sudden reappearance makes me jump in the bed.

"That was *one* time," I say, returning the frame back to its place. "And sneaking a peek into one's *open* toiletry bag in a shared bathroom is hardly the same as snooping through their childhood belongings."

"Mm-hmm, sure it is," he says with a wink. Theo closes the space between his now-shut door and the bed and rips back the warm covers, sliding in next to me. "Hi again," he says, lying on his side to face me, a smile brewing beneath his dark stubble.

Instead of letting me respond, Theo crashes his lips into mine. I melt against his touch, wrapping my arms around his neck and looping my fingers into his wild hair, and pull him even closer to me. There's an urgency to the way he's kissing me. Like he has been a man starved and my lips are the only things keeping him going.

He rolls me onto my back and presses the full weight of his broad body against mine. My legs naturally wrap around his waist, an invitation to make me his whenever and however he wants.

I hate how much time we wasted in those hotel rooms *not* doing this every chance we got.

"Mmm, baby, I've missed you," I groan against his lips, feeling his smile against mine. "I don't think you realize how badly I missed you." I run my hands down his muscular back as his hungry lips claim mine again, my fingers continuing to trail along his side. I marvel at how hot his skin is beneath my touch. He presses his forehead to mine when I reach between us, cupping him in both hands and giving his now-throbbing cock a squeeze.

"I've fucking missed *this*."

"It's yours," he whispers, his voice hoarse against my ear. Planting kisses along my neck and on each cheek, he repeats the words my heart has been longing to hear over and over again. "It's yours . . . It's yours . . . I'm yours."

He's mine.

My head is swirling at his admission. Theo Fernandez is mine.

Right now, the only thing I care about—the only thing my heart and body and mind are capable of focusing on—is the way Theo's kissing me. Like he's trying to make up for lost time. Like his hands need to relearn every inch of my body.

Like finally, I'm his.

29

THEO

The Fernandez Residence
1201 Stone Hill Lane
Monona, Wisconsin

We've fallen into a lovely routine on the lake: Waking up with enough time to sneak coffee back into our room. Walks along the water, hand in hand as we talk about nothing and everything. Quiet moments on the dock with the water slapping against the wood as our soundtrack. Anything to maximize our alone time. Not that I had any concerns about Asher and my family getting along. In fact, they've become as thick as thieves. And I couldn't be happier.

This morning, he dutifully followed my mother's instructions at the stove when she explained the steps required to make her famous pozole, the rich stew boiling on the burner between them. He asked all the right questions and the two of them went back and forth, laughing, chopping, and mixing the afternoon away.

He also didn't hesitate to join my father on his mission to

gather some wood for the firepit. I'd spent the last few weeks traversing the globe with this man who practically groaned at every mention of physical activity, so I watched in borderline disbelief as he voluntarily walked into the woods with an ax slung over his shoulder and a genuine smile on his face.

We had family meals every day, ran errands in town with Mom, and checked out my favorite places as we drove to visit Elise at her clinic. I could not be prouder to see everything she's accomplished in our hometown.

When the delayed and rather unimpressive finale of *The Epic Trek* finally streamed, the entire family gathered around the television. Lola found her place in my lap and Frankie insisted on curling up in Asher's. He didn't seem to mind.

We watched Bianca and Jackson stand opposite Jenn and Ellie, and after what felt like an eternity, our friends' names flashed across the screen.

My heart just about shot out of my chest with joy. Everyone was on their feet, cheering loudly as we watched our sobbing Midwest friends hug on-screen, confetti and balloons surrounding them like the happiest of snow globes.

Today was spent at the zoo as a family—Lola's hand in mine and Frankie on Asher's shoulders at his request. They bombarded Ash with questions about the animals and exhibits, which he happily and rather animatedly answered. Even if some of his explanations were above *my* head, my niece and nephew hung on to every word.

"Look, Tío Dos, it's you and Mr. Asher," Frankie shouted, pointing excitedly when the zookeeper in charge of the penguins pointed out two male penguins who had been bonded for years. A not-rare occurrence in the animal kingdom, we were told.

The two little penguins stood side by side away from the group with their matching little tuxedo markings, and occasionally, one would nuzzle into the other. A subtle check-in but a clear sign of affection nonetheless.

"But did you even exchange pebbles?" Lola asked, her face smooshed up against the glass. Her question prompted Asher to lower Frankie to the ground before bolting out of the exhibit, leaving the three of us scratching our heads at his sudden disappearing act.

He raced back in before we knew it, though, dramatically panting and drawing looks from the nosy zoo-goers.

"Theo Fernandez," he all but shouted, an over-the-top formality in his voice. He knelt and a collective gasp erupted from those who had definitely stopped what they were doing to watch our very public, very comical spectacle. "I searched every corner of the world to find the perfect pebble to present to you."

He lifted his closed hands and opened them slowly to reveal a partially dirt-covered black rock the size of a misshapen marble that I wasn't entirely convinced wasn't a broken-off chunk of pavement from the penguin exhibit walkway.

"Will you do me the greatest honor of accepting this pebble as a token of my affection?" he asked, his eyes gleaming with mischief and a spontaneity that is so unlike him.

"How could I possibly say no to that?" I said, taking the pebble from him, knowing it would quickly become one of my most prized possessions. It's already safely wrapped in a pair of socks to be put somewhere special. Everyone around us clapped in a congratulatory cheer as Lola and Frankie, both seemingly giddy with excitement—I was beginning to think the double scoop of mint-chocolate-chip ice cream was a poor choice—launched themselves at us.

"It looks like a potato, Tío Dos," Frankie said.

"Leave my potato rock alone."

Lola reached for Asher's hand, leading the way out of the exhibit. If I hadn't been falling head over heels for this man before, seeing Lola and Frankie fawn over him the way they did definitely solidified Asher's hold on my heart. New and exciting, like all relationships begin, but with a permanence that makes my insides melt.

When we got home, we ate dinner as a family, and then Stefan got the kids to bed while Ash and I helped clean up the kitchen and Mom and Elise sipped wine by the fire. I didn't think twice when my dad nodded his head from in front of the sink for us to sneak out the side door for some much-needed alone time. I love my family, but this is what I've been craving all day—Asher wrapped up in my arms, his skin sweet and mine to touch.

"What was it like growing up here?" Asher asks, his back now firmly pressed against my chest as we sit in the uncomfortable familiarity of the metal rowboat my family has had for as long as I can remember. The weather could not be more perfect, and every cricket west of the state of Michigan is out in full force tonight singing their summer song.

"Kinda like this, I guess," I say against his temple, pulling him tighter against my chest. The soft movement of the lake creates a subtle sway of the boat. "I think I spent more hours on this lake than in the house."

"Mmm. Sounds nice." He's trailing his fingertips across my forearm again. It's something he does absentmindedly or intentionally when we're intertwined like this, but either way, each stroke of his touch reaches directly into my core.

"This is nicer."

He turns in my arms, quickly locking his hands around my neck as he does. "I don't want to leave." Asher kisses me once on the neck and then three more times slowly, his lips lingering longer and longer with each pass against my skin. We haven't talked about how all this is and will be coming to an end. I think we both just decided it was far more fun to stay in this imaginary bubble of blissed-out kisses and the warmth of family.

"Then let's not," I say, my lips now against his temple. I can smell the sunshine on his hair and if I could bottle up this very moment, him in my arms on the lake, I'd want to live in it forever. "Let's just stay right here until we're old and gray."

"Wouldn't that be something," he says, his thumb slowly gliding along my cheek. I lean my hand into his touch, realizing that I've found myself in the middle of a moment I thought only existed in movies and daydreams—wrapped in the embrace of someone I can no longer envision a future without.

I love this man.

It's as simple as that. And on some level, I think he loves me back. Neither one of us has said those words yet, but I feel them each time Asher pulls me close and savors every inch of my skin. I feel them when he reaches for me in the middle of the night, finding solace and comfort with my hand in his.

Clear as day, I feel them here on the lake, the changing colors of the summer sky dancing around us as we cling to each other, willing our bubble to last a little longer.

30

ASHER

The Fernandez Residence
1201 Stone Hill Lane
Monona, Wisconsin

Our last night on the lake is one I'll remember for the rest of my life.

Theo, Stefan, and Alejandro huddled around the grill. Elise and Carla laughing at the table. Frankie passed out in my lap and Lola losing her own battle with sleep.

I take as many mental pictures as I can of every detail so I never forget this feeling.

Of home and warmth and looking over at Theo, eyes bright and alive in the summer night; of the feeling of love. I *have* fallen for him, hard, and I think on some level, beyond the jokes and the charming bravado, there's a part of him that still may not believe it.

After dinner is cleared away and everyone begins to settle down for the evening, I extend my hand toward Theo, and he doesn't hesitate for a second to take it in his. I lead him across the lawn toward the water, and when we reach the wooden dock, we sit side by side and let our bare feet dangle in the crisp water. The lake that Theo's family's home sits on is calm. It reflects the light of the bright moon almost perfectly on its smooth surface—I could spend hours out here, counting the stars in the clear night sky and listening to the sounds of summer swell heartily around us.

Theo doesn't rush me.

One of the things I've come to admire, and envy, about him is his ability to just *be*. For someone so full of life and energy, whose job demands that he constantly be on the go, he has the uncanny gift of being fully present in any given moment. He seems to savor the moments he's a part of.

"You're different here," I say, leaning my head on his shoulder.

"How so?"

"I don't know . . . You just seem more at ease." There's a lingering sweetness of campfire smoke and sun on his skin that I wish I could bottle up.

He slowly brings his lips to my temple, planting the softest of kisses there. "That makes sense. Being here—with them—is like exhaling. I guess I get to be the real me, quirks and all."

"I like your quirks."

"Yeah?" He puts his hand on my thigh, his skin warm and comforting against mine.

"I could do without the snoring, but . . ."

"Hey, now," he says, nudging me in a way that forces our bodies even closer together.

I can't help but smile at all the traits of his I've discovered during our time together. Like how he always takes a deep inhale of a freshly clean towel before using it or how he's incapable of falling asleep unless he's made sure that the closet and bathroom doors have been properly shut.

Or how he has consistently reached over in the middle of the night to hold my hand, and in those moments, I never feel more content.

"What I'm *trying* to say is that everything about you has been one giant surprise after another."

He allows a few moments before responding, the silence between us accented by the chirps of a nearby cricket. "In a good way?"

"The best way." I can feel him exhale next to me, and knowing my words are a relief to him makes my heart ache. "Theo, meeting you changed my life."

Removing his hand from my thigh, he puts an arm around me now. "I was hoping you'd feel that way."

Turning to him, I gently plant a kiss on his jaw. "My life is infinitely better because you came into it." I think back to everything that has happened since our paths crossed at the airport, and it's hard not to believe fate brought this man into my life when I needed him most.

"We really have been through it," he says, his lips pressed to my temple. It feels like an understatement, all things considered. "So . . . now what?"

"Now, we go back to our lives," I say, slowly kicking my feet back and forth in the cool water. "No more cameras and living out of our suitcases. No more nonsense with Bianca and Jackson or having to put up with Dalton McKnight . . ."

"And us?" he asks, interrupting me.

The fact that he wants an *us* is more than I could ever ask for.

"Us?" I repeat, turning to face him. Reaching up. I place

both of my hands on his face and stare deep into his eyes—eyes
that are radiating concern for a future neither one of us has
really talked about before. "We can do anything we want, but I
don't care what we do, Theo . . ." He cocks an eyebrow at me,
which only makes me smile. "As long as my mornings start
wrapped tightly in your arms and my nights end with your
hand in mine, I'll be a happy man." And it's true—if I've learned
anything the past few weeks, it's that I require far less than I
thought to make me happy. Really and truly happy. And Theo
just might be at the center of it all.

But who knows. Maybe all this was never about him.

Or us, even.

Maybe sitting here with this magnetic force of a man was
never meant to be my destination. Instead, the whole point of
him and us and the undeniable way he makes me feel is that I
needed to come apart. Seam by narrowly held-together seam,
rough edges and all. Maybe I needed a moment of unbecoming
to shake loose everything I've been carrying all these years.
Shedding bits and pieces of who I thought I was supposed to be
in order to find myself again.

To love myself again.

And Theo? I think the hands of fate were onto something
weaving his life into mine like this. Not as some prize to be
won, but as someone to share the journey with, together.

"It's that simple, huh?" he asks, the smallest smile tugging
at the corner of his mouth.

"You and I have been gallivanting all over the world these
last few weeks, doing things *well outside* both of our comfort
zones. Doesn't *simple* sound pretty amazing right about now?"

Theo shakes his head, the smile he's been holding back finally making its reappearance. He places his full lips to mine,

and as the crickets carry out their joyous tune and the soft breeze coming off the lake dances on our skin, I am left in awe at the lack of urgency to his kiss.

Because now, maybe for the first time ever, it's not lost on either of us that we have all the time in the world to figure out what comes next.

"Simple sounds more than perfect, actually," Theo says, and I couldn't agree more.

///////////////////////

Theo and I FaceTime with Jenn and Ellie in bed on our last morning. Their faces smooshed together on the screen, hair wild and eyes still in disbelief that they'd actually won. We pass along our infinite congratulations and make promises to see one another soon, especially since Ellie will be heading off to college next year. My heart swells with the knowledge she'll now have the means to go to whatever school she gets into, and while she grimaced when I tried to sell her on different biomedical engineering programs, I'll be cheering her on as loudly as I can regardless.

After waving a tearful goodbye to Theo's family, who make me promise many times that I'll be back soon, I hop in the car, where Theo is waiting, his head down but a soft smile on his face.

Driving to the airport together feels different this time.

He holds my hand, alternating tracing tiny circles and hearts with his thumb over my knuckles like he did all those times on the show. Without even having to look at him, I have a pretty good idea that he's feeling what I am.

Sadness that our time on the lake has come to an end.

When we arrive, I learn my flight back to Boston has been

delayed, so there is still some time for us to linger outside the terminal. Theo leans against his parents' sedan, and I stand fidgeting with my bag's strap again, trying and failing to string together a sentence to articulate exactly how I feel.

How much he means to me.

How much I need him.

What do I say to the man who has felt more like home than any place ever could?

He must sense my inner turmoil, or maybe he just can't bear to not be touching me any longer, because Theo takes me in his big arms and holds me close. I take a deep breath and commit every note and subtlety of his scent to memory.

"This isn't goodbye, Asher Bennett," he says into my temple, his voice soft but filled with so much love. I squeeze him tighter. "We're going to figure this out. Together."

"Promise?" I say, craning my neck so I can look him in the eyes.

"Of course. I'm all in." He kisses me—again and again and again—and I know the second I turn away that I never want to say goodbye to this man. I couldn't possibly. I know it without any reservations and with judgment as clear as day. Because meeting Theo the way I did was no accident. No logic or rational thought could convince me otherwise.

Sometimes, a life detour comes along when you least expect it.

And if you are brave enough to lean in to it, that little detour—or the right person—can change everything.

Like Theo has.

Like only he could.

EPILOGUE

THEO

TWO MONTHS LATER
Asher Bennett and Theo Fernandez
3440 W. Lake Drive
Chicago, Illinois

s that the last of them?" I shout over the mountain of boxes we've somehow accumulated.

After hours of arranging our belongings, I'm ready to be done. To officially settle into our new home and start this next chapter for both of us.

I think back to that last time at the airport. The second Asher walked through those airport doors, I had to fight the urge to run after him. Question after question bounced around my skull: What if he changed his mind? Should I have gone with him? What if he had just stayed?

But he had loose ends to tie up. We both did.

So, I went through the motions of my life those first few weeks without him, trying to return to some sense of normalcy.

On more than one occasion, I had to remind myself it would all be worth it in the end.

That he was worth it.

We spoke every day. Most days, Asher enthusiastically told me about every detail of his work. We'd argue over who missed the other more and make a running list of the things we wanted to do when we saw each other. We exchanged an infinite number of selfies, both clothed and, well, not, and when someone would tag us in a #Thasher picture, it was a race to see who could send it to the other first.

He usually won.

Nighttime was the hardest.

I had gotten so used to curling myself around Asher, the feeling of his soft skin pressed against mine. The way our curves and edges lined up so seamlessly without even trying. On those nights when I couldn't sleep, I reminded myself that soon, I'd be able to reach my hand out and feel his waiting.

So now, standing together in *our* Chicago town house, knowing that everything we've quietly been waiting for has finally arrived, it's nearly impossible to contain the excitement that has been building. We spent the first couple of days waiting for our things to arrive, marveling at the view of Lake Michigan and the newness of each other, the novelty of never having to say goodbye again. I'm pretty sure I kissed every inch of Asher's skin, twice, to ensure I knew every trace of him. Every perfect little detail of the man I loved. We ate Thai food and drank wine—which Asher ordered from that little place in Italy we'd stumbled upon—in our underwear on a thick blanket on the floor listening to legends like Gipsy Kings and the Cranberries and, of course, Ashley Tisdale.

I just might make a fan out of him yet.

But isn't that what you do when you're madly in love?

Throw yourself headfirst into each other with everything you've got?

Diving headfirst into Asher feels like coming home, and our home, with his things and my things and *our* things, has quickly become my favorite place in the world.

"I think that's it," Asher says from behind me, setting down the box he carried up the steps onto the kitchen island.

"Are you excited for tomorrow?" I ask, closing the short distance between us and joining him in the kitchen.

"And nervous," Asher quietly admits, his gaze remaining on the plates he's begun unwrapping one by one and neatly placing in the kitchen cabinet above the stove. His new job at the research lab starts tomorrow and despite my insistence that everyone on his team is going to love him, the first-day jitters are getting to him.

Moving in together is a big step for both of us.

But this chapter feels like a much larger one for Asher.

Even without winning the prize money, our online popularity garnered a lot of attention from potential investors who expressed interest in funding his Own Voices in STEM program.

After weighing his options and a lot of intense back-and-forth on Asher's part, his program ultimately found its home with the University of Chicago's Knapp Center for Biomedical Discovery, where he will serve as the newest project manager. I could not be prouder. His drive and work ethic are some of the most impressive things about him, but it's his devotion to the training and empowerment of future LGBTQIA+ biomedical engineers that leaves me standing in awe of the man before me.

"You're going to change the world, Asher Bennett," I whisper against his temple after pulling him away from the box he was unpacking.

"How can you be so sure?" he asks, dipping his hands into my back pockets, pulling me even closer.

"Because I love you, obviously. I know these things," I say matter-of-factly, letting my lips brush against his hair. Those three little words still make me giddy. Even more so when they're accompanied by a blushing Asher Bennett. "Besides, you've already changed mine, so you're already winning."

He laughs, but it's the truth.

Meeting him in the airport opened my eyes to a life I hadn't even realized I was missing out on.

What started off as a mutually beneficial ruse turned into one of the most significant life lessons for me. After the competition, I was quickly able to get back in the cockpit. The social media frenzy that followed us was more than enough proof that I had in fact taken the necessary steps toward a healthier work-life balance. Diving headfirst into work was no way to live. At least not in a healthy way, and it's definitely not how I want to live anymore.

Mark was right, as always. There *is* more to life than work. He and Amelia kept me company, and sane, until Asher got here, and I couldn't help but notice they seemed lighter, happier, than the last time I saw them. They'll tell me when they're ready, whatever it is.

I've also started giving flying lessons as a way to share my passion for aviation with others. Asher doesn't know it yet, but we've got a day trip up to Madison this weekend. Elise said the kids have been incessantly asking when they were going to see us again, so we figured now would be as good a time as any to rent a twin engine and fly up to see everyone before Asher's schedule gets too complicated. It's the benefit of being this close, something I will never take for granted again.

Asher pushes a box of carefully wrapped glassware in my direction, which I make quick work of unpacking and putting away. Standing side by side in our kitchen, amid a growing pile of discarded packing tape and Bubble Wrap, it's easy to envision what this life could look like.

A life spent loving him and being loved by him.

But an unexpected knock at the door pulls me away from my thoughts.

We shrug at each other, and Asher plants a kiss on my jaw before sauntering off to the front door to see who it is. He returns with a grin on his face and a welcome sight—

Jo.

"Hi, friends," she says quietly, a nervous edge to her voice. She's holding a potted money tree in one hand and a bottle of champagne in the other. We haven't seen each other since I stormed off the show's set, but I've never blamed Jo for anything. Not for a second.

We go in for a hug awkwardly, her hands still full, but she wraps her arms around my waist regardless, seemingly relaxing like she's been unsure of how her reunion with us would go.

"Your sister gave me your address," she says, handing the gifts to Asher and hopping up on the kitchen counter, making herself right at home.

Asher laughs. "Of course she did."

I'm going to need to have a conversation with Elise about boundaries. But in this case, I am deeply appreciative of how much she takes care of me.

Even if she goes about it in the most interesting of ways.

"While I'd love to chitchat . . . we want you back," Jo blurts out. Right to business in typical Jo Bishop fashion.

Asher and I exchange confused looks.

"I'm not following." I move from where I was leaning against the kitchen island to stand next to Asher.

Jo reaches over the counter to snag the bottle of champagne she'd brought and begins opening it. "The show," she says. "We want the two of you back. For real this time."

The *pop* of the champagne cork makes Asher jump against me.

"I know it's a lot. Trust me, no one would blame you if you wanted to kick me out of here right now and tell me to shove off," she says, setting the cork down beside her.

Asher rummages through a random box on the counter, procuring a coffee mug, a wineglass, and a tumbler that's missing its lid, shrugging when Jo raises an eyebrow at our drinkware selection.

"But hear me out," she says, generously pouring the champagne into the glasses. "Everyone is dying to know what #Thasher is up to. Our socials have been incessantly blowing up about you two idiots since everything went down. What Dalton did . . ." she says, her voice trailing off.

It was impossible to tune out the news that Dalton had been let go from the show. Good riddance. "Well, let's just say things would be different this time. The entire *Epic Trek* family is on your side, so if there's any part of you that's at all interested, we'd love to have you."

Her sincerity is touching.

But what she's asking is a lot to take in.

"What do you think, babe?" I ask, squeezing Asher a little

tighter against my chest. I have no idea where his head's at with all this, but I'm sure he'll surprise me. He always does. "Do you want to wing it again?"

A smile grows across his face, slow at first and then all at once, and I'm pretty sure there isn't anything I wouldn't do for him just to keep him smiling like this.

"With you? Always."

ACKNOWLEDGMENTS

Hi, friends—thanks for sticking around. As a reader, I always look forward to a book's acknowledgments. Seeing all the people who had a hand in putting a book I love into the world spelled out. Like little puzzle pieces in an author's life who fall into place one by one along the way, and after a while—after celebratory milestones and publishing highs and lows, self-doubt and the all-too-familiar impostor syndrome—something truly beautiful happens.

A work of art is put out into the world.

But now, as an author, acknowledgments mean even more. Because I get to publicly share the love I have for the people who made *this* happen.

That's why you, my sweet readers, feel like the perfect place for me to start. Because without my fellow romance lovers, none of this means anything. Without you, I wouldn't get to be living out a dream I never knew was within reach, nor would I have felt brave enough to put these words down on paper to begin with. There is no me without you, and for that, I am eternally grateful. Thank you for showing up and for wrapping me in your kindness and for being some of the most special relationships in my life. Each one of you has impacted my life in ways I don't think you'll ever be able to understand, so brace yourself for awkwardly long Chip hugs, because they're coming.

In writing this book—and every one that will follow—I hoped to craft a love letter to the community that has given me so much: my vibrant, resilient, and beautifully perfect LG-BTQIA+ family. As a gay author, my hope is that the characters I write reflect the joys and complexities of our lives, and each reader feels seen and celebrated within these pages. Queer joy is a powerful force, and I believe with every fiber of my being that every person is so damn worthy of their own love story. Despite the loudness and ignorance of the world around us, never forget that.

To my brilliant, superhuman of an agent, Jess—you have fundamentally changed the trajectory of my life. Getting to work with you, to learn from you, and to have you in my corner has been such a privilege. I still have the sticky note I nervously wrote in 2021 that has your name circled at the top of my *Dream Agents* list, and all these years later, having you in my life is better than I could have ever imagined. Thank you for holding my hand every step of the way, but more important, thank you for taking a chance on me.

To Tarini and Kate—my powerhouse editing duo. I will never be able to thank you enough for seeing the magic I'd hoped was in this story. You've pushed and challenged me as an author, kindly guiding me along the way as we uncovered more and more about Theo and Asher. Together. I have so much love and appreciation in my heart for every moment of this experience and I just hope you know how much your mentorship, expertise, and unwavering support of my vision have meant to me.

Sending massive hugs and air kisses to everyone at Team Putnam for being absolute joys to work with and the best in the business.

If you've stuck around this long, please know I have now reached a point where I am writing this with tears in my eyes.

One thing no one told me about publishing was the friendships with authors that spring up when you need them most. So many of my favorite authors—writers whom I admire and adore—have now become friends. Family, even. And so much of my own publishing journey wouldn't have happened without this phenomenal group of humans who extended a hand and showed me the strength of community: Livy Hart, Julie Soto, Elena Armas, Hannah Grace, Torie Jean, Christina Lauren, Marley Valentine, CE Ricci, Erin Connor, Tarah DeWitt, Jessica Joyce, Ray Riley, Steven Rowley, Lyla Sage, Ashley Winstead, Millie Perez, Andie Burke, Lindsey Kelk, Hannah Bonam-Young—each of you inspires me every single day and I am so honored to have you in my life.

Oh, and a special thank you to Lana Ferguson for keeping me sane throughout all of this by swapping screenshots of our favorite Instagram boy. (And also for answering every single panicked publishing question I had.)

To Courtney Kae—thank you for celebrating every milestone with me and for loving my boys as much as I do. Your friendship and support have made all of this worth it.

To Becca, Chloe, and Sarah—I'm still trying to figure out how I weaseled my way into this beautiful group, but guess what, you're stuck with me. Watching you soar and shine makes my heart just about burst right out of my chest. No amount of thanks will ever be enough to convey how much your friendship, check-ins, and unconditional encouragement have meant to me. But just know . . . I love each of you forever and ever.

Psst—Sarah? Thanks for encouraging me to pitch myself. I one hundred percent wouldn't have my agent—or this book—without you.

I'm sure most of you are aware, but on the off chance you're new here, I entered this lovely book community as a Bookstagrammer who just so happened to love screaming about the romance books I adored. I've made some of the most impactful friendships along the way. To the beautiful and quirky and one-in-a-million bookish community—I love you endlessly and I pinky promise I'll always want to talk about book boyfriends and Taylor Swift with you!

To Lil, Kayleigh, and Sophie—I'm pretty sure you've read this book in every iteration, sometimes out of order and with zero context, and have done so enthusiastically despite your busy lives. But if I'm being honest . . . each of you was the glue that held me and this book together at one point or another. Your love for Theo and Asher—and for me—kept me going when I really, *really* didn't want to, and for that, I'll owe you for the rest of my life. Forehead kisses and a lifetime of gratitude to each of you.

To Phil—thank you for encouraging me to dream and for fiercely advocating for queer romance and for simply being you. My world is a much better place because you are in it . . . and I mean that with my whole heart.

To Rachel—you have been the reminder (rather forcefully—hello, you're a Taurus) to believe in my art and advocate for myself, and you have unquestionably been there for not just me but my husband too, in more ways than I can count.

A special thanks to the one and only Annie Meagle for

swooping in, as only she does, and helping me see the heart of this story through a different lens. You are pure magic and I cannot wait to continue working with you on many, many more love stories to come.

Asher and Theo's love story—or anything I write, really—wouldn't exist without my Chelsea. You were the first person I ever shared anything about this book with, and every moment along the way, you've never once stopped believing in me and what this story could become. You hold me up without even trying, and if it's not clear after all these years, you're the best friend I've ever had. Ready for round three?

Tears update: They are flowing quite freely, tbh.

To my family and friends—thank you for enthusiastically supporting this weird little dream of mine. For checking in and for being excited every step of the way and for pretending you didn't read the sex scenes. Thank you for making me brave and loving me anyway when I'm not. I am surrounded by the best and most beautiful people a guy could ever dream of, and I hope I've made you proud.

And the biggest and most important thank-you goes to my husband. My better half in every way. My loudest cheerleader and my fiercest defender and my ultimate book boyfriend. Because without you, sweet man . . . I quite literally would not have the ability to believe in love. I wrote this book in honor of the leaps of faith we all take in the pursuit of love. And honey? That leap we took together all those years ago was the best damn thing that ever happened to me. I look forward to *winging it with you* until we are old, gray, and still as wildly in love as we are today.

DISCUSSION GUIDE

1. *Winging It with You* makes for the perfect armchair travel as we are vicariously flown across the globe to some of the most vibrant destinations. Which of the locations en route Theo and Asher's journey on *The Epic Trek* would you put at the top of your travel bucket list and why?

2. *Winging It with You* features the ever popular fake-dating trope. Discuss to what extent this trope best fosters intimacy between Asher and Theo over other possible romance tropes, especially within the setup of this competition. Put simply: In the battle of tropes, which one wins out?

3. Asher and Theo engage in an emotional game of tug-of-war. At what point did you observe either one of them fully giving in to their feelings, and what was the discerning quality that gave them away? Discuss to what extent the story being told through both perspectives clarified your understanding of where the couple stood at each moment.

4. Theo and Asher have their bags packed, both literally and metaphorically, as it relates to their emotional baggage. Dis-

cuss how Theo and Asher each hold themselves back in love and in life. In your experience, what does it often take to open yourself up again, to *unpack your bags* if you will?

5. In writing this book, author Chip Pons was intentional in illustrating queer joy on the page, despite Theo and Asher's emotional hiccups. Discuss where you as a reader found these moments of queer joy, and why illustrating such moments is important.

6. From the title's allusion to wings and the tagline's reference to catching flights to Theo's occupation as a pilot, the motif of *flight* makes a notable mark in this novel. Discuss how this motif shows up in Theo and Asher's relationship as it starts to take form.

7. Family plays an important role in the book. Discuss to what extent family often factors in to one's decisions in love. Where is the line between support and influence?

8. Clint is a vibrant character, to say the least, and makes an appearance in some of the story's most dramatic moments. To what extent do you believe Clint basks in the theatrics of a relationship? Can someone like Clint ever be ready for real, mature love? Discuss.

9. Throughout the course of the competition, Asher and Theo adopt the phrase "winging it with you." Discuss what this means to you in the context of a relationship. In what ways did the title prime you for Asher and Theo's love story?

10. What's next for Asher and Theo?

WINGING IT WITH YOU PLAYLIST

- "Hold On Tight (Acoustic)" by R3HAB & Conor Maynard
- "Big Jet Plane" (feat. Vancouver Sleep Clinic & Amelia Magdalena) by Pop Goes Ambient
- "Shakes" by Luke Hemmings
- "Acting Out" by Ashley Tisdale
- "Kiss Me" by Ed Sheeran
- "Juliene" by Daya
- "10,000 Emerald Pools" by BØRNS
- "past life" by elijah woods
- "Fade Into You" by Blonde Maze
- "Hesitate" (feat. OSKA) by Hazlett
- "affection" by BETWEEN FRIENDS
- "Someone to You" by BANNERS
- "Where do we go now?" by Gracie Abrams
- "Are You Even Real?" by James Blake
- "Mess Is Mine" by Vance Joy
- "Be Slow" by Harrison Storm
- "Roses" (feat. ROZES) by The Chainsmokers
- "Animal" by Troye Sivan
- "Part of Me" by By The Coast
- "Let Down" by Michigander
- "Nervous" by Maren Morris
- "When You're Gone" by Shawn Mendes
- "chance with you" by mehro
- "Labyrinth" by Taylor Swift
- "Bend the Light" by Acceptance

Chip Pons grew up in a small lake town in Northern Michigan before eventually traveling the world as a photojournalist in the US Air Force, where he met and worked alongside his dream of a husband and better half. He's spent his entire life swooning over the love stories filling up his shelves, until one day, he was brave—or delusional—enough to write his own. He currently lives in the heart of Washington, DC, and when he is not writing or chasing around his pup, Margot, he can be found daydreaming of untold happily ever afters or on Bookstagram shouting about the books he loves. And snacking, like, all the time.

chippons.com
BooksOvrBros
X ChipPons